Into the Woods:

INTO THE WOODS

Kathleen Kerridge

Edited by Sam Flaco & Emma Stedall

Visit www.facebook.com/OfficialKathleenKerridge to keep up to date with forthcoming releases, news and occasional weird rants about the British Weather

Into the Woods: Searching for Eden, Part One.

Contents

Prologue 11

Part One 19

I 21

II 45

III 71

IV 91

V 115

VI 129

VII 151

VIII 160

IX 171

X 188

XI 202

XII 231

XIII 245

XIV 267

XV 281

Part Two 307

XVI 309

XVII 327

XVIII 339

XIX 350

XX 364

XXI 378

XXII 386

XXIII 395

XXIV 409

XXV 423

Part Three 463

XXVI 465

XXVII 467

XVIII 489

XXIX 493

XXX 498

XXXI 503

XXXII 519

Epilogue 525

Acknowledgements 529

A Small Note. 531

For Ninja Lady.

Into the Woods: Searching for Eden, Part One.

PROLOGUE

"There he is!"

The victorious yell sounded with the same effect as a hunting horn or a starting pistol. A fox hunt, perhaps, or the more sinister echo of a long dead past.

Once Upon A Time...

Earlier still, the same call would have been heard, by a villager or a farmer. The yell, shrill and eager for blood, could have been an invader, spying a native. Hungry with lust for the riches the hunted ones—and the land—held.

The cry, whoever it may once have been used by, was enough to make Eden's heart pump in his chest. The painful suddenness of rushing adrenaline left him breathless for a half an instant.

"Shit," Eden said, hearing the gang advancing. He did not waste time looking over his shoulder to make sure it was him the shout was directed at. The sun was still in the sky. The wind still blew. While that much was certain, he could say with the same surety that the cry was aimed at him, no one else.

"Oi, Paki!"

"Faggot boy! Wanna suck my dick?"

"Get the Paki fucker!"

"Get him!"

Eden scooped his backpack from the ground and shouldered it as he broke into a run. He vaulted a bench to flee down an alley and scrambled over an eight foot wall with enough agility to make a marine proud. He thought, briefly, of the library book he had left behind, open under the swaying branches of a weeping willow, close to the children's play area of the park. It was only a brief thought, though. He would just have to buy another one as a replacement. Again.

"Fuck," Eden said, pushing himself to run onward.

His goal was the thick line of trees at the edge of town. Woodlands as old as England, the old folks joked. Magic woods, others said, spinning yarns. Woods where witches were created and deals with the Others were made. Souls sold and changelings left alone, to be taken back by the Fae, the stolen human child returned. Exchanges were made in those woods, some hippies joked, heads filled with mystery and cannabis as they practised their New Age nonsense, chanting under the diseased old alders. Humanity was given to the Fae in return for powers not quite dreamed of. Knowledge of the Auld Ways. The unknown.

The idea of magic meant the woods had become a sanctuary for Eden. It was a place where the hunters would not go. A place he would be safe. It helped that the Blair Witch Project had, for some reason, done the rounds at his college during his first year. It had spooked a lot of people and now fewer students than ever were willing to enter the woods. A rumour here and a well-placed lie there, and Eden had soon found himself with a *haunted* wood to hide in. It was his haven, one which he knew as well as his own bedroom.

The Fae, while a cute story, were a damned sight less terrifying than the reality of Ridley Stuart and his gang of testosterone-fuelled council-estate dwellers. The Fae had done nothing to Eden. Last time Ridley and the gang had caught him, he had been left with broken ribs and several nasty fractures to his hand and ankle, where they had stamped on him. He would take his chances with the Fae, he decided, pushing himself to run harder.

"Eden!" a familiar voice shouted, as he ran past a café. He didn't look around, dashing across the road instead. He narrowly avoided being smeared into the tarmac by a speeding van.

"Eden! Damnit, not again," Eden heard Lacey shout over the noise of the traffic and the blaring horns that heralded Ridley's dash across the road. "You leave him alone, you bloody cowards!"

Her only reply was the hoots of the gang as they continued in pursuit of their prey.

The voices and sounds behind Eden faded as he darted into the woods. He had to force his legs to carry him further through the trees. Running had become a battle against the fire ripping through his muscles. The agony of lactic acid burning into his thighs and calves was making his vision cloudy. He knew he was going to have to stop sooner rather than later. He glanced left and right. The brown and the greens of the surrounding forest started to flicker and flash silver. Lights sparkled at the edges of his vision. Yet on he ran, stumbling now, deeper into the woods.

A few more minutes and he would be safe. He would be in his sanctuary, where he would be able to rest until his legs stopped feeling watery. He would sit, hidden from the eyes of his enemies, until he was able to heave himself to his feet and not have to try to balance on legs turned to jelly.

He just had to get deeper.

Eden shook his head, hoping to clear his sight and stop the visual disturbances. He bent his head and dug in further, pushing his feet against the ground with the last vestiges of his energy. He saw, at last, the stream he had been trying to reach. It cut the woods in two. All he had left was a leap for his life and he would be safe.

Well, safer than he was now, anyway.

He pushed himself from the ground and soared for a precious moment, hanging in the air as he jumped the stream. It was not an easy distance, but it was possible to jump the stream. So long as the run-up was long enough and there was enough speed behind the launch. Luckily for Eden, the threat of being caught by the council-estate gang was enough incentive to ensure he always had both speed and run-up.

After the jump, the gang's fear of the unknown was enough to keep *them* the other side of the stream. No doubt they would find the jump an easy one, if they had the nerve to try it.

Eden landed without grace on the opposite bank of the stream. Thudding into the ground, his foot slipped down to break the surface of the flowing water. He hauled himself, panting, up the steep bank and back to his feet.

He turned in place, unable to hold back a small grin of triumph as he watched Ridley come into view. Eden raised his middle finger, silently insolent, and shrugged his backpack higher on his shoulder, walking away from the cursing gang of boys. Ignoring the insults they shouted at him, he wandered deeper into the woods with the tired tread of a man sixty years his senior.

Staggering, once he was sure he was out of the gang's sight, Eden held a hand out, finding the trunk of a silver branch tree and using it for balance. He caught his breath, head hanging low. He drew a deep breath in, let it out as slowly as he could and repeated the process until his breathing was no longer a harsh ragged gasp for air. Dizzy, spent, all energy was sapped from his body. It was as though he had been harvested for it. He sank to his knees, hitting the soft ground with a heavy thump, staring at his palms. He frowned at the beads of blood smeared over his skin, turning sticky and darkening to a crusting maroon under his gaze.

Eden lifted his gaze to the birch tree, looking at his palm print, stamped on the peeling bark in crimson bloody paint. He shook his hair from his face, slipping sideways to lie curled on the leaves scattering the ground. He looked blankly into the surrounding forest.

The light changed from the brightness of an early spring afternoon to purpling twilight. The sky turned mellow, darkening to be streaked with soft pinks and deepest blues. An alien sky, whose sun was a red giant, huge and pregnant, sinking downwards in the sky, looking close enough to touch. It rested, heavy and lazy, on the horizon, shrouded by the unnaturally hued clouds, which added to its mystery.

Eden watched the trees. They reached out for him with hand-like branches and waved skeletal arms up to praise the light of the blood-red sun. Clawing fingers and arthritic knuckles skimmed his head as he battled a dazed haze of disbelief and told himself he should run. Run faster than he had ever run before. Get the hell out of the forest. Get the hell away from whatever was happening—if there was still the slightest chance it was possible to do so.

It was only a small part of his mind, though, telling him to escape. The bigger part wanted, very much, to stay right where he was. Warm and comforted by the beautiful sky. He wanted to stay on the forest floor, watching the woods transform around him. To stay and watch the world change from ordinary, into something *new*. Something *Other*, something *more*.

They were changing into something more beautiful than Eden had ever imagined. He watched the spreading branches and the blossoming flowers, blooming with colour so vibrant they stung his eyes. The ancient trees grew larger still, thin fingers of branches stretching and uncurling to touch the sky and feel the air, which flowed purple around them. The leaves on the ground now lay on bright green spongy moss, not bare brown earth. The moss was vivid, fresh and fragrant. Vines crept up the trunks of the trees, caressing the bark with the soft touch of a long-known lover. Birds sang louder, the water rushed by, no longer a gentle flow, and the leaves rustled noisily overhead. The faint sounds of traffic had faded entirely, leaving nothing but the music of nature in its place. Mother Nature playing her own instruments of the forests.

Eden rolled onto his back in awe. He looked upwards at the orange tinted sky thought the thick canopy of leaves. He looked again at his palm. The blood was cracked and dried, now, stuck to his skin. He must have sliced himself as he had ran. Either on the wall he had scaled, or when he had landed on the bank, when he had jumped the stream.

He had come into the forest with blood, he had touched his blood to a tree.

Closing his eyes, Eden let his hand fall to the earth at his side. "Well," he said to himself, under his breath, "it's the Forest of The Fae."

He sat up, tailing his hair, and glanced around with both hands held to the crown of his head. The woods were beyond recognition. It was unlikely they ended after a two mile trek. The motorway was probably not three miles to his right and he doubted that his city was the other side of the—wide, rushing— river.

"Shit. I finally crossed over," he said, dropping his hands into his lap. "I actually did it."

Into the Woods: Searching for Eden, Part One.

PART ONE

Into the Woods: Searching for Eden, Part One.

I

First things first. Eden dusted himself off and got to his feet. *Find water*. He looked at the rushing waters of the wide river and gave a small snort of amusement. Water, it seemed, wasn't going to be one of his problems. He walked to the water's edge and crouched to scoop a palm of crystal clear water, tasting it to make sure it was fresh. It was. He rinsed his hands and splashed his face, drying himself with the hem of his T-shirt. Wide eyed, he took in the vibrancy of the world he had found himself in. He had imagined, dreamed, for so long. His mind had created paintings of the Forest of The Fae, but nothing could come close to the reality, or the intensity of the woods he found himself in.

A furry mammal scurried through the trees, fat bellied and light footed. Eden wondered if it was a creature that would have been seen in his own forest. A mole? A badger? Something he could name and recognise? His eyes drifted, fixing on a cluster of dark plum berries hanging heavy on a bush. They looked like blackberries. He walked over to the bush and picked one to look at closely before nibbling the edge of the berry with hesitant teeth.

It tasted like a blackberry. He picked several and put them in the front pouch of his backpack, where they wouldn't get too squashed. It was hardly a meal, but it was better than nothing. Eden opened his bag, rummaged through his books, sweater, spare T-shirt and all the other junk, to finally reach his lunch. Typically, it was squashed at the bottom, under everything else. He drew out the tin-foil wrapped sandwiches he had packed for himself that morning.

"Eat...keep your energy levels stable," he said to himself like a mantra, biting into a cheese and ham sandwich. It was squashed and battered, and the juice from the tomato had run into the white bread, making things soggy. The cheese had got warm and been melted, while the ham was a bit worse for wear.

It was the most delicious sandwich ever. Eden ate one half, carefully packing the other half back into his bag; he could eat that one later, if nothing else presented itself. He turned slowly in a circle, frowning.

"Which way?" he asked himself quietly. "Hmm?" He closed his eyes as he turned around, arm outstretched and finger pointing. He opened his eyes and looked at the gap in the trees facing him.

"That'll do nicely. Well...nothing ventured, right?" he said, walking with as much confidence as he had, lending himself what courage he could find. He needed all the help he could get—even if he was the only one around to give it. Firmly pushing his fear and uncertainty down, he followed a thin deer path through the trees. Maybe he would find someone who could help him. Maybe a town?

Who knew. He had never, after all, thought he would ever manage to get into a Fae Forest and break through whatever veil separated the two worlds. It had been a dream. An escape. A way to make his life more tolerable and see him through the long hours of school, then college, with some lovely daydreams of elves and fantasy creatures. A dream. It had never been *real*.

Now, though, he was in a woodland that bore absolutely no resemblance to the one he had ran into from the motorway. There was no motorway, he reminded himself. It was not the wood he hid in to escape the bullies, and was not the forest he had spent so many hours mapping and exploring. The sky was wrong. The sun was too big, the clouds were the wrong colour. The trees were too old, and the plants too bright. The water tasted too clean and the moss was too soft. It was all too *perfect*. That he had slipped, somehow, into a place of myth he had no doubt at all.

The question was, how was he going to get back out? Could he get back out, more importantly.

Sighing, Eden pulled the band from his hair, catching all his hair back into a scruffy tail halfway up his head to knot into place. Almost immediately, a few strands broke loose to hang in front of Eden's eyes. He flicked them behind his ears and walked onwards, trying to keep the river a few metres to his left while he scanned for smoke from a fire, or the noise of a town. He hoped he wasn't the only person in the world—that way would lie madness.

Suddenly fearful, he started to jog along his path, hurrying to be anywhere but a place where he was alone. He glanced over his shoulder, taking a mental snapshot of the way he had come, then faced front and ran faster, always keeping the river to his left.

What if he was the only person in this place? What if there was no one else here for him to find? Not the Forest of the Fae, but a ghost world, where he would live and die alone, unremarked and unknown.

No one to love him, no one to grieve for him? What if that was what this place was? A highly sensual forested hell? Enforced solitude, until the day he laid down under one of the perfect trees, next to a perfect bush, on a perfect bed of moss, where he would close his eyes on the perfect sky above his head, and die. Alone.

Fear rising, he decided, with the benefit of hindsight, that the broken ribs might have been better. He used his hands to hold thick branches out of the way as he plunged deep into the forest, never losing sight of the river. If there was a town, it would be near the water source, right? If there were people.

If, if, *if.*

His breath tearing in his throat, Eden shook his head in mute denial of his thoughts. Not that. Anything but that. He had to find someone. Anyone. His terror was complete.

He ran for what felt like hours, but was probably only minutes, before he stopped and fell to the ground to hunch into himself against a tree trunk. He tried to get a grip on his panic. He was shaking, sobbing and heaving in each breath with a loud wheeze. Eden knew enough to know he was going into shock. He could hardly blame himself, all things considered. This was a lot bigger than sleeping on a train and winding up in London by mistake.

Eden held his face in his hands and concentrated on his breathing again. In through his nose, hold it, let it go gently...slowly. Hyperventilating was a real threat and he did not want to pass out in the woods alone. He had watched too many horror movies to risk making that mistake. As soon as he passed out, some knife-wielding maniac would come alone and—

"Fuck, Eden," he said. "Stop scaring the shit out of yourself." He leant back against the tree trunk and bent his legs, curling into himself so he could fold his arms atop his knees. He rested his chin on his forearms and looked around at the trees surrounding him. Nothing but trees, forest and more of the same for as far as he could see through the trunks. He shook his head gently.

"Got enough to be scared of, I reckon," he told himself. "Don't add the made up stuff. Not today. Stay calm and just...work it out. Breathe. Remember to breathe," he added, focusing on his breaths once more.

He closed his eyes on the oppressive forest to listen to his breathing, concentrating on the beat of his heart slowing back to a normal rate and the feel of his pulse in his veins. It beat steadily in his wrists and neck, comforting him as it stopped pounding and quietened to a soft rhythmic thump. At least all systems appeared to be working and going back to normal, he thought, sleepily opening his eyes again.

"I'm going to be hating trees, sooner rather than later." Eden picked up a small stone at his side and flicked it at a vine covered trunk.

"You best get used to them," a soft voice said from behind where Eden sat. "There's not much else for miles."

A lithe woman, only a few shades lighter than Eden himself, stepped into view. Eden immediately thought of Mayans or tribal princesses from the pages of history. Although they were probably looked less imposing. She wore her light-brown hair in tight individual braids, a loose faded-umber shirt, tucked into tight leather trousers that were in turn tucked into slouchy knee-high flat boots.

Eden scrambled to his feet, staring at the woman and at the arsenal of weaponry she wore strapped and belted to her body. A bow, arrows in a quiver, two swords, a handgun—which looked oddly out of place, holstered to her sword belt—several wicked looking knives and a pair of Egyptian Sais. There were even a few throwing stars hanging near her hip and a belt around her thigh, with another knife tucked against the leather of her trousers. Eden looked back at her face, finding a pair of startling blue eyes studying him in silence. He looked at her ears, following the elongated point at the tip.

"Uh...I'm..."

"Eden," the woman said. "I heard. I'm Takana Jarlen. *General* Takana Jarlen."

Eden waited, scared in case her friendliness belied a more vicious core. Military ranking explained about a fifth of the weapons Takana had attached to her. She looked as though she was expecting to single-handedly fight a war. She turned, looking at the trees surrounding them. Eden saw a grenade clipped to the back of her thick leather belt and clapped a hand over his mouth to stifle an unmanly gasp of terror.

"Are you quite well?" she asked, looking back at him. "Do you have some kind of mental retardation? Are you need need of medication? I heard you talking to yourself. You are right, you shouldn't scare yourself." She frowned at him, peering closer. "You look gormless."

Eden swallowed his fear and drew his shoulders back, eyeing the woman. "That's a first," he said. "No, I'm not gormless, retarded, or needing medication. I was talking to myself so I wouldn't go insane." He looked around, waving a vague had at his surroundings. "I was worried I was the only one here. I was scared I was alone. This isn't my world." Remembering himself and his manners, stupidly, all things considered, he held out his hand to Takana. "It's a pleasure to meet you, General Takana, ma'am." He blushed, wondering if he sounded as stupid as he felt.

Takana took his hand, rocking on her heels as her warm skin came into contact with his. She staggered back, dropping his hand, then drew a deep breath and approached him again, eyes wider than before. She picked his hand back up from where it hung at his side, looking at his fingers before folding both her hands around his, holding him captive.

"Where am I?" he asked, letting her hold his hand. It seemed unwise to try and take anything from someone with so many weapons, even if that something *was* his hand. It comforted him, without him knowing why it would.

Takana's eyes were a compassionate dark blue in her light brown face. It was nearly as striking a combination as his own silvery-green against his dark skin. She patted his hand, turning it over between her own so she could look at his palm and trace the lines with a pointed nail.

"Are you all right?" she asked quietly, not looking up. "All jokes aside, I think you've had quite a shock, Eden."

"Yeah. Reckon I have at that." He waved at the trees. "Am I in the Forest of the Fae?"

Takana shook her head. Bells Eden hadn't noticed tinkled prettily at the ends of her braids, chiming with the softness of a breath before they fell silent.

"No," she said. "No more than it is Eden's Forest because you happen to be standing in it. You are in Alfheim. We call this country Bordenthal. The Border Lands. An apt name, as it is one of the many places where the Divide between my world and yours is at a weak point."

"You live here?"

Takana looked once again at Eden's open palm before pressing it back into his chest, effectively allowing him to have it back.

"I am a Border Guard. Yes, I live here. For over quarter of a century, I have not been called by these trees, alerted to an alien presence. It has been a long time, Eden. A long, long time."

Eden rubbed his hand down his face and blew out through his mouth, whistling softly. He was where he had spent years trying to get to. His emotions were spiralling out of control, again. He shook himself and took a deep breath, facing Takana. Now he was with someone who probably had the knowledge of how to get back to his world, which scant hours before he would have traded anything for, he was suddenly sure he did *not* want to be returned to his world.

"Your job. It's to send people back, isn't it?"

"And make deals," she said. "Once Upon A Time..."

"Exchanges? You are given humanity in place of something *other*?"

She tossed her braids over her shoulders to make them chime again in the stillness of the forest. "Too much Marlowe, my dear boy," she said, grinning. "What would I want with humanity? Short-lived and weak. No, I would not want humanity, not for anything."

28

"You make deals," Eden said, thinking. "So people can stay here?"

"Many seek the Fae," Takana said. "Only a handful every thousand years are strong enough to cross our Divide as you have done. Humans do not stay here, Eden. It is not their world. But to cross the Divide cannot go unremarked or unrewarded. They cannot bide here, though."

"You send them back...take payment and give gifts," Eden said, seeing images in his mind as clearly as they would have played out on a television screen. "You take payment and see people back across the river. You give them power, sometimes. Abilities. You police the Divide and keep the realms separate."

"Bingo," Takana said, eyes on his face. "Not so gormless after all."

"What do you ask for?" Eden asked, intrigued.

Takana studied his face for a moment, stepping forward to hold her palm to his cheek. She watched him for several heartbeats. "A lover's kiss, a breath, a sigh in the light of the morning. The touch of a hand on my own. The smile of a friend and the laughter of an ally. A night and a day of you...to have your company, and your closeness. So I may say I have known it. Known you."

Eden lifted Takana's hand from his cheek, holding it in his own, and raised it to his lips. "A breath, a sigh, the touch of a hand and the smile of a new friend," he said. "You get lonely."

She closed her fingertips around Eden's. Her blue eyes proof of her sadness. "I thank you," she said, squeezing Eden's hand before letting it fall. "You're but a child, but you see more than men ten times your age. How old are you, Eden?"

"Eighteen. Nearly nineteen," he added, as though a few months would make any difference. He studied Takana again, telling himself he was in the presence of an actual Fae-Creature. "May I ask how old you are? If it's not too rude, I mean. You look my age, but I'm betting my grandparents would be young, as far as you're concerned."

"They would be children, to me," she agreed. She looked at the sky and waved a hand at a small path to her left. "Will you take supper with me, Eden? Before you cross back? I shall not hold you to the night time, I think you will not be able to give me what I desire from you."

He took her hand when she held it out to him, walking behind her as she led him through the wood.

"My age?" he asked.

Takana looked at him. "I would hope you are old enough for *that*, Eden. No, I think I am lacking what you desire."

Eden frowned, shrugging his backpack higher on his shoulder. "What do you mean?"

"I'm female," she said, chuckling softly when she looked at him.

"What? That I'm gay is written on my face, now? How the hell?"

"Age and experience," Takana said. "And you have a rainbow badge on your bag. I spend a lot of time in your realm, Eden. I'm aware of your symbols and meanings. Silent statements and stands, shouted by something as simple as a badge."

"Oh," Eden said, face warming. "Yeah, seeing the badge makes sense. You've been to my realm?"

"Many times. I have a home there, which I like to visit when I am on leave. And I'm partial to the nightlife and amenities there, although this world is home."

Eden felt stunned that there were Fae-Creatures crossing into his world and he'd never known about it. Although, now Takana had told him, it was as though he had always known it was so.

"Will you take supper with me?"

"I'd like that, yeah," Eden said. "I'm not ready to go back yet, though. Not yet. Will you answer my questions? I've been trying to find this world for so long. I'm not ready to go back to my own. Not yet." Realising he was repeating himself, his lingering panic short-circuiting his brain, Eden clamped his lips together. He inhaled through his nose, rubbing his eyes with one hand. He looked at Takana. "Please don't make me go home," he finished quietly. "I don't want to go."

Takana trailed her fingers along the leaves of a vine, crawling up the gnarled trunk of a tree.

"I will answer those questions to which I know the answer," she agreed. "But you have many questions I cannot answer. They are not my answers to know, Eden. You may as well ask a rock, for all the wisdom I can share with you. I'm sorry. I'm a soldier—I don't have the answers to all your questions.

"Yet you know I have questions," Eden replied. "You seem to know a lot about me, considering we just met. You know more than people who have known me my whole life, so I'm betting you're more than just a simple soldier."

The laugh of Takana's reply was let go on a whisper of wind. "So much wisdom," she said, "yet you think to ask of me—*me*—your destiny. I am no god, Eden. Your destiny is not mine to know, but there are some things I may be able to help you with. Others, no. They are not mine to see and nor are they my secrets to guard."

"Fair enough," Eden said, shrugging. "Do I get to choose to stay here? And if I do stay, is it forever, or can I go back one day?"

"For most people, there is no choice. They are sent back across the Divide and may never return. There is no way back for someone I cross over the river. The Divide is closed to them forever." Takana walked along the deer path, linking their fingers together. "There is no way back, once they leave."

Eden followed Takana, past rabbit warrens and ground-nesting birds he could not name. "I can return?" he asked after a while. "If I go, can I come back? You speak of *they* as though *they* don't include me. I don't want to go, if I can't come back."

Takana looked back over her shoulder at him. "You walk where you choose. I do not see a door that is strong enough to hold you, Eden. You will never be shut out from a world you wish to be in."

"What do you mean?"

"What I say, Eden."

Crossing a rickety planked bridge spanning a winding brook, he stepped onto dry land and looked around the clearing. There was a stone fire-pit in front of a simple wooden cabin. A lean-to, filled with chopped logs and fallen branches was nestled near a clump of rowans. It might not have been much, but it was welcoming and homely. He let go of Takana's hand, sitting on a low three-legged stool when she waved at it in silent invitation. He folded his long legs, resting his forearms on them. He thought for a moment before remembering his manners and opening his bag, pulling out the second half of his sandwich and a Mars bar. He handed them to Takana with as much ceremony he would have used for a wine of the best vintage.

Takana smiled. She placed his meagre offerings next to her own stool.

"I thank you," she said. "It is a poor guest indeed, who brings no gift for their host." She lifted the lid from a ceramic casserole dish next to the fire and poured water into it, sprinkling herbs and seasonings before gently placing a small joint of dark meat into the liquor and placing it on the fire with the lid in place. "Soup." She tapped the pot. "For tomorrow, if you're planning to stay we will be fed well." She poured from a clay bottle, filling two hand-beaten pewter goblets, and passed him one. "Berry wine."

"Thank you," Eden said, taking the goblet. He sipped. The wine tasted of a thousand summers, lighting the inside of his mouth with sunshine. He cocked an appreciative brow at his goblet and sipped again.

"What did you mean?" he asked, once Takana had finished poking the fire and ministering to another open cauldron. "Not a door strong enough to hold me?"

"I mean what I say, Eden," Takana said. "You will walk where you please. When you are wise enough to know your own power and accept the man you are yet to become."

"So I can come back?" he asked, not understanding. "If I go...I can return?"

"If you choose to be here, then here is where you will be. There is no way to close a world to you. You have the right to come and go at your will."

He murmured his thanks when his wine was replenished. He could not remember draining the goblet. Telling himself to sip slower, he placed it next to his foot and leant towards the fire. He could come and go as he wanted. He had opened the world he had wanted to see for so long. He had opened the door, and no one could shut him out again. Getting home was somehow unimportant, knowing that he could walk from one to the other, as he wished. He grinned at Takana.

"That's cool. I was scared I would be stuck in one world or the other."

A shadow flitted across Takana's face, but it was gone fast enough for Eden to tell himself it was a play of the light, cast by the low hanging sun in the sky. She laughed. It did not sound forced, so Eden relaxed.

"I doubt you could ever be stuck, Eden," she said under her breath as she looked at the growing flames of the fire. "One may as well try to catch the wind in a child's butterfly net." She flicked her fingers. "Catch a breath of a sigh between your palms, and expect it to stay there. Some things are not there to be caught or held. I think you are one of those things, Eden."

Not understanding her words, he shrugged to himself. Most people would be odd if they were left alone for years, he supposed.

"I dreamt of this place," Eden said. He picked up his goblet and drank again, letting the summertime burst on his tongue and slide down his throat. "This world. The sky. It *was* this world, wasn't it?"

"It was this world, yes," Takana said. "You hold the secret of it in your eyes. You have seen it, and seen it often. Walked it and smelled it. Touched it with your hands and heard it with your ears. You have the stamp of the Fae on you."

"There is someone," he said, almost to himself. "In my dreams. In my mind. I can hear his voice calling me, but I don't know who he is. I can't see him in the dark. He's in the dark, calling me, trying to draw me to him. I can touch him," he continued, looking at the flames of the fire, licking the logs and kissing the pots "I touch a hand. There's a brush of a fingertip across my face. Moments. Stolen touches from an idea I have in my head." He looked at his wine, into the depths of the deep berry-coloured liquid, seeing his unsettled reflection in the liquid, too vague to make out details. His face shimmered and vanished as he tilted the drink and sipped again. "Is the dream...is it real? Is there a face behind the voice? Here?"

Takana grabbed his hand with an intensity that startled him. "Never doubt yourself," she said, her voice as urgent as her grip.

For the first time since Eden had met her, she looked as wild and lethal as the Fae were said to be. She looked dangerous as a tornado—beautiful to watch...from a distance. Not something he wanted to be too close to. He gulped at his wine, rearing back, away from her.

"It is not mine to know all your answers, Eden," she said, sighing. She shook her head, patting his hand as she loosened her grip. "I cannot tell you your destiny, but I *can* tell you to listen to yourself. To listen to and follow your heart, and your heart alone. It will lead you to where you long to be. It has the power to take you there, but you must *listen*. You must *trust* yourself."

"And follow a voice into the dark?" Eden asked,

clasping Takana's hand as though he might tame her wildness, soothing her like he would an agitated cat. "I should follow a voice that wants to lead me into the dark?"

"So you can reach into the darkness and shine a light," she said, pulling her hand free. "He is not calling to lure you in...he is calling to be set free."

"Takana," he said, standing as she strode away from the fire. "Takana?"

"No more." She spun where she stood, making her braids fly out around her head and chime. They sounded discordant. "Ask me no more, Eden, please...this is not mine to tell you. I don't know enough. I can't see enough. I am not a god—this is not for me to talk about."

"Takana...calm down." Eden jogged to stand in front of her and take her hands. "I'm sorry. I know I shouldn't pry too far, or too deep. My mama always used to say it would be my downfall...I simply ask and ask, without thinking," he said, babbling to try and smooth down the hackles risen on Takana's shoulders. "You have the sight...like most of your folks, I guess. It's new to me to be with someone who might have the answers to what I want to know, is all. I am sorry...please. I won't ask nothing else from you, okay?"

Takana pulled her hands free. She looked him for a long moment. "You truly have no idea, do you?" she asked, walking slowly back to the fire and refilling her wine goblet.

"No idea about what?"

"Oh, save me from fools and the meddling of the gods." She held her pointed chin in her hand, lifting one finger wrapped around her goblet to point at him.

"You," she murmured. "You're here, searching for what?"

"Answers."

"No. You're seeking a lot more than that. I have a question for you."

Eden waited.

"When you open your own equivalent of Pandora's Box, are you ready for whatever might be inside? Some dreams turn into nightmares, Eden. Are you prepared, say, to be drawn into the dark...if you cannot pull the face behind the voice free? You have crossed the worlds for someone you have never seen, and yet, I can see, in your eyes...in your soul...that this is only the start, and that you would have crossed more than a world to find the one calling you. You do not know him. You have never seen him...and it matters not?"

"It don't matter a damn, no," he said, draining his wine. He took the bottle when Takana held it out to him, pouring again for both of them. "I've been hearing him, been called by him, every night since I was eight years old." Eden drank wine, shaking his head. "I've been seen by doctors and shrinks. I've been drugged, examined, and I'm ridiculed by most people who know me. I've been thinking I'm mad. Called names," he said, speaking to the fire. "I've had a decade of being called to a world I was told repeatedly doesn't exist. Now, the way I'm seeing this, is that I've either finally broken and I'm having one *hell* of an episode, or it was all real, right the way along. Am I ready to open Pandora's Box?" he asked. "General Takana, ma'am, let me tell you straight— finding the contents of that box ain't gonna be nearly as weird as my life up till now. Open a nightmare? I just ran from the nightmare. Yeah, I'm ready."

Takana merely watched him. She waited until he had regained most of his composure before she reached to pat his arm. "It doesn't sound easy."

He pushed his fingers through the length of his hair to knot it at the back of his head in a scruffy bun. He met Takana's eyes, slumping where he sat. "Sorry for the outburst," he said, looking down. "I'm a bit overwhelmed by all this."

"I should imagine you are," Takana said gently. She refilled their goblets once more. "Drink." She waited until he had taken a healthy swig of the wine. "So, you're ready to leave your world? Ready to turn your back on all you know, to chase a dream and find a voice in the darkness? While you *can* return, Eden, doesn't mean it will be easy for you to leave, if you start on this path. What if you lose your way and can't find the right path back?"

"I..."

"Do not speak rashly." Takana waved Eden into silence. "Take the time to listen to more than your first impulsive thoughts. You owe it to yourself to tell yourself the truth, don't you think? To give yourself the time to make sure you know what the risks you face are?"

Eden bit his lower lip, gazing at the flickering flames of the fire. About to say he didn't care, that he simply had to seek the face behind the voice—find the one who called to him in his sleep—he thought about what he would be leaving behind. Not college. He would not miss college, or anyone in it. He had few enough friends for them not to be a concern. He wouldn't miss his mundane weekend job in the local grocery store, either; stacking shelves and straightening cans was hardly his career of choice after all.

Could he leave his father, though? Yes, he could leave and walk away from everything in his life and not be filled with loss. His life in his world had been unravelling for too long for him to hold many ties to it.

"Forgive me for prying," Takana said. "I just think you need to be sure of what you're doing. You look *well-to-do*, we used to say. You will be missed. Your family? Friends? A lawyer?" she joked, grinning over the fire at him. "You are not coming here from off the streets, from the wrong side of town, are you? You are not the usual stray that I might meet here, in Bordenthal."

Eden chuckled. "Not much gets past you, does it?"

"*Nothing* gets past me. You're wearing jewels that could be sold and feed a large family for a year." Takana shrugged, waving a hand to encompass his ear and eyebrow piercings. She moved her eyes to his mouth. "Is that a four or a five carat diamond in your tongue?"

He clicked the diamond ball against his front teeth and poked his tongue out slightly, showing off the piercing. "Four. It was my mother's. Her engagement ring; when she died, she left me everything and I wasn't gonna wear her rings, so I had the gems made into jewellery I could wear."

"Hardly a street urchin," Takana said thoughtfully, "yet you dress with less care than one, for all you may be a rich-kid stepping out of his comfort zone. You care little for what others may say...or what they think about you."

Eden shrugged. "They all think I'm mad anyhow. Why should I bother trying to get their approval, when

they can't stand me? I might as well be me and dress
how I'm happy. Look how I want to look."

"Hmmm."

"Appearances ain't what's important."

"No, but it takes more than a little bravery or a
bigger than usual ego to turn against the tide and
stand out among a crowd."

"Perhaps."

"You're prepared, Eden, to leave a life where you
are plainly affluent and well cared for, to walk this
world alone?"

"Reckon so," he said. "I'll miss my dad, but I
think he'll guess where I've gone. He's the only one
who really believed me. Kind of, anyway. Him and my
mum. He never thought I was mental, at any rate.
When I don't show up in a couple days, he'll know I
haven't been caught and killed by Ridley."

"You seem to have made your choice, Eden. It's
not my place to either judge you, or try and change
your mind. That's not to say I won't try, of course."
Takana swept her braids over her shoulders, leaning to
the fire with a cloth in her hand. She lifted the
varnished, red-clay cauldron from the fire-pit and
placed it in the embers at the edge of the stone circle
with a glance at the sky, as though gauging the time.
Satisfied, she stirred the contents of the pot and ladled
stew into two deep bowls, passing Eden one with a
carved wooden spoon.

"There are things you will need, and knowledge
you cannot do without, if you mean to enter this
world," she said, spooning stew into her mouth. "Eat.
You cannot tell when your next meal will be, nor
where it may come from. Never pass up the
opportunity to either eat or sleep when you have the

chance."

He ate obediently. The stew was delicious, full of subtle flavours with a savoury sweetness that made eating it a joy. He accepted a heel of bread, soft and fluffy, from Takana and followed her lead in dunking it, chunk by tasty chunk, into the stew, finally using it to wipe around the bowl, leaving it as clean as it had been before being filled.

"I can offer you a bed, for a night," Takana said, wiping her bowl with a wet cloth and drying it, before she placed it next to the fire. "There is a lot about this world you should know, before you make a decision to stay, Eden. To you, in your world, you mistakenly believe this realm to be one of fantasy and light. Of magic and intrigue. You falsely believe that this world is one where singing, dancing and happiness abound. A utopia, of sorts." She shook her head. "It is no utopia, Eden. Many of the Fae detest humans and anything from that world. They are not cute, not loving and, honestly, a lot of them would rather dance with your head on a pike than let you pass their towns unmolested."

Eden frowned. "Why? What have humans done, to deserve that?" he asked, a suspicion of a thought growing in his mind even as the words left his mouth.

"The Fae had the Human Realm first," Takana replied. "The humans hounded us—the magical folk— from our world, burning us alive and hanging us as criminals, simply because we have magic in our blood. We were *ungodly* and killed for it. Persecuted. We have had to watch our world be raped and pillaged. Humankind are not welcome to do the same here."

"But...you spend time in that world, you said." Eden looked at the handgun holstered to Takana's

41

waist, and pointedly at the grenade she wore on her belt. "It seems you don't have qualms about using human weaponry—manufactured in that realm with means the Fae disagree with?"

"While we might make use of the human creations for our benefit," she said, grinning widely, "we are unwilling to start mining this world for fossil fuels and precious stones. You will see no high-rise buildings here, Eden. Nothing more modern than water-driven and wind-powered machinery. Clean energy. Don't make the mistake of thinking us backwards because we do not have satellites and computers, and our roads are free from motor vehicles. We live by a slower pace, absolutely, but we are more advanced than the Human Realm in many ways." Takana picked up the wine bottle, shaking it to check the level. "The technology is here, in this world. We simply choose an easier life. When we want to play at modernity, we cross the river and pretend to be human. The best of both worlds."

"Which humans can't have," Eden said, understanding. "You won't have a human here, in case they begin to rape your world for the riches it holds. The Fae don't need to have the material riches to be rich, do they?"

"You are quick."

"I won't change my mind," he said, lifting one foot to rest on the stool so he could hug his leg into his chest. "I can't fully explain it, not in a way that makes sense, but if I've made it this far and all this is real, then the guy I hear might be real too. I have to at least look. I have to find the one who's been calling me, Takana—I can't not search."

"This isn't a land from the pages of a storybook,

Eden."

"I know. I still have to look for him."

"Orien save me. A noble quest," she said. "What do you have in the way of supplies and weapons?" she asked.

Eden blushed and hoped his dark skin would disguise it. He looked at his wine, lifting his shoulders. "It's not like I planned to come here," he said, glancing up. "I got a can of Diet Coke, a handful of berries, a cereal bar, some books and pens..." He rested his eyes on his backpack. "If I'd thought I'd break through, I'd have packed," he said, frustrated at being made to look stupid. It *was* stupid. He couldn't be expected to pack for quests when he had expected a normal day at college. "I have the clothes I'm wearing and a spare hoodie, as well as a sweater. No weapons—if you spend that much time in my world, you'd know there's no need. I live in England, not America or Kuwait."

"As I said," Takana said, "save me from noble quests. Stand up and let me look at you. I might have a spare set of clothes that will fit you. Please tell me you can use a sword? A bow?" she asked as Eden shook his head, lower lip between his teeth. She groaned, standing directly in front of him. "Nothing?"

"I shoot," Eden said as she started circling him, assessing his size. "Um...you know. Target shootin' and such?"

"Which will be handy, if we happen to be ambushed by ten green bottles, standing on a wall," Takana quipped. "Or if an enemy is kind enough to stay still and hold a bulls-eye for you."

She held her hands on his hips, muttering under her breath about narrow hips and wide shoulders. She looked down at his tattered old Converse baseball boots and shook her head in resignation, telling him he needed new boots, urgently. He tried to absorb what he assumed was going to be a training schedule.

"You must have *some* skills?" Takana asked.

"Yeah, some."

"What are they?" she asked, exasperated.

"I learn as fast as I run," he said, "and I run real fast."

II

Eden wondered how he had ever had the preconceived idea of swords being a light an elegant weapon. Sweat was pouring down his face, chest and back. His hair was plastered to his scalp and he was trembling as he circled, trying to keep a wary eye on Takana and struggled to keep his double handed grip on his sword. It easily weighed twelve pounds and was three feet long. He occasionally went to the gym and played on a weight machine, but his exercise regime had mostly consisted of standing up to fetch ice-cream from the freezer, an occasional tennis match with his dad and, mainly, running away from Ridley. He had thought he was fit and, for a human, in the Human Realm, he was. In the Fae Realm, he was woefully inadequate.

Takana prowled around him, like a lethal cat, searching for an opening before darting forward and swirling her own heavy blade in a two-handed arc that came close to decapitating him. He jumped backwards, swiping instinctively with his weapon. The steel clanged loudly, ringing in his ears as the vibration of the impact sent painful shockwaves up both arms and into his burning shoulders.

Gritting his teeth, he shook his fringe back and charged, knowing that he did not have it in him to hold off another offence from Takana. He had the joy of seeing shock register on Takana's beautiful face, and her slanted eyes widen, and then metal hit metal and thoughts of beauty were gone from his mind. There was nothing except the absolute *need* to disarm the woman, before he was killed. Even if it was meant to be training, Takana showed no quarter. He had several wounds, smeared with healing balms, to prove just how hands-on Takana's teaching style was.

Takana watched him, dancing and twisting around in front of him. "Well done," she said. "That's not a bad move. Keep going and I might get tired. One day."

Eden backed away, sword held in front of him. "Do you even get tired?"

"I think it's possible."

"Never happened?"

"Nope," she replied, lips smacking on the word with satisfaction.

"Damn," he said, still walking backwards, taking a wide circle while he thought about his options. Brute force was, apparently, not going to work. He would pass out exhausted long before he had an effect on Takana's unlimited source of energy. He let his shoulders slump and held the sword with one hand, swiping his soaked hair from his eyes.

"Don't bother trying that ploy," Takana said. "I know you're not that tired."

"Getting there," Eden said. He held his sword loosely in his hands, trailing a line in the dirt as he backed away from Takana. He glanced over his shoulder at the trees, formulating a plan.

"You're going to be trapped, Eden. Then you're dead."

"Yeah, maybe," he agreed, "but you ain't gonna stab me in the back, if I'm up against a tree, right?"

"I could take you down as easily as a child."

"It's likely, yeah."

He turned away from her and, running as fast as he could with the sword clasped firmly in his left hand, he grabbed for a tree branch with his right and swung himself upwards and outwards. Spinning with his own momentum, he twirled around the trunk to land just as Takana approached the tree. He touched the tip of his sword to her back, poking her gently between her shoulder blades.

"I run fast. Bang, you're dead," he said, leaning to whisper into her ear. He reached around her to take her sword. "I win."

"How did you...?" Takana asked, staring at him in open astonishment. She opened her hand to let him grasp the hilt of her sword. "You caught me unaware. I've never seen anyone move like that who isn't an elf."

Eden bowed with a flourish, flipping her sword so the hilt was on offer. "I told you I'm fast."

Her hand closed on the metal hilt and she rolled her eyes. "Let me see you do that trick again tomorrow. You'll have to come up with something better than that, Wonder-Boy. It won't work on me twice."

"No, but I don't need it to. I just need it to work on an enemy once, right?" Eden asked, using a balled up cloth to wipe the sweat from his face and chest. "In the meantime, I think extra weight lifting might come in handy," he added. "Need to work on lifting this little beauty." He examined the sword Takana had given to him. It was anything but beautiful, plainly constructed from dull metal without any embellishments or unnecessary adornments. Function over prettiness—it had been made to do a job, not be hung on a plaque and be admired. He was slowly falling in love with it. What it lacked in beauty, it made up for in character and lethalness.

"It's hardly Merlin's Excalibur," Takana remarked as she wiped herself with a linen towel and flapped her shirt away from her stomach. "For a beginner, Eden, you did exceptionally well, but I think you have a lot more to offer, yet. You need to work harder—practice makes perfect."

He still wondered what he was going to be facing that would require him to become some kind of warrior, but hummed agreeably. "Okay, I'll practice," he said, "Uh...do you have somewhere I can wash up? And you mentioned you might have some trousers I can wear?"

"Possibly. You're about the same size Cole was. A bit shorter, but his clothes will suffice."

"Cole?"

"Cole," she repeated.

"Who is Cole?"

She waved a hand at the woodlands. "He got bored of being here. Elves. Flit about wherever they choose to be, for as long as they choose to be there, then they're gone again. Not so much as a goodbye. Not that you can expect much else from an elf, of course."

Eden raised an eyebrow, polishing the dull metal of his blade with the cloth he held. "He was your boyfriend?"

"If you could put it like that, then yes. Yes he was a boyfriend. For a while. As I say...elves can't be pinned down or be asked to be faithful to one person. I should have learned that from my father. It was fun while it lasted, though. With Cole. At least I knew full well what I was letting myself in for. Still...it would have been nice to know he was leaving. I had made dinner," she said, eyes darkening. "He left between meals."

"That's harsh."

"You think?" she asked quietly. "Well, it's ancient history. And he *was* an elf...can't trust them as far as you can throw them. I should have learned that by now. Orien knows I'm old enough."

Taking a mental note, Eden made a small sound of sympathy. "Who's Orien?"

Takana stilled, blinking at him as though he had asked something impossibly stupid. She closed her mouth. "Orien? He's the...well, I suppose you wouldn't know, would you? Goodness. I would have thought you would...but no, why would you? Orien is the original god. The creator, who brought everything into being. He created the worlds."

Eden looked back, adding a few blinks of his own to the conversation. He hoped that he hadn't fallen into some kind of world as fixated on religion as the one he had so recently left. Keeping his atheistic views to himself, he looked back at the sword again. Maybe the religious beliefs of the Fae were different to the Human Realm. Maybe they had definitive proof their god was real. Who knew?

"Anyway," Takana said, "you want to wash. Let me fill the kettles and get you some water heated. The bath is hanging in the woodshed, if you don't mind dragging it indoors to the kitchen?"

"Kitchen?" Eden looked at her.

"You don't think I have an outdoor fire and nothing else, do you?" she asked. "What about in the winter, or when it rains? This is a permanent camp, not somewhere I stay for a couple of nights, Eden. I live here. I do have some amenities."

Embarrassed, Eden looked at the cabin. If it had a kitchen, then he had no idea where Takana fit her bedroom; it was smaller than his wardrobe. Realising she had seen him looking, he blushed.

"I'll be happy to fetch the bath. Thank you."

"Yeah, yeah, Wonder-Boy," she said, walking across the clearing to her cabin. She looked back over her shoulder. "It's big enough for two," she called. "Deceptive."

"Okay."

"I prefer an outdoors life."

"You don't have to explain yourself to me."

"I'm betting you're used to bigger and better things, aren't you, Wonder-Boy?"

He shrugged. "Bigger, yeah. Don't know if that makes it better or just means I had more room to be lonely in."

She kicked open the front door of her house. "I'm kidding no one," she said, flinging her sword onto a narrow cot that was pushed against one wall. "This place is hardly big enough for the rats I share it with. No one's been here for so long that I stopped seeing it for what it is. A small prison at the edge of the Borderlands. While Cole was here, I never saw it. Not at all," she said, blue eyes distant as she looked at her home. It softened her sharp features and took away the hard light glowing from her pupils. "When Cole was here, it felt like a palace. Love can blind you like that. Now, though, it is nothing more than my prison. Self-imposed," she said, "but a prison all the same."

"Oh, I don't know." Eden stood in the doorway to look around at the interior of the small building. Once his eyes were used to the darkness within the cabin, he reached for one of the oil lamps, looking around for a box of matches. Seeing none, he placed it back on the small shelf next to the door and walked inside. "It's cosy," he said.

He glanced at the few drawings sketched on parchment, pinned to the bare wooden walls. There were items scattered across a scrubbed table, just the right size for two people to share a meal. A quill, parchments, a fountain pen, a biro that looked so totally out of place it made Eden look twice, several books—the sort of paperback romance that could be picked up in a train station newsagents, further proof that Takana did cross over to his realm—a half-made origami animal, bright against the plain surface. Small things that spoke of habitation.

Pushed against one wall was a double bed, covered with a bright patchwork quilt. At the furthest wall, opposite the front door, was a small but serviceable kitchen, with hearth, copper pans, pots and a stone sink. The kitchen fire was the only heater for the room, but the cabin was not big enough to warrant another. Eden looked at the chimney breast and the small figurines that danced their way across the mantelpiece. In a small silver frame, there was an old photograph, further exciting Eden's senses. He walked closer, seeing Takana dressed in wartime fashion, a scarf around her head and overalls grimy with earth, a spade in her hand. Next to her stood a tall, stunningly handsome man wearing shirtsleeves and braces to hold up trousers that could have only been tweed.

Happy memories, the same in any world and any home. Eden touched one of the ornamental dancers with his fingertip. He could sense their movement, for all they stayed still on the shelf. Turning, he saw a pile of cushions next to the table, a book next to them with a feather to hold its page. The cabin might have been small, but it was the most homely place he had been in. It held a warmth and welcome that was lacking from other homes. It didn't need to be big or ostentatious—it was perfect as it was.

Eden bent and picked up the largest steel kettle from next to the hearth and turned to Takana. "Do you fetch water from the stream? Or is there a well?"

"There's a well," Takana said, pointing at the left wall of the square room, as though Eden could see though it to where the well presumably stood. "You don't have to be polite about my home, Eden. I know it's small and nothing like you are used to."

"I like it," Eden said, leaving the room to walk to the well. He lowered a wooden bucket, heaving it back to the edge of the well to tip water into his kettle. "It's cosy."

"Poky."

He shrugged. "Semantics. It keeps the rain off and the heat in? Keeps you safe and out of the elements?"

"Mostly."

"That's good then." Eden carried the kettle back inside, hanging it on a hook above the dead fire. He reached for a brush and crouched to start sweeping out the hearth. It didn't take long to clear the fireplace and stack fresh kindling and wood. He looked again for matches, or a tinderbox, if there was no other option. There was nothing. He frowned, wondering what to do, just as a scent of ozone filled the air in the room. The soft hairs on his arms rose, and there was a moment where he could have sworn he was held in stasis, somehow. Time stopped for the briefest of instants. Just long enough for his mind to tell him he was in the presence of magic. He looked at Takana, who was staring at the fire. Eden leant back just as she narrowed her eyes.

A *whoomph* of sound, muted and soft, marked the fire flaring to life. Flames licked the logs and kindling, catching easily. In moments, the fire was roaring brightly, lending an orange cast to the gloomy home, cheering it up with its light.

Takana lit a spill from the fire to touch it to the oil lamp next to the door. She carried it to the table, setting it down.

"You just...the fire. It..." Eden took a deep breath while his heart skittered and jumped jerkily behind his ribs, startled into palpitations. "Gosh," he said, holding his hand over his chest. "Could warn a guy, next time. What did you do?"

"You find a witch in the woods, you expect a bit of magic."

"Witch?"

"I like to dabble," she said, sitting at the table. "Witchcraft amuses me."

"Yeah...right. So, is it really rude to ask what you are?"

"Wood Nymph. What are you?"

"Human." Eden sat opposite her. "What else would I be?"

She eyed him in silence for several moments, then snorted and shook her head. "What else, indeed. Save me from the meddling of Gods and noble quests," she said under her breath. "You're sure you're human?"

"As sure as I can be, yeah." He sat opposite her. "I come from the realm of the humans, and I was born to human parents, went to a human school, and have a human doctor who likes to jab me with human vaccines, so I reckon I'm human. Wood Nymph, huh? You can talk to the trees?"

"I can," she said. "Some of them, anyway. They are quieter than they once were, but some still speak." She reached behind her for a squat rough green bottle and drank from the neck. Wiping it, she passed it to Eden. "Go easy—it's not as weak as the wine."

He tilted the bottle in silent toast and sipped, spluttering as the harsh whiskey seared its way over his tongue and burned its way down his throat. Home-distilled rotgut was easier on the palate. He held the bottle out to Takana, coughing violently as he tried to catch his breath.

"Holy shit," he coughed out between gasps for air. "You *drink* that? I'd use it to polish the goddamn swords."

"Keeps the cold out of my joints and helps me sleep," she said. "Gets better the more you drink. The more you drink, the more you forget the taste."

"Yeah, I bet," he said, taking back the bottle and drinking with a lot more caution. Warmth flowed through his veins and muscles with the drink, pleasantly heating him from the inside out.

"So, where are you from?" Takana asked. "Apart from the Human Realm. I'm guessing America, from the accent?"

"Yeah, originally Alabama. England for ten years, now, though," he replied, accepting the bottle when Takana passed it back again.

"I thought the Deep South," Takana said. "You have the drawl. It's faint, but it's certainly there."

"Dad moved to Portsmouth. In England," he added for clarification, "for work when I was eight, so I'm a half-and-half, I suppose. Still have an accent, though. Can't seem to lose it, although it's faded some. Comes out when I'm drunk." He looked at the bottle and drank again. Part of him was ready for Takana to ridicule the way he spoke. It was a favourite pastime for the bullies where he lived and at college.

"It's unique. Musical," Takana said, eyes watchful. "There's another accent there too. Not just American or British. I can't place it..."

"Indian," Eden said. "Punjab. My mama was Indian, but she moved to the States for college and met my dad. Like me, she never managed to lose the accent, though—had it until the day she died. I guess I sound like a mongrel," he finished. "Guys at school take the piss at the way I talk. Where I ain't all that bright sounding, you know? They call me *Bubba Gump*, or whatever they think is clever any particular week. I get mixed up, at times, between English and Punjabi – the grammar is different. I tend to sound a bit slow, I guess."

"It's a nice accent. Perhaps they're jealous. When I was younger, I sounded more common than you'd give credit for."

"Really?"

Takana sipped at her whiskey. "I think they're jealous."

"Okay, sure, whatever."

"You sound just fine, ignore whatever they said. Be you."

"Well," Eden said, sipping, again, "I'm a mixture anyhow. Sound weird, talk odd, but hey. It's who I am. Guess I picked up phases and accents from all over."

"I hear what you're saying," Takana said. "A lot of us, in the Border Guard, have picked up the phrases and colloquialisms from Southern England. We have crossed back and forth for so long, that our languages have blurred together. At least you'll not find us hard to understand, unless you pass through Alfheim and into the Dark Lands. We all speak English and sound much like people in your county."

"Farmers?" Eden joked.

"Farmers, indeed."

"It's hard to believe you go through to my world. The Fae, I mean."

"All the time," she said. We keep up with current affairs, Eden. The time of the Fae being backwards forest creatures is long gone." Takana looked around and nearly choked on the whiskey. "Contrary to how it might look, we are far from backwards forest creatures."

Eden laughed with her, taking the whiskey when it was passed back to him.

"My old speech raises its head when I've been drinking, also," Takana told him, smiling. "I know what you mean. I ain't nothin' but a half-breed from Florenthal, after all. No good me putting on flowery airs, making meself seem more than I am." She smiled again, sipping her drink. "It took fifty years for me to lose my accent. You're young yet. It still comes out, when I'm drunk."

"Talking of drunk, are you trying to get me pissed?"

"Oh, you'll get drunk with or without me trying," she said. "Please tell me you can handle your liquor better than you can pack for a heroic quest?"

"It's an *heroic* quest, now?" he asked. "Thought it was a noble one."

"Bad enough it's a quest, I would have thought."

"You don't like quests?"

"I don't like seeing attractive young men risking their lives."

Eden folded his arms on the table in front of him. The cool breeze blowing through the door danced over his bare back, brushing his skin in a gentle caress and drying the last of his sweat. "You say that as though I'm going to walk into danger at every turn. I just want to find the face behind the voice," he said, lifting his shoulders. He linked his fingers together on the table top. "I don't see how I'm risking my life. I'm not a child."

"You are a child," Takana replied. She drank from the green bottle again, her eyes fixed on his face as she gulped. "You're a child, and you have no idea of what events are waiting to conspire against you. The path you will walk, Eden, is not one I would wish for anyone, but it is yours to walk. You are risking your life. Risking it," she continued, drinking deeply again, "for someone you have never met. Never seen. Yet you are so *sure* you love them that the knowledge is tangible."

"I am sure, yes," he replied. "I have no doubt about what I feel for him."

"He may scorn you, Eden. You could leave all you know, and risk all you have, for nothing at all. And the way through these lands is hard enough for those of us born to the Fae—you have the smell of the Human Realm imprinted on your soul as much as you have the light of our magicks in your eyes. With each step you take, you are risking your life. To many people, you would be worth a lot more dead than you are alive...and to others, you would be a valuable slave, to be traded and sold like a pup bred for market.

Eden opened his mouth, ready to object, but Takana held a hand up, speaking again.

"Please, Eden, see what you are risking. For a dream? I've played along. You've played with a sword, and beaten me in battle. You have shared food and drank with me. You've seen the land you desired to find. Now go home, Eden. Go home and try to forget this place. Live the life that is yours, if only you reach out and take it. This is the crossroads. You may be able to get back to your world, if you choose to stay here. There is *every* chance you will become lost and meet your end, here, in a land filled with those who would own you or kill you. Leave, now, and live the life you have the chance to live. It will be easier than the path you seek to step onto."

"I don't have anything to return for," Eden said, almost to himself. He shook his head, raising his shoulders. "It's just me and my dad, and he would rather I was here, he knows this is what I wanted. He'd rather me gone and happy, than be at home, lonely and...and sad. You know what loneliness is, Takana, living here. Imagine the same loneliness, yet being surrounded by people. People who can't stand the sight of you, who are scared of you, who don't understand you. That is what I would be returning to, and honestly? Damn." Eden took the bottle from Takana and drunk deep from the neck. He shook his head and focused on the feeling of the raw alcohol burning its way down his gullet.

"I would be happier here," he continued, looking at the bottle. "I don't have much to go on, I know I don't. I know I haven't seen a face, or anything like that, but at least, *here*, I am in the same world as someone I love...and someone I truly believe loves me,

Takana. Whatever I might face, here, it has to be worth more than living an empty life in a place where I'm as trapped as surely as if I'd been caged?"

"Caged?"

Eden shrugged and drank. "Yeah. Don't matter if I can escape my town, I don't reckon. There's something about *me*, I think, that people just...I scare them." He shook his head at the bottle before sipping once again. "I—I'm kinda psychic, I guess. Telepathic, perhaps. Hell. Even I don't know what it is I have, but I know that there's times when I can't keep it all back, and I'll say something...answer a question that ain't been asked out loud...that sort of shit. It makes me a freak, I know that."

"How so?" Takana asked.

"I hear thoughts, I think," Eden replied, daring to glance at Takana's face, gauging her reaction. It took courage to meet her eyes. Seeing only compassion, he took a breath and looked back at his hands. "I see things. Images. They don't make much sense, but there's been a lot of times when what I've seen has happened. I've thought people have been speaking to me and I answered them—but they hadn't said a thing. They were just thinking and I was hearing them. I went to a church once. That was...well, it was interesting."

Takana made a small noise and Eden lifted his head, looking at her. He shrugged one shoulder dismissively and handed her back her bottle. "Reckon I'm getting maudlin," he said. "Let's just accept that I'm going to fit in nowhere. Not in the world I came from. Better I take my chances here, where I won't have no special abilities as far as most folks are concerned. If I can get back to my world, one day, then that's just great. If I can't?" Eden sat back in his chair, thinking. "If I can't, then I can't, huh? Don't see as it matters none."

Takana's eyes were cool and assessing, and she sat in silent appraisal of him for several long minutes before she turned away, leaning to pluck two small wooden cups from a narrow shelf behind her. She set them firmly on the table, in the centre, and poured whiskey to the brim of each. She slid one across to Eden, a silent challenge, and lifted her own cup.

Eden narrowed his eyes at her, mutely picking up the cup in front of him. He held it up in salute, then tossed the contents down his throat, never looking away from her face. Her eyes changed subtly as he placed the cup back on the table to be refilled, as though she had seen something she had been searching for inside him. He picked up the newly filled cup and repeated the salute before drinking. She had been right. The more one drank, the less one noticed the taste—or the burn.

"How serious are you?" Takana asked, as he downed the third full cup.

"Deadly so," he replied, before tossing back the contents of another cup.

She narrowed her eyes at him, forcing more whiskey down her own throat, and refilled their glasses. He took his cup from the table and downed the harsh liquor.

"You won't get me so drunk I'll want you to send me back where I don't wanna go," he said, gesturing for his cup to be filled again. "You aren't going to make me agree to something I don't want to do. I can see the plan in your eyes. I can feel what you're planning to do, and I'll save you the trouble now. It won't work." He sipped, putting the cup down. He spread his hands on the table, assimilating the wooziness brought on by the strong liquor. Sure he wasn't going to be sick, he wrapped a hand around the cup and concentrated on being sober. It had some success. "I'm not going back," he said to Takana. "You can't make me."

Takana sat back as though he had slapped her and slammed the bottle onto the table.

"Fine. You want to throw your life away, and there's nothing I can do to stop you. Is that about it?"

He drank, just a sip, from his whiskey before setting the wooden cup down in front of him. He hoped he didn't look as sick as he was starting to feel. The whiskey was some of the worst he had tasted.

"Not throwing it away," he said, shuddering as the hard liquor ran down his gullet. "I'm not throwing my life away," he repeated. He wasn't. Not if his hunch was right—a hunch that had been slowly forming itself in his mind over the course of the day. His mind, somehow, felt clearer, here in these lands than it had ever done in the Human Realm. Already, it seemed as though his old life was something that belonged to someone else. Nothing he could connect to himself with any sense of familiarity. This life, here and now, made more sense than the other had ever done.

Far from throwing his life away, he was making one begin. *Here* was where he was meant to be. As though ever having been in the other world had been a mistake. He belonged here, as much as Takana did. It felt like home.

The water over the fire started to boil, letting out huge plumes of steam that heated the inside of the small cabin. Takana reached over and moved it from the gridiron, standing to tip it into the wooden tub. She stalked outside, filling the kettle with more water from the well. Sitting back down, she looked at Eden. Resting her chin in her hands, her elbows on the table, she frowned, as though working something out.

"There are clothes in the box under the bed," she said, standing up to walk to the door. "Soap is next to the sink," she added, pointing to the stone sink in the far corner of the room. "There's a scabbard for your sword hanging in the cupboard, and an extra bow. A knife that will fit your hand is in the box with the clothes. Take the whole box. You'll need everything in there. I'll make a start on a pair of boots for you." She looked once more at his battered Converse. "Those will fall apart sooner than would be convenient. I expect you washed and dressed—fully armed and looking like you might live longer than a week—in thirty minutes. We will get you to grips with the basics of a bow and arrow, before supper. Then you can sleep—you're in for a long day tomorrow."

Eden watched as she lugged more water into the cabin and prepared the room for him to bathe, chatting amicably all the time. He stood, bowing his head in deference to her as she readied to leave him alone. "Thank you. I won't let you down...thank you."

"Yeah, yeah, Wonder-Boy," she said, turning away. "Just don't get dead. I can't have your death on my conscience. Might as well blow up the realms myself," he thought she said as she walked away.

He sat, frowning at the small wooden bathtub for another few minutes, then heaved the warming water from the fire and set it down next to the bath, using a pitcher of cold water to cool the water in the tub. Stripping out of his jeans, socks and shoes, he pulled the band from his hair. Fleetingly thinking of his power-shower, he sat down, his knees folded under his chin, and decided he could live without amenities. They were unimportant, in the grand scheme of things. Scrubbing quickly with a rough linen cloth, he jumped out of the rapidly cooling water, wrapped another length of linen around his hips and bent to wash his hair over the bath. Rinsing with the clean warm water from the kettle, he wrung his hair out, twisting it tightly until nothing but a few beads of water formed along the length of the thick raven strands.

The box under Takana's bed was filled with items that had the scholarly side of Eden's brain in raptures. He was holding items that could have been hundreds of years old. The handle of the knife was so worn, so frequently held, that the wood was as smooth as ivory. Sleek and comfortable in his hand. He set it, along with its sheath, on the bed. A hairbrush was similarly set on the bed, along with a hand-carved comb for lice and several leather thongs, plainly hair-ties. No underwear, though. He searched again, then gave a small mental shrug, dismissing it from his mind. The Fae, it seemed, didn't bother with underpants.

He wondered about Cole as he shook out one of the two pairs of trousers and a fine lawn shirt, dyed lightest blue. Tall, he thought, pulling the trousers over his bare hips. He stood at six foot one, maybe six-two if he stood straight, and Cole's soft brown leather trousers were long in the leg by a few inches. Otherwise, the fit was perfect—snug, but not too tight, around the hips and bottom, but with enough flexibility for full freedom of movement. He smoothed them over his thighs, satisfied, and pulled the shirt down over his head, tucking in the billowing yards of light blue fabric. Sat on the bed Eden slid knitted woollen socks, made of the finest thinnest yarn he'd seen onto his feet. He could hardly wait for the boots to be made—the baseball boots, while good with anything in the Human Realm, were not fitting for an ensemble of such fine quality. He laced his Converse with an internal sigh and added the sword belt to hang over his left hip. He assumed it would go there as he was right handed. The knife holster he buckled around his right thigh in the same style Takana wore hers. He frowned at the bow in the cupboard for a moment, wondering how one was meant to wear it, or carry it around, without it getting in the way. He had a small pang for his guns, but pushed it aside and grasped the bow, pleased it was a short one and not a longbow—he had no idea how he would have been expected to deal with a six and a half foot tall bit of wood. Knotting his hair, he pulled his shoulders back, and held his hand on the door handle. The whiskey had left him light-headed. He hoped there was more food than just the single bowl of soup—he needed something for substantial. Still, he wasn't drunk, not by any stretch of the imagination. At least he wasn't going to embarrass himself in front of his host.

"Well," he said to himself, "you wanted this. Time to reach out and make it your own, I guess."

"Elf-made clothing suits you," Takana said, eyeing him as he walked across the clearing to the outside fire. "Not many men can carry the look as well as you can."

"Thank you." He folded himself onto the short stool near the fire. "I wasn't sure how most of the weapons were meant to be worn," he admitted, placing his bow at his side.

Takana checked him over. "You have them on correctly. The bow, in fine weather, can be slung over your back. In the rain, you will have to store the bowstring separately, where it will not get wet. Dry feet, dry bowstring. Got it?"

"Got it. And eat when I can—same as sleep where I can."

"And fill your water bottle whenever the opportunity presents itself," Takana said. "Drink as much as you can, when you find fresh water and fill your bottle—then drink as sparingly as you possibly can. Like food, one cannot always know when water shall be freely available."

"Okay."

"You have a lot to learn, Wonder-Boy."

Eden knew he did. He met Takana's eyes and pulled back his shoulders. "I'm willing to learn what I need to know," he said. "I'm not playing around. I want to learn. I want to stay in this realm."

"I know. That is why I am willing to teach you as much as I can," Takana said. "I don't believe you should be walking the path you seem to be choosing— you have two paths, clearly marked, and the other will be a lot less painful for you. I don't agree with your choice, but you...well, let me just say you are not a soul that should fall and be lost to us." She looked down at her long fingers. "To lose you would be a tragedy beyond bearing, so I will teach you all I know. At least then I can say I have done all I can to help you along your way. You are so young," she said, sighing to herself. "So, so young. Still," she said, looking at him, "it is an honour to be able to sit where I sit, tonight, and I suppose that I should at least try to be worthy of it. That *I* should be sat here," she said, her voice floating away on the wind. "Who knows what this is the start of. Right!" she said, standing up and clapping her hands together, rubbing her palms. "Bow and arrow. This is the nocking point," she said, tapping the bowstring. "You need to fix the arrow to it, holding it between your fingers, like this..."

"Excellent!" Takana called a few hours later, actually smiling at Eden as she clapped with uncharacteristic enthusiasm.

Eden grinned and jumped down from his vantage point atop the woodshed to jog around the fire. His bow was held loosely in his left hand and his eyes scanned the trees. A flash of white caught his eye and he raised the bow to fire in one swift movement. His arrow pierced the flapping cloth to one of the trees. He *loved* his new bow. Guns had been fun and he had enjoyed target shooting, but this? He had been born for this weapon, he thought.

He dropped and rolled to avoid a stone thrown by Takana. She had decided that, as any enemies would almost certainly not be staying still with a helpful target painted on their fronts, he should learn to duck and cover. Loosing arrows as he darted around the clearing with missiles thrown at his head and scraps of cloth flying through the trees to be shot down. Takana had thought he might hit one target in ten and get himself brained in the first five minutes.

Eden had been training for an hour, had missed

three targets out of a possible three-hundred and had not been hit once. More than that, he was having more fun than he could ever remember having before in his life. Exhilarated by the simple joy of hitting targets and avoiding missiles, he felt more alive than ever before. He also had to admit that it was nice to have impressed Takana with his gymnastics. And to show off a bit for an appreciative audience, somersaulting and cart-wheeling to avoid Takana's rocks, while learning to fire an arrow almost at the same instant.

"Alright, Wonder-Boy," Takana called, holding her hands up. "Enough. You're impressive, I'll give you that," she said, walking over to him. "Well done—you look as though as you were born with a bow in your hand and a quiver on your back. And, Eden, you sure can move. But it's late," she said, glancing at the darkening purple sky. "Time to eat and sleep—you need to conserve your energy, even if it might seem limitless."

"All right," he said, walking to the fire and sitting down. He stroked his hands over his bow and placed it gently at his side, patting it to reassure himself it was safe and close to him.

Takana gave him a knowing look. "If it feels like an extension of yourself already, then I think you may have found your weapon of choice."

He smiled at her, feeling shy. "It feels as though I'd forgotten how to use it, is all," he said, stroking the bow like he would a lover, his fingertips skimming the smooth wooden curves. "As though I knew, the moment I pulled back the string—I just had to remember, that's all."

"Previous life?"

He dipped his head to look at the ground between his feet. "Who knows."

"Indeed," Takana said. She touched his cheek with a gentle hand. "I learned, many moons ago, not to question what is not mine to know. Sometimes, the knowledge that something simply *is*, is enough of an answer. Maybe it's a previous life, maybe it's an innate skill you were born with and never had the chance to discover until now. We will likely never know, so just accept it for the gift it is."

"Wise words," Eden said, resting his hand over her fingers and squeezing. "Thank you, Takana. For letting me stay."

She shook her head, eyes thoughtful. "I doubt I could have made you leave." She dropped her hand and picked up a toasting fork, looking away from him, and into the flames of the fire. Methodically spearing a thick slab of white bread, she held it out to the flames and reached sideways for a earthenware pot of what Eden assumed was some sort of dripping. When the bread was toasted, she smeared it with the gelatinous animal fat and handed it to him, spearing another doorstop of bread onto the fork.

"Thank you," he said, taking a large bite. He was hungrier than he had realised. The exercise on top of the whiskey had drained his final reserves of energy at the end of the most emotional day of his life for years. Leaning forwards so the fat did not drip onto his shirt, he studied the sky for several minutes. "How does time work, here?" he asked, swallowing the mouthful of delicious toast and washing it down with the mild berry wine.

"The days are longer," Takana said quietly. "Time slows while you are in this realm, though. It's odd.

Nothing that can be fully explained until you have experienced it for yourself." She looked at the sky. "The days are longer here. Our times works differently to the Human Realm. It's hard to quantify how it passes. It's meaningless, almost, in this realm. I think you have been here a couple of days, as you understand time."

"But I've not got sleepy."

"You won't feel sleepy at first. Your body will adjust and the magic in the world will keep you alert. Well, more alert than had you been in the Human Realm."

"So you don't measure time? No clocks?"

"Gods no. One might say that they shall meet at sundown, but no clocks. We don't rush. We take our time. If we wait a few hours for a person to show up, then that if a gift. To take time out and enjoy the period of nothingness. It can be therapeutic to sit and watch the world go by."

"Okay. I'm liking this place more and more, the more I discover. No clocks. Perfect." Eden finished his toast. Takana brandished the toasting fork in invitation, as if he was going to deny himself the best toast he had eaten. He waited while she cooked, taking the golden brown slice of bread when she passed it over. "Is there anything I can help with?" he asked, catching a drip of fat before it slid down his chin. "That you'd normally do at night?"

"You can collect wood that has fallen from the trees," she said, pointing at the tree-line across the rushing stream. "Just what has fallen to the ground. Do not harm the trees."

Eden looked at Takana, then at his quiver, filled with arrows. He felt the colour drain from his face as he looked back at Takana. "I shot them. They can *feel*?"

She snorted. "Everything that is not rock can feel. Yes, the trees can feel, as can the vegetables you pluck from the ground, and the sheep you slaughter for your dinner. Yes, they can *feel*. However, few are sentient. Try to avoid setting anything that looks like me on fire, won't you?" she asked drily. "Asking you not to cut the limbs from the standing trees is not the same as making you feel bad for piercing a few with an arrow. Do not concern yourself with shooting at trunks, Eden. Concern yourself with not cutting into my homeland to gather wood for a fire. Go...collect kindling and branches. Then you can fetch water and bring it to the cabin. We will need to wash in the morning, and make tea. Then, Eden, you can sleep."

III

"I know you're there," Takana called into the trees, glancing over her shoulder at her cabin to make sure that Eden slept on. Unaware and innocent—for now, at least. "There is no one who can walk in these woods and not have me know they are there." She folded her arms. "What do you want, Toleil?"

A soft sigh was followed by the crunch of hooves on the undergrowth a second before a slightly built faun stepped into Takana's view. He met her eyes across the clearing and walked forward, picking his way across the rickety planks that served as her bridge, his hooves tapping on the ancient wood. He stopped in front of her and bowed.

"You are not the only one who the trees talk to," Toleil said, pitching his voice low as he leant closer to her. "You have a visitor. One you have not sent back."

"Damn," Takana said, closing her eyes briefly. "Damn their gossipy leaves. How far has the knowledge spread?"

"To me," Toleil shrugged. "Mayhap further still."

"Elves?" she asked.

"Perhaps."

"Oh, shit." Takana looked back at her cabin and calculated furiously in her head. As far as she was aware, there were no elves—no large gatherings anyway—for at least a three day ride from her camp. A *hard* ride, at that. She had purposely asked to be given a position far away from the nearest elven town. It was easier to get on with life without constant

71

questions about her blood and the distrust the elves had for nymphs. The less she had to do with elves, the better. They had hurt her enough with their cutting words and sanctimonious judgements. Better that she avoid them and keep away from them. Out in the isolated border towns, she could pretend she had no elven blood running through her veins. It hurt less, then, when they shunned her for her nymph-blood.

Faeries, Nymphs and Hobgoblins held no fear for her, but the elves scared her and not just because they stood in judgement of her. They were terrifying. Even Cole, damn his black heart to...no. No, she couldn't curse him. Not for following his nature, and it *was* in their nature to roam and never settle. Still...even Cole had held a quiet lethalness that had scared her as much as it turned her on. Elves thought they owned the land.

Damn them all, they *did* own the land. She was answerable to them, the same as every other creature in the realm. And if they found out that she had not forced Eden to return, then it was her head that would be resting on the executioner's block. No explanations, no trial, nothing. Her job was to make sure that the two realms stayed separate, and no one from the Human Realm had the chance to ruin the last refuge of the Fae, as they had raped and pillaged the Auld Lands.

Toleil watched her in silence for several minutes. "Takana," he said, quietly, "tell me you have since sent the creature back to the world it came from?"

"It is not so simple as that." She scanned the forest with alert, watchful eyes. "Those who open the lands have the right to—"

"Oh, for the Love of Orien!" Toleil hissed. "You know as well as I do that there is *no one* in these lands who will accept that claptrap, Takana! On paper, I have the *right* to ask for audience with the King and beg for the hand of his daughter...if he had one. In reality, were I to go trotting into his castle, I would be slaughtered by a guard, most likely, for trying to attack his Majesty's person. And if I asked to marry a princess, I would be placed in the stocks and ridiculed at the least. So don't give me that crap about this creature having the *right* to walk these lands, because there is no right at all, and well you know it."

"I know how to do my job, Toleil."

"Then do it. Give the creature some residual power, or grant it a longer life and send it back the way it came. Send it on its way. Do what has always been done. The Human Realm will gain one more witch, and you may yet save your neck."

It sounded so simple, Takana thought. Do what had always been done and what the Border Guards were destined to do. Give the human a gift and send them on their way. One more druid. One more witch. One more mage for the Human Realm. The who had crossed would become gifted—no harm done to the Fae.

"Takana, you know your job."

Takana slumped and bowed her head. "I know. But it is not that simple, Toleil. I can't send Eden back."

"Eden? What manner of name is that?"

Takana shot Toleil a withering look. "You should read more," she snapped. "Eden is the name given to the utopia called into being at the beginning of the worlds. Both our realm, and the Human Realm have the same story, if one can be bothered to interest themselves with a small amount of history, Toleil.

Eden is the name of the promised land."

Toleil shrugged one bare shoulder. "What of it?" he asked. "Send the creature back, and claim you were delayed—you may yet keep your head."

"Damn your eyes," Takana hissed, turning on the faun. "If I were to force him back, if I *could* send him back, then I would be committing a worse crime than disobeying the elves...I *cannot* send Eden back. He has chosen to remain in this world."

Toleil watched her as though she had grown another head. "If either king learns of this deception, Lady, then you shall be executed. Both Airell and Jaizel have this law. You speak treason against the realm."

"I can't send Eden back. This is bigger than Airell and much bigger than Jaizel—may Orien consume his soul to whichever hell spawned it." Takana spat reflexively on the ground. "I cannot send him back," she repeated. "He has chosen to stay in this world.

Toleil looked at her as though she had gone insane, frowning as he studied her face. "I know it's been a long time since Cole was here," he said, narrowing his eyes, "but you never came across as the sort who would be turned by a good fuck."

Takana had drawn back her arm and whipped her hand across Toleil's face before she had even thought about moving. The faun staggered back, holding his cheek, and licked the blood from the corner of his mouth, staring at her.

"You take that back," Takana said harshly, stalking towards him. "How *dare* you?" she asked, shaking inwardly as she advanced. The anger pulsed through her veins like the strongest powdered Paheka-Root, leaving her high and dazed. She felt the power of the land under her feet, and stepped in time with the beat of the earth. Stretching out her hand to grab Toleil by his throat, she shook him hard. "You accuse *me*, the greatest guard this realm has ever *known*, of thinking with my cunt, is that what you are saying, Toleil?"

"No," the faun gasped, shaking his head quickly. "No, Lady...I spoke before I...I should not have...I am *sorry!*"

Takana opened her hand and let him fall to the forest floor, staring down at him with hard eyes. "You will never mention Cole to me again, do you understand?"

Toleil rubbed his throat with his hand and drew in deep breaths. He heaved himself to his knees. "I apologise, Lady. Forgive me."

She glared for another moment, before holding out her hand to help the faun rise to his feet. "Speak no more of it," she muttered, guilty now her anger had abated. She dusted Toleil's shoulders off with her hands and turned away from him, walking towards her home. She looked back over her shoulder.

"I need your help, Toleil," she said quietly, beckoning him to follow her. "Jaizel cannot find this boy, do you understand? If Jaizel finds him, then we are lost."

"No, I don't understand. Not really," Toleil said, trotting along in her wake. "It's just a human, isn't it? Begging your pardon, Lady," he added, bowing, "but if you are not bedding it, why do you want to keep it?"

Takana pushed open the door to her cabin, eyes on Toleil as he looked around the small room and rested his eyes on Eden, asleep on the bed. His eyes widened and he held a hand to his chest, then glanced at Takana with fearful—hopeful—eyes.

"No," the faun said, barely breathing the word. "No...it can't be..."

Takana pulled Toleil back out of the cabin before he could creep closer to her precious charge and closed the door. She held her hand on Toleil's shoulder. "You force him back," she said, challenging the faun. "You try and send him back across the river, Toleil. You tell him that he cannot walk this realm."

"I would not dare," Toleil croaked, stepping back, away from the cabin. Away from Eden.

"Jaizel cannot—*cannot*—find this boy," Takana said, her voice low and urgent. "Help me, Toleil. If you have been told, then it is too late to stop the trees talking. I cannot silence the forest. That would draw Jaizel's attention more than a vague rumour of a human in the land." She thought for a few minutes, pressing the heel of her hand to her head. "How fast can you get word to Alexander?"

"Alexander?" Toleil repeated, as shocked as if she had asked to speak to Cole. In the faun's defence, to ask for Alex was on a par to asking for Cole.

"Yes, you fool. We need *help*, and Alexander is the only person I can think of who is even slightly equipped to assist in this. How long will it take you to reach him?"

"I will reach him and bring him back by next moonrise, if I leave now," Toleil said, glancing at the cabin. "Should I tell him what I have...what I have seen?"

"No. He will think you're mad. Tell him that I need his help." She reached up to unclasp a delicate silver chain from around her neck and handed it to Toleil. "Tell him that I call on the fealty of our shared blood. That if he cares for me at all, then for the love of Orien himself, I need him to come to me—and come prepared, Toleil. Tell him to come prepared. I am in trouble, and I call on him to save me."

Takana watched Toleil run from the clearing as though he had banshees on his tail. She leant back against the wall of her cabin, closing her eyes with a quiet groan. She held her fingers to her forehead, rubbing gently above her eyes. It didn't help, but she never expected it to. She sank down to the ground, pulling her knees into her chest, and rested her chin on her knees to watch the trees that surrounded her.

"You bastards." She narrowed her eyes at the trunks that seemed to close in on her small cabin. "You don't have a fucking clue what you might have done, do you? You stupid, stupid bastards," she bit out. "All of you. When you are razed to the ground by Jaizel...when your burnt and dying arms are stretching to the skies, imploring the gods for their mercy...remember this night, and remember what you have done. Remember that with your talk, and with your rumours, you may have taken the chance you had of salvation. I'm done with you," she said tiredly, leaning her head back against the wooden wall. "I'm done with all of you. I revoke my protection," she said, closing her eyes. "I revoke my protection, and I withdraw my fealty. Do you hear me?"

The leaves around her rustled in agitation. A wind stirred, whistling through the branches, the sound the scream of the forest. Takana did not open her eyes to watch the branches whip back and forth, or watch the leaves fly into the turbulent air.

"So long as you understand," she said under her breath. "I leave with Alexander, when he comes. If he comes," she added. "Then you are on your own and I don't care if it is the vines that strangle you, the insects that eat you, or Jaizel burning you to ashes. Whatever your fate, you will remember this night, and you will weep, knowing it was your own doing. Pray...oh, Orien save you all...pray that I am enough to keep that boy safe. Or it could be the end of us all."

Takana slid her hand sideways across the splintery wood of the ramshackle porch, and reached under the single chair that was pushed under the glassless window. Drawing the crossbow out from hiding, she checked it over carefully, adjusted it here and there, then laid it over her knees. Ready for a *long* duty, she relaxed into herself, feeling her features grow wooden, and prepared to defend the boy asleep inside her home to the death.

Eden ate his breakfast in silence, keeping one wary eye on Takana as she prowled around the clearing, shooting glances at the forest. He scooped another spoonful of minced meat to his mouth, chasing it down his throat with some boiled barley and a swig from his mug of sweetened tea. He could not figure out the change in his host since the previous night. He hoped to God it wasn't because she might have actually expected him to sleep with her.

No, it couldn't be that, he thought, meditatively chewing more minced meat. Takana had made it clear she knew he was gay and that he was off limits to her. She had said her role would be entirely that of teacher and host. He had kept the relief from his eyes, so he knew she could not have seen it written there to offend her. Besides, he thought, she would not have made him footwear if he had offended her. He felt a small smile tug at his mouth, looking at the boots covering his calves. Soft and slouched, they fitted like a second skin and were the most comfortable thing he had ever worn on his feet. Made from deerskin, Takana had used stitching smaller than his eyes could easily see. Layering the sole from several pieces of skin, they were lined with soft sheepskin between each layer, effectively making a cushioned sole that felt as soft as a cloud underfoot.

Takana turned where she stood, and looked at him for a moment, then span away and stalked back to her cabin, slamming the door behind her when she went inside. Eden jumped, frozen where he sat, eyes on the closed door. It opened again a few seconds later as a bag was tossed out onto the small porch, followed by a couple more sacking bags, another bow, a few pots, utensils, blankets and water-skins. He frowned and started to place his bowl of half eaten breakfast at his side, only to have Takana shout at him from inside the cabin.

"What did I tell you, Wonder-Boy? You *eat* when there is food to put inside you!"

He picked the bowl back up and hastily spooned food into his mouth. Takana seemed to have issues with him not eating anything she put in front of him. It was better to eat than make her angry—especially with her mood so unstable. He wondered again what had happened the previous night.

"Thank you! Orien save me from the mentally deficient," Takana called. "When you have eaten your fill, I want you to melt the fat in the large clay pot.

Just put it next to the fire," she continued, walking out of the cabin with a bundle of clothes in her arms. "When it's melted, add the ham to the chicken pot, and then cover it all with fat. It will last a few days, then. Fill water skins, and make sure we have a bag of suitable feathers for arrow fletching, all right?"

"Uh...sure," he called to her. "But why?"

"Because I feel like bloody looking at a bag of feathers and fatty chicken," Takana snapped. "Why do you think, Eden?"

"Wow, you're snippy in the mornings," he retorted. "For all I know, Takana, you're doing housekeeping and want me to run around fetching feathers and painting fences so you can turn around in a few weeks and show me how I've learnt Kung-Fu by scrubbing the table in your cabin!"

Takana looked at him, glaring for a heartbeat, then laughed helplessly. "Point taken, and sorry for snapping your head off. We have to leave by moonrise, tonight. A lot sooner than I would have liked to leave, but it's unavoidable."

"Oh. Oh, okay," he said, scraping his bowl clean and putting it down. He slid the pot of fat close to the fire and looked around for something that could be used as fletching, his eyes resting on the three chickens pecking peacefully in their coop near the stream. He looked at Takana, frowning.

"Can't leave them," she said with a shrug. "Wring their necks—we can cook them and eat well for the next few days, at least. I refuse to travel with a live bird, however handy the eggs might be. In the woodshed, Eden, are you listening to me?"

He turned. "In the woodshed?" he asked, waiting for instructions.

"There's flour." She grunted, packing one of the bags. Fill a smaller sack, hmm? We might need it sooner rather than later. Then pack your clothes. The ones I gave you, and the ones you arrived in."

"So, kill and pluck the birds," Eden said, "pack the feathers, pack my clothes, fill water bottles, get a smaller sack of flour, get the cooked chicken covered in the fat, with the ham...okay. Anything else?"

Takana glanced at him. "How much can you carry, Eden?"

"A fair amount."

"All right," she said, "then pack up as much of my home as you can carry and still be able to run. The less I have to burn, the better."

He gaped at her. "Burn?"

"There will be some *bad* people coming this way," she said. "Some people are said to be able to link themselves to others, using their presence. a presence can be found in anything one has owned. Whilst I have no proof that it *is* possible, I would rather not take the risk and find out they are able to use that particular skill to burn me from the inside out, Eden. What we can't take, we shall have to burn. The more we can take, the better for us in the long run. The more we have, the more self-sufficient we can be. Besides," she added, looking down, "it is my life. I want to bring as much of it with me as I can."

Eden jogged to the chickens and winced at the mere thought of the task ahead. He bent into the run and cradled one of the birds in his arms, stroking the feathery head. He closed his eyes and ran his hand down the delicate neck then drew in a breath and moved quickly, tipping the bird upside down and yanking the head away from the chunky body. He grimaced as the bird flapped under his arm, pinned to his side; dead, but moving violently as its nerves accepted the fact.

"Damn," he said, dropping the carcass to the grass. He reached for the second bird, which eyed him and squawked, flapping to get away. He snagged it and dispatched it quickly, then the third. Heavy-hearted, he held all three birds by their necks in his hand and walked back to Takana.

"I don't got a clue how to gut them," he admitted, putting them next to Takana's bag. "If you can do that, I'd be thankful."

"Thank you," she said, touching one of the lifeless bodies with a tender fingertip.

"It's okay," Eden replied, mixing ham into the cooked minced chicken and filling the small pot with liquid fat, making sure all the air pockets were banged out. He looked at Takana from the corner of his eye. "Something happened, since last night," he said quietly. "Someone came here. Upset you."

"I can see why you piss people off. Yes, someone came. My closest neighbour, if one could call him that. Toleil. He's a faun."

Eden blinked. A faun? He pictured a faun in his head and wondered if Takana could possibly mean...

Takana slapped him. "A faun. Goat bottom half, human top half. Hooves. Try not to stare if you meet him."

"Does he have horns?"

"For goodness sake! He's a faun! Of course he has horns."

"Oh...okay. He actually has goat legs?"

"And hooves."

"Okay," Eden said. "Faun. Got it. So he came

here, last night?"

"He did," Takana said. She did not sound pleased. "The trees have been talking, and your presence is known. We have to get you out of here, before anyone comes to see if there is truth in the trees' gossip. I've called for help...if help is to come, it will be here by moonrise. We have until then to clear the camp and get ourselves ready to leave. And burn what we plan to leave behind," she said, almost to herself.

"If help is to come? You think it might not?" he asked, stilling her busy hands by laying his over them and squeezing. "I should leave. Point me in the direction of the nearest town, and I'll leave. You don't have to leave your home, Takana."

"Oh, dear boy," she said, resting her forehead on his shoulder. "It was too late for me the moment I found you. I have to leave here, because if I am found, then I will be killed, Eden." She turned her head and kissed him lightly on his cheek. "Do not worry about me," she said next to his ear. "Do not worry about anything you cannot control, and give your attention to the things you can. Come, pack with me and help me prepare for the journey and we will talk and share stories. I'll start," she said. "My name is Takana Jarlen, and I am, for the purposes of the most recent census, a Wood Nymph. I am also half elf, but I have always tried to ignore that," she said. "My mother had the same weakness as I did when it came to a pretty face. Elves can't be trusted." She winked, grinning brightly. "But *damn*, they're good between the sheets."

Eden chuckled, and started plucking the first of the chickens, carefully putting each feather into a small cloth bag. "Who is Jaizel?" he asked. A chill slid down his spine as he said the name, as though the simple sound of the word could conjure up a sense of foreboding. He shook himself. It was no different to a million other times something had walked over his grave. The name, though, rang a bell somewhere, deep inside. As though he should know it, but why, he could not have said.

"Are you all right?" Takana asked, watching him.

"Uh, yeah. Sure, I'm fine. I thought I'd heard the name before, that's all. Who is he?"

"An Elven King. One of them."

"Oh?"

Takana shrugged both shoulders and sat up straight. "The realm we're in can be looked at as one world with different countries. Different clans, and different kings. Jaizel is an elf—the most powerful elf ever known in all of history. The most wicked man ever known in all of history," she said, shaking her head sadly. "He is a Dark Elf. Now, if the Light Elves are bastards, then the Dark ones are a hundred times worse. And cruel. Cruel but powerful."

Eden plucked the chicken he held although he kept flicking his gaze upwards to watch Takana as she spoke.

"Jaizel is...he is the culmination of generations, and thousands of years, of cruel and tyrannical breeding programs. He has the power of a thousand average elves, and sits on his throne, unchallenged and unquestioned. He is a true tyrant, and rules these lands with a law of steel."

"We're in his country?"

"We're in the Borderlands," Takana replied. "Bordenthal. Neither his lands, or King Airell's. These lands belong to Airell, technically, but they are cared for by Cole. They were gifted to him a couple of hundred years ago. King Airell does not interfere with Cole's lands."

"King Airell?" Eden asked, hearing the shift in Takana's tone. No longer hateful as it had been for Jaizel, her voice had softened as she spoke of the other king.

"Airell is the king of the lands to the west and south. Jaizel's lands stretch north and east. We are central, here. Now, it's obviously a bit more complex than walking either east or west, as to whose land you will be in, but that's a rough guide for you. It serves its purpose. Airell is a Light Elf."

"Also not to be trusted?" he asked.

"Oh, Airell is different," she said, not meeting his eyes. "When that man says he will do something, then it will be done. If he says he will be somewhere, then he will be there, and if he promises you the moon from the skies, then it will be because he has found a way to pull it down to you."

"You respect him?"

"Very much," Takana agreed. "And fear him for the same reasons I respect him," she added, sighing. "He may not be as cruel as Jaizel, but he has several laws the same—and the first of those is that no human will be permitted into the Elven Realms. He would kill me just as swiftly as Jaizel would, for not sending you straight back across the river."

Eden sat back, feeling as though Takana had punched him, hard, in the gut. "You said that by crossing the river, I had earned the right," he said. "I have to go back?"

"It's too late. Oh, my dear, dear, Wonder-Boy," she said, "it was too late long before this. This is your path, and it is the path you must walk. Me crossing your path does not change *your* journey—it just means that I will have to change direction. The problem I have, is that I will not be able to get you close enough to Airell for him to see *why* I did not—*could* not—send you back. If he could see you, he would understand. And we have to keep you as far from Jaizel as we can, because he would likely see into your soul, far deeper than I can see, and then, my dear, you would be lost. We can't lose you. You would be a prize beyond measure for Jaizel. You are...goodness. You are more special than you can imagine, Eden. You will find out how special, if we can keep you alive long enough. Crossing back to the Human Realm, now, would not be enough to keep you safe from Jaizel. We have to get you out of here, and hide you as best we can.

"I am sorry. I cannot tell you more, and at the same time, I have told you too much. Eden, all I can do is promise you that I will die to protect you, if that is what it takes to keep you safe. I give you my bond, and my fealty. Until my death, I am now sworn to you, bond and fealty. Neither is given lightly, and my words are my oath. Do you understand?"

"I understand that I'm just a regular kid from a small town in the middle of nowhere," Eden said, taking both her hands again between his own. "Sending me back won't help you?"

"No, Eden. Sending you back would just break your heart—the outcome for me would be the same. Do you accept my oath?"

Eden frowned at her. "It...I...Takana, I don't know what's going on. I don't know what...why would you offer this? I'm just *me*, Takana!" he cried. "Nothing special, no one of much consequence. Just plain old Eden."

Into the Woods: Searching for Eden, Part One.

"And so much more besides," Takana said. "It will be clear, one day. Do you accept my oath, Eden?"

"Do I have a choice?" he asked, sighing as he let go of her hands. "Reckon you'll go where you want. And you're my teacher. I was taught not to argue with my elders and my betters. If you will be happier swearing me an oath, then I accept it, and thankfully."

She exhaled heavily and smiled at him as though he had given her the greatest gift in any world. Leaning forward, she met his mouth gently, pressing her lips to his in a brief kiss before sitting back. "Thank you," she said, sounding calmer than she had all morning.

Stunned by the fleeting pressure of her mouth on his own, Eden held his fingers to his lips and drew a breath of his own.

"This oath," he asked hesitantly. "Don't mean I just married you, in Fae-Speak, right?"

She laughed loudly, startling the birds from the trees. Blue eyes twinkling at him as she shook her head, she gripped his shoulder and squeezed once before letting her hand drop.

"No, Eden," she said, still grinning broadly. "No, we never just got married, and I give you my word that your virtue is safe with me. I have seen where you are meant to be, and that place is not in my bed or between my legs. Stop looking so *scared*." Takana snuffled brightly to herself as she took the plucked chicken from Eden's lap and slit it easily open with her knife, as though giving her oath had lifted a weight from her shoulders.

Eden looked at his knees. He couldn't help touching his lips again. He could feel the ghost of Takana's kiss there, on his skin. He hoped he didn't look as stunned as he felt. After all, he had never imagined his first kiss would be given by a Fae-Creature from another world. Takana was beautiful, though, so that was a bonus. He stroked his fingertip over his lower lip, more in awe, now the shock of immediate intimacy had passed. Takana was still giggling. She tapped him on the knee, catching his attention to grin at him.

"Married!" She snorted. "Goodness me, if I ever have a bridegroom, then I hope he doesn't look a quarter as scared as you did, then. Come—let us hurry and get ready," she said, "then I'll do your hair. While it suits you very much, we do not have elastic bands here. I shall braid it for you. Not that it will matter a damn if we're caught, but perhaps, if you look like one of my kind, Eden, then we can keep you alive for longer. Just pray our help arrives."

"Can I ask what help it is you're expecting?" He sat still while his hair was brushed.

"You can," Takana said. "I have called on my oldest friend. Alexander. Alex. He is a warrior, a soldier, a survivor. An elf. A well-bred, royal elf. He sits at King Airell's right hand, when he is at court. Very powerful, and he has the ear of his cousin, the king, who also happens to be his best friend. They are as close as brothers. Closer."

"If I might say so," Eden said, "he sounds an odd choice. A dangerous one."

"Yes. There is some risk."

"But?"

Takana lifted one shoulder in an eloquent shrug. "He is my brother," she replied. "We share a father. Shared. I'm calling on family fealty and hope I can count on his eminent common sense. He has always been sensible—I think he was cursed with it at birth. Joking aside, Eden, I have always believed it is better to die a fast death at the hands of one you love, than be burnt or beheaded as a traitor. At least, if Alex comes here, he will see you and understand why I have made this choice. Whether or not he chooses to kill me for treason, which he is within his right to do," she said, sighing, "you should be protected. I can but hope."

Eden bowed his head, wishing he had never found the way into the lands of the Fae. He shook his head and closed his eyes when Takana rested her hand on his back, between his shoulder blades. He had walked—ran—blindly into her world and for reasons only she knew, she was willing to risk everything to protect him. He could not begin to hope to understand why she was making the decisions she was. Nor could he argue with the choices she was making. She was at least a couple of hundred years old, and he was a child. He was at the mercy of her decisions, and had to trust and pray that she knew what he was doing.

"I'm sorry," he said. "I can't turn back the clock. I can't not have come here. I'm sorry I've gotten you into this. I wish I hadn't."

She patted his back. "Eden?"

"Yeah?"

She leant into his field of vision. "I tried to turn you back. I tried to cross you over the river. But not because of any laws, and not because I could face danger. I wanted you to turn back for your own sake. I hoped to turn you from the path you are set on, but I was wrong to do it. And I am pleased beyond measure, Eden, that I am here with you, and that you are walking this realm. Do not apologise to me. Not now, not ever. Not even if I am dying in your arms, having given my last breath for you, Eden. Never say sorry to me again, but know that you have made the sun come from behind the clouds, and have made me very happy. And given me a reason to live, not just exist. Cheer up! It will be a great quest!"

"You hate quests," he said. "Is a great quest as bad as a noble or heroic one?"

"Oh, it's much worse than that," she said happily. "The great quests are the ones where legends are born."

N

By the time the beat of hooves floated through the trees to reach Eden's ears, the moon was high and pregnant with mystery. She hung, softly tinted pink, with clouds of dark purple shimmering across her glowing face.

The trees were quiet. Subdued, Eden now knew. They were scared too. He turned slowly in a circle, looking at the line of ancient sentinels guarding the secrets of the elder sentient trees, protected behind them. The gossipy old men, cursed by Takana to be left to fend for themselves.

Eden shared a glance with Takana and was pleased when she reached for his hand, gripping it firmly in her own as she raised a crossbow and pulled her shoulders back and her chin up. Proud and warrior-like, a protective shield who left no doubt of her ability to fight.

A horse, silvery-white in the moonlight, emerged from the trees. Its rider rode bare-back, both hands raised to rest on top of his head. The man was lithe, tall, and one of the most beautiful creatures Eden had ever laid eyes on. He had long dark brown hair, plaited down his back to frame a pointed and sculptured face, saved from being sharp by only a few degrees in the set of the nose and the slope of high cheekbones. Wide slanted eyes scanned the clearing and the cabin, then rested on Takana. The rider tapped his knees to the horse's sides, hands on his head as it walked, slowly, to stand in front of Takana's crossbow.

"It is impolite to greet an invited guest by pointing weapons at them, sister." Alexander's voice was musical and pitched just *so*. The sound reverberated in Eden's skull for a moment. "You did invite me, yes? The faun was not mistaken?" Alex's eyes flicked over Eden and widened for an instant, then the bland neutral expression was back in place. He looked back at Takana. "My dear, you will not shoot me, so you may as well lower the bow," he said, sliding from his horse. "You invited me. Trouble, the faun said."

Takana lowered her weapon and bowed her head. "It has been a long time, Alexander."

"Too long," Alex replied. "Far too long. I have missed your company. I wish you could have called on me in more pleasant circumstances than these." He reached, as though to take Takana's hand, then checked himself and let his hand fall back to his side. "You look well," he said, softly. "You are well?"

She shook her head, once, from left to right, shoulders lowering. "Alex, I need you. I am to stand accused of treason, both sides of the border."

"You are," Alex agreed. "You are said to have allowed a human into our realms, and not forced it back. Those are the charges, Takana."

"I'm a he," Eden muttered. "Not an *it*."

"I know," Alex said. "I was stating the formal charges against my sister, to my sister. My apologies." Alex looked at Takana. "I am pleased to discover that you are not turned traitor, after all," he said.

Takana let out a breath and slumped towards her brother, who reached out and circled his arms around her back, holding her for a long moment before he let her go.

"You can save me? Save us?" Takana asked, her voice breaking. "Alex, please tell me you can help us evade those who would see me dead, and Eden captured."

"I can, now that I know, and have seen with my own eyes, that you have not betrayed this realm, Takana. I prayed that the rumour was untrue. I thought...would you *really* allow a human in, and to stay? No, I could not see you doing such a thing—committing such a crime against the Fae. However...revolutionary...you may be, I could not see you risking our life, and our ways, Takana. But we will have to move fast, my dear. Rumour spreads quickly, and others are not far from here. What is your name, child from the Human Realm?" he asked Eden, formal and polite.

"I'm Eden, sir," Eden said, inclining his head and offering his hand. The man clasped his fingers, swaying as they shook hands. Eden frowned at the reaction of the elf, wondering at it. However, he let the long slender hand drop and took a step back. Alex seemed friendly enough. "I'm honoured to make your acquaintance."

Alex looked at him closely and took his hand again. "The honour, my dear boy, is mine entirely." He met Takana's eyes. "Orien's Blood, Takana."

"Quite," she replied. "Was I meant to toss him in the river when he refused to return to where he came from?" she asked, smiling widely at her brother. "What say you, Prince Alexander, soldier of the Crown?"

"I say, my dear sister," Alex said, "that we throw him on Jinx and bloody run as fast and as far as we can from this place. The trees?"

"Are to be silenced."

"Good," Alex said, looking around at the circling trunks. He glared at their branches and narrowed his eyes. "Curses on you all," he said. "You will be heard no more by my people. Wood and leaf forever more. Heard no more, ignored, and left to petrify where you have taken root."

"Is that necessary?" Eden asked, his voice quiet in the night. "They thought they were doing good. I'm human, and I'm in this land, where I sure ain't meant to be. They thought they were doing good."

"And they have risked the life of every man, woman, and child in this world," Alex said. "They know what they have risked. *Do you argue your punishment?*" He shouted into the lines of rustling leaves and swaying trunks. "*Do you argue the sentence?*"

A deep rumble came from under Eden's feet. He stepped back as quickly as he could, trying to escape the tremendous noise and violence coming from the earth. Takana grabbed his arm and held him next to her.

"*We shall speak no more,*" a thousand voices said, as one. "*Until The End of Days is over, we shall be silent. We shall not be heard. Our voices shall be ignored. Until the End of Days is over, or until Orien's Heir forgives us this wrong, and commutes the just and fair sentence handed this day to us, by you on behalf of the Light Elves of Alfheim. You have our fealty, and our oath, and we shall speak no more.*"

Eden watched the leaves still, and the branches freeze. They turned to petrified stone as he gazed around, struck dumb by what was happening to the forest. He turned in a circle and watched every tree,

94

young and old, thin and willowy or thick and squat, turn to stone.

"No," he said, shaking his head. It was too much to take in. Too abhorrent to witness the trees be silenced. Frantic, he spun to look at the hundreds of trees turning to stone. He felt wetness on his eyelashes, but did not care. He looked at Alex. "No...not this," he said. "Please. They have to be able to talk to each other! You can't do this. Not a living death. Let them speak to each other, please?"

"Knowing they would have had you killed?" Alex asked.

"They thought they were doing good," Eden repeated. He ran over the bridge to the trees and held his hand to one of the frozen stone trunks and shook his head. "Not this—this is too much. Please? Let them talk to each other? Don't mute them, please?"

Alex watched the forest for a minute. "You will hear each other," he called. He waved a hand at the trees. "It is more than you deserve," he added as the life slowly returned to the petrified forest.

Eden rested his forehead against the slender trunk of a birch tree, stroking his fingers over the live bark, sensing the life within ebbing back.

"...*thank you*..." The whisper was nothing more than a breath of wind skimming past his ear, but he heard the joy in it. He patted the trunk once more before he jogged back to Takana and Alexander.

"Thanks," he said. "Truly, thank you. I couldn't have that on my conscience."

Alex looked at Takana. "Deal with what you are leaving behind," he said. "Eden, get on Jinx. She's friendly...do you ride at all?"

"He was born in the Deep South of America, Alex,"

Takana said, lighting an oil lamp and walking to where she had set wood and oil soaked hay to fuse the cabin. "Boy was probably put on a horse before he could walk, and a gun put into the hand not holding the reins."

Eden chuckled and vaulted up onto the tall horse. She must have been seventeen hands at least. She was beautiful. He stroked her silvery mane. There was a *whumpf* of heat as flames burst into being, fuelled by magicks and the more mundane oil from the lamps inside the cabin. Eden stayed still as the fire roared higher, licking the wooden building and consuming it as it found it liked the taste of old wood and ramshackle furniture. He caught the glint of one of Takana's tears, reflecting the flames, and looked away, not wanting to intrude on her moment. Her goodbyes. There was a lump in his own throat; he may have only been at Takana's camp for a few *human* days, but it had been safe, and warm, and homely.

Now, it was gone.

He shouldered his bow, and settled the quiver against his back. Making sure his sword was safe in his scabbard, he lifted the scarf Takana had made him wear from around his neck, upwards to cover his head. He wore it Arabian-style, like a Bedouin from the pages of history. It covered his face, turbaned around his head in deep swathes of folded grey fabric. Alex lifted a similar length of material from around his own neck, draping it easily around his face and head. Eden decided if he looked half as good as the elf, then he had no complaints about the fashions. Alexander looked cloaked in mystery and like an extra in an action movie or video game. Eden forced his eyes from the man, heat rising in his cheeks at the direction his thoughts had taken regarding the older man. With luck, the headscarf would hide his blushes, he thought, shifting on the horse

"It will be all right, Eden," Alex said, patting his leg.

"Starting to think I shoulda gone home," Eden said. His mood changed again, as suddenly as before. He felt as though he was filled with all the possible emotions he could experience and was going through them all, one by one. Surreptitiously wiping his eyes on his sleeve as they moved away from the camp. He steeled himself and straightened his spine. The last thing he wanted was for these amazing people to find him weak. "Don't feel much like an adventure, now. it feels..."

"Real," Alex said. "I know. But do you doubt that you are where you are meant to be? If so, then I can see you back to the Human Realm."

"Or throw me in the river."

"I have not done enough good in my four-hundred years to balance out a sin so great as that," Alex said seriously. "Do you wish to return to the world you knew as your own, Eden?"

"The world I knew as my own? It was my own."

Alex stopped walking and looked up at him. Stepping the three paces it took to reach Eden's side, he reached up and took Eden's hand in his own, staring at his palm, then at his face.

"Did that world ever feel as though you belonged?"

Eden glanced down at the perfect elf, the lie ready on his tongue. He shook his head, unable to lie. "No. No, sir, it never did."

"How long did it take you to break past our wards

and barriers? To see past our glamour and jump our river? How long have you *known* we were here, Eden?"

"I've known this was the Forest of the Fae since we moved to England. My mama, she told me, when I was small, that this was my place and that there was magic. That I could dream and pray, and hope. That magic would be mine, one day. I figured it was something to distract me from the voices I heard, and the things I would see happening." He tapped his heels to Jinx's sides moving off once more, with Alex walking on one side of Jinx and Takana on the other. "I knew, on the surface, that it couldn't be more than a fairytale. Nothing more than a pretty story to take my mind off the *real*. But deep down, I knew it was all here. Been trying to get in since I was fourteen, for real. Five years."

"So," Alex said, "do you wish to return to the world you knew as your own?"

"That's still my world."

"I beg pardon. They are *all* your own, Eden. You misunderstand what I am asking. Do you wish to return, right now, and leave this *adventure*? Live and die a human life, to forget this all happened. You will live, work, meet someone, grow old, like a human, and die, like a human, or you can stay here, with us, and maybe find your destiny."

"Alexander!" Takana said. "Mind your words." She narrowed her eyes at her brother across Jinx. "Be mindful of what you say."

"The child has a right to know," Alex said, holding Eden's eyes. His own were clear hazel, without shadows. Without malice. Kind eyes that spoke of a trustworthy soul. "You have a choice, Eden. But you will not have it for many more hours. You can still live as a human. You can go home, and this will be like a dream to you."

"You're saying, if I stay, I won't be human?" Eden asked.

"No," Alex replied. "I'm saying if you go back to the realm you know as your own, you will become one."

"I'm not human," Eden said. It was not a question. Even his own mind held no incredulity at all. He had known he was something *other*. He had seen the glances his parents gave him, and each other. He had heard the whispered conversations, about him. About his telepathy and visions—and about the dreams. He had known. Right along, he had known. Still, the *knowledge* was like having a weight lifted from his chest. He was not insane; he had never been insane. He had just been out of his place. Out of his world.

"What am I?" he asked.

"Special." Takana squeezed his calf. "You need to know no more than that. Rest now, Eden, we have a long journey. Sleep on the horse. We won't let you fall. Remember what I said—and I am still your teacher, young man. Sleep when the opportunity presents itself, and get used to doing so."

"Sleep sitting up?" Eden asked, yawning behind his hand.

"You'll be able to sleep standing up before this is over," Takana promised. "Just wrap your hands in Jinx's mane and lean forward. We'll be moving fast, but you won't fall."

"You have my word," Alex said, his voice lilting even more than before. It became musical. Hypnotic.

"Let your eyes grow heavy, and your body relax. Sleep, Eden. You are young, and we are old, let us look after you for tonight...sleep..."

"Alex," he heard Takana say, "he will sleep in his own time..."

"I want him rested, and I want to move faster than he would be comfortable with. Sleep, child..."

Eden struggled with his eyelids. He wanted to lift them and say that he would be fine—that he didn't need to sleep. That he wanted to talk. But Jinx's mane was soft against his cheek, and his body too heavy to lift. He could not open his eyes. Moaning softly, he felt the world drift away and nothingness reach for him with gentle hands, ready to carry him away on a cloud of dreams.

"You will tell Airell?" Takana called as they galloped through the Borderlands on newly acquired horses, Eden, sleeping, on Jinx between them. "Tell him that I should be spared?"

"You took one *Hell* of a risk, Takana!" Alex snapped. "What if this boy had been able to fool you? What if I had arrived to find a *human*? A human! In this world? Orien's Blood! I understand that your life has been...harder...than most, with your bloodlines, Takana, but you really do try my patience sometimes!"

"You can ram my fucking bloodlines up your arse, Alexander! I'm not one of your horses! Your father had every chance to say no to my mother—he chose to screw her. If he felt so strongly about having a half-breed bastard, then maybe he should have kept the royal prerogative in his pants! Then again, if rumours are true, I'm not the only one, am I? And His Majesty has his own *mistake* hidden away."

Alex glared at her. "You talk out of your arse and have no *clue* what poor Airell is going through."

"It's true?" Takana asked, taken aback. She had not expected any kind of confirmation of the rumour. "He has a hidden bastard?"

"No, the child is not hidden, and no, the child is not a bastard," Alex said, looking straight ahead.

"But if there is a child, and Airell is unmarried?"

Alex glanced sideways at her, across Eden's body. "He is not...was not...unmarried."

"If he has divorced, then the brat is as much a bastard as I am."

"Takana! You are an *intelligent* woman. I know you are. You're half elf for crying out loud! You are as far from stupid as I am, aren't you? I have already said the child is no bastard. He was married, legally, before Orien, to the boy's mother, and they consummated that marriage, legally, before Orien. And the union produced a son."

Takana ran a hand over her braids. "All right. So he has a son. How could that have turned into a rumour that reached *me*? A hidden bastard child—a gargoyle, by all accounts. Mentally deficient and an embarrassment, I hear from the east."

"Damn their Dark souls,."

"Is it true?"

"I hope not."

"You don't *know*?" Takana asked, gaping at her brother. "You said he is not hidden. The child."

"He is not hidden," Alex repeated. "He's in

Chiearatul."

"A half Light Elf?" Takana all but yelled, aghast. "Alex! A half breed Light Elf, in Jaizel's lands? Airell's *son*? What the hell is he doing there? What if Jaizel finds him?"

Alex slowed their horses and looked into Takana's eyes.

"Jaizel has found him?" she asked. "Airell's son?"

"Jaizel knew about the child before we did," Alex said, quietly. He leant over Eden to speak into Takana's ear. "Airell married the Princess Relaizia. Twenty years ago. As you are no doubt aware, Relaizia also had her own brother's child, twenty-two years ago. Airell met her, fell in love and married her when the child begat by her brother was a babe-in-arms."

"I am aware. Airell *married* her? She's a *Dark* Elf."

"She was lighter than I could ever hope to be," Alex said. "She bore their son, but she never told Airell she was pregnant—she told Airell she was going to fetch the Prince. Her son by Jaizel. She said would come back to him. They were to make a life together. She never returned and Airell assumed she had left him, but the marriage is as valid today as it ever was."

"But she left him...that's adultery."

Alex shook his head impatiently. "No. We discovered Relaizia died at Jaizel's hand, when the child, Gray, I believe he is called, was young. She left behind Prince Gray, and the other boy, her son with Airell. We do not know anything about him, not even his name. Just that he was born and survived. As you know, Takana, rape is not recognised as being grounds for adultery—and that poor woman endured her brother's attentions through no fault of her own. We found out about the child, Airell's son," Alex clarified, "just under a year ago. We do not know where he is, and we do not know how to fetch him out from that place. We do know that he has been used...most vilely...by Jaizel. By Jaizel's army, if half the rumours are true."

Takana held her hand over her mouth, disgusted. "No...not even that bastard would do such a thing to a mere *child*. What could he hope to achieve?"

"The boy was born under Orien's Star," Alex said, looking around. "We need to move—even with the trees silenced, I do not feel safe, here. Wait until we reach my house, Takana. Then I will tell you all—I need your help as much as you need mine."

She tapped her heels to the horse's sides and sped up to a gallop once more, her mind spinning.

It was strange to be returned to civilisation after so many years in the forests of Bordenthal. Alex's hunting lodge was luxurious by any standards, but especially by those of Alfheim. It was more than worthy of the richest man in the land. An imposing residence, constructed of golden brick, the lodge was actually a mansion, looming over the small town which Alex owned.

They had managed to get Eden past the town-folk without too much trouble and into the lodge. Alex's housekeeper, a woman as sensible as her master, had taken one look at their precious charge and had immediately sent for blankets and ordered a bed to be made up on one of the couches in the dining room, while a room was hurriedly prepared.

"Dinner?" Alex asked, carrying Eden in his arms as he walked along one of the wide hallways, past portraits of family members Takana had never met.

They would never admit to her existence, so meeting them was unlikely to happen, despite her rank in the army and Alex's public acceptance of her relationship to him. Alex had embraced her as his sister, from the moment he had found out about her. It was damning to the family's reputation, but Alex did not care. He was like that. He went his own way and be damned to anyone else. He seemed determined to acknowledge he had a sister—whether Takana chose to acknowledge she had a brother. An elven brother at that.

She followed Alex. It was impossible to dislike the bloody man. Kindness seeped out of his pores as most men would sweat. There were exceptions to every rule and Alex was just that. No elf could be accused of honesty. Everyone knew never to trust an elf.

And then there was Alex. Airell too, of course. Damn them for making it impossible to distrust all of the race, the way she longed to do. It would be easier to discount the elves as whoring bastards, like her father had been, and yet she had to admit, even if only to herself, that there might be some good men.

"You must be hungry, Takana?"

She blinked, looking at Alex as he gently laid Eden onto one of the deeply cushioned brown-leather sofas placed around the informal dining room. It was Alexander's go-to room. He ate, studied, read and entertained close friends in this room. Not opulent in any way that could be immediately seen, it was a warm and comfortable place. Sparsely furnished, heated by a great roaring fire, it was Takana's favourite room in the house—the one she had spent many weeks in when she had been seventeen years old and at death's doorstep. The room had changed over the intervening two-hundred years, yet it always would speak softly to her of *home*.

"I ate," she said, trying to keep some distance. If she allowed herself to be lulled back into Alexander's way of life, there would be no hope. She could not live as a princess and be expected to return to the harsh life she had taken as her own.

"We have roasted pork," Alex said.

Damn him. He was smiling lopsidedly at her, knowing she couldn't refuse a hot meal.

"A roast would be nice," she said, conceding defeat to her brother—and her stomach, which rumbled happily at the thought of a roast dinner. She looked at Eden to avoid looking at her brother.

"He is amazing, Takana."

"I know," she said, covering him with a soft patchwork quilt. "I'm still trying to make myself believe he is here. That I found him."

"He's in my house," Alex said, grinning like a schoolboy. He rubbed his nose, his eyes shining brightly with irrepressible joy as he looked at Takana. "Wait until Denny sees him. Orien's Blood."

Takana let her defences fall. History would have to be let go, for now. The future was going to be a lot more important.

"Let's hope we are not forced to see Orien's Blood. I would much rather it stayed inside him." She said. She sat at the weathered old dining table. It had once been in Alex's garden, she remembered, following a deep gouge in the wood with the edge of her nail. He had only brought it indoors because there had been a bad storm and he didn't want the table to end up rolling into Chainia City, lost forever.

A serving maid came in with a bottle of wine—a human-made chardonnay, which Alex favoured above most elven wines. Takana said yes with alacrity, when the maid asked if she wanted a glass. In for a penny...

"Admit it," Alex said, sitting opposite her. "You're tempted to stay and take me up on my offer. Stay here. Lead the army, sister. Be the princess you have the right to be and lead Airell's army in comfort. There is no need for you to hide, skulking in the forests of Bordenthal, as though you are ashamed to be royal."

Takana held up a hand. "Stop. I would rather not become your enemy, Alex, my dear. I do not wish to be part of...this," she said, gesturing around the room. "A guard. That is all I am and all all I wish to be, Alex. Speak of it no more. Let us eat and be friends. Tell me of Airell's child. Tell me what is to come. And call for more wine," she added, draining her glass. "I intend to take full advantage of your cellar."

"The boy vanished, with Gray—the prince—a few years ago," Alex said. He glanced at Eden, making sure he still slept. "We can only work on hearsay," he continued, "but the information we have gathered tells us that Jaizel's son ran from Asanthai Palace with Airell's child. They have neither of them been seen since."

Takana frowned. "They have not, perchance, been murdered in a tower?"

The light in Alex's eyes shone bright for a moment. "I think not. Airell's boy is wanted alive by

106

Jaizel. Much as this one would be wanted alive," he added, pointing at Eden. "Neither child would be much good to the man if they were dead, would they? However..."

"However?"

"However," Alex said, "this child is in a more dangerous position than Airell's child is. If Airell's child is, of course, alive. But then, I should think he is alive, because the rumours surrounding him are just beginning to grow into something more than a whispered piece of gossip in the back of a tavern. Were he dead, then the rumours would have ceased, long ago."

"And the boy was born under Orien's Star?" Takana asked. "He would be the prophesised child? Half Light, half Dark...of course," she murmured. "*From Dark and Light combined.* How could we have all missed the inference of mixed breeding? How could *I* have missed it?"

Alex raised one perfect dark brown eyebrow across the table. He sat back as their meal was brought into the room and placed in front of them both. He waited until the maid had left the room before he shrugged and sipped from his silver wine goblet. "I doubt, Takana, you thought a Light Elf would ever take a Dark Elf to their bed. No one would have thought it would happen."

"No one thought an elf would lower themselves enough to fuck a wood-nymph either," she retorted, starting her meal. It was, as always, delicious. "And yet here I sit, the outcome of such a liaison. How did you find out about all this, Alexander? You are certain it is true?"

"I'm Airell's best friend," Alex said simply. "He

heard the rumour that he might be a father and saw his people laugh at the idea. He could have let it be a tale. He did not. I saw in his face that it could be true, and I spoke to him about it. He loved Relaizia, Takana. Truly loved her. He has been hurting, and nurturing his hurt for nearly two decades, believing she had deserted him, and yet he had never sought to have the union nullified. That alone shows how deep his feelings for her are. So, I was sent to find out how much of the rumour held truth."

Alex finished the final morsel of food and laid his knife and fork side by side on his plate. He steepled his fingers, looking at Takana over the tips. "The facts, as I know them, are that the princess did indeed bear another son, a couple of years after Prince Gray's birth. She withdrew from court shortly before her confinement, and was only seen on occasion by palace servants and the odd distinguished guest—a glance of her from a window, you get the idea."

"She was Jaizel's prisoner, you mean?"

"Yes. Her brother took it as a personal affront that his *property*, as he saw Relaizia, should be used by another. He made her life hell after she returned." Alex drank more of his wine, tapping the table with his fingertips. "Facts," he muttered. "She was beaten repeatedly and kept prisoner in the palace. She endured a nightmare and was left to cope alone—no women-in-waiting. She survived, though. By all accounts she forged as much of a life as she could for herself and her sons—right up until Airell's child grew older," Alex said, his voice dropping to a low murmur. "Jaizel deemed it unlikely that the child would die from the experience, and decided to put the prophecy into action."

Takana laid down her cutlery, tasting bile. "The bastard...joined...with the poor child?"

"After killing Relaizia to get to him," Alex said. His hazel eyes were dulled and sad. He looked at the table, thinking about his words. "The two brothers were imprisoned—Jaizel's own son fared little better than Airell's, if my information is accurate. Then, both boys vanished. One night, they were there, the next they were not. Common theory has it that Gray ran with his younger sibling from Asanthal. There were several deaths that were never fully explained on the night this is said to have happened. There are rumours of their presence, in the Tarenthian Forests, past the Wastelands, but they cannot be verified. We cannot get there to find out. It is a mystery. They vanished into the night, and no one heard of them again."

"Until recently," Takana said, folding her arms. She flicked an eye at Eden to make sure he slept on, and that there was no piercing silvery-emerald eye staring back at her, seeing into her soul. She chewed her bottom lip, shaking her head slowly from side to side as she thought on her brother's words. "The child has possibly emerged from whatever place he was hidden, from the sounds of it. Although it is doubtful that he is declaring his parentage to the world at large, I am imagining that if a prophesised child is walking around, people are starting to notice him, whether he wants to be noticed or not. Am I correct?"

"You usually are." Alex said. He looked at her over the rim of his goblet. "I see I have your attention with my mission. As you caught my attention with yours."

"You have," Takana conceded, inclining her head.

"But I do not see how I can help the great Prince Alexander."

Alex's eyes were calculating. "I need someone who can get me through the forests, unseen, to Chiearatul. You need someone to protect you from everyone who wants you dead."

"You don't mince your words, brother," she said drily. "You want me to get you through the Wastelands, onto enemy soil, is that what you are asking?"

"It is," Alex confirmed. "More wine?"

"Thank you, yes," she replied. "Correct me if I am wrong, but what you are suggesting is that I lead you through the ancient routes of the nymphs, into hostile territory, where you will stand out like a beacon among Dark Elves...you plan to find Airell's son, yes?"

"I have to. Airell has asked it of me."

"I thought as much. Are you forgetting we have one, rather large, impediment to our gallivanting through the world on what is sure to be a wild goose chase for a boy long dead?" Takana pointed a finger at Eden and raised her own eyebrow to match Alex's. "We have Eden with us. You would drag him along with us?"

"Oh, I would not dream of leaving him behind," Alex said. "Goodness gracious, no. He cannot be left, Takana, my dear. As well you know. He comes with us."

"If I refuse?"

"Then he comes with me, and we part ways at dawn," Alex said simply.

"That would mean my death!" she cried, chilled by Alex's impassive gaze. "You can't leave me."

"Then you better not refuse," Alex said, leaning

forward to take her hand. "Takana, I love you, and I would have come to you even had you not called on the fealty of blood. I would fight to the death for you, and you know I would—that you have chosen to be estranged from me is your decision, and one that I have respected, but we are brother and sister. You called, and I came running to you, as I always have and will always do. But, Takana, this is bigger than us. Bigger than your life or mine. If we can both emerge from the days to come alive and unharmed, then it will be through the grace of Orien himself, because the chances are minimal...you know they are. We have to keep this boy safe, Takana, and we *must* find Airell's son before Jaizel recaptures him. He holds the secrets of the gods, if he is the One."

Takana turned her head and studied Eden's face. He was stunning, she had to admit. Truly beautiful. Tanned skin, the colour of pale burnt umber, eyes that flashed silver and emerald, when they opened on the world, set above a regal straight nose. He had lips that were full and giving, begging to be kissed—she had been unable to stop herself stealing a single kiss from the boy, despite her resolve—and he looked every inch a king-in-waiting.

She tossed her braids over her shoulder and turned back to face her brother. "What if Airell's child is not the Chosen One? What if the Chosen One is right here, in this room?"

"I don't doubt he is," Alex said, quietly, his hazel eyes softening to rest on Eden's face. "I have no doubt at all that we are holding one half of a complicated puzzle."

"Yet you think the other child is as important?"

Alex picked up his goblet and drained the rich

111

wine in several steady gulps. Placing it back on the table, he met Takana's gaze with full honesty. "A lock needs a key. The question is only whether we hold the locked box, or the key to open the mysteries."

"I would bet my last ecru on Eden being the former."

"Oh?"

"Yes. There is something about him, Alexander. Wait and see."

"All right," Alex said easily, lounging back in his chair. "I'm in no rush, after all. How did he get into this realm?"

"Blood and tears," Takana said, helping herself to the wine. "He has been running into the Edge for years. He used it as an escape from those who would terrorise him in the Human Realm. He would run to our woodlands, terrified, as though the hounds of hell were on his tail, Alexander. But I managed to keep the glamour in place, and he would return to his place eventually, unseeing as ever. And then, this last time, I cannot fully explain it. I started to lose my hold on the glamour even before he entered the Edge. He was beating down all the barriers and all the charms before he even reached the trees."

"So easily?"

She winced and rubbed her head, remembering the disorienting sensation of having her control ripped from her grasp. "It was fast, this time. It hurt to feel it. He entered the forest, as always. Jumped the river from his side, as he always did. And then he slipped...bleeding into the ground. His tears fell. And then he pressed his hand to a tree, and that was it." Takana looked up, drawn abruptly from her reverie. "The forest answered his call, and I could not stop it."

"It was not a moment of weakness on your part?"

Takana shook her head firmly. She had asked herself exactly the same question and took no offense at her brother asking it. Could she had possibly been lax in her focus? Had she let her iron grip on her glamour slip?

"No. It was nothing like that. As he came running towards the Borderlands, everything faded and flickered around me. The whole world lost its sharpness, and then, there he was," she said, shrugging helplessly. "His blood in the soil, on the trees. His tears falling into the ground, Alex. He broke through enchantments older than any race with ease, and I don't think he has a clue just how momentous what he has done actually is."

"Why has he been trying to get into this world?" Alex asked quietly, speaking to himself almost.

Takana grinned and folded her arms on the table to lean over to Alex. "You're going to love this."

"I am?"

"He has been plagued by voices attached to ghostly beings," Takana said, sitting back as Alex's eyes widened. "A voice, calling to him, from out of the darkness. Unseen...hurting. Wanting him. Needing him, he says. *Loving* him, although they have never truly met. Eden is willing to break through realms, walk all the worlds, and battle whatever comes his way, but he will not be swayed from his aim, which is to find the person behind the voice."

Alex frowned for a few moments, before sitting back in his chair and crossing his legs at his ankles. "If the boy is in love, Takana, then we know that he cannot be a part of the puzzle involving Airell's son. We will help him on his quest, but the chances are that he seeks some princess in the outer reaches...damn. It was too good to be true, that he should be linked to Airell's son, somehow."

"Oh?" she asked. She lifted her goblet and gazed at her brother over the rim, smiling with her eyes. "Who says Eden is seeking to rescue a princess from an ivory tower?"

"You are joking?" Alex asked, sitting up to look at Eden, his mouth pulling into a wide joyful smile. "Really?"

"Really." Takana raised her goblet and tapped it to Alex's. "In this case, dear brother, the role of this particular princess is to guide our knight in shining armour. So he can rescue his prince."

V

Eden opened his eyes and glanced around the Elysian cream-toned bedroom, his hand closing to grip the thick silk of the eiderdown he had been covered with. He had a frightening moment thinking he had woken up in his room, back in the Human Realm, then breathed out a long and slow whistle of relief when he realised he was still in the Fae-Lands. Rolling onto his side, he propped himself up on one elbow and looked at the muted colours of the artwork hanging on the walls. Landscapes, in the main, they held nothing that caught his interest. No fantasy creatures, or fire-breathing dragons.

Eden pushed down the crinkled unruly mop of his hair. He wondered when the tight cornrows Takana had braided had been taken out and if he had been drugged. The last thing he could recall with any clarity was sitting on Jinx—magnificent animal—and Alex telling him to...

"You sneaky bastard," Eden said under his breath. "Knocked out by hypnosis, huh?"

He flopped back onto the soft pillows and looked at the ceiling, unable to stop the curve of his mouth. Knocked unconscious by the words of an elf. Well, it was another thing to add to the ever growing list of new experiences, he supposed. He let his eyes fall closed, only to open them with a start when the door to the room opened.

With one hand holding the quilt to his chest, he fleetingly wondered where the hell his shirt was. Eden sat up and looked at the strange woman who was looking him over from the doorway. Another elf, he decided, taking in the elongated and pointed ears of the woman, not at all concealed by her curly blonde hair. She folded her arms over her chest and intensified her examination. The quilt seemed, quite suddenly, rather thin. And Eden had a horrible feeling his own hair was puffed out from his head like a dandelion in seed. He ran his hand through it again in the hope it might lay flat, but by the small amused smile that touched the stranger's face, he guessed it was a hopeless task.

So much for looking good. Undressed, bleary from his sleep, with hair sticking out in all directions, and covered in healing scratches from his training with the sword. He was a mess.

"Every bit as glorious awake as Takana said you are," the stranger said, sashaying into the bedroom. She smiled a greeting and held out a hand. "Denita Jarlen. Denny, for convenience. And you, I am told, are Eden."

Eden took her hand and shook once before letting go. He pulled the quilt higher around his chest. "A pleasure, I'm sure," he said, spying his trousers on a chair pushed up against the opposite wall. "Um...you'll have to excuse me, not getting up for you. It appears I've been stripped."

"You can't sleep in your clothes," Denny said. "Besides, we needed them so we could get the measurements to make you a spare change of clothes, while you slept. I wouldn't worry—you're not made differently from my kind. There was nothing seen that we had not seen before. A little more, perhaps," she added, winking at him, "but nothing new."

Eden rolled his eyes and snorted, shuffling across the bed. Holding the quilt around his waist, he stood up and crossed to the chair that held his trousers. With a pointed look at Denny, who showed no signs of leaving, he shook his head and pulled them on under the quilt, laughing when she pouted.

"Spoilsport," she said, flinging herself into the chair and resting her foot on her knee. "You certainly have nothing to be ashamed of."

He tugged his comb through his hair and wet his hands in the basin to run over his face—and then his hair. It had to be tameable. Had to be.

Denny stood to take the comb from his hand, pushing him down into the chair. "Let me," she said. Her hands worked sure and swiftly, plaiting and twisting until the wild shoulder-length mop of snarly hair was subdued into neatly woven braids. She added silver clasps and clips, then stepped back looking satisfied.

"It is shorter than most men would wear their hair," she said. She opened the door at the sound of a quiet knock, admitting a small man bearing a tray with a silver domed plate and a pot of something, as well as a cup. "Thank you. On the dresser will be fine," she said, waiting until the man had left again. She looked at Eden's head. "Your hair is short for my kind, yet longer than normal for the Human Realm, I think?"

"Uh, yeah." He watched Denny lift the dome from the plate and was pleased to recognise a couple of chops and fried potatoes. "Thanks for braiding it. Um...where is Takana?"

Denny passed him the plate of food and a fork. "Sleeping." She poured the coffee. "She needed to rest, after getting you here."

"Where is here?" Eden asked, biting into a chop. Lamb cooked to perfection. He chewed, swallowed and took another bite, suddenly ravenous. "The last thing I can remember is Alexander telling me to sleep. Don't got a clue where I am, now."

"You are at Alexander's hunting residence. Safe." Denny leant against the wall to consider him. "And you are going to be lucky to stay safe, Eden. You have so much to learn."

"Yeah, I know," he muttered through a mouthful of lamb chop.

"Oh, I do not mean hand to hand combat, Eden," Denny said, leaning over to look into his eyes. Her face did not look nearly as friendly, or as beautiful as it had before. Her eyes narrowed, and her lips thinned, stretching over her teeth in a grimace that was more snarl than smile. She showed her teeth; small points of needle sharp whiteness that looked more suited to tearing flesh from bones.

"You do not know where you are," she hissed. "You have no idea who I am. You do not know the cook. You do not know who can be trusted, and yet here you sit, at ease, eating *poison* for all you know! Unarmed. Stripped naked, and possibly in the hands of an enemy. Who is to say that I am not here, sent by Jaizel, to bring you back to his lands? I could have killed Takana and dispatched Alexander. I might not have known Alexander was, indeed, the mighty Prince Alex...you gave me his name, Eden!"

Eden leant back, trying to get away from the lethal looking creature. She was nearly nose to nose with him, and angry. He rolled backwards on the mattress, landing quietly on the other side of the bed to face Denny. Barefoot and bare-chested, there was little enough to hand to be able to fend her off. He could not see his sword, and his bow was nowhere to be seen either. He looked at the snarling elf again and knew he had been played. It had been a test, and he had been found wanting.

"Damn." He closed his eyes. "You could've killed me ten times over already." Opening his eyes again, he gazed unflinchingly at Denny. "Where are my weapons?"

"Outside," Denny said. "I came in while you were sleeping and took them. You were so susceptible to Alex's suggestion that you were in a coma, almost. We have been able to move you, undress you, ride with you, and could have used you as a puppet if we chose. Takana could have been anyone, too. You trusted the first face you met. Blindly. You, Eden, are a liability. A gullible naive boy who will serve himself to the wicked king without any of his soldiers leading you there in chains. Orien help us."

"I'm kinda new to this," Eden snapped, glaring at Denny. "I can't wrap my head around the fact that most folks here would want me dead, okay? Even the assholes back home generally just wanted to beat the shit outta me, not kill me. I'm new, I'm green, and I'm sorry," he said, holding his hands out to his sides. "I told Takana I don't got a clue about what to do—not yet. She said she would teach me. Give her longer than a few days, huh?"

"You have fire, at least," Denny said meditatively. "You are too trusting, and I have seen lambs harder to lead to slaughter, but at least you have fire."

"Wow, good to know," he said, stung. He spotted his shirt, crumpled at the end of the bed, and snatched it up from the floor to yank over his head. Tucking in the yards of excess material, he sat and pulled his socks and boots on. "Let me guess. There's a line of folks, all waiting to come and stare at the *creature* from the Human Realm, and have a laugh at how stupid it is, right? Is that how it works?"

"Not quite," Denny said. She sat next to him. "Alexander was rightly concerned by how easily you accepted his suggestion that you sleep. And how well it worked. You have been unconscious for over a day. I can help you learn to block suggestion. It will be a great help to you, in a land where mental-magic is commonly used as a weapon against those from the realm you came here from. I can teach you to close your mind and shield against attack. Takana can teach you weaponry and combat. Alex can teach you about the land you find yourself in—and all about the creatures herein. And then, who knows, maybe you'll survive."

"Who do I get for survival lessons?" Eden asked. He took the chop Denny passed him with a sigh, but bit into it and chewed, in case Takana was outside the door, waiting to see him waste an opportunity to eat. "The faun? A centaur?"

"Don't be flippant," Denny said. "We've got you the best..."

"I'm sensing a *but*."

Just then, from somewhere else in the house, Takana screamed. Eden bolted to the door and pulled it open, ready to run along the brightly painted hallways to see what was wrong, when Takana's irate shouts started to make sense.

"You can get the fuck out of my sight, you fucker!" she screamed. There was the sound of whistling steel, and several thumps. "How *dare* you even come *near* me, you bastard!"

"Takana...I..."

"I don't want to fucking hear it, you tit-sucking *cunt*!"

Eden looked at Denny to see an irrepressible smile was tugging at the corners of her mouth, even though sounds of swords being swung and clanging against each other rang through the hallways.

"I was called away, you mental fucking *bitch*!" a man yelled, as china smashed and something thumped onto the wooden floor. "Will you stop trying to kill me? *Orien's Blood*! Takana! Stop!"

"I'll stop when I have your testicles mounted above my fucking fireplace, Cole!"

"Ah," Eden glanced at Denny again. "She doesn't sound happy. I assume Cole is a survivalist?"

"We'll see how good he is. If Takana actually kills him, then obviously, he's not as good as his reputation says he is."

"Look," Eden said, turning to face Denny fully. "I appreciate your help, and I am grateful you thought to get me the best, but I won't have Takana upset for the sake of me learning how to live in a wood, or whatever. I can do that anyway—I'm from mountain territory originally. Learned things that aren't so easy forgotten."

Takana whirled into sight at the end of the hallway, and met Eden's eyes as she swung her sword in a graceful arc, causing Cole—just out of sight—to cry out in panic.

"Good to see you awake, Wonder-Boy," she said, before she looked back at the elf rounding the corner.

Cole was armed with a sword, Eden saw. He also saw that he could only use it as a shield; Takana was giving him no chance to use it as a weapon. Cole was tall, as Eden had thought. Six-five, at a guess. He, unlike Takana and Denny, wore his hair tailed loosely and tied with a thin leather thong at the nape of his neck. Dark blonde, he had olive toned skin, and if Eden had thought Alexander handsome, then Cole was truly beautiful. Even dodging the violent frenzied strikes aimed at his head by Takana, he was stunning enough to leave Eden feeling flustered.

"Takana, please listen to me!" Cole said, narrowly avoiding a swipe that would have seen his guts spill onto the floor. "I was called away—I had no notice myself. No time to tell you goodbye. I would never have left without a word! What do you take me for?"

"A promiscuous git," Takana hissed. "A bastard fucking elf with less morals than a dog scenting a bitch in heat."

"Okay," Cole blocked fast as Takana's sword came downwards with enough force to sever his arm at the shoulder. "I don't deserve that, I don't think." He looked at Eden, in between sword blows. "Hi. Nice to see you awake, Princess. Cole. Me, I mean. I'm Cole. Uh. Ouch, shit, Takana! That one nearly hurt me!"

"Um, hi," Eden said, mesmerised by the man. "I'm Eden. Nice to um..." He watched the sword play for another couple of heartbeats, and then took his own sword from where it was rested against the hallway wall, next to the door. Holding it firmly, he waited for Takana to swirl her own long shaft of steel in a wide arc, then pushed Cole backwards and stole his sword, blocked Takana's blow, and held Cole's sword to her throat. As moves went, he was impressed with himself, but tried to hold back his grin of triumph at Takana's sudden motionless stance; she stood as though shot, staring at him without comprehension.

"Calm down," he said, lowering Cole's sword from her neck. "You want him gone, then it's fine."

Cole gaped at Eden, mouth open, as did Denny. Eden glanced around and lowered Cole's sword a little more, moving his own sword to push Takana's down by her side. Her arm moved easily, obeying the slight pressure from Eden's sword. She opened her hand and let her sword drop, causing Cole and Denny to gasp.

Takana looked sideways, away from Eden's eyes, and found Denny. "Two lessons," she said. "And I am disarmed." She looked at Cole. "You are still a tit-sucking git, Cole Jarlen," she snapped, glaring over Eden's shoulder. "Keep out of my way. And if you hurt him, Cole, then I will make your life a hell the likes of which you cannot imagine."

"Takana...please listen to me..."

She shook her head and raised a shaking finger to point at Cole. "I loved you, you bastard," she croaked. "I believed your words, and swallowed your lies. You betrayed me."

"I was called back, urgently, Takana," Cole pleaded. "I had no notice, and I planned to come back as soon as the mission was over."

"And you didn't, did you, you fucking—"

"It still isn't over," Cole interjected, holding his hand up. "Takana, I haven't been called back, don't you get it? I was called away from you...from us...and damn you, woman, it killed me to leave! But I had to!"

Takana lifted her chin in challenge. "Where were you called to, so urgently, that you could not come back to me to say goodbye?" she asked. Her eyes glittered in the sunlight streaming through the window. "Why should I believe you?"

"Because I say so," a quiet voice murmured. "I called him."

Eden spun around to see the speaker; his spine tingled with a thousand sensations the voice awoke within him. Deep, lilting, musical and hypnotic, it was a voice Eden would follow happily into the fires of Hell.

He needed Denny, if she could save him from this, he decided.

The man was special. Eden could not have said why that was, exactly, but the first word that came to his mind was *special*. Average height, the man was good looking, but nothing spectacular—not compared to Cole and Alexander anyway—he was brown haired, hazel eyed, with lightly tanned golden skin, which made him look as though he spent his summers running along Californian beaches. Nice, but nothing that could possibly account for the sense of deep attachment Eden felt. It was an irresistible pull, from the bottom of his deepest subconscious soul.

Aware the others were all down on one knee, heads bent, and right fists held over their hearts, Eden walked slowly and faced the man, scrutinising each feature; slanted eyes, long eyelashes, high cheekbones and a strong chin. He held his head regally, but his mouth was soft and full. His back was straight, yet the set of his shoulders was tired. As though he had walked too far, for too long, and seen things he wished he could forget.

His eyes held a sadness beyond comprehension. He looked back at Eden, but the life in his eyes was dimmed. He looked young until one saw the pain in the soft hazel of his eyes, then he looked ancient.

Eden bowed elegantly, and looked up at the king. "Your Majesty. It is an honour to meet you, sir."

"The honour is mine," Airell said, holding out his hand for Eden to shake.

This time, the touch of the elf rocked Eden, more than it did the king. Eden took a step sideways, stunned by the electrical jolt that flew up his arm to his neck. The sudden clenching of his jaw made him worry, briefly, for his heart. Then, though, the sensation passed and he felt normal again. He was still pleased when Airell let go of his hand. It was discombobulating to feel so up in the air. For a second he could have sworn he floated.

Airell looked at Takana's bowed head, then Cole's. He shook his head. "I called Cole back, Takana," he said, still quiet. "I sent him to find my son."

Takana bent her head lower. "I understand, Your Majesty."

Airell nudged Takana with his foot. "Get up, cousin. Submission sits ill on your shoulders, Tree."

Takana looked up and grinned. "Up yours, Elf."

Airell grinned back and held out his hand to haul Takana to her feet. He clasped her briefly in a close embrace, then pushed her back to look her over. "It is good to have you back, cousin. You are back? Or are you dropping off your precious charge and then going back into self-enforced exile?"

"Back, it would seem."

"Good. I have missed you. You are well?"

Takana looked slowly at Cole, then at Airell. "I have been better."

"You could have gone back to tell her where you were going, Cole." Airell looked at him. "It would have delayed you by what? An hour? Two?"

Cole looked at his feet. "You sounded scared. I didn't think—just ran."

"I understand," Takana flicked her gaze over Cole. "Had I been called, I would have likely acted the same. I am sorry for your...I don't know what to say, Airell. I am sorry."

"Thank you. Alex says our guest here might be of some help?"

Eden, feeling all eyes rest on his face, knew he was turning deep red under his cinnamon skin. He frowned. "Me? Um, sir, I don't mean to be rude or nothing, but I just got here, and so far, I ain't doing all that well."

Airell appraised Eden silently for several long heartbeats, then waved a casual hand, dismissing all company.

Eden watched Takana leave, feeling exposed and alone. He crossed his arms over his chest and waited for whatever was coming his way. To tell this—so, *so* special—man he could be of no possible help was galling.

"Walk with me," Airell said, turning away to walk along the hallway, his booted feet silent on the raw wooden boards. "I don't bite, and I don't want you dead. Come, Eden. I would talk to you."

"I don't know what I have I can offer." He followed Airell. "Really, Your Majesty...I don't know my ass from my elbow."

"You know your dreams," Airell said as Eden caught up to walk next to him. Airell glanced across at him. "I have a feeling we're looking for the same thing, Eden of the Human Realm. I saw your face when you saw me. You felt a connection. It went both ways, Eden. You seek my son, and he seeks you. I am of his blood...but you, Eden, if I am not mistaken, are of his soul. Will you help me get him safe, Eden?"

Eden stopped walking and held his hand against the wall, caught off guard. "Your son? Me? Where is he? Who is he? You know the voice I'm seeking? You know who it is talking to me? Calling me?"

"I think so. I cannot say for sure, but I have a feeling, and my feelings rarely lead me wrong. It has been enough of a feeling that I have travelled here to meet you...and see you with my own eyes. Eden, my son was born in Chiearatul—the Dark Lands. I had no idea. I heard a rumour of his existence a year or so ago...too late. Far too late," he said, shaking his head. "He was born in Asanthal Palace—Jaizel's palace. Of all the places he could have been born, I think he was born in the worst place imaginable, Eden. His brother, Gray, escaped with him when he would have been nine or ten."

Eden held his breath. His chest felt strangely tight—that he could *possibly* be close to the voice that called his name in the dead of night? Impossible dreams that were, after all, real? He could find the man behind the hands that reached for him, holding him close and stroking so gently down his cheek, before his mouth was found by gentle lips that had the power to take him out of himself?

Airell said, "I do not even know his name" He drew his lower lip between his teeth and shook his head slowly from side to side, hopelessness evident in every line of his body. "My son is out there. He needs my help. He needs protection. He needs *love*. And I do not even know his name, Eden. He may, or may not, be the same person; your dream and my son could be nothing at all to do with each other, but..."

A growing sense of certainty was growing inside Eden's chest. A physical assurance that he was heading on the right path, whether or not this king's son was the one he had crossed the worlds to find or not, he could not tell—but he had to find him all the same.

"Only one way to find out, I reckon," Eden said. He held his hands out at his sides, offering himself. "If you want me, then here I am, Your Majesty. Still hold that I don't got a lot I can offer you folks, but what I have, is yours."

Airell's eyes fixed on Eden's face for several long heartbeats. There was an unreadable glint behind his hazel irises. He turned away.

"I assure you, Eden, what you offer, we will gratefully accept. Come—we shall eat, and then Denny will want you. Then Takana. And then, I should imagine, Cole and Alex will likewise insist on having some hand in your, um, training, shall we say? You will be a busy young man, Eden of the Human Realm. Best keep your strength up while you get used to our ways."

M

"Not too tired?"

Eden turned to Takana, taking his eyes off the road leading further away from Alexander's luxurious lodge. They had been travelling for over a week, along the wide road. That it was an Elven road, in another realm, still popped into Eden's head at the strangest times. Maybe so his sense of wonder would stay in place. His mind wanted to ensure he would stay awed.

"I'm okay, but thanks," he said to Takana. "I'm enjoying the scenery. It's beautiful."

He looked around at the landscape; rolling fields of pastel grasses that could be seen through the trees when they travelled close to the edges of the woodlands. Cole had mapped out a route, which wound around the villages and towns of Bordenthal. It meant that occasionally, like today, Eden could look though the scant trees at the edge of the Borderlands and tell himself he could see forever across the fantasy plains of the Elven Realm. It wasn't unlike the English countryside, except everything was so much more vibrant and colourful, as if someone had turned up the contrast on his vision.

"We can stop if you need us to. We've been travelling for a long time, Eden. If you need to rest, we can take a break."

"Really, I'm okay," Eden said again, tipping his head toward the sky. His hair slipped down his back. Worn loose for once, he was enjoying the sensation of his hair falling around his shoulders and tickling his neck. "Not getting tired as easy as I did," he said. "Getting used to it, I guess." He patted Jinx's mane and shifted his seat, checking for his bow, arrows, quiver, swords and knives without conscious thought. As he could now fight with his sword without thinking about it, and mostly block Alex or Cole trying to *suggest* things to him, he knew where his weapons were at any given time—they were a part of him.

Each passing day took him further from the boy he had been. He could barely recognise his former self, now; mentally and physically, he knew he had changed beyond all recognition. His newfound strength of mind had been matched by his body as Takana and Cole had made him train until he dropped, and then kept trying to beat him while he was down. He had soon learnt not to fall. His sword no longer felt heavy. It was feather light to him, an extension of his arm as he swung it easily through the air with deadly speed and deadlier accuracy. His muscles had also changed from the good-looking bulk gained from occasional trips to the gym and a few press-ups in his room. Now, he was a lithe athlete, corded with tight muscles that had got there through hard work and training. Useful strength, which could be used. Not the fakery of his old physique, good for nothing except to look fine without a shirt.

Takana looked front again, but not before Eden saw the pleased smile that touched her lips.

He watched her tap her horse on his sides and trot ahead so she was next to Cole. It was great to see her happy. After the small battle in the hallways of Alex's house, Takana and Cole had spent most of the day talking in low voices, in the corners of rooms. That night it had been obvious to everyone in the house—

and maybe in the nearby town—that they had settled whatever bad-feeling had settled between them. The noise of their love-making had been enough to make Eden cover his head with a pillow to try and get some sleep. Cole and Takana had a passionate relationship—and a very physical one.

"Having fun on your day off?" Alex asked, nudging his steed closer to Jinx.

"Day off is relative," Eden said. He grinned at Alex. "Although, only two hours being worked into the ground by my highly respected teachers, not four...yeah, guess it is a day off. But," he added, chuckling, "you have to take into account that it means another two hours in the saddle, which ain't a day off for my arse. Gonna have a hide tougher than shoe leather soon."

"We can stop whenever you need to, Eden."

Eden flicked his eyes at Denny's back. "I'll do for now, but thank you. I will let you know if I'm gonna faint from exhaustion, and ask to stop before I get there."

"Stubborn bugger," Alex said, but grinned his approval as he bent to the side to rummage in his saddle bag. He sat up holding a small bread roll, wrapped in rough-spun muslin. Unwrapping it, he broke a chunk off and popped it into his mouth, chewing thoughtfully. He held an offering out to Eden, who took it with a quiet word of thanks. Alex nodded at Denny. "My wife's a good teacher."

"Yeah," Eden said, agreeing. "She is. Scary as fuck, but good."

"It's good she is—at least you know what you are dealing with, with the Fae. We are not, contrary to the human myths you would have heard, all prancing, dancing cobblers, wishing to clean houses and mend shoes while you sleep."

Eden tipped his head back and laughed gleefully. The last thing he could picture his travelling companions doing, was housework in exchange for milk. They might, possibly, concede to washing up their own dinner plate, in return for some strong spirits, loud drum music and a night of dancing around a fire.

Their dancing was, in general, hedonistic rather than prancing gaily around a workshop. So much so, that he had spent more than one evening of their journey staring at his knees, or into his wine, wondering if Takana and Cole would actually bother to take to the relative privacy of the trees surrounding them, or if he was about to become an unwitting voyeur. So far, most of their clothes had managed to stay on until they were alone, for which he was thankful. Not that their being dressed stopped them expressing, clearly, what they were planning. Eden could not help but think he was watching foreplay, each time Takana and Cole started to dance to the beat of Alex's drum.

Alex lounged back in his saddle. "The honeymoon phase. It can get tiresome," he looked at Eden, rolling his eyes. "Seriously, though, Denny is doing right in scaring you half out of your wits. We are Elf. We are Fae. We can shift shape and change your perception of us. We can lure you in with beauty and you will not see the truth behind our false smiles until you are snared in our trap and slaughtered like a sluggish spider. Learn to always see the truth behind the facade, Eden. Do not be drawn in by lies; see instead what is truly in front of your eyes, and face that truth head on. It is the only way you can hope to survive us. At least until you learn your own power."

Eden managed, just, to avoid rolling his eyes. He had to accept, in the light of all evidence, that he may not hold pure human blood. He had entered the lands of the Fae, for one, and he was learning skills that no full human could ever hope to achieve. However, he *felt* human. He looked human. And he could not see how he could be otherwise, as his parents were, as far as he knew, as human as human could get. He was not adopted, he knew that for sure, and yet...

And yet, any time they met another traveller, and the stranger found Eden with their eyes, huddled in the centre of the group of warriors, their eyes would widen and they would stare at him as though they were trying to see inside his soul. They would flick an unreadable glance at Alex, then back away from Eden with sweeping bows before turning on their heel and running through the forest, both elated and terrified.

Takana had soon decided he no longer had to have his hair braided, nor should he have to try and hide his essential strangeness. It didn't matter what he did, he was not going to fit in, she said, so he may as well look how he liked, and not bother trying to conform with the ways of the elves. He was not going to change back into his jeans and tee for anyone, though—he adored the clothes he wore, and his boots were the most comfortable thing he had ever owned. Nor was he willing to let any of his Elf-made weaponry out of his sight. He was pleased to have his hair back to normal, though, it had not liked being made to conform any more than the rest of him, breaking free of the cornrows several times a day to stand out from his head as though he had been rubbed with a balloon.

Hilarious, it might have been—dignified, it was not. He was pleased to have his own unique brand of messiness back.

"Denny's good," he said, looking at his teacher's back. "I'm pleased I'm starting to see past her illusions, though. She sure can look monstrous when she chooses to...fangs, and such? Can you do that?"

Alex turned to look at Eden and drew his lips back from his teeth, transforming from beauty to beast in a heartbeat. His almond shaped eyes became elongated, while his chin extended downwards, stretching his mouth to show two rows of sharp pointed teeth that looked capable of ripping Eden's flesh from his bones, and grinning as they did it. His finely sculptured nose became pointed and his cheekbones sharpened. He reached out a hand that was transformed from elegant to claw-like, talons in place of nails.

From pal to predator in seconds.

Eden drew in a deep breath and focused his mind, forcing himself to see *behind* the horrific facade and find the real man he knew was hiding behind the terrifying illusion. The man behind the animal.

Gradually, slowly, he saw the flicker of Alex's real face behind the mask, and let out a sigh of relief as he used his mind to peel away the final layers of the elf's disguise until the stunning man he knew faced him once more.

"You're better at that than Denny...but don't tell her I said so. Scared the freaking shit outta me for a moment then."

Alex finished the last remnants of his roll. "She can teach you to see past it, though. I can't."

"How do you do that?" Eden asked. "The morphing."

"I'm not entirely sure. I just think of it, and that's what you see. It's a glamour, really. I do not actually *change* myself...I don't think. Or I might do, and then others can learn to see my true form? I can't be sure, Eden. I know that when I *become* a wolf, I am not *actually* a wolf—I do not have canine thoughts, nor do I understand barks and growls...and yet, as far as I am aware, when I speak, I will snarl and howl. I *speak* English, but others will hear a wolf. I am a shape shifter, Eden, as are all of my kind, except Cole...to ask how I do it, is like me asking you how you made your skin so dark."

Eden nodded his understanding. "Thank you. I just wondered, you know? If you had to train, or something, I mean?"

"No. Practice, perhaps. As you would learn to pull any funny face? I can pull myself into the form of a cat as easily as you could go cross-eyed."

"Very cool," Eden said, taking the flask Alex passed him. He sipped at the diluted whiskey and handed Alex back his drink, wiping his mouth on his sleeve. It might not have been the best matured bourbon, but he was used to the taste now, and it did keep the chill from his joints through the long hours of travel.

"Cole can't shift?"

Alex hesitated, glancing at his cousin, then shook his head. "No. He's weak, magically. He finds it difficult to use any power. His skills lie elsewhere."

"Oh, okay," Eden said, eyes on Cole's straight back. He wondered if the man was seen as backward, to the other elves. Alex's tone told Eden it was not normal for an elf to be without magic. He filed it away for later perusal, in the back of his mind, and looked back at Alex. "Can anyone learn it? Or is it an elf thing?"

"Hmmm...I don't know," Alex said, thoughtfully running his eyes over Eden. "Try it and see."

Eden shook his head. "I would look stupid."

"Yes, very likely...but I could do with a giggle."

"Ha, ha, bloody ha," Eden said. Alex playfully punched his arm, making him chuckle. "That would have worked last month."

"I know. It's no fun, now you can block suggestion. Here," he said, passing his flask once more. "Drink. We will stop soon and eat. You must be getting tired?"

"Really, I'm okay. I'm getting more...hmmm." Eden shrugged, thinking. "More awake?" he asked. "The longer I'm in this realm, the less I feel the need to rest and sleep. I know I would have had to stop twice, by now, even just a few days back...but I'm awake. Kinda dreamy, but not sleepy. I could happily just ride and let my mind drift away, but I ain't *tired*. Does that make sense?"

Thoughtful hazel eyes rested on Eden as Alex appraised him. "I do not sleep, Eden. I know what you mean, but...Eden?"

"Yes?"

"Hold onto your sleep, and your humanity, for as long as you can...once it leaves you, you will grieve for it. The total absence of the present. The blackness behind your eyelids as your body sinks and falls into dreams and worlds where you can be anyone and anything. With the absence of sleep, you find the death of dreams, and when there are no dreams, you only have the real to hold you...and the real is not always enough to carry you through the dark days.

Rest," Alex said, "sleep...and take joy in it while you still have the gift of nothingness."

Eden rested his hand over Alex's long fingers when the elf gripped his shoulder and squeezed in silent reassurance.

"I won't look weak?" he asked, looking to the side to find Alex's eyes. Something about the man inspired confidence. Over the weeks of travel, Eden had realised that Alex was fast becoming one of the best friends he had ever known. He shrugged.

"I don't want the others to think I'm weak," he admitted. "Whether we're all looking for the same person or not, I don't got a clue, Alex, but you have to find Airell's son, right? I don't want to be the weak link in the chain that means you're held back and slowed down because I have...human...needs."

"You won't slow us down," Alex replied. "You are not weak. And we need you to rest, Eden."

Eden shook his head. "No...you need me to keep going, so you can find Airell's son."

"No, Eden. We need you to rest so you are strong enough for what we could face when we head out of the Tarenthal. You are far from weak. You are not slowing us down. But we might need you to fight—and I still believe you hold something more special than I can start to explain, inside of you, and we will need you to have the power to draw on it. When the time comes. Until that time, Eden, please enjoy what you have left of your humanity. Let us enjoy being around you, and let us remember humans as we once knew them. Before their bibles told them to believe magic to be evil...when they were still our family. Rest, little one, and let us remember what it was to dream."

Eden held Alex's eyes for several long heartbeats.

He called out softly, without looking away from Alex.

"Can you stop, please?" he asked. "I should rest."

"Oh, thank Orien," Denny said, reining in her horse. She slid from his back to land on the fallen leaves of the forest floor. She rubbed her backside. "I thought you'd never ask. I'll make a fire."

"I'll cook," Cole said, stretching tall as he dismounted. He winked at Eden. "You okay with salt-cod, Princess?"

Eden rolled his eyes. "Fool. And, yes. Thank you. I'd eat a shoe if it was cooked long enough. Your cod ain't all that bad. Not compared to your beef."

"I thought it *was* shoe," Alex said under his breath as he swung his leg over his horse's back to land quietly next to Eden's leg. "Sure wasn't a bloody cow."

"I heard that, Alexander!" Cole called, as he sauntered away from the horses, hand in hand with Takana. "Want to starve?"

Alex grinned and walked after the couple. He looked over his shoulder at Eden. "I have more bread," he mouthed, holding a finger to his lips. "I'll cook tomorrow."

"Thank Orien," Denny said, smiling up at Eden. "Come on. Dinner and bed for the nominal human."

"Yes, ma'am," he said, sliding down from Jinx's back.

Eden surveyed the clearing, frowning at the spaces between the trunks of the tall trees. He looked upwards, following the spindly branches to the sky, which reached like skeletal digits near the top of the trees, bent and gnarled fingers pointing to the heavens with a promise of eternity. He shivered and pulled his shawl from his saddlebag, draping the rough wool around his shoulders as he turned in a slow circle, concentrating. His right hand slipped down his thigh to check his knife was in his sheath.

A flash of movement caught his eye. He span on his heel, trying to follow where it had fled. He saw nothing. His heart beating hard in his chest, he forcefully made himself breathe slowly and turned again in a circle.

"Eden?" Alex called, walking back towards him.

Eden held his hand up, palm outwards. "Stay there," he said in a muted warning. He saw Alex reach for his bow and shook his head. "I don't think that will help," he said, watching the darting ghost from the corner of his eye.

It was nothing he could focus on, it was too fast. Whatever it was, it flitted through the trees and flew from branch to branch faster than his eyes could follow. It sped across the mulch of the forest floor, and launched itself into the air with equal agility. As soon as he could make out an arm, or a leg, it had vanished; too quick for him to keep up with.

He turned, by slow degrees, and faced Alex, lifting his hands out to his sides with infinite slowness. "Where I come from," he said clearly, "this means I ain't gonna harm you. I have no weapons in my hands. You're a darn sight faster than I am. I ain't a threat...I won't hurt you."

Alex frowned and took a single step forward. Eden shook his head as the wind picked up to whip his hair around his face and sting his eyes.

"Alex...no," he said. He looked at Denny and shook his head again. "No weapons. Takana, Cole? Come here and stand like me. Trust me. I don't got a right to tell you what to do, but...just this once. Do it. Just stand still."

"And be killed?" Takana asked, her hand on the hilt of her sword.

"Yeah—because I'm so dead. Show you ain't gonna hurt no one, and let him see you, is all I'm asking."

"He?" Alex asked.

Eden turned again, slowly, carefully placing one foot behind the other as he span and scanned the trees all around him. "He," he repeated. He held both hands on top of his head as he continued to rotate. "I will not hurt you," he said, closing his eyes. He stood still. "None of us will hurt you. For the love of your gods," he muttered to the grouped elves, "I hope to hell you're all doing what I am?"

"I'm insane," Takana said, but Eden heard the stillness as his companions stood motionless in the woods.

"Thanks," he said to the silence. "My name is Eden," he said, quiet but clear. "I'm not here to hurt you, or your land, or your people."

"You are from the Human Realm," a voice said.

"Yeah. I was born there. Don't mean I'm gonna hurt you."

"...get Khari..."

"Who?"

"Be quiet," the voice said, singing next to Eden's ear. There was a whisper of movement, then the voice said, from close to Alex, "Light Elves...in Chiearatul. I know you—I have seen your likeness, painted and plastered in taverns. The mighty prince, Alexander. And the hunter, Cole. There is quite a price set upon your heads, aye? Your bodies do not need to be attached to them. And you have with you the witch, Denita Jarlen, Princess of Chainia...and...what's this?"

he asked, circling Takana. "A nymph? Wearing the clothes of a soldier." There was a small intake of breath. "A nymph...with elf-blood," the voice said, mockingly. "Do you have a name, Nymph-Warrior? I haven't heard of you."

"Because all those who would speak of my name in bars and pubs are dead. By my hand. I could kill you where you stand. Show yourself to me," Takana snapped. "Eden?"

"She is called Takana," Eden said, turning to face the direction of the voice. He kept his eyes closed lightly. Through the redness of his eyelids, he could make out the shadow of a willowy figure, hovering close to Takana. There was a knife in its hand, and it danced on light feet around the stationary elves.

"Don't hurt no one. We never came here to hurt you."

"Oh?"

Eden shook his head, looking through his eyelids at the shadow. The more he concentrated, the clearer he became. Tall, but not overly so, the man was slim and athletic, with long hair worn loose down his back. A defined but not sharp face sat atop a swan neck. Well bred, and regal.

Bowing, Eden bent his left leg and half knelt, although he kept his chin raised. "I mean no harm," he said, his closed eyes fixed on the elf in front of him. He couldn't be invisible, surely?

Fine hair was lifted by the breeze blowing through the branches of the trees. Eden watched as the elf stalked closer. He lifted his chin before the delicate hand could touch his jaw. As he was touched by gentle fingers, Eden swayed and drew a breath. He held his balance by touching the ground next to his knee, and bent his head.

Touching Airell had made him breathless. This man left him spinning out of himself.

The elf gasped and drew back his hand. "Orien's Blood...who *are* you?"

"Eden."

The elf took a deep, deep breath and straightened his shoulders. "You may all camp here for the night. There is a stream half a mile west; the water is fresh and gives strength. I will leave food for you next to the stream. You will not leave this camp—if you try, I will kill you. I will be back this time tomorrow." There was a sharp wind, and a sense of movement.

"Hey! You got a name?" Eden shouted.

"You can call me Gray!" came the reply. Already it was faint. "Graghz, of Chiearatul. Stay there—I *will* kill you, if I have to."

Takana held her hand out and clasped Eden's arm. "I could have killed him. Now we are captive!"

"Eden!" Cole groaned, "what were you thinking?"

Eden looked at Denny. "Did you see him?"

Denny turned to face him. Pale faced, she was sweating. She wiped her top lip with the back of her hand and sat down suddenly.

"Denny?" Alex asked. "What is wrong, my love?"

Denny looked up at Alex, her eyes bright. "That was Prince Gray. Relaizia's son. The one born of incest. He's Airell's stepson."

Eden crouched next to the stream and plunged his

142

hands into the flowing water, bringing the icy fluid to his face to drink. It was, as promised, refreshing and therapeutic. He doused his face and neck with more handfuls of water, wiping himself down with an inefficient handkerchief. He hoped he looked cleaner than he felt, but doubted it. He would have liked a bath before Gray returned. He would have settled for stripping naked and swimming in the stream, but he had a feeling that it wouldn't be taken well by Gray, however good his intentions.

He turned when Takana coughed to get his attention. She held out a plate of the food that had, as Gray had said it would be, been left close to their camp—or prison, depending on one's point of view.

"Not poison?" Eden asked, taking the plate and straightening himself from his crouch. "Sure it's safe to eat, and he never decided to kill us with poison instead of stabbing us where we stood earlier?"

Takana narrowed her eyes. "I could have..."

"No, I don't reckon you could," Eden said. He picked up a chunk of curried meat with his fingers and popped it in his mouth. "Not one of us could have stopped that man from killing us where we stood. However hard that is to hear."

"I couldn't even see him," Takana admitted, sighing. "Never even knew he was there. Yet you did."

Eden scooped up some rice, chewing thoughtfully. He swallowed before speaking, taking the time to consider his words.

"I felt him before I saw him," he said. "He...you know when you're a kid, and you just *know* that the shadows in your room move when you're not looking at them? The flitting movements that set the hair on the back of your neck to rise? The knowledge that if you close your eyes, the monster watching you will dart out and gobble you up...a sure knowledge—one that all the adults say is dumb. But it feels so real that it can't be ignored, and if you *do* ignore it, then you are denying the essence of the animal you really are. I felt all that, and then some," he said, sitting down on the leafy mulch next to the stream. Eden ate another couple of mouthfuls of food. "To move would have been death. My only chance was in talking my way out of danger." He looked around the camp. "At least I talked him out of killing us without thinking about it, I guess."

"It was quick thinking, Eden," Alex said, joining him and sitting at his side. He held out a wooden tankard of frothy fresh ale.

"Thanks," Eden said, gulping down the ale and passing back the tankard. "We're fucked, right?"

Takana snorted. "No," she said. "It's just the son of the single most powerful being to walk this world. We'll be fine."

Alex raised his tankard. "Only the son who outwitted that powerful man and has evaded him for a decade. Doubly powerful, bred from Jaizel's loins and Relaizia's spirit. May Orien have mercy on us, if he finds us wanting. I don't think we can fight with any hope of winning."

"It's doubtful," Takana agreed, sighing. "Fuck. We're the best of the best, and we got caught like sitting ducks. It's embarrassing. Captured by a kid."

"A kid with an excellent ale-maker," Cole said, wandering over to them with Denny. He held up the clay jug and filled tankards. "His hospitality certainly isn't lacking, is it?" Cole asked, sitting cross-legged at

Takana's side. "Fantastic food, great ale, and I can't wait to taste the wine, this evening. If I'm going to die, I plan to do it with a full stomach, drunk."

Eden accepted the offer of ale with a nod of thanks and a smile at Cole's words. Dying drunk, among friends, was better than a lot of alternatives. He drank some of the ale. It was as good as Cole said it was.

"What happened when he touched you?" Cole asked. "I saw you—you nearly fell flat on your face."

"It was weird," Eden said quietly, looking at his hands. "I know him. Just hadn't met him."

"That makes no sense."

"Don't have to, does it?" Eden asked. "Nothing else seems to lately. He touched me, and it was as though a part of myself was touching my soul. It happened with Airell, too, but it was stronger with Gray. We...connected."

"Leave it, Cole," Denny said. "We're all swimming unknown waters. It makes sense that we'll find things that are strange and new."

"Hmm. So, Princess," Cole said, grinning at Eden. "Any second sight to tell us if we're gonna get the hell out of here, or going to die in a pot, being boiled for stew by Dark Elves?"

"Idiot," Alex said, rolling his eyes at Cole. "You really are a fool."

Eden snorted, amused at the byplay. "Don't reckon we're gonna be dying in a pot."

"Oh, good. I'd be chewy," Denny said, lying on her back and folding her arms under her head. "Besides, I can think of better ways to die than being boiled alive."

"Me too," Eden said.

145

"He can't die," Cole objected, punching Eden playfully. "He's still a virgin."

Eden rolled his eyes and ate another ball of rice and curried meat, looking around at the trees thoughtfully.

"Are we being watched?" Alex asked under his breath.

"No," Eden said. "I was just looking around. Don't reckon he's watching."

"But I'm guessing leaving wouldn't be bright?" Cole asked, looking at Takana and holding out his ale for her to drink. "What do you think, sweetheart?"

"Don't call me sweetheart," Takana said, but shrugged and shook her head, taking the ale and gulping steadily. "Staying put is the only sensible option. As much as I hate to concede a point, Eden is right—Gray could have killed us all where we stood. If he says we will stay alive the whole time we stay put, then I vote for staying put, for now, and reassessing the situation when we have something to reassess."

"Well, we could do with the rest," Denny said. "There are worse places to pitch camp."

"As though we have a choice," Takana snapped, smarting at the fact that she had been captured.

Eden rested his chin in his palm, absently fingering the remains of his rice into his mouth. He nodded when Cole held up the ale jug in silent invitation, filling the tankard Eden held out to him. The sound of the water rushing past calmed his nerves and he felt the residual fear slowly fade as the sun sank down in the sky. He wrapped his thick shawl around his shoulders and leant back against one of the wide tree trunks, watching as a fire was lit and the group of elves uncorked the clay bottle of wine, drinking with approval as they watched the rising flames, bright in the twilight. He shook his head when Takana held out the wine, holding up his ale to show he wasn't without a drink.

She watched him for a couple of seconds, then turned away, allowing him to be alone in his own space. She sat with the others, listening to a story Cole was telling to pass the time.

Hours passed and the sun vanished entirely as the moons rose in the darkness to light the camp in a soft pink glow. Takana gave up her watch, swapping with Alex so she could lay near the fire at Cole's side. Alex pulled his knife from his belt, slicing into an apple. He snared a slice with the tip of his knife and knelt forward, offering it to Eden in silence.

"Thanks," Eden said.

Alex patted his arm. "You should sleep. Who knows what tomorrow will bring."

He shook his head slowly. "I feel like I'm standing on a tightrope. One wrong move could send me falling into an abyss...but I don't know the right move to make, so I'm trying to stand still. Hold time still. And I can't." He leant his head back against the tree to close his eyes. "I don't know the right move to make. If I don't know the right move, how can I make myself avoid the wrong one?"

Alex crawled across the small space separating them and sat at Eden's side. "What are your options?"

"I don't know," Eden said, softly. "It's all clouded, but I'm on a precipice."

"What is in the abyss, Eden, if you fall?"

"The unknown. Dreams...nightmares," he mumbled, shaking his head. "Pain...hurt...death." He opened his eyes to look up at the moon. "The promise of all I ever asked for, and all I ever wanted." He looked at Alex. "Not that I asked for, or wanted, pain, hurt and death, obviously."

"Obviously," Alex agreed.

"I dunno, Alex. I know that if I move, then everything will change. And when I first tumbled into this realm, then sure, it was fun, and it was all a bit of a game. And now, it's my life, you know?"

"Eden?"

"Yeah?"

"What happened when Gray touched you?"

Eden looked sideways to meet soft hazel eyes. "It was as though I had reached out and touched my own soul. I was unprepared for it. I've only felt that happen in my dreams...when I'm being called. When I see that hand, reaching for me, out of the shadows, beckoning me and calling for me. I reach out," he said, quietly, holding his hand out as though his dream would be there, reaching for him too. "I touch his fingers, as they reach for me, and the hand will touch my face...and I know I am where I am meant to be. I am anchored, and I feel such a sense of belonging that it's beautiful, Alex. All the doubts and all the questions I have always had, they go, you know? There's nothing but the knowledge that I am *exactly* where I belong, with him. When Gray touched me, I was nearly knocked flat by the sense of *knowing* his touch...but it wasn't quite him. So close, but I'm not looking for him."

"So you think the dream is his brother?"

"I do, yeah. But I'm scared. This isn't a game anymore. This isn't a make-believe heroic quest, Alex. If I find the guy I've been dreaming, then I know I won't ever be able to turn my back and walk away from any of this. All I know, and all I've left, will be gone. I'll be falling into the unknown...and I have to hope that him anchoring me will be enough. Because...in finding him, Alex, I will have found the dream. But the dream may well hold a nightmare. There's danger in taking the step towards him, but I will lose my soul if I walk away."

"Do you think you can turn back, now, and not know what happens?"

Eden shook his head. He felt helpless, but there was no way he could turn back. Not now. Not when he was possibly so close. He had to be close—he could feel it, deep within him.

"I can't walk away," he said. "No more than I can tell myself to stop breathing, Alex. But that don't stop me shitting myself about what's going to be coming my way. I know that nothing can be all plain sailing and pain free...but the flashes of the future I see heading my way?" He shivered, pulling his shawl tighter around his shoulders, and lay down to curl up on his side, looking at the flames of the fire. "I'd like to find a way to stop some of what I'm seeing happening," he said. "Pain and bloodshed. Death and war. I can see it, but I don't know why I'm seeing it, or what's gonna bring it about, you know? The future holds everything I dreamed of. And some dreams are dark. Nightmares and terrors. It's all there, if I stay."

"We can get you out, Eden," Alex said, close to his ear. "We can open a pathway, and send you back. You don't have to carry on along this path...you can still turn back."

Eden let his eyes fall closed, forcing the images of an uncertain future from his mind. "I can't go back," he said.

"You can. Eden, you don't have to be here. It will hurt us all to send you back, but it will hurt us more to see you suffer. We can send you back."

"No. If I go back, now, then I will die never knowing what it is to *belong*. If I stay, then I will at least have that knowledge, Alex. I will know what it is to truly love someone. Everyone dies. By staying, I get to live first, at least."

Alex moved, inhaling as though he wanted to say more, then stopped himself. "Goodnight, Eden. If I can help it, you won't get hurt. You have my vow."

Eden let the darkness behind his eyelids overwhelm him, taking him to a place where dreams and nightmare combined, to show him all he would gain by staying.

And all he would lose.

VII

"Up."

The voice was harsh, drawing Eden out of slumber with a start. The foot in the base of his spine was far from gentle, and he skidded away, reaching for his sword, which had vanished from his sight. Scrambling to his feet, he saw the others were all being subjected to the same treatment; hooded figures surrounding them in the pre-dawn light of the forest. Alex, Eden saw, was leaning, dazed, against a tree trunk, a bloodied cloth pressed to his left side and his face blackened from eye to jaw. Takana stood nearby, struggling with the ropes that bound her arms behind her back. One of the hooded people reached for her and she turned her head violently to spit in their face. Eden shouted out as a hand appeared from under the hooded cloak to whack Takana with enough force that her feet left the ground and she was catapulted into a tree.

Dazed, she staggered upright and turned her head to spit out blood, glaring at her attacker.

"Gag it," one of the other hoods snapped. "If it does it again, slit its throat."

"Takana," Eden called, shaking his head as she kicked out. "Stop. For the love of the gods, just stop!"

A fist, or club, hit Eden's back as he spoke, hard enough to bring him to his knees. His hair was grabbed, twisted into a knot by a hard hand. His head was jerked back. Something cool was pressed to his throat. Eden froze, trying to see into the shadows of the deep hood to make out a face. Features. Anything. Something he could maybe use to make a connection with the man. Nothing—his assailant was faceless.

The cool metal of the knife pressed harder against his throat, and Eden felt his skin split; hot blood ran down from near his ear onto his shirt. He heard Takana scream past her gag, and Alex cry out. The thud of a boot connecting with flesh penetrated the terrified fog Eden was surrounded by, and he heard Cole grunt, Takana's muffled screams growing frantic.

"Kill the prince," his captor hissed. "Send Airell his head. How dare he send his soldiers into this land. With a *human*!"

"Ngh," Eden managed, scared to shake his head in case the knife should sweep further across his skin. "Don't..."

"Shut up, human!"

"He's not fucking human!" Denny yelled. "Don't hurt him."

Eden saw his attacker nod at someone, and there was a soft popping noise, then horrified silence before Alex's scream pierced the clearing.

"Oh, gods, no," Cole cried. "Denny! No...*no, no, NO!*"

"Do you want to be next, little soldier?" Eden's hood asked, his voice a soft hiss of malice. The knife pressed harder to Eden's neck once more causing more blood to flow. "Your neck seems just as delicate as your friend's. Take the prince's head," he said again, the hood turning in the direction of Alex's keening. "Was that your whore, my prince?" he mocked.

"She was my guest," a steely voice said, close to Eden's back. "And you are here uninvited."

Eden heard the unmistakable sound of a sword

being swung, and the knife pushed deep into his neck. He closed his eyes, waiting for the blade to move another half a millimetre and slice open his artery, then the hand in his hair relaxed and the blade fell. He heard a thump and opened his eyes.

Scrambling back from the head staring up at him in front of his knees, Eden hauled himself to his feet and caught a sword tossed in his direction without much thought. The long steel blade was dripping with fresh blood. Eden swiped tears from his face with his left hand, then got a double handed grip on his sword, swinging it in an arc either side of his torso as he approached a hooded man about to take a swing at Takana, helplessly backing away from the flashing weapon, bound and gagged.

"Khari! Your left!"

Eden saw a blur, his head and face hidden by a tattered grey scarf, spin into action. A long sword in each hand, he cut down several of the gang without stopping to see them fall, dead, to the forest floor. Turning, Eden faced another assailant, almost freezing again when he felt something press down the length of his spine.

Eden darted forward, lifting his sword as he ran across the clearing to bring down at the join of neck and shoulder of another hood. There seemed to be hundreds of them, more appearing with each that was felled. He met Cole's eyes and hauled him to his feet. Cole bent to grab the felled attacker's weapon, joining ranks with Eden and Takana.

Cole glanced over Eden's shoulder and looked at whoever was there. "Thank you," he panted, chest heaving.

"Thank me if we get out of this alive, aye?" the

musical voice said, almost singing the words. Each syllable hit Eden deep in his gut, as though he was being punched by sensation. He longed to turn, pull away the grey scarf and see a face, but forced himself to continue slashing through the hooded men who had attacked the camp and had killed his friend.

He could see Denny's body lying several feet away from the fire, Alex fighting with a skilful speed that was astounding, whirling and slashing at the hoods close to her feet, slaying anyone who approached his wife's lifeless corpse. Gray appeared next to Alex, darting in and out of focus, moving too fast for the naked eye to follow.

The last few hooded men turned, running into the trees. Eden lowered his sword, panting, clasped his hand to his neck and watched them flee. An arrow was lifted next to his face, the silver head bright in the corner of his eye, then it was loosed and one of the fleeing men fell. Gray lifted his own bow and fired, bringing another to the ground.

"Alive," he said, glancing to whoever was behind Eden.

"Ah, fuck, Gray," the lilting voice moaned. "I hate keeping them alive." Another arrow was let loose and the last man staggered and fell, screaming, to the ground, an arrow lodged behind his knee.

Gray raised a brow. "Good shot, Khari," he said.

"Aye, it was, but I was aiming for his arse. Thigh wound? That sort of thing."

"Liar," Gray said, swinging his bow over his shoulder. He looked around the camp at the bodies, and ran his hands through his hair to leave streaks of blood in the fairness. He walked to where Alex was knelt at Denny's side and crouched next to him, resting a hand on Alex's shoulder. "I'm sorry," he said. "We came swiftly, but it wasn't fast enough. There was a wide front of soldiers and we could not get here sooner. We shall bury her with the honours she deserves."

"Oh, gods," Cole cried, skidding over to Alex and pulling the older man into his arms. "Alex...oh, gods, Alex..."

Eden closed his eyes, feeling the hot wetness of his tears run down his cheeks into the corners of his mouth. Swaying, he felt the world tilt even as he heard voices calling his name, then he hit the ground and the lights went out.

"Blood loss and shock. He'll be okay soon enough."

Eden blinked his eyes open to look up into the branches of the tree he was sprawled under. A blurred shadow bent into his line of sight and his hair was smoothed back from his forehead. A damp cool cloth was pressed to his neck and the shadow moved again.

"He's coming to."

"Good. Just fainted," Gray said. "The wound?"

"They nearly took his head."

"Nearly isn't *did*," Gray replied. "He'll live. Does it need stitching?"

"Think it might. Keeps coming open. He's immune to being healed."

Eden forced himself to lift his hand and press over the cloth being held to his neck, applying as much pressure as he could and still breathe. Warmth flooded through the fabric to wet his hand and he groaned, lifting his fingers to see bright blood soaking his skin.

"I think...stitches are needed, yeah," he breathed. Feeling himself start to tremble, he squeezed his eyes closed and held his bloodied hand to his head, trying to get a grip on himself.

A hand touched his own, sending him spiralling out of himself. His head was jerked to the side, splitting open the wound once more, and he realised he had been resting on firmly muscled thighs. Thighs which were attached to the body now half lying on the ground while their owner tried to catch his breath in deep heaving gasps.

"Khari?" Gray called.

"I'm...I'm all right," came a flustered reply as a hand clasped the cloth back to Eden's neck. "Came over faint. Are...are you all right? Eden?"

Eden managed a small nod as his breathing came easier once more.

"Your name...it's Eden?"

"Yeah."

"I'm Za'akhar," the voice said gently. "Khari. Don't move. It's a bad wound. Deep."

"Denny," Eden said, remembering. He closed his eyes against grieved tears. "Oh, god. Denny."

"Sorry." Khari brushed his fingers over Eden's chest. "We were waylaid by another couple of dozen bastards near your camp."

"Who were they?"

Gray leant into Eden's field of vision and held a hand to his head. "Soldiers," he said, checking Eden's eyes and pulse. "Trackers, sent by my father."

"You kept one alive..."

Gray's eyes grew hard. "I had to know for sure where they were from and how many there were."

"Okay. What happened to him? The alive one?"

Khari held a hand on Eden's chest, stilling his questions. "The alive part of the equation was fixed before you came round."

"You killed him?"

"No—Alexander did," Cole said, kneeling at Eden's side. Blocking his view, if he should try and turn his head. "You okay, Princess?"

"Not a bit," Eden said. "You?"

"No. Denny was an old friend. We were close."

"Where's Alex?"

"Concentrate on you, Princess," Cole said, bowing his head for a moment. "Alex will heal." Looking up, he glanced at Gray. "Thank you. Another minute and we would have all been lost. Did you lose many men?"

Gray raised an eyebrow. "Men? It is only Khari and myself—we have no men to lose."

"Just the two of you?"

Gray looked at Eden again. He touched his jaw with gentle fingers, lifting his chin as Khari moved the cloth. Frowning, he pushed Khari's hand back down. "Keep applying pressure," he said. "I'll set some water boiling and fetch my kit. You'll be all right?"

"I'll be all right, aye," Khari said. "Be quick—I don't like the amount of blood."

"Had my throat cut open. It's bound to bleed some."

"It's not cut open, as such," Khari said. "More a puncture wound. You were lucky."

"Don't feel it."

"A more experienced soldier would have known

157

how to cut a throat." Khari touched his cheek. "You were lucky, Eden."

Eden tried to find Khari's face with his eyes, looking upwards as much as possible until it ached. Khari's breathy chuckle was soft as he patted Eden's cheek again and leant forward into his line of vision, pushing the covering from his head and pulling down the fabric swathing the lower half of his face.

"Easier to see me, now?" Khari asked. He gazed down at Eden.

Eden ran his eyes over a face that was, to him, perfection, and gazed into slanted eyes that blazed with all the colours of an autumnal forest; golds, browns and yellows merged together in a pool of pure sunlight, bound in place by a rim of thinnest, purest inky black. They sparkled, filled with life, above a long straight nose which, in turn, was placed *just so* above full pink lips that were turned up at the corners in a smile Eden knew was never far from the surface. Khari's face was filled with a subtle joy that seemed to laugh at the world around him, but held enough sadness behind his eyes to break Eden's heart.

"You called me to you," Eden said, lifting a hand like lead to hold against Khari's face. "You called me."

Khari bent over him until their faces were inches apart, and stroked the back of his fingers down Eden's jaw. "You came," he said. "From the Human Realm. You were in another world...and you came."

"I had no choice," Eden said, unable to look away from Khari's eyes. "Sorry...it took so long," he breathed, his vision blurring again. Squeezing his eyes closed, he drew in a sharp breath as the sodden cloth was pressed, hard, to his neck by Cole.

"Keep still, Princess," Cole said, his voice firm and

urgent. "Takana—come and hold this compress for me? Eden, you concentrate on staring into Khari's eyes, eh? Just stay with us a bit longer and we'll have you patched up in no time."

"He's lost a lot of blood," Takana said.

"Gray will fix him up," Khari said, looking away from Eden's face for a brief moment. He lifted Eden's head, shuffling his legs out from under him to lay him flat on the ground. Moving to sit fully at Eden's side, Khari held his hand and squeezed, his other hand stroking along the curve of Eden's eyebrow.

"I dreamt your face," Khari said, resting his forehead against Eden's. "I dreamt your face, and heard your voice. My impossible...impossible, dream. Just hold on, okay? Keep looking at me. It will be all right, soon. Eden? Open your eyes...Eden? Stay with me...Eden..."

VIII

The smell of earth filled Eden's nose before his mind woke sluggishly. Deep earth, the sweet scent of decaying leaves and soft mulch; a clean smell, if an odd one. He sniffed, smelling peat burning nearby, and then more subtle aromas; soup, some roasted meat, stewed vegetables, rich spices, and damp linen. Moving, Eden felt the weight of blankets covering him and the softness of a mattress beneath him.

He hissed in a breath of pain as his wounded neck made itself known. A hand immediately touched his face.

"Don't move too much," Khari said, his voice quiet. "We've had to stitch you up, and you have a poultice in place. We couldn't heal you properly, for some reason. You've lost a lot of blood, so just lay there and rest, all right?"

Not seeing as he had much choice, Eden opened his eyes to find himself in a space dimly lit with a few floating balls of glowing orange light. "Okay," he murmured, looking at Khari. "You're still real."

"Aye, I am," Khari affirmed, standing. His head nearly brushed the earthen ceiling, and Eden realised he was in a cave of some kind.

Eden looked at the walls—packed rich brown earth—and followed the lines of thousands of thin roots that wove together down the walls and across the ground to form a interlaced wooden floor. The trees were a part of the room, cleverly used to create the space. Eden realised he was underground. A doorway was a few metres away to Eden's right. His bed pushed up against another wall run through with tree roots. He wondered how deep underground he was as he watched Khari move towards a fire, built into the same wall as the doorway.

Taking the time to study the man who had only been a shadow in his mind until now, Eden took in Khari's blonde hair, noting that it was unusually cut for an elf. Short back and sides, it fell into a slight left-side parting to brush down over his forehead in long soft spikes that ended just on his eyebrows. He was tall, wide shouldered and slim hipped. Dressed oddly for his kind too. A frayed tightly fitting navy woollen sweater, which clung to Khari's torso and hips. A creamy long sleeved top showed beneath the raggedy ripped and torn wool of the jumper, accompanied by a dark grey pair of rumpled trousers and slouchy calf-boots.

In short, Za'akhar—Khari—looked nothing like any of the elves Eden had met as he had travelled through the land and into Chiearatul. He looked more like he had stepped out of a movie; a renegade or a mercenary, mixed in with a bit of Prince Charming. Eden snorted at himself for fanciful thinking.

Khari crouched in front of the fire and straightened holding a wooden bowl of steaming liquid. He sat back down next to the bed, picking up a spoon.

"Eat," he said. "It will help you make more blood. Replace some of what you lost."

"Guessing it was a lot," Eden said, his head spinning as he tried to lift it from the pillow. "Feel as weak as a newborn kitten, if I'm honest."

"You lost about half of what you had in you, yes.

Eat."

Eden obediently opened his mouth, eyes once more fixed on Khari's face as he swallowed the spoonful of delectable broth.

"This is tasty."

Khari smiled at the compliment. "Thanks. Are you comfortable?"

"Yeah. Where am I?"

"In my house. My room."

Eden clenched his hand around the thick blanket covering him, and Khari nodded.

"My bed," Khari said, lifting the spoon once more for Eden to eat. "It's not much, compared to what you're probably used to, but it's home."

"I've gotten used to a shawl and a rough forest floor," Eden chuckled. "This is paradise after a few weeks of being cold and rained on. We're underground?"

"Aye. Safe and hidden."

"The others?"

Khari tilted his head at the doorway. "They're with Gray. Alex is next door, resting and healing."

"Healing?" Eden asked. "He was hurt bad?"

"Aye, he was. He nearly spilled his guts out over the ground to join your blood. When the soldiers ambushed him, they nearly cut the man in half—he's a strong warrior to have lived through it. He'll be all right in a few days, same as you. Well...it'll take longer to deal with the loss of his wife, but he'll live."

Eden closed his eyes briefly, an image of Denny flashing into his mind.

"You were close?"

"She was my teacher," he said. "Training me to see past enchantments and prevent folks controlling my mind. We were pretty close, yeah. Cole and Takana are all right?"

Khari put the empty bowl down next to the bed. "Takana had a few teeth knocked out, but Gray found them and they should set back in place."

Eden winced at the thought of pushing teeth back into his gums. "Ouch."

"Aye. Ouch indeed. You've all impressed my brother." Khari slipped his hand under Eden's, thumb stroking his palm. "Gray isn't easily impressed—most people are weak, in his eyes—but you lot have impressed him. You're all strong."

"He's decided not to kill us, then?"

Khari's eyes twinkled at the humour in Eden's tone. "You're safe enough here," he promised. "I won't let him kill you. What were you all doing in the Tarenthian Forests, though? Chiearatul is suicide for Light Elves. And for someone from the Human Realm, Orien's Blood...you might as well have held up a sign saying you would like to be killed! Did you upset the King? The Light King, I mean...not, not Jaizel." Khari pressed his lips together as though saying the name made him ill, and looked down at Eden's hand in his own. Standing suddenly, he turned to the fire and knelt, moving the wood around in the hearth with a poker. A kettle was swung over the flames and two clay mugs appeared from a small low cupboard. "Why are you here?" he asked again, not looking around.

"Me personally, or us as a group?" Eden asked quietly.

"You."

Eden rolled, carefully, onto his right side and curled his arm under his head, trying to minimise moving his neck in case the wound should split open.

163

He looked at Khari's straight back, at his long neck and fair hair, drinking in the sight of him. "I've been trying to get into this realm for years," he said. "I heard you, and thought I was mental, but I had to try and get in, to see if you were real. I finally broke through..." he frowned, realising he had lost all track of the days, and had no real idea just how long he had been in the realm. "I reckon it's been a couple months, maybe. Got through to the Borderlands, and, well...here I am. I was looking for you."

Khari turned to look over his shoulder at Eden. "The others?"

"Actually, they're looking for you too," Eden said gently, watching Khari's golden eyes flash with fear at his words. He shook his head. "You're not in any danger," he murmured. "The opposite, as it happens. They were sent by your father to see if they could find you and, if they could, to see if you were okay...if you wanted to go back with them. You and your brother."

"My...my father?"

Eden held his free hand to the left side of his neck, over the poultice. "He found out he had a son, and asked Alex and Cole to try and find you," he explained. "Takana is here more because of me, but as we were all looking for the same guy, I don't see as it matters."

"You know who my father is? Gray won't tell me."

"No?"

Khari shook his head and turned to move the boiling kettle off the heat, pouring water into both mugs. A fragrant herby smell immediately filled the earthy room. "Who is he? My father?"

Wondering whether to speak, Eden hesitated. Deciding if he owed anyone loyalty, it was the one who had haunted his dreams, he waited for Khari to turn and face him again.

"King Airell," he said, glancing at the door. "He was in love with your mama...never knew she was pregnant when she left to fetch Gray. She never returned—he only found out what had happened a year or so back. He's had folks looking for you since."

Khari sat back on his heels, speechless, and ran his hand over his head, then combed the long spikes back into place with his fingers. "That's quite a claim," he said, glancing like Eden at the doorway, making sure they remained alone. "Truly?"

Nodding, Eden watched as Khari closed his eyes and breathed out heavily, then grinned at him.

"I always wondered. It's good to know he's not some faceless nameless goat who abandoned mum. She said he wasn't, but I was never sure if she was saying it for my benefit, aye? After all, parents lie to their kids, after all. I think it's a rule somewhere that no parent ever tells their kid the truth. Save them the hurt of knowing they were unwanted and abandoned."

"You weren't abandoned," Eden said softly. "And you were wanted. You and your brother. Airell said your mama—mum—left to get Gray. She was meant to go back to him. They were going to run. Try and find somewhere safe, I think. It was too risky for them both to try and get Gray, she told Airell, and convinced him she could get her son. She left to get him and that was the last Airell saw of her. He had no way of knowing what happened when she left him...he never knew anything of what came after. He found out he had a son and immediately sent out folks to find you."

"Hmmm. Well, it's good to know. Do you think you can sit up a bit and drink?" Khari asked, changing the subject. He waved a hand and two of the soft orange globes of light floated closer to where Eden lay on the bed.

Eden looked at the lights and then at Khari. "Magic lights?"

"Heatless flame," Khari said, sliding an arm behind Eden to lift him carefully, arranging pillows with his other hand to rest Eden against when he was satisfied with the angle.

"You have heatless flames? How did you get them?"

"Created them. Here, drink."

The mug warmed his hands as he sipped at the sweet liquid. Heat flooded through his veins, pleasantly relaxing his muscles. The pain in his neck faded as he drank, and he raised a brow at Khari. "Are you drugging me?"

"Painkiller, aye. You looked as though you could do with some. It's harmless, as long as you don't drink too much." Khari drank from his own mug, watching Eden carefully. "It's really not going to harm you," he said. "You can swap if you want, and drink mine. I promise it's not poison."

Eden chuckled and drank the rest of his drink. "Why do you need it?" he asked. "Were you hurt too?"

"By those bastards? No. No, they never hurt me."

"Then why..." Eden shook himself. "Sorry—I'm too nosy. It ain't my concern."

Khari shrugged. "I was nearly killed by Jaizel and his army, just before Gray escaped with me. It left lasting damage where I didn't heal everything right. I was too young, and Gray was too weak when we ran...never fixed it up properly. I can't walk or run easily without potions to numb it all."

"Damn," Eden said. "I'm sorry...that's..."

"Not important, right now," Khari said, closing the subject. "How are you feeling?"

"Stunned, mainly. You're really real. I ache, and my neck hurts like a bitch, and I can absolutely feel that I was kicked and punched in the back, but mostly I'm stunned. For years, Khari, I've been thinking I was going mad. Hearing voices and seeing visions...I've been living to sleep, just to feel you close to me, and here you are."

"Aye...and here you are. It's amazing."

"It is," Eden said softly, closing his hand around Khari's as it was placed over his palm. He studied Khari's features, drinking in all the details he could, from slanted eyes and long eyelashes, to the firm jaw and wide mouth that looked as though it was made to be kissed. Golden eyes flicked over his face in return.

Reaching out a hand, Khari traced the curve of Eden's lip with his fingertip. The touch was as gentle as a butterfly lighting on his flesh, yet it seared Eden to the core, burning into him with an intensity that set a fuse alight deep within his soul. His eyes were glued to the golden lights of Khari's irises as he was held immobile on the bed, overwhelmed by sensation just at the touch of a finger on his lips.

"By the gods," Khari said, his mouth barely moving as he breathed the words, "who *are* you? It's as though I have known you for a billion lifetimes...but I've never met you until now. It's...I have never felt anything like this, Eden."

"No," he replied, "me neither."

"I don't want it to stop," Khari said, trailing his fingers down Eden's cheek, past the poultice and along his shoulder, gently skimming across his skin as though he could see with his hands. "I longed to have you in my life, real, with me. Just to see you, for real, is fantastic. To be able to touch you, after so long..."

Sliding down the bed in a daze as Khari slipped under the blanket and laid on his side facing him, Eden traced the line of Khari's chin, feeling the softness of his skin as his hand skimmed under his ear and down the side of his neck. Exploring in silence with his fingers like a blind man committing a face to memory. Khari silently wrapped his arm around Eden's waist to pull him closer. The globe-lights dimmed to leave the room in a comfortable gloom, silent but for the sound of their breathing.

"You're shaking," Khari said.

"I know. So are you."

"Trying not to faint again. My head is in a whirl. Lying down helps. If I was standing, I'd be flat on my back by now."

"Yeah. Me too."

"How's your neck?" Khari asked, holding his palm over the padded poultice.

"What neck?" Eden asked, his hand resting over Khari's heart. He could feel the beats echoing his own. He stroked Khari's sweater, surprised by how soft the frayed and worn wool felt. He ran his finger along a rip under his rib. His cheeks warmed with pleasure at the indrawn breath he got in response to his touch. Khari's eyes were suddenly ablaze with fire, leaving Eden breathless and unable to look away as Khari closed the small distance between them and kissed him, his mouth as soft as a sigh on Eden's. So gentle he was barely touching him, Khari's lips had the power to leave Eden gasping, his hand clinging to the fingers linked to his own. He groaned deep in his throat as the touch of Khari's tongue swept along his lower lip, lifting him out of himself to fly and scatter into a thousand small sensations as though he had no body. As though he had been ignited, a torch that blazed suddenly to life, burning with a desire so fierce he wondered if it would consume him.

Khari drew his head back, just enough to break the contact of their lips, and gazed at Eden in stunned silence, his breathing ragged. "I think...I think the world just shifted. What was that?"

"I have no idea," Eden answered, catching his breath. "What did you do to me?"

"I..." Khari held Eden close to his chest. "I haven't got a clue," he said, "but whatever just happened, I liked it."

"Me too," Eden said faintly, closing his eyes. If he had been lightheaded before, now he was ready to pass out—lying down or not.

"Are you all right?"

He shook his head. "I dunno," he said. "I feel real woozy, but if you do that again, I sure ain't gonna complain!"

Khari ran a hand down his side, under the blanket, and pulled Eden towards him, pressing against him. He laughed quietly, a deep rumble that echoed in Eden's ears. "Maybe you should concentrate on making more blood before I do it again," he said. "You need your blood flow elsewhere than where I can feel it. Your head, instead of your cock maybe?"

Eden chuckled, quieting when Khari stroked his face and cradled his head, holding him gently against his chest. He let the feeling of wholeness wash over him and held his hand on Khari's hip, sliding it over the crumpled fabric of his trousers to rest gently on the curve of his backside. Just to hold him, and be held, was a form of heaven after so long dreaming. Never allowing himself to believe it could all be real, unable to speak to him, to find out his name, hear his voice: he had waited so long.

"Sleep," Khari said next to his ear, his musical voice soft. The small glowing balls of heatless flame blinked out, leaving just the glow from the fire to light the room; the flames casting red and gold shadows on the earthy ceiling.

"I'm scared to," he replied, just as quietly. "I don't want to sleep, then find all this has been another dream. Scared you'll go. Scared the hoods will come back..."

"They can't get to you. Not here," Khari said, smoothing his hand rhythmically over Eden's hair. "You're safe to sleep and get your strength back. And I won't let you go. I promise."

"You'll stay?"

"Aye, I'll stay, Eden. You're safe, and I won't let you go...sleep."

IX

When Eden next woke up it was to a stomach that thought his throat had *actually* been cut, painfully empty and loudly letting him know that he had slept much longer than was usual. His neck ached. Bruised and tight, it felt as though it was swollen to twice its normal size. He could feel each individual miniscule stitch holding his skin closed beneath the poultice—a fresh poultice. It was cooler and lighter than the one that had been in place when he had fallen asleep.

Fallen asleep in firmly-muscled arms, against a wide chest.

He moved his hand in a panic, sure for an instant that he *had* dreamt Khari appearing. He had imagined the tall blonde elf with flashing golden eyes.

His hand touched warm flesh and soft wool, and he heaved in a breath, letting it out in a long sigh of relief. He opened his eyes. The room was softly lit by the magical lights and the fire, enough light to see Khari's sleeping face on the pillow next to him. Eden studied each feature as Khari breathed evenly and quietly, his face relaxed and peaceful.

The blanket had been pushed down to their hips while they slept. Eden cuddled further into the soft and giving fleshy pillow above Khari's armpit, looking down his chest at their legs, entwined under the covers. He trailed his hand across the warmth of Khari's stomach, hard and flat with strong muscles. Pale against the darkness of his trousers, Khari's skin was like alabaster, lit by the light of the fire and heatless flaming lights so it glowed. Unable to stop himself, Eden ran his fingers across the soft skin.

Khari moaned in his sleep and lifted his arm to slide under his head, stretching out and arching. Eden grinned as Khari's woollen top lifted further, revealing more skin and muscle, so pale against Eden's own cinnamon colouring that it held him captivated for a long moment. Hypnotised by the darkness of his hand against the paleness of Khari's stomach. Smooth white flesh with a scattering of dark blonde hair around his navel that led down in a thin line to the waistband of his trousers.

Bolder, Eden ran his hand upwards under Khari's top, exploring on his way to rest his palm over his heart. He stopped just under Khari's rib, his hand stilled as his fingers met raised and puckered skin. A long stripe and a wide crescent moon shaped scar, along with several other long slashes slicing upwards along his ribcage. Eden frowned, watching Khari's face as he moved his hand higher, following the path of the scars to Khari's armpit and then around to his back.

Khari grunted in his sleep, wincing. Moving his hand back to his chest, Eden looked downwards to see the edges of the scars peeping out from under the long sleeved creamy top worn under the ragged jumper. They shone pale in the firelight; old and well healed, but spoke of deep and brutal wounds. Eden's mind skittered away from what they must have looked like when they were first inflicted.

"They're hideous," Khari said quietly, his eyes still closed. "You're not missing much by not being able to see them. Do you feel better after sleeping? You've slept over a day. We were going to try and wake you up if you hadn't come round by lunchtime. Must be hungry?"

"Some," Eden agreed, holding his hand splayed over Khari's stomach. "You could never be hideous. Nor could anything about you. Did this happen...before?"

"Aye. Before." Khari opened his eyes to treat Eden to a full golden stare. He studied him in silence for a moment, then gave a shrug and lifted his top and sweater upwards, exposing his chest so Eden could see the ridges and valleys of the scars crossing his ribcage and right breast.

"They go round to my back," Khari said. "My back is worse. Jaizel thought flaying me might be fun. He skinned about a quarter of my back—it's at its worst across my shoulders, but the scars are pretty much all over."

Eden stroked his fingertips back over Khari's unblemished stomach, below his navel, and propped himself up on his elbow. The room swam out of focus for a moment, but soon righted itself, so he sat up. He held his hand on Khari's abdomen again. "No scars here," he said, running his eyes up his chest. Despite the damage, Khari's torso was beautifully built; flat planes and curved musculature that Eden ached to explore.

Khari looked at him and brought his knees up into his chest, scrunching into a defensive ball. "No scars on my thighs at the front, or my belly, no," he said simply. He sat up and pulled his sweater and long sleeved top over his head, glanced at Eden, then swung his legs off the bed so Eden could see his back, leaning to rest his elbows on his knees. He turned to look at Eden's face.

Eden reached a tentative hand to follow one of the deepest ridges across Khari's left shoulder. A valley of a wound, it cut into his flesh, sunken like a river bed. It was deep enough that Eden could make out bone beneath the fragile skin. Oddly, Khari's skin was not puckered and silvery, like the scars over his chest. Here, the skin was opaque, laid over the webs of scarred and flayed muscle like frosted glass or tissue paper, as thin and fragile as a butterfly wing.

He traced the lines of Khari's muscle under another section of devastated flesh, trying to grasp that he could actually see each individual tendon and network of muscle groups stretching over Khari's wide shoulders. It was indescribable damage, and had been inflicted with the deliberate aim to destroy the beauty of Khari's body.

Eden shook his head, leaning forward to touch his lips to the worst of the damage. "I wish I could stop the pain," he said under his breath, kissing his way down Khari's shoulder blade. "I'm sorry you were hurt so bad." He met Khari's eyes and lifted his face to find his mouth, kissing him. "You're still not hideous," he said as Khari pulled his cream top back down over his head. "Strong, and a fighter, to survive that...not hideous."

"Thank you." Khari turned so he was fully facing him and lifted Eden's chin, staring at his eyes to gauge if it was hurting or not. Satisfied that Eden was not about to pass out again, he gently pulled the poultice away from his neck, stopping when Eden hissed a gasp of sudden pain.

"Shit. How bad is it, Khari?"

"Not as bad as it feels, I don't think. It was deep, but not too wide. We were hoping to be able to heal you, at least a bit. In fact," Khari said, "we were relying on healing you inside the wound, Eden. But none of our magicks worked on you at all. So we had to just close you up and then use herb-lore." He held up the poultice. "Not as effective, but you're not infected at all. The main thing is for you to try not to move your head too much—don't pull the stitches out and reopen the wound. It was close to the artery and we had to work hard to make the vein join together again. I'd be happy if you could not bleed to death, after I waited so long to actually *be* with you."

Eden rested back against the pillows when Khari pushed him down to the mattress.

"Your job is to rest and heal," Khari continued, stretching out his booted foot to swing the kettle over the fire on its hook. "We're not sure what you are, but you should be able to heal faster than a human can. Gray says that humans can take weeks to heal after a bad injury...is that true?"

Remembering that Khari would have never seen a human, Eden nodded. "Months, sometimes."

"Wow. Do they really have no magicks at all?"

"None."

Khari raised a sculpted eyebrow. "Really?"

"Absolutely. Some claim to, but they're mostly frauds. They don't got them real magicks, not how you mean. Why?"

Khari shrugged. "I always dreamt of living in that realm," he said, blushing. "I like the sound of living amongst people who can't spell-cast, or attack me with powers. Humans sounded like a tale, when Gray told me about them...I wondered if they were truly real, that's all. Not that it matters," he added, shaking his head, "it's not like I'll ever be able to meet one."

"For what it's worth," Eden said, "I was raised as a human, by humans. I don't know what I am either, but until I managed to break through to this realm, I never thought I was anything but human...so you can tell yourself I'm one, if you want." He grinned. "I don't have any powers, really. I can see past enchantments, if I concentrate...Denny was teaching me. She was teaching me to ignore suggestion, too. But they're learned skills, not magical powers. You want a human, I'm as near as damnit."

Khari chuckled. "Aye, all right. Until you find out what you really are, you can be a human." He knelt in front of the fire and ladled broth into a bowl, then sat on the edge of the bed and passed it to Eden. "Drink that—it will help you heal and strengthen you."

"Thank you." Eden tilted the bowl to his mouth and sipped. It was delicious; savoury and delicately flavoured with unknown herbs, it coated his taste buds and slid down his throat like elixir. "Did you make this? Or Gray?"

"Me," Khari said. "I like to cook. Well, I like to eat, right? So I learned to cook as a means to an end. It reminds me of when I was young." He lifted his legs onto the bed and rested next to Eden on the pillows. folding his arms he crossed his legs at the ankles. "Mum kept me and Gray really well fed, aye? Then when she," Khari glanced at Eden quickly. "Jaizel killed her, when I was ten. Me and Gray were slung into the cells under the palace. The food there wasn't good," he said. "When we got free, I learned to cook. Trial and error, but I've managed to recreate quite a few of my mum's recipes. I'd watch her when I was a baby, and I guess a lot of the memories stuck with me. It's peasant food, sorry, but it's filling and good for you."

"Why do you keep assuming I'm used to silver plates and gilded bedsteads?" Eden asked, draining the last of the broth with relish. "This is all amazing."

"You have a diamond in your mouth that could buy a house and keep a family fed for about five years, Eden. Your shirt was finest lawn, and the laces were silk. Your trousers are made of Alfheimian leather, and the boots you wear are crafted by a genius." Khari touched Eden's earring. "This sapphire could clothe a dozen servants. This," he added, pointing to Eden's necklace, "could buy a farm. You don't have to pretend you're not rich, wherever you have come from."

Eden pulled out his earring, handing it to Khari. "In my world, it's worth a bit less than a farm," he remarked. "The clothes are Cole's...where is my shirt?"

"It was ruined, sorry. Too much blood—we couldn't wash it out."

"Oh. Damn, I liked that one most. It made me feel like a hero from a pirate film. I'll have to wear the other one, I suppose. Takana made the boots," he said, glancing at where they were placed close to the hearthstone. "The diamond was my mama's. It was a ring, but I had it made into this when she died. The necklace isn't worth as much in my world as you think it would be here," he added. "It might buy me a meal in a nice restaurant, but it sure wouldn't buy me a farm."

Khari held out the sapphire earring to Eden.

"Keep it." Eden looked at the small gold hoop Khari had in his own ear. "It'll suit you. I like what you wear," he said truthfully, picking Khari's sweater up from where it had been left on the bed near his legs. Shaking out the folds, he held it up to look at the frayed wool and the slashed tears in the knitted garment.

"It's falling apart," Khari said with a sigh. "It's hard to get wool, so I can't make another one. It's warm, but it's nothing but a rag, now. Worn it to death, and got caught in thorn bushes one too many times over the years. But, as I said, it's warm. Gets cold here at night and in the winter. Layers are the way to keep warm."

"You made this?" Eden asked, looking at the wool. "Knitted it?"

"Uh...is that what it's called? Couple of sticks and you sort of weave the yarn?"

"Yeah, it's called knitting," Eden said. "Wow...clever. Did you make this too?" he asked, touching the sleeve of Khari's shirt. Close fitting, he could see now the sweater had been taken off that it was much like a T-shirt he could have bought back home. Soft jersey-like fabric, clingy and warm, it was cut and tailored to perfection.

"Aye, yes. We have to make all our clothes," he replied. "Make do with whatever materials we can get our hands on." Khari said. "This is the easiest pattern to make quickly," he admitted, "so all my tops are cut like this."

"I like how it looks on you," Eden said, meaning it. He looked at the doorway as Takana appeared. "Takana. It's good to see you," he said, holding out his hand as she approached the bed. Khari stood up, bowing his head, glanced at Eden, and left on silent feet. Eden frowned at the door, before patting the bed for Takana to sit. He held her hand between his own.

"I am so, so sorry about Denny," he said. "And Alex getting hurt...and your teeth."

Takana shook her head and pulled the side of her mouth away from her teeth with a crooked finger to show her teeth were all in place and present. "Hurts a bit to chew," she said, "but it's nothing. I've had worse. So has Alex."

"Khari said he was nearly cut in two."

"He was. Nearly lost his fucking intestines. They all came from nowhere, Eden. I am so sorry...we were meant to protect you, and we got captured, first by Gray, and then by those Dark bastards. We should be strung up for failing in our duty."

Eden shook his head, carefully, and laid down to rest his head on her thighs, closing his eyes. "I'm just pleased you weren't killed," he said, holding her hand to his mouth. "I was so scared, when I saw you get hit. I couldn't get to you, Takana...I'm sorry. I shouldn't have slept. I never *saw* them coming. I was so busy wrapped up in my own thoughts, that I..."

Takana's finger rested over his mouth. "Shhh," she said, stroking her thumb over his eyelashes. "This was not your fault. All right? I came to see how you were," she added, smiling down at him when he opened his eyes. "We have been worried. A lesser man would have died from this injury. I thought, for a ghastly moment, that I had lost you. Then your prince swiped off a few heads. Beheading the bastards was one way to stop them killing you. He's the one you dreamt of? He carried you here and wouldn't let anyone else look after you, so we assumed he was the one you were searching for."

"He is, yeah."

"He seems nice. Quiet, but a nice boy. Good

179

looking."

"He's fucking hot, ain't he?"

"He certainly is," she said, giggling with him. "Eden, he's amazingly hot." She nudged him gently as he grinned, but sobered, gazing into his eyes. "He is Airell's son, isn't he?"

"He is," Eden confirmed. "You could've asked Gray that—I'm sure he would've told you."

"I wanted to make sure, by asking you," she said. "He's my cousin, then..."

"Sorry," Khari said, standing in the doorway with a tray of food. "I know you probably don't want a half-breed Dark Elf related to you...I won't tell anyone," he said, walking to the bed.

Eden sat up, taking the tray from Khari.

Takana stood and faced Khari, studying him for a full five seconds before she bowed gracefully, her leg bent behind her, knee nearly touching the floor. "Your Highness," she said, her voice soft and modulated, as it had been when addressing Airell. "It is a pleasure to meet you, at last. I am Takana. Your *half-breed* Wood Nymph cousin. I bring you the true regard of my King, your father. I am obligated to offer you the hand of friendship and family on his behalf, and to sincerely invite you to come to Alfheim, to meet him.

"Should you, as is your right, refuse this offer, Your Highness, then I am to inform you that you may call, at any time, on the King, or his armies...both shall be at your disposal. Should you want, for anything, it will be yours, if you ask. Be it loyalty, men at arms, or shelter. Call us, and we shall be at your side."

Khari, looking stunned, backed up against the tree-root wall next to the bed and shook his head from side to side. "I don't know what to say," he said.

"Um...please stop bowing? I can't concentrate with you being all...bowed."

Eden laughed under his breath. Takana shot him a glare and he picked up a small morsel of richly spiced fish from his plate, hurriedly popping it in his mouth. "I'm eating," he said, waving a hand. "Look...eating. Gosh." He looked at Khari. "She gets real mad if there's food and I'm not eating it. Reckon the two of you would make a good team. You cook it, she can watch me eat it. Although, while Cole's not around," he said, leaning towards Takana, "Khari can *actually* cook, so if he wants to come back with us to Airell, then him cooking would be cool...I swear Cole has actually been cooking leather and passing it off as jerky. I grew up with jerky, and it ain't what Cole thinks it is."

"The man hasn't a taste bud in his head," Takana conceded. "But, Khari, the offer I bring you is serious. For you and your brother. Airell, king of Alfheim, would like to meet you, and offers the hand of family and friendship."

"To a bastard child he's never met?" Khari asked.

Takana blinked. "You're not a bastard."

"I am. By the law of these lands, I am a bastard. Nameless."

"You are no bastard," Takana repeated. "Airell and Relaizia were married, by Orien's law. With witnesses. And you, Khari, were born a full ten months after that marriage. You are no bastard. That's my job. You are the legitimate heir to the throne of Alfheim, should you choose to take it when the time comes. You are Airell's only child, Khari, and you were conceived after a marriage that was held, and witnessed, under Orien's law. And," she added, "under our law, the law in Alfheim, your brother is made legitimate, although he cannot sit on the throne. Nominal parentage is automatic when the marriage is completed, for all previous children born to either party. Airell is as much his father, as he is yours, under our laws. Your mother knew that. So did Airell. He made Gray legitimate...Gray legally bears Airell's name."

"Why would he have done that?" Gray asked. He flickered into sight, and glanced at Takana, ignoring her startled gasp at his appearance next to the fire.

Eden dropped the bite of fish he had been about to eat. His brain was telling him that the man had just appeared from nowhere, but it wasn't something he was inclined to believe, just because his eyes had been witness to it. He looked at Khari, as though what he had seen would be confirmed as an illusion. Khari, however, seemed to see nothing amiss. Gray *had* appeared from thin air and it was nothing unusual, if Khari's lack of reaction was anything to go by.

"Why would he have done such a thing?" Gray asked. "I am Jaizel's son. I am born of incest. Why, for all the *worlds* would he choose to give me *his* name?"

"You...you can become invisible!" Eden said, stating the obvious.

"Inbreeding morphs abilities," Gray said, as though he was stating that the sky was blue. "Why would King Airell choose to give me a name as old as the realm itself? Is he insane?"

"Sometimes I wonder," Alex remarked, clinging to the doorway, Cole supporting him with an arm around his waist. He looked at Gray, then Khari. "He loved your mother with a passion. He planned to give up his throne and live with her, bringing you up as his own, Gray. He never knew about Za'akhar." Alex made it to the bed. He sat down heavily on the edge, catching his breath with his hands held to his side. "He planned to have a family, of course. He would have been overjoyed to know Relaizia was pregnant, but overall his initial plan was to run away with your mother, and make a home away from Jaizel. Away from these lands entirely."

"He became invisible," Eden hissed. "Am I the only one freaked out by it?"

"Don't masturbate," Cole said, smiling when Gray snorted and shook his head. Cole bowed from the waist, looking at Gray. "Your Highness. I am honoured to meet you and call you cousin. And it will be an honour to stand at your side to get your throne from the bastard currently sitting on it. Two thrones, two brothers." Cole winked. "Feel free to give me some kind of title. I live in hope of one."

Eden frowned. "Aren't you a prince?"

Cole shook his head.

"But isn't your mama Airell's sister?"

"Different fathers. Airell's father was a king. My grandfather was a poacher. My mother was born to the old queen—she remarried when Airell's father died. Married her gamekeeper," Cole said. His eyes had darkened. "Her brother made damned certain that no offspring from a gamekeeper could hold a title."

"My father was a piece of bloody work," Alex said. "He was a horrible old goat. It's his fault Cole has no title."

"Oh. Oh, okay, then."

"You're my first cousin?" Khari asked, looking at Cole.

"I am, Your Highness," Cole murmured, bowing to Khari. "And it is an honour."

"You're all fucking mad," Gray said, holding a hand to his head and looking around the room. "There's no way to tell if Khari is Airell's or Jaizel's child. I'm sorry to be crude, but I remember...I was young, but I was old enough to know what my animal of a father did to my mother. From the moment—the *moment*—she returned to the palace, he was on her like a rutting goat! He thought Khari was his. That *he* had created the chosen one, for the gods' sake! Now here you all are saying Airell claims parentage? Telling me, now, that I have a legal name? *Ugh!*"

"You need to see Airell," Takana said. "Khari looks like him. Blonde, not dark, but they look alike. Look at him next to Cole. Next to Alex. It's the eyes. I know Airell. He adopted you when he married your mother, Gray. And he isn't the kind of man to do anything without thinking about each and every consequence of his actions. That he never met you," she added, looking at Khari, "is killing him. He blames himself, but he knows that to have stopped your mother leaving him would've meant Gray was left behind, and he isn't able to want her to have stayed with him. Not at the cost of Gray."

"Za'akhar is Airell's," Alex said. "Ask Eden what happened when Airell touched him."

"He's your dad," Eden said. "He holds your blood. I felt it."

"That's good enough for me," Khari said softly, looking at Gray.

Gray hesitated, running his hands down his face. He looked at Cole, then Alex. "If this is a trick, I can promise you that you do not have an army strong enough to kill me and I will not allow you to hurt my brother."

"No trick," Alex said, shaking his head. "Airell holds my oath. As such, that oath is sworn to his sons...while they are under my care." He drew in a slow breath, pale faced and sweating. "I'm in no condition to trick you, love." He slipped sideways on the bed, curled up on his side next to Eden's legs. "No condition at all. I think moving might have been a bit ambitious," he said to Takana, lifting his hands to show his shirt was slowly being soaked with blood.

"Oh, gods," Takana said, kneeling next to her brother, "stay in bed...that was *all* you had to do, you stubborn old git." She lifted his bloodied shirt as Cole joined her and Gray poured water from the freshly boiled kettle, adding herbs and singing quietly under his breath.

"Lay him flat," Gray said, glancing at Khari.

Khari pulled his shirt over his head and folded it carefully to place on the low cupboard next to the fire. He knelt, shouldering Takana and Cole aside, and held his hand over the foot-long gash across Alex's abdomen, smearing blood across sweat-soaked olive skin. He murmured something too low for Eden to catch, closing his eyes, and then let out a breath, long and slow.

Silver mist, pure and light, seeped from Khari's hands. It covered Alex's torso to bathe him in a subtle glimmering light. Dancing across his torn and injured flesh, the lights span and whirled, kissing skin and skidding across the hideous slash. Gray leant over and tipped the contents of the bowl he held over the backs of Khari's hands. The scent of chamomile and lavender floated around the earthen bedroom. Khari ran his hand across the bloodied wound, watching as the silver mist lit the herbs and made them glow briefly, and the skin knitted back together under his touch.

Takana's amazed gaze bore into the side of Khari's face in silence, her wonder echoed in Cole's eyes, and Khari lifted his hands away from her brother, glancing at the elves either side of him.

"He should heal now," Khari said, standing up to wash the blood and herbs from his hands. He dried his fingers on a scrap of cloth and wiped a few specks of blood from his chest, then pulled his shirt back over his head, followed by his torn sweater. "He'll sleep for a few hours," he added, waving his hand at Alex. "You might want to move him back to Gray's room—he won't feel it."

"That was...gosh," Eden said to Khari. He felt awed by what he had witnessed, and he could tell by the looks on Takana and Cole's faces that it was beyond any magic they had seen before. "You fixed him. That was beautiful."

"That's what never worked on you." Khari turned and picked his bow up from its place in the corner, swinging it over his shoulder, and wrapped a scarf around his neck and head. "Move him back to your room, Gray," he said, heading to the door. "I need to check the traps. He'll need something to help him get strong, when he wakes up."

"You're going out?" Eden asked, pushing himself upright. "Is it safe out there?"

"Aye it's safe. Has been for years. We're hidden, I told you."

"We found you," Takana said.

Gray snickered. "No. You were stumbling around

making enough noise to scare the birds from the trees. I found you. When I went to find out what all the commotion was about. You were a good few miles away from finding us."

"Damnit!" Takana snapped. "I need retraining."

"You and me both," Cole said. He stood up and faced Khari. "Would you like a hand? I'm not, and have never claimed to be, a soldier or a warrior...but I can gather and forage like you wouldn't believe. If you're hunting and trapping, then I can help."

Khari flicked his golden eyes over Cole's face and turned to leave without a word.

"Chatty bugger, isn't he, Princess?" Cole said, grinning at Eden as he followed in Khari's wake. "Mind he doesn't talk your ear off...well, up and out, I suppose," he said, his voice growing faint. "This is a regular warren...dig it yourself? Are you always this quiet?"

"Do you ever shut up?" Eden heard Khari ask. "When you hunt, I imagine the animals jump on your arrows just to escape the incessant blathering, aye?"

"We're going to get on just fine, little cousin," Cole said. "Show me where to go..."

X

The following days, while Alex healed and regained his strength, and his own wound knitted together were an oasis of calm for Eden. The serenity of Khari's underground home was absolute. All stresses and rigours of life were strictly left in the forest above their heads; in the sprawling warren underneath, it was peaceful. Leaving Khari's bed, Eden had explored the rambling house, astounded by the high ceilings arching over his head, the thick roots of ancient trees woven together to form structures of awesome beauty.

The clay earth under the forest had been lovingly shaped and carved around the snaking foundations of the woods. The spaces naturally left by the trees had been utilised and turned into rooms and passageways. The floors were made up from more roots and from woven and plaited branches and rushes. Carved cupboards and tables held small tumblers filled with wildflowers and bright leaves, all lit by the softly glowing balls of heatless flame Khari had created. The light they gave could vary from anything as dim as a candle flame to a blazing light more akin to the electric lights Eden had known in his previous life.

Eden picked up a carved statue, running his fingers over the white wood, wondering what tree it was made from. He placed it back on the table in the high-ceilinged hallway and walked onwards, the ground sloping upwards towards the unseen exit. He hesitated, then turned back and started to walk back down, not ready to leave the underground haven. Not yet. He had thought he would be claustrophobic, but the spaces below the forest were large enough and well lit enough that he could have stayed in them indefinitely. Spacious or cosy, the room could be found in the warren of spaces Gray and Khari had carved out from the earth herself.

Wandering slowly, in no rush and with no place to be, he passed a library of books, stolen from Jaizel's palace and other places by Gray on his travels. He had learned that Gray would leave the sanctuary of his home to fetch supplies, when they were in desperate need of them. In the dead of night, he would cover himself from head to toe and walk as an invisible ghost through the forests to the closest towns. Bringing back wool and cloth, metal items, blankets...and books. Hundreds and *hundreds* of books.

He took a step into the library and gazed upwards at the soaring ceilings and high shelves. There was a huge fireplace built into the right hand wall and two cushions on the floor near a low table. The standard cauldron and kettle were placed on the hearthstone in front of the fire, along with a couple of mugs and two plates. Eden had learned that the brothers would cook and eat in whatever room they happened to be in; they did not bother to move to another place simply to fill their stomachs. Although there was a larder filled with hanging meats and stored root vegetables, they did not have a designated kitchen. For the brothers, a bedroom worked as well to prepare a meal as a kitchen.

Walking to the fireplace he studied the books on the shelves carved into the clay beside it. Ancient and handwritten, the manuscripts were made from vellum, covered in leather. His hands itched to reach out and hold one, wondering how old they were. He knew that the Fae were much, much older than humanity. He could not begin to imagine just how old some of the faded scripts actually were. He wondered if the hands that had held the quills were still alive. If the authors of these books could possibly still be breathing and walking the world. It could be possible, elves were immortal, after all. He reached out and stroked his knuckle down the spine of one of the manuscripts, turning to a sound in the doorway. He met Khari's eyes, hooking his thumbs in the pockets of his trousers.

"I couldn't resist a look," he said. "Sorry. I'm naturally nosy."

Khari crossed the floor and handed him a jug of ale, bending to pick up the mugs, which he placed on the table by his knee. Taking the ale back, he poured both mugs full and held one out to Eden.

"You like to read?"

Eden nodded. "Love it. You can leave whatever world or life you're in just by opening a book. They hold their own kind of magic, I reckon. They call me with a promise of escape, and so far they ain't failed to deliver."

Khari pulled the leather-bound manuscript Eden had touched from its place on the shelf. "Not sure how much escape this one can bring you," he said wryly, reading the cover as he drank from his ale mug. "Metalwork and Methods of Sword-Making? Handy information to have, aye sure, but maybe not the kind of romance to read as you're falling asleep. Unless you can't sleep...then it might have a use at night."

Eden chuckled, looking through the pages at the

diagrams and small script beneath the pictures. "It's not exactly a riveting plot, I grant you," he agreed, putting it back on the shelf and patting the spine. "I guess I was wondering if the books in this realm would be anything like the ones I would have known, back home, you know? I doubt that a fairytale would be called a fairytale, here."

Khari sat down on a cushion and crossed his legs. "Fairytales? About fairies?"

"No," Eden said, as he sank down to the second cushion. "I guess they should be called folk-tales. That would be more accurate. Although most have a wicked witch, or a fairy godmother...some sort of magic. Magic flutes, that sort of thing." He shrugged and sipped from his mug again. "I have some in my bag," he said. "Some Shakespeare, and a compilation of fairytales. Not much, but if you like books, they might be fun to look at."

"Stay here," Khari said, standing up. "I'll get the bag."

Eden waited, sipping at his ale and flicking through another large book. Squinting at times to try and make out the unfamiliar script. He looked up when Khari reappeared, his bags and backpack hung over his arms. Pushing the book aside to make room, he took his backpack from Khari and flipped it open to reach inside and pull out his copies of '*Romeo and Juliet*', and '*King Lear*'.

Khari took *King Lear* from him reverently, studying the embossed print of the paperback with the same awe Eden had felt staring at the leather bound books surrounding him. It made Eden smile to see the simple pleasure on Khari's face as he felt the pages and turned the book over in his hands to read the blurb on the back.

"This came with you from the Human Realm?" Khari asked, opening the cover with a reverence that made Eden feel a bit guilty when he thought about the times he had bent the spine of the book, or casually tossed it into the corner of his room.

Like most of the others in his English Literature class, he held a certain contempt—close to loathing— for William-Goddamn-Shakespeare. Two years studying his work for an A-level, was, to Eden's mind, two years too long. However, seeing the way Khari was examining the book was making him see it in a new light.

"I ran from my college straight into the Borderlands, yeah. There was a gang of guys. They found it great fun to gather together with the sole aim of finding me and trying to beat the living shit out of me on a weekly basis. I went to school with them, and they hate me. So they chased me, and I ran...next I knew, Takana was there in front of me. For once, I wasn't even trying to break through to this realm—I was just running and trying to save my ass from a beating."

"I saw you fight Jaizel's soldiers," Khari said, not looking up from the book in his hands. "Why not just stand and kill them?"

"It don't *quite* work like that in my world," Eden said, chuckling. "Besides—only been learning to fight since I met Takana. As a general rule, back home, folks don't go around armed with swords and bows. No need to arm yourself. Not where I lived."

Khari glanced up. "Sounds odd. Considering you were at risk of being attacked by gangs."

"A gang of bullies isn't quite the same as what

you're thinking it was like," Eden said, explaining as best he could what it was like to live in his world. He could tell by the incomprehension on Khari's face that he wasn't doing a great job of it. "Maybe, one day, you might see it yourself," he said, refilling his mug with ale.

"I'd like that," Khari replied, golden eyes thoughtful. "Who knows what might happen. You made it through to this realm...who's to say that I can't make it through to that one?"

"Exactly." Eden fell silent as Gray walked into the room with a small sack. He passed it to Khari.

Gray smiled back when Eden said hello. He passed a few minutes exchanging pleasantries, making sure Eden was comfortable, then left again. Leaving him alone with his brother.

"Lunch," Khari said, opening the sack. He passed Eden one of the plates from the hearth, filling it with bread, cheese and fruits. He swung the kettle over the kindling of the fire and flicked a glance at the dry wood, giving a small shake of his head when Eden jumped, wide eyes on the roaring flames that now licked the kettle. Biting into a dry roll with strong white teeth, he pulled a wide clay pot from the sack, pushing it close to the edge of the newly lit fire.

"Soup," he said in explanation, his golden gaze flashing in Eden's direction. "I keep forgetting that you don't have powers where you come from. It's alien to me to think that no one can light a fire without an hour with a flint and some tinder. Very strange."

Eden reached to the bottom of his bag, sitting straight again with his hand clasped around a disposable lighter. He flicked the flint and grinned smugly at Khari. "It don't take hours where I come from," he said, passing the lighter over the table. "We have lighters and matches. And lighting fuel," he added honestly, remembering the debacle of trying to light his barbeque the previous summer. No matter how many balls of scrunched up newspaper, or fire-lighters—which had smouldered under the coals for ten minutes then gone out—he had used, in the end he had resorted to smothering the whole thing with lighting fluid and throwing a match at it.

"Your way is cooler," Eden admitted, accepting his lighter back and tucking it back in his bag. Realising Khari was looking at the bag with interest, he pulled out his Hans Christian Andersen book and laid it on the table, then passed his bag to Khari with an apology that it held only items he would have used for college and random junk that was picked up over the course of the week.

Khari pulled Eden's hoodie from the backpack and shook out the creases to study Elmo. He glanced at Eden and pulled his sweater off, replacing it with the grey sweatshirt. Looking down his chest at Elmo, he grinned brightly and continued exploring the few items Eden had brought with him. Jeans were closely scrutinised, as were his baseball boots. His college folders and notes were fastidiously examined, the paper rubbed between thumb and forefinger; a pen was cause for several moments amazement as it was clicked on and off, then laid on the table gently.

Friendship bracelets, bought from a market stall; cartridges for his fountain pen; his wallet, holding a bank card, library card and driver's license; a crisp packet and half a pack of chewing gum; his boxer shorts and socks—thankfully clean; his old T-shirt, still stained from his fall on the riverbank as he had passed between the worlds; a calculator and math-set...all the mundane items that he carried around every day without ever thinking about them, now held up to the light and examined as though they were relics or gifts of more value than gold. He grinned when Khari looked at him, reaching to straighten the hood of his sweatshirt so it rested straight across Khari's shoulders.

"It suits you," he said. Khari held his hand, eyes uncertain. "You look as though you could almost pass for human." Eden looked at the small but pronounced point at the tip of Khari's ears. He had seen bigger, stranger, ears in his world than Khari's. They might be a bit...pixie-ish...but they were nothing to cause anyone to look more than twice, if they looked at all.

"Almost?"

Eden grinned and leaned over to kiss Khari gently. "You're too good looking to be human."

Khari's eyes flashed with unspoken pleasure at the compliment. He picked up the jeans again, his silent glance at Eden speaking volumes.

Eden grinned. "Try them, if you want. Reckon you'd look hot."

"Why didn't the mermaid just leave her prince a note?" Khari asked, rolling on his cushion to lay on his stomach, his baseball boot clad feet lifted in the air. He propped himself up on his elbows and reached for the tall bottle of berry wine, slopping some into a roughly blown glass. He waved the bottle at Eden in invitation, pouring when Eden held out his glass. Khari squinted, turning his head onto one side to better see Eden in focus. "Why didn't the idiot just write a note? She died for no reason, didn't she?" Khari poked Romeo and Juliet, nose crinkling. "And Romeo was a fool."

Eden rolled onto his back to look up at the library ceiling. Drunker than he had thought he was, his head was nicely spinning and he felt warm and relaxed. He folded his arms under his head and bent his legs at the knees, shuffling closer to Khari.

"They're tragedies," he said, arching like a cat when Khari combed his fingers though his hair. "They're not meant to have happy endings. Guess that makes them true to life. Happy endings are rare."

"But striving to find a happy ending is what makes us alive," Khari argued. "And when there are obvious solutions, it's not right that people—or mermaids—don't use their heads and end up dead, foam on the waves, for no reason. Poor stupid mermaid. They're meant to be intelligent creatures, I thought."

"Mermaids?"

"Aye."

"They're real?"

Khari looked at him. "Yes, Eden, they're real," he said. "The same as elves, fauns, dwarves, banshees, the skinfaxi...all the *mythical* creatures. I will tell you if one I mention is *not* real, all right?"

Eden giggled, shrugging awkwardly. "The succubus?"

"Real," Khari said, exasperated. He turned the page to read with one eye closed for a moment as Eden moved closer, resting his head next to Khari's arm. "Are you sure you don't mind me stealing your clothes?" he asked.

"I'm sure," Eden replied. In all honesty, he thought Khari looked fantastic dressed in jeans and hoodie. When he smiled, he looked like the teenager he was, even if the warrior was barely hidden below the surface. "Why don't you have long hair, like all the other elves I met?"

Khari rubbed a hand over his head, fingering the long blonde spikes into style, then shrugged. "It was long, when I was young," he said, his voice quiet. "But it was matted and vile when Gray ran with me...and I had been picked up by it, had it used to swing me against walls and to control me...so I had Gray shave it off. I get uncomfortable, now, if it's longer than this. I like it long on other people, but hate mine feeling knotty and messy. Besides," he added, "this is easier to wash over a basin, and I wash it a lot," he said. "Are you hungry?"

"Do you ever stop eating?"

"Not really," Khari said. He knelt up, then stood, bending to hold the table for balance. "Oh...made that wine stronger than usual," he said, managing to straighten, only staggering a little. He held out a hand to Eden, helping him to his feet. Losing his balance, Khari leant against him for a moment, breathing a laugh next to his ear before lifting his head to look straight into Eden's eyes.

Eden drew in a sharp breath, mesmerised by the flashing spectrum of colour in front of him. Khari found his mouth, kissing him deeply and he wondered if he had been bewitched, somehow. Powerless to do anything but respond, he staggered backwards, pushed gently but insistently to lean against the wall, Khari's body shielding him from the room while he was kissed with a previously hidden passion. A hand came up, touching the line of stitches under his jaw, following their path across his neck, then leaving them to glide down Eden's throat to the open vee of his unlaced shirt, tracing his collar bones, then his chest.

Eden raised his hand, trembling. He felt the thick fabric of his own sweatshirt as he trailed back down to the hem, sliding his hand under the layers of T-shirt and hoodie to feel his way upwards once more, Khari's skin hot under his palm. His heart beat hard, thudding in time with the pulse in Eden's ears. Skimming his thumb across Khari's nipple, his senses were ignited by the indrawn breath he got in response. Khari's moan was enough to send his mind reeling. Scattering into a thousand shards once again.

His knees weak, Eden clung to Khari, panting against his neck. Trembling, just as breathless, Khari held on, using the shelves to keep them both upright, his breathing harsh and ragged. Khari looked at him, confusion and questions written clearly in his eyes.

Eden shook his head. Whatever happened when they kissed he had no answers for. He did not even know the right questions to ask. He just knew that when Khari's mouth touched his he felt as though he was flying. As though he had lost himself, and found himself, all at once. As though he was soaring high out of his body, nothing but pure sensation, unable to live unless he was touching the amazing elf he had searched for and dreamed of.

There was nothing but Khari and without Khari he would be lost. He had never wanted anyone so much in his life.

His hand still held over heated skin, he rested his

forehead against Khari's and closed his eyes to catch his breath. "What are you doing to me?" he asked.

"I...I could ask the same," Khari breathed, getting a hold of himself by degrees. "It feels like I'm nothing but tinder...and you touch me, and I'm going to explode. But I *can't* explode. Exploding would be a relief," he said with a quiet chuckle, lifting his head to look into Eden's eyes. "It feels as though I will never be able to be me again, when you kiss me. When I taste you..." He leant forward to gently track the curve of Eden's lower lip with his tongue, "I lose all sense of who I am." Khari moved, his breath hot against Eden's ear, "I am nothing, but I am everything. Everywhere, all at once. A knotted ball of desire, ready to spring open...if we don't stop. But if we don't stop..."

"We'll explode. To not stop will mean...more than we're ready to bear."

"Aye," Khari agreed. "Uncontrollable...unknown...something. I can feel something inside me, straining to get free. Pulling away from me...wanting you," he said, holding Eden close to his chest. "It feels as though there's a part of me that just wants you...and I will die if it can't have you. But it's nothing I've known...it scares me as much as it brings me to life."

"I know. Me too. There's a part of me screaming to stop, even while there's another telling me to never stop. I don't know what it is. I'm scared too."

"Go...slow," Khari mumbled, as he skimmed his lips across Eden's mouth.

"I like slow," Eden replied. "This is enough. Just to be with you. After so long, just to hold you is more than I imagined I would ever know. This is enough. I'm in no rush." He moved shakily, straightening his trousers and shirt. Pushing himself away from the shelves, he kissed Khari once more before stepping away to clear his head. "Do you have more of that wine?" he asked. Khari dressed in tight jeans, mussed and flushed was too much for his mind to take in. He wondered if the guy had any idea just what he did to him.

Khari scooped the bottle from the floor, drank from the neck, and pressed it into Eden's chest. "There's loads, aye," he said, grabbing Eden by the hand to drag him from the library. "Let's go where there's other people, and get drunk. Because, may Orien help me, I don't know if I can stop myself...not with the way you're looking right now. Starting to feel as though I might have to sleep in another room."

"Don't you dare," Eden said. He gulped from the bottle. "I've been with you at night for close to a decade...you can't leave me now. I think I'd die," he said, not joking.

Khari looked at him from the corner of his eye. "I know. I wouldn't be able to be without you either." He walked quickly along the hallways of the warren, pulling Eden in his wake. "I'm just scared I won't be able to stop, and hurt you. I *would* rather die than hurt you."

"Hurt me how?" Eden asked.

Khari hesitated, but looked at Eden with an honesty that made his heart skip a few beats. "I want to lose myself in you and feel myself be a part of you. I want to hold you and mould you to *me* and be part of *me*...and the thoughts I'm having?" he asked softly, "Orien's Blood, Eden...I want to make you scream my name and make you *mine*! I have to be able to stop. I can't...I can't do that. Be like that."

Eden staggered when Khari dropped his hand and walked rapidly down the hall, away from him. He raised an eyebrow and drank from the wine bottle again. He slumped against the earthy wall, waiting for Khari to turn around and face him. When he did, Eden raised the bottle, bending his head in a small bow.

"Sounds like a plan, to me." Eden murmured the words, knowing Khari could hear him, even with the distance between them. "When you're ready...I don't have an issue with you making me scream your name. Sounds...fun." Khari heaved in a breath, captivated. "Make me scream, when you're ready," he breathed. "Make me yours."

Emerging into the weak sunlight, Eden felt the nip of the encroaching winter in the air and gratefully shrugged into the cloak Alex passed him, then jumped up onto Jinx's back. He watched Khari climb through the round opening to his underground home and cover the entrance with sawn planks of wood, scattering heaps of earth over it.

Khari knelt, holding his hand to the ground, and watched as vines and bracken grew from the earth, snaking across the small clearing to cover the hidden entrance completely. He whistled, holding his arm out. A white, black spotted, bird of prey, with a wickedly sharp and hooked beak, landed on Khari's wrist. Stroking his fingers over the feathered head of the bird, he fed it a strip of bloody meat and transferred it to his shoulder.

"Oliver!" Khari called, his voice a melodic song.

Hooves sounded in the near distance. Eden watched a huge black stallion appear from the trees and walk to Khari, bowing his massive head to have his nose stroked.

"Ollie," Khari said, tilting his head at the horse, eyes on Eden. He pointed to the bird on his shoulder. "She's called Fain."

"Friend of yours?" Takana asked, eyeing the bird of prey.

Khari nodded, swinging himself onto Ollie's bare back. He gulped down a good measure of the painkilling potion he had brewed that morning, recorking his flask with precise movements, and drew his cloak together to fasten at the neck with a jet brooch.

"Nice horse," Eden said, walking Jinx to stand at Ollie's side. Khari was sat about a foot higher than him, and Jinx was hardly a small horse. "Have you got everything you wanted to bring?"

Lifting his shirt and woollen jumper with a small secretive grin, Khari showed Eden a flash of Elmo. "The rest is in your saddlebags. I thought you wouldn't mind me wearing the top, but tell me if you get cold."

"I'll steal your woolly before I ask for Elmo back." Eden held out his hand to Fain, letting her peck the side of his finger while he searched in his bag with his other hand for the ham roll he knew was there. Finding it, he fed the bird a strip of meat. "Is she an eagle?"

Khari raised a brow. "No. She's a gyrfalcon. I assume you don't hunt, then?"

"Nope," Eden grinned. "Not with birds. She's bigger than I thought birds of prey would be. Big wings," he added as Fain chose that moment to stretch out her wings, as though showing off.

"Aye," Khari agreed. "She's a beauty. Keeps us fed, hey, girl?"

Fain pushed her head to Khari's cheek, folded up her wings, and settled down comfortably on his shoulder.

Gray appeared between the trees, mounted on a chestnut horse that was only slightly smaller than Ollie. He, like everyone else, was dressed for travel; his cloak, bag and weapons worn with a regal dignity that left Eden in no doubt, if he had any to begin with, that he was in the company of a future king. Gray's hair was no longer loose, braided instead into an intricate design to hang in a plaited tail down his back to his waist.

Eden had seen Khari's eyes widen when Gray had made an appearance, and knew that his hair, and the braid, signified *something*, but had not wanted to ask what that something might be. It looked as though his hair had been twisted and looped together, woven and plaited in lattices and ropes that span around each other with a complexity that made Takana's braids look mundane, even with all their chiming bells and silver clasps.

Gray lifted his head a fraction of an inch and looked down his long straight nose at the forest around him, checking that all trace of his occupation had been erased. He looked at Khari.

"You are sure this is what you want?" Gray asked.

Khari lifted his chin, staring at his brother. "It is what I want," he said, clearly and formally.

"We may never be able to return, Khari. Be sure."

"I am sure, Gray."

Gray held a hand twisted in his horse's mane. "All right," he said, turning around to face the forest. "I warn you, mighty Prince Alexander," he called, trotting away, "I *will* kill you if this is a trick to get my brother."

"As if I'd doubt him," Alex said, following the Chiearian prince through the trees. He glanced left, at Denny's grave, and bent his head in farewell, then faced front, head straight and eyes dry.

Cole and Takana bowed to the piled rocks covering the burial place of their fallen friend, then vaulted onto their horses. Takana waved Eden in front of her, with Khari.

"We'll take the rear," she said to Khari. "No doubt you will have to save me from your place in the middle of the cortege," she added, "but give an old warrior the pretence of protecting you, eh?"

Khari turned Ollie to face the direction Gray had gone. He tapped his feet to Ollie's sides, his left hand barely resting on the horse's wide shoulders, and took off through the trees.

Takana grunted and raced after him. "Come on," she called to Eden and Cole. "Looks as though there's no end to his talents! Of *course* he can ride as though he's a fucking jockey...bloody show-off!"

"I think she likes him," Cole said, breaking into a canter. He grinned at Eden. "I know I do. Kid has spirit—I like spirit."

Following Khari and Gray was relentless. Whatever the ground was like, whatever might happen to be in their path, the brothers rode as though they had the hounds of hell on their tails. Jumping hedgerows and streams, racing across open fields and rocky passes, they kept a pace that left Eden and the Light Elves flagging far behind. Mostly, they could only tell which path to take when Khari, or Gray, doubled back and jerked their head in the direction of travel. It was easier on open ground—at least then Eden could just make out the shape of a distant figure on horseback to tell where they were.

He estimated that they were going back at about

four, maybe five, times the speed that they had travelled on the outward journey. Jinx, bless her soul, was managing to keep going, but he had no real idea how. He was exhausted riding her, so the poor horse must be close to falling.

Far in the distance, Eden saw Fain circle and swoop down to the ground at a dizzying speed. He glanced breathlessly at Alex, looking sideways at his friend.

"Reckon that's dinner?"

"I do hope so," Alex replied. "They can't keep going for much longer."

"We said that five hours ago," Takana said, her voice shaking with the pounding of her horse's hooves. "At this rate, we're going to arrive at the palace tomorrow in time for tea."

Eden looked ahead once more. He saw Khari heading his way and sat straighter in his saddle, watching as he approached, not holding onto Ollie at all; no reins and no saddle, Khari sat astride the magnificent beast with the same ease as he might have sat on a chair. In his hands he held his bow, arrow nocked and at the ready, and slung over his right thigh was a string of rabbits, wildfowl and a goose. Eden cocked a brow at the catch as Khari slowed in front of him.

"Gray has found a place to camp," he said, looking at Takana, Cole and Alex. "Just through those trees," he added, pointing at the distant tree-line. We can eat and rest for the night. Rest the horses."

"And yet your horse looks just fine," Eden said, looking at Ollie. The black stallion glared back at him and grunted briefly as though insulted that Eden could think he would be anything *but* fine; as though he had been for a nice relaxing afternoon canter, not a gruelling ten hour race across rough and unforgiving ground.

"He's a good boy," Khari said gently, patting Ollie's neck.

"He's a beauty, I'll say that," Alex agreed, leading his own horse in a trot across the fallow field. He looked at the string of dead animals. "You hunted as well, even going at that pace?"

"It was mainly Fain," Khari replied. He studied Eden for several silent seconds, then sidled Ollie next to Jinx, reaching out to lift his chin and examine the neat row of stitches. He nodded approval that they were holding, and that Eden had nearly healed, letting go of his face. He turned back to Alex. "You are well?"

"Thank you, yes," Alex said, inclining his head. "Not even an ache. You have some skill with healing, don't you?"

Khari looked at him for a moment, then nodded.

"Is there anything you can't do?" Takana asked. "Just out of curiosity. Let me guess...you can't play an instrument, and are tone deaf?"

"I play flute, guitar, lute, harpsichord and can drum. And I can sing," Khari said, looking mildly affronted that anyone might think otherwise.

"Of course you can," Takana muttered. "So what can't you do?"

"Not much," Khari said, galloping away.

"Take a joke, maybe?" Takana called after him. "Don't be upset, Khari! I was only playing around!" She looked at Eden. "He's way too uptight. I was joking."

"He's nervous of you all, I think," Eden said. "It's just been him and his brother for so long, remember.

He had no idea about who his father was, and he's come out the other side of hell, if his back is anything to go by. I know the other...rumours...about what he went through at Jaizel's hands, and I'm starting to wonder if they might be true. So all in all, I reckon he's pretty together, really. Well, I say that, but it's all relative," he said. "He's good fun, when he decides it's worthwhile opening his mouth to speak." He shrugged. "Remember too that he's having to leave the safety of his home, knowing that he has armies searching for him, wanting to take his head back to Jaizel. He said Jaizel won't ride into the Tarenthian Forests—superstitious, I think—but he sends his men regularly to try and capture Khari and Gray. I'd be nervous out in the daytime, too. Maybe that's why he rides like a madman."

"Or he is simply a madman," Cole said thoughtfully, lowering his voice as they neared the trees. "I haven't worked it out, but he's a bit odd to say the least. And he has some *serious* skills when it comes to hunting and trapping."

"And armed combat," Alex added. "Gray had a huge role in fighting off that ambush, but Khari? I've never seen anyone so young fight like that."

Eden remembered the whistle of the sword above him, and the thump of the decapitated head as it landed in front of his knees like an offering, and closed his eyes briefly. He saw again the windmills Khari had made with his swords, one held firmly in each hand, as he span and danced his way across the campsite, cutting through flesh and bone with a grace that he had not seen anyone else display. Khari had moved almost lazily, knowing what his attacker was going to do before it was done; he had been where he had needed to be. Ready to slash and swipe his long and wicked looking swords, moving and twirling them like batons in front of him, at his sides, over his head. They had never been still, and anyone who had come close to them had been cut down without so much of a blink when they fell.

"He's a warrior," Eden said. "He's had to make himself strong, so he's made himself the strongest he can be. Maybe then he won't be hurt again." He dismounted from Jinx, rubbing his arse to ease the numb pain in his buttocks. He looked up at Takana. "It's all an act. He has to be strong, be apart from everyone, be detached. He has to be prepared to kill, and be able to fight...but he's gentle, and he's kind, and he *is* good," he said. "He's scared of you. But he's had the guts to come with you all the same."

"Yes," Takana said, sliding from her saddle and rubbing her backside. "He's had a lot to deal with, I know. I'll give him time." She grinned at Cole. "He's bound to learn how to take a joke eventually." Walking to where the aroma of cooking meats was already floating from the dense forest, she stretched her arms above her head. "That smells bloody brilliant, Khari," she called. "We'll have Cole cook for you tomorrow, then you can marvel at how we made it as far as we did in one piece...what *are* you wearing? Is that Eden's jumper?"

"Aye...Elmo," Eden heard Khari say softly. "He said I could wear it."

"It looks strange, but suits you well," Takana said, her voice gentle. "You would have never been to the Human Realm, would you?"

"No," Khari said as Eden entered the small campsite. "I've never left Chiearatul."

Takana looked thoughtfully at Khari for several seconds, then at Eden before she looked back at Khari. "I am a border guard," she said, sitting down to accept a large tankard of frothy ale from Gray. "That means that I have to guard the borders between this realm, and the human one. I have to stop humans entering our lands."

Khari glanced up, flicked his eyes at Eden, then sniggered. "You're running before you get killed for failing in your duty?" he asked, drily. He watched Takana bristle, then grinned. "It's all right," he said, looking back down at the onion he was slicing, "you're bound to learn to take a joke, in time."

Gray chuckled, looking into the fire but grinned when Eden whooped.

"You got *burned*," he sang, pointing at Takana. "Oh, that was classic!"

Takana laughed and shook her head. "Okay, I deserved that," she admitted. "What I'm getting at, Khari, is that in the right place, I'm able to walk from this world to the Human Realm."

Khari jerked his head up, staring at her. "You've been there?"

"Lots," she said. "I have a house there, as does Cole."

"I lived there for decades," Cole said, chiming in. "That realm is a perfect home for one without many powers, such as myself. Airell uses Glamour to disguise my ears and off I go. I have several properties there."

"Cole and I have made lives in both realms. Also, as a Border Guard, I have to let quite a few of our kind through, for one reason or another. It's free passage for the Fae—my job is keeping humans *out*, not keeping the Fae in. Maybe, if Airell is agreeable, I can take you, and Eden, back to the borders and see you across the river. I am sure that Eden would like to see his father and let him know that he is all right, and as safe as he might be, all things considered. Alex? Can you see a reason why Khari might not be allowed to cross with him and see the realm he has dreamed of?"

"I was thinking the same thing myself, as it happens," Alex said. He is of age, and he is a prince. If anything, it would be wrong for him *not* to see that world."

"I can go through to see the humans?" Khari asked. He looked at the faces surrounding him, meeting and holding Eden's eyes. "I can walk between the worlds too?"

"If Takana says so, then I guess you can. I would have asked, a few weeks back, what on earth you would want to go there for, but I think I can understand what the draw might be, now. I never knew that the Fae could cross back and forth, though. I guess it makes sense that they can, but I never thought of it before. There have to be conditions, though, right? You can't just have, I dunno, a faun prancing about in the town centre. That *would* be noticed."

"Eden, you will learn," Takana said, "has a slight obsession with fauns. He missed a visiting friend, and cannot quite grasp that there is a race with goat-legs and human everything else."

"Fauns are weird," Khari said with a shrug. "You know they're, like, *naked* at the bottom, but you never see...anything." He looked around the fire at everyone. "I always wondered if male fauns have to tuck their cocks away or something. And why wear a coat in the cold, but forego trousers? Odd creatures. But then, mermaids," he said, smiling brightly at Eden. "Fish arse and flippers, human top half? That has to bring its own set of complications when it comes to making baby mermaids and mermen. Do they lay eggs, like fish, or have live young, like people? And again...where do the males keep their cock and balls? Or...is it *really* like fish, and they have to, I don't know, fertilise a pile of roe?"

"And, suddenly, I will never be able to look a Mer in the face again," Alex said.

"Not without wondering if it all gets a bit kinky when it comes to making babies, anyway," Cole agreed.

"They have belly buttons," Takana said, frowning, "but I have to admit to never having thought where the babies might appear from. And I confess to never giving fauns and their parts much thought. I shall have to ask Toleil when I see him next."

Alex raised both eyebrows to gape at his sister. "You cannot simply ask Toleil where he hides his penis!"

She shrugged, flashing her white teeth in a brilliant grin. "I have to, now. I swear I shall never be able to concentrate on a card game with the man until I know!"

Khari laughed. The sound was bright and musical, pure enough that everyone fell silent and turned to look at him. He closed his mouth and glanced around nervously before looking down at his hands.

"You have a beautiful laugh," Alex said. "I haven't heard it before. The sound took me by surprise."

"I haven't heard that laugh in years," Gray said,

staring at his brother. "You sound like Mum."

"It was funny," Khari muttered, looking at Takana. "Will you actually ask him?"

"Only if he pisses me off," Takana replied. "So yes, most likely."

Eden moved around the fire and sat down at Khari's side, drawing his knife from its sheath and slicing a carrot into the pot next to the fire. "I can't cook to save my skin," he said conversationally, "so if I go really wrong with the slicing and dicing, tell me. You have a great laugh."

"Thanks," Khari said, looking sideways at him from under long dark-blonde eyelashes. "Do you want some bread? It might be a while until this is okay to eat."

"Bread would be nice, thanks. Are you all right? This has to be a big change for you."

"I've never left our home," Khari said. "I've been a day's ride away before, but only when we had a really bad winter, and we had to forage further afield for anything edible. That was a few years ago, though. And it didn't end too well."

"Oh?"

Gray leant forward to look around Khari. "We ran into a large group of Jaizel's men. Experienced ones. It was a close call, that day. We made it out, but barely. I haven't taken Khari away from home since. But it *was* years ago. We have more experience, strength, and power nowadays."

"I don't think I would like to run afoul of anyone who could possibly beat you in combat," Cole said. "If they can battle you, and win, then they must have supreme powers, the like of which I dread to ever know exist."

"You haven't met my father," Gray said, looking away. "As strong as I am, he makes me look like a weak babe in arms."

"Ah, but," Cole said, popping an almond into his mouth with a grin and a wink, "he's a cunt. He doesn't count. I was talking about *real* people, not that arsehole."

"Oh, real people?" Gray asked. "Then no, I'm about the best there is."

"Thought so," Cole said. "Would you like to come and help me gather some plants and herbs?" he asked. "I noticed that although we seem to have the meat and protein side of things sorted, we're going to be living off a single turnip and a withered carrot in less than two days. And I think Khari might like to brew up some more of his painkiller?" Smiling at the small nod Khari gave him, Cole stood up. "Have you tried a lotion made of Paheka tree sap and poppy oil?"

"No...just the potion."

"Well, it takes a bit of preparation," Cole said, "but when it's made properly, it numbs where it touches. Massaged into your back, it will stop all your pain. Just don't confuse it with your potion, because it will kill you, after sending you mad."

"I'm already mad, I thought," Khari said, looking up at Cole.

"Bloody hell. Are you a bat?"

"I have very good hearing, aye."

Cole groaned, and crouched down next to Khari. "In that case, I think you might possibly be totally bonkers, but you're good looking, and I hope you make Eden happy, and he makes you happy. I think you ride like a lunatic, and you could do with going slower tomorrow, before you kill the marvellous creature you have as a steed. I think you cook brilliantly, but lack social skills. You don't mean to boast, but you're making us, the best of the best, feel like children next to you. Take your foot off the pedal a bit, Khari, and slow down. Life isn't a race, and the one who reaches the finish first is the loser, so take a breath and ease the pace. You're going to live for a good few thousand years, if you can evade Jaizel. Enjoy the ride." Cole snared a slice of onion from Khari's knife, outing it in his mouth. "Now you don't have to strain your pretty ears to hear me, do you? You're cutting those carrots way too thick, Princess," he added, patting Eden's head as he stood up. "They'll take an hour to cook like that. Ready Gray?"

Gray stood next to Cole. He looked down at his brother. "Ready camp while I'm gone," he said, shouldering his quiver and picking up his bow.

"Cabbages don't need shooting!" Cole sang from somewhere in the bushes. "You don't need a weapon to hunt vegetables."

"No, but I need one to kill you with if you don't shut up," Gray said, jogging away. "It's for protection, all right? You can't be too careful."

"Sure, all right...I guess parsnips can get violent if they don't want to be pulled up from the ground. Touchy sod, aren't you, Gray? Learn to relax."

"I'm as relaxed as I can be. I don't like leaving my brother alone. I haven't left him since..."

Khari listened to his brother's voice as it faded away. He sliced into the second onion, holding it in his hand and using his thumb to guide it along the blade of his knife.

"He's protective," he said, not looking up. "He gave up everything to protect me. He worries if I'm not next to him."

"I think I would, too," Alex said. He drew his sword from the scabbard on his back and knelt with it across his thighs, using a stone from his pack to hone the curved blade. "I think, had I fought as your brother has fought to keep you safe, I would be exactly the same. And I would be extremely proud of the man I had raised," he said, looking over the flames of the fire at Khari's bent head. "I never had the pleasure to meet your mother, Za'akhar. Sorry, Khari," he corrected, "but I know Airell. He would not have given his heart to anyone less than worthy...I would have liked to have met her. I am...I am so sorry for your loss, Khari," Alex murmured. "I am sorry for Relaizia's death, and I am sorry that it was left to your brother to find a way to save you from Jaizel. I know what happened to you..."

Khari looked up, eyes searching. He glanced at Alex, grunted, and looked back at his knife.

"You know nothing," he said tonelessly. "You have heard rumours and gossip from those who think my name and my story has worth and can be used as currency. You don't know what happened to me, but you think you do, and you believe that asking me might hurt me more than Jaizel managed to do...or offend me," he said, glancing up.

Looking into Alex's eyes again, Khari nodded to himself, seeing something in the older elf's face that was invisible to Eden.

Without thinking about it, Eden reached out his hand. He rested it silently on Khari's knee, unable to leave him in his own space. Khari glanced at him, the building tension fading. He looked back at Alex.

"You are scared to offend me. I'm an unknown

quantity to you, and you do not want to push me over the edge, in case I might be too delicate to speak of the memories I live with daily inside my head. As though speaking of any of it could make it happen again. As though speaking of it will hurt me all over again...by hiding it, it gives Jaizel power over me, and I refuse to give him more power. Ask what you want to know, Alexander, Prince of Alfheim...but do not presume to know a past that only I have the truth of."

Alex dipped his head. "I am sorry, Khari," he said softly. "You are right. I know rumours, and I have heard tales. I give you my apology."

"I accept it," Khari said, tossing his onion into the pot.

"It's said that Jaizel raped you," Takana said. "To try and get the power you're thought to hold."

Eden peeled another carrot, watching as Khari's fingers clenched near his knee. Only slightly, and they relaxed again almost immediately, but the reaction had been there. He closed his eyes for a moment, feeling pure hatred grow in his chest, filling him. He had known that it had happened, maybe, but to *know* it was different.

"He kept me as his whore for three years," Khari said, his voice low and devoid of all emotion. "He thought he could make me release my powers by fucking me. When that failed, he passed me to his army, to see if any of them could make me release the powers of a god. They failed too...if I had what they were seeking, I would have given it, and gladly, to make them stop. They flogged me, flayed me, and tried to break me. I have been hanged, and I have been starved. I was almost buried alive, and I lived in a dank prison, naked and cold, after being torn from my mother's arms and forced to watch her murder. I think *rape* is an understatement, for what Jaizel did to me."

"He tried to destroy you," Alex said, voice thick.

"He failed," Khari replied harshly. "I refuse to let him destroy me."

Eden didn't dare look up. He swept his wrist across his eyes, blinking to clear his sight as he looked at the half-peeled carrot in his hand and the glinting blade of his knife.

"I will kill him," he ground out through clenched teeth, shocked to hear the malevolent violence in his voice. He heard thunder in the distance, a low rumble of ominous foreboding and let go of the carrot, the blade of his knife pressing into the soft flesh at the join of his thumb and forefinger. He watched the blood well up and drip into the dark earth beneath him.

"I will kill him," he said again. "Whatever I have to do, I will see this man knelt at my feet, and his blood will run."

Khari touched his arm, pulling his hand back when Eden lifted his head. He gazed at him.

"Your eyes..." Khari breathed, dumbstruck. He looked at Takana, then Alex. "Eden. Your eyes. You're *shining*."

"Holy Gods," Takana gasped, fumbling for a mirror. She shoved it into Eden's hands. "Look!"

Eden frowned at the stunned expressions surrounding him and lifted the small hand mirror. Studying his face, he saw that the silver in his eyes, normally a thin ridge around his pupil, had expanded to make his irises look like mercury. The emerald green that was normally the predominant colour had all but disappeared.

He passed Takana back her mirror. "Yeah—it happens when I get upset. I can control it, mostly. But right now...I want to kill someone. I want to have him in front of me and tear him apart," he spat. "If it takes me a thousand lifetimes, I will bring that man to his knees and laugh as he screams for mercy."

Eden closed his eyes and saw, clearly, a flashing image of Jaizel. He held a hand to his head, seeing a million futures flicker behind his eyes; saw outcomes and possibilities and chances. He saw each pathway, and every turning. Focusing again on a face that should have been deformed and sickening, but was as sweet as an angel's, he inhaled deeply and waited for his future—all possible futures—to stop playing for him. He felt himself slip to the side and heard Khari's worried cry, then his hands scooping him up from the grass to be held over strong thighs.

"What's happening?" Khari asked, panicking. "Is he having a fit? Eden?"

"Leave him...he's psychic, we think," Takana said, laying a cool hand on Eden's head. "Just hold him and wait for it to end."

"His eyes turned silver..."

"The boy has the power to break through shields and defences that have held for thousands of years. He learned to see past glamour and block his mind to suggestion in hours. He opened our world to himself with his blood. He can see things that no mortal man should ever see. His eyes changing colour is fairly dull, all things considered. What else is going in this pot?" Takana continued. "Do you have any mushrooms? I'm partial to mushrooms."

"No, Gray said that most can kill you, so not to touch them," Khari said, smoothing his hand over

Eden's head.

"He'll be all right, my love," Alex said from nearby. "The best thing one can do during these kind of episodes is to wait and let it pass on its own. He isn't hurting."

Eden tried to move, to let everyone know he was all right, but he was frozen in place, unable to move a muscle. He wondered if he was learning what a coma felt like, then managed to twitch a finger. Relieved, he did it again, and curled his toes, getting control back slowly. Khari tightened his hold around him and squeezed gently, bending to press his lips to Eden's forehead.

"Are you all right?" Khari asked, quietly.

Eden moved his head in what was meant as a nod. Khari understood. He straightened Eden's clothes, holding him in place with one arm while he tucked in his shirt and arranged him more comfortably across his lap.

"Just rest a minute, aye? You're all right."

"Thanks."

"You could have warned me that you have...episodes," Khari said. He lifted Eden's head and held an ale tankard to his lips. "Scared me for a moment."

Eden opened his eyes. "Sorry."

"It's all right. I thought you were having some kind of fit, like Gray can have sometimes."

"Gray has fits?" Alex asked, passing a small square of caramel into Eden's hand.

Eden lifted it and bit into the corner. Khari rubbed his chest, looking up at Alex.

"Aye, he does. Not bad ones, but sometimes he comes over funny. He says he sees the world around him as veils and curtains, and everything flickers...he thinks he sees other worlds, sometimes."

"He's a seer," Takana said. "That's what happens to me—it's why I'm a border guard. He can see the pathways between the worlds. I can help him learn what it is he's seeing—until he learns, it will overwhelm him, sometimes."

"Oh," Khari said. "That will be good, if you can help him. I don't like it when he takes bad. It scares me a bit," he admitted, looking away from Takana and Alex.

Alex reached for Khari's hand and squeezed it before letting go. "It's natural and okay to be scared. You don't have to hide it, Khari. Everyone gets scared unless they're fools."

"I can't afford to be weak. Or...I'm not *used* to allowing myself that weakness," Khari amended. "I've come from a place where being weak means death, and I refuse to die. But thank you," he said to Takana, "if you can help Gray, then thank you."

Eden sat up, nodding when Khari looked questioningly at him. "I'm okay." He drank down the remaining ale in the tankard and wiped his mouth. "I'll be okay," he repeated. He turned his head and looked into Khari's eyes, touching his face with his knuckles. He saw again some of the visions from his future. The world around him faded, only Khari remaining in full focus.

"You are amazing, Khari," he said, stealing a gentle kiss. "Not weak. Never weak." He held his hand over Khari's heart. "You hold, in here, more power than you can ever imagine. It's endless. Limitless. You just have to accept it."

"Is this a psychic thing?"

Eden let his hand fall from Khari's chest. "I don't need it to be. Anyone with half an eye can see it in you, they don't need any special abilities. You are a survivor, and you will be able, one day, to stand and watch Jaizel fall and die. He will fall at your feet, Khari, and you will watch him die."

"That's a psychic thing, aye?"

"That was a psychic thing," he confirmed. He stood up. "We better get the camp set up for the night before Gray and Cole get back," he said, unbuckling bedrolls from his saddlebags. "Is there more bread? I'm hungry still. Know what I really want? I want some cheese and tomato on toast, with pepper and some chocolate milkshake. But," he said, taking the soft bread roll Khari passed him, "as that ain't likely to happen, dry bread rolls and ale will do nicely."

Takana shifted her bow to her left hand and stretched against the trunk of a tree, her eyes scanning the woods surrounding her, listening for any sound that could have been out of the ordinary. She tapped a drawn arrow against her thigh restlessly, checked her guns were in place, and looked left at Cole.

Cole had an arrow already nocked to his bowstring, gun-holster unclipped and semi-automatic ready to be grabbed, if needed. His beautiful eyes twinkled across the space separating him from Takana, and he winked at her. No warrior, Cole was still the best marksman she knew. He might not be able to fight well, should their camp be attacked, but he could take out a fly at a hundred yards with one of his arrows. With a gun, he was even more deadly.

Becoming still, she scanned her surroundings once more then looked to her right, at Alex. He was as alert as she was. His chin was high and his eyes narrowed as he searched the trees and climbing vines surrounding their small camp. Still a warrior, even two-hundred years out of the army. Some things were never forgotten, but Takana could tell he would rather have an army guarding the precious teenaged boys sleeping in each other's arms close to the embers of the fire. Takana looked at Gray and felt herself relax.

They would be all right, while Gray was on guard. They might not have hundreds of fully trained Alfheimian soldiers watching the woodlands with them, but they had Gray, and she was sure he might just be better than an entire Alfheimian army. If anyone threatened Khari, Takana did not doubt that they would be cut down in a heartbeat by the regal and composed prince standing opposite her in the inky-blackness of the night.

She pulled a hollowed-out hard roll stuffed with shredded goose from the bag at her feet and bit into it. Catching Cole's quick look, she tossed another over to him, watching him catch it easily with one hand. Takana turned and quirked an eyebrow at Alex.

"I'll eat next," he said, the first words any of them had spoken in close to five hours. Alex rolled his shoulders and lifted his bow, ready to spring into action, should it be needed while Takana ate in her normal fast and business-like manner.

Gray held up his own snack when Takana looked at him, his well-bred features amused as he tore into it with strong teeth. Takana knew she had impressed him. For some reason it made her absurdly pleased to know that she had not been found wanting by the boy. And he *was* a boy, compared to her two-hundred years. No more than a babe in arms still. Until one looked at the life he had lived and known under his father's tyranny. When that was taken into account, Takana wondered who might actually be the eldest of the group. She watched Gray's eyes rest on his brother and saw the barely concealed adoration he felt for Khari. Looking away, she left the young warrior to his silent contemplation of the two sleeping boys.

"He is more than I thought it possible for one child to be," Gray said. He met Takana's eyes when she looked back at him, and tipped his head at the sleepers. "Eden."

Takana nodded.

"You are fortunate indeed to be tasked with his care. To have found him."

"I was not given the task," she said. "And he tumbled into my back garden with as much grace as a baby deer trying to ice skate. I never found him. He found me."

"I think he did. I doubt one could find Eden, unless he chose to be found."

"He does not have a clue who he really is," Alex said. "I think it wise to keep it that way, for now. He is coming to terms with the knowledge that he is not human, and that his magicks and abilities are waking up within him. He does not need to have added weight to bear on his shoulders. Let both of them be the young men they are, at least for now. Let them have their ignorance for as long as possible."

A small frown marred Gray's forehead as he glanced at Eden once more. "He really has no idea?

You do not think that it could be dangerous to have him so ignorant?"

"I think he is slowly putting the pieces together in his mind." Takana shrugged. "He is far from stupid. Young, yes. Naive, yes...but not stupid. I think he has an inkling, and that the suspicion is growing the longer he is in this realm." She ate the last of her roll, standing tall with bow and arrow at the ready once more, her eyes flicking over the trees behind Gray and casting about in the dark to make sure they were still as safe as they were likely to get.

Alex caught the roll she tossed at him and ate swiftly. Drinking down a full mug of weak ale, he stretched tall.

"I think it is rather amazing," Cole said, "to be privileged enough to stand here, knowing that we are at the change of all we have ever known. That this is when everything becomes different, and when the ages switch from one era to the next. And here we are, standing at the hub...at the centre of the universe, nearly. It is humbling," he ended, smiling at Takana. "It's a story to tell the grandchildren, isn't it?"

"Whose grandchildren?" Takana asked, one brow lifted.

Cole eyes settled back on the woods. "Ours."

"I thought children had to come first, before grandchildren," she replied, but her heart skipped a beat, stuttering in her chest. She straightened. "It is not possible," she said,. "You cannot father children on a half-nymph, royal bastard."

Her reply brought an impatient huff from Cole. "I am sure I could have children with the woman I love," he retorted, "if she were agreeable. When all this is over."

Alex grunted, looking around into the darkness. "You'd have my sister responsible for your bastards?" he asked, his voice deceptively soft.

Takana closed her eyes for a moment, wishing that the two men, for once, would manage not to snipe at each other. It was never-ending. Just when she thought they might leave the subject of her relationship with Cole alone, it was brought up and all hell broke loose. Every time. Alex would not, *could not*, accept that she was content to simply have Cole in her life and Cole, in return, could not stand it when Alex seemed to question her honour. She waited for the storm to break as the bickering grew louder.

"You would have her responsible for your bastard children, and likely get bored and leave her alone and shamed, with no job to keep food in their stomachs, Cole? You think her life has not been difficult enough, that you think adding nameless children will help?"

"What the fuck do you take me for, Alex?" Cole hissed. "I do not plan on having bastards running around half starved with no clothes on their backs. I am not your father."

Takana groaned. "Shut up, both of you," she said. "Sorry, Gray—there's a bit of residual bad feeling regarding my birth and childhood, as you may gather."

"Don't worry about it," Gray said. "I hold the monopoly on strange familial situations. Royal bastard?"

"My father had a wandering eye," Alex said, the words clipped. "He left Takana's mother pregnant."

"Royal Prerogative," Takana said, leaning her head back on the tree trunk. "Alex found out about me when the old goat died, and sent Cole for me. It's thanks to Alex that I am a guard, with a small degree of status, and not a wench in a tavern somewhere flashing my tits and sucking cocks for a few coins. There's not many career choices for a half breed girl-child without a father."

Gray shifted his weight and lifted his foot to rest against the tree, his bow held loosely at his side. "You enjoy being a guard?"

"Mostly," she said. "It's fun when you get a random prophesised heir break through the veils to land in your back yard. Mainly it's a bit boring. Lonely. Cole was with me for years, but he had to leave, so it's been lonely the past couple of months. Just me and a few chickens. The company was poor, but they laid eggs, so I forgave them the lack of conversational topics." She smiled at Gray's quiet chuckle. "It was a good post to have—one I was lucky to have."

"You should have lived as the princess you were meant to be."

"Where would the fun be in that?" she asked, glancing at Cole. "Last time I wore a gown, I tripped over the hem and nearly broke my neck."

"Last time you wore a gown, it got badly torn," Cole grinned with a flash of white teeth in the moonlight.

Takana smiled with him. "Oh, yes. Quite," she said. "You found the laces beyond your skills."

"You were sewn into it."

"By definition, a gown is a garment able to be lifted at the hem, my dear. There was no need to tear it from my back in order to get to me."

"Orien give me strength," Alex said, his voice low. "It is only at my sister's demand, Cole, that I have not had you horsewhipped."

"Oh, will you shut up, Alex?" Cole asked, looking at him with narrowed eyes. "Your sister is more than capable of defending her own honour. And her honour does not need defending, as I keep telling you. I wish you'd get that through your thick head, Alex," he added, glaring over the small clearing. "If I had my way, I'd marry her. Orien only knows I have asked enough times."

"Takana?" Alex asked, mouth opening and closing as he looked at her. "Is this true? Cole has asked you to marry him and you have *refused* him?"

"I would not have him married to someone like me," she snapped. "Stop staring at me like that."

Alex frowned and switched his gaze to Cole, who shrugged and leant back once more against his tree, checking his weapons absently before settling into place, comfortable despite the hours he had been on guard.

"Do you want to marry Cole?" Alex asked, looking at Takana again, his hazel eyes soft now.

"What difference would it make?" she asked. "It would disgrace him. It can't happen."

"Bullshit," Cole snarled, angering as he glared at her, the same as he had a thousand times before. He deflated when she set her jaw and glared back at him. "Fine", he said. "Don't marry me, Takana. But you're not getting rid of me, and I will act as though we are married. In my mind we are, anyway. In my mind, we were wed two centuries ago and nothing you say can make me feel differently."

Alex stared between them once more. "You'll be married when we return to the palace," he said, tone brooking no argument. "This is ridiculous, and frankly, Takana, I have never heard such a pathetic reason to deny yourself the person you love. With Gray as witness," he said, "I pronounce you Handfast...by *royal prerogative*...until we reach the palace, where you shall be bound together in marriage, by Orien's Law."

Takana looked at her brother, speechless. She looked at Cole, seeing the same shock written on his face. She glanced again at Alex, at the glint in his eyes and the amusement plain to see on his face. He knew, full well, what he had done. He knew that he had just given her away in wedlock to Cole. And he knew that she could not fight the *order*, even if she really wanted to—and she did not want to. She turned slowly to face Cole, suddenly shy. His eyes shot to rest on Alex several times, as though searching for the joke, before fixing on Takana and staying there. She lifted her chin.

"Fool," she said, when he bowed. She was feeling giddy.

"Your fool," Cole answered, eyes still on her face.

Gray coughed behind his hand. "If you would like to go and...patrol the perimeter," he said tactfully, "I am sure Alexander and I can guard the camp. Go," he said. "Congratulations, both of you."

"Thank you," Takana said, still stunned. She squeezed hard when Cole slid his hand in hers, looking up at him. "You have time to appeal," she said softly.

Cole brushed a thin braid from her face, looping it behind her ear, and bent to kiss her gently on her mouth. "Come on," he said, leading her past Alex and into the trees. "You only get one wedding night."

"It's not the wedding."

He flashed a grin at her, pulling at the laces of his shirt. "It is to me."

XII

"Hold your hand out," Takana said to Gray, "and try to touch the gauze you see."

Gray frowned, waving his hand in front of his face with an expression of intense concentration. Eden looked at Khari and suppressed a giggle.

"He looks mentally deficient," Khari said, starting to laugh. He covered his mouth with his hand, eyes flashing brightly at Eden, filled with humour. "Is she really going to have him open the worlds, or is she just making him look deranged?"

Eden turned his face away from Takana and grinned. "I have no idea," he said, breaking apart his roll and passing half to Khari. "Do you see anything gauzy keeping you in this realm?"

"If I see anything gauzy, then I'm drunk," Khari said. He walked to Ollie and vaulted onto the huge stallion. "Fain!" he called, holding out his hand. He brought her to his face and kissed the falcon gently, placing her on her normal perch next to his ear. "I don't generally see misty veils that are waiting to be pushed aside. I feel positively normal," he added, pulling a stunned expression. "Me, normal? The world will end!"

"Gods help us all," Eden said, swinging his leg over Jinx's back. He walked her over to Khari and Ollie, leaning to cross his arms on Jinx's neck, Gray and Takana forgotten. "How are you doing?"

Khari sat back, propping himself up on his elbows and lifting his leg so he was lounging easily on his horse's back. Ollie looked at Khari and whuffled gently. Eden swore the animal smiled.

"I'm all right, aye," Khari said after a moment's silent thought. "It's strange to be away from home, and I'm still a bit...nervous, I suppose, but I'm all right. It's been a nice journey." Khari looked around at the forest they had left, at the flatlands in front of him, and at the distant mountain that held the pass to what would soon become his home. He gestured to it, glancing at Eden. "I will relax when I get there," he said. "I'm still worried that we're going to have to fight an army of thousands and I'll be dragged back to Jaizel's citadel."

"Will the soldiers come this far?" Eden asked. "We're practically out of Chiearatul, aren't we?"

Khari's eyebrow lifted. "How the bloody hell would I know, eh?" he asked. "I was locked in a single suite for ten years, spent three in a cell, and then lived underground since. I'm not uneducated, but my geography needs some work." He looked at the mountain again and bit his lower lip between his teeth pensively. "I've never been to a town, or a city. Not even a hamlet. I've hardly seen *people*, except the few who might have been scavenging in the woods and spotted me. Then I would, you know, say hello and pass the time of day. But they'd give me really strange looks and leave pretty fast...but then, that could be because there's normally a few dead soldiers around when you start getting within ten miles of our home, right?"

"Hanging corpses are likely a good deterrent," Eden agreed, remembering the rotting hanged men scattered through the woods. They sent a clear enough message, that was for sure. He reached out a hand and squeezed Khari's thigh gently. "It must have been lonely, sometimes?" he asked, rubbing the thick rumpled grey fabric of Khari's trousers.

"Sometimes," Khari said. "Then, I would lie down and pray to sleep...and be with you. And the loneliness would vanish with the dreams. Kept me sane. But I had Gray," Khari continued. "We had to cling together more than most brothers might need to. We were the only hope of survival for each other. I couldn't have lived without him, and there have been more than a few times since we escaped that he would have died without me being there to save him. And we had books, too. The escapism helped immensely."

"I hear that," Eden agreed. He looked over at Alex, hearing him saddling his horse and kicking out the fire. Cole was close, crouched down to spread salt over layers of glistening rabbit flesh. Eden hoped he wouldn't be asked to eat *that* any time soon. Cole might be able to survive indefinitely, but his body's survival had come at the cost of his taste buds lives. "Tell me you don't eat preserved salted rabbit, Khari?"

"It's not been on the menu, so far," Khari said, watching Cole with a frown. "Before I get that desperate, there's leaves and pickled berries...and my own arm."

Eden giggled, discussing the merits of arms, mud and leaves over the taste of salted rabbit while Khari relaxed, coming out of his shell. He stated anything was better than rabbit, full stop and salting wouldn't help, shuddering as he took a reflexive bite of his roll, as though taking away the imagined taste of salted rabbit. Khari quietened, but the smile remained on his normally impassive face. Eden decided he would move the heavens, if it would make it stay.

"Takana might whip his cooking into shape," he said.

"I have the idea that Takana could whip anyone into shape," Khari said, sitting up straight and drinking from the flask that held painkilling potion.

Eden frowned, reaching into his saddlebag to find the small precious clay pot of numbing lotion Cole had made for Khari's back and hips. He held it in his hands, looked at Khari, then jerked his head back at the trees, walking away from the horses. Without the lotion, however well he might hide it, Khari was in agony.

Khari glanced around, sliding off Ollie's back to land silently on the mossy ground. He moved Fain to Ollie's neck with a tender pat of her head and grabbed his bag. He walked after Eden to the trees, lifting his shirt over his head as he vanished from sight.

Eden waited until Khari was stripped down to his trousers. Scooping a generous amount of the lotion from the pot, he felt his fingers go numb. It was strange to be so completely anaesthetised without the use of what he still thought of as *modern* medicine. He spread the lotion across Khari's shoulders, circling gently over his back to his waist.

Khari turned his head, looking at Eden from the corner of his eye. "This stuff is amazing," he said, "but I'm not sure if I wouldn't prefer to actually feel you touching me."

Eden looked up from his fingers, meeting Khari's eyes. "It'd hurt you," he murmured, looking back at the horrific scarred muscles, so visible under the fragile skin.

"That's not the point I was trying to make," Khari said. He drew his knees into his chest, and curled forward so Eden could massage around his sides and down to the waistband of his trousers. "I just meant I would prefer to be able to feel you touching me. Not...not like this."

"Maybe, when we're not under armed guard and being watched every moment of every day, there'll be a chance to be *able* to touch you without needing an excuse." He patted Khari's shoulder, then remembered he couldn't feel it and leaned forward into his line of sight. "Get dressed, before you get cold. That should last you until we stop."

"Will we make it to the pass today?" Khari asked. He opened his bag and pulled out a clean shirt. Worn and frayed like all of his clothes, this shirt was a soft flannel, once black, now faded to grey from constant wearing and washing. Khari pulled it over his head, followed by his jumper. Happy, once he had arranged the folds of fabric comfortably around his hips, he belted on his sword and swung his cloak around his shoulders. "That pass marks the border, doesn't it?"

"I think so."

"Alfheim is at the other side?"

"The Wastelands," Eden said, handing Khari his bag. "No Man's Land."

"Safe?"

Eden considered it. His mind scuttled away from the thought of the Wastelands, even though their journey through them had been uneventful. The darkness of the woods, with the skeletal branches of long dead trees and the howls of night-creatures had left him terrified. He folded his arms, unconsciously trying to comfort himself.

"Not really," Eden said, "Takana led us here via the ancient Nymph pathways. Even Alex wouldn't try and come here, into Chiearatul, without her leading him. There's bad things in the woods. I think it's filled with all the folk that are banished from both realms. Gangs. Evil spirits? I'm not totally sure, but if it scares Alex, then that's a good enough reason why it scared the living crap outta me."

Khari looked at the distant mountain, his eyes narrowing. "Did you have to fight, on your way here?"

"No—the Nymph paths are safer. Takana knows the way through...I think her mother might have taught her, when she was young. It's not without danger, from what I picked up from their conversations," he murmured, "but it's safer than attempting to go through the forest, and it's the only pass between the lands. Then you hit the Borderlands, and that's where I came through. It's safer, there. For the Fae," he added, "mostly, if a human is found wandering, then they get taken back to their own realm. Or tossed in the river, depending on the guard who finds them."

"Humans aren't exactly popular," Khari said. He jumped onto Ollie and settled his bird on his shoulder.

Eden shrugged lightly, swinging into his saddle.

"It doesn't bother you?"

"I know that the Fae lived in the Human Realm before humans came along," he said. "I know that it used to be wild and unspoiled. To the Fae, they see it as humans have raped their world in order to survive, and they sure as hell ain't gonna let the same happen here, in their new home. Better to protect it, than risk it happening twice because they don't want to harm a human. Sure," he added, "I would rather those who got through weren't killed, but to a lot of the Fae, they're so much vermin. Like rats. A sub-species, without powers or any real knowledge, as far as the Fae can tell. I would prefer it if they weren't killed, though."

"I like humans," Khari murmured.

"You only know one."

"I don't know any, but I like the pretend one I've met."

"Are you ready to set off?" Alex asked, crossing the clearing to stand at Eden's side. "If we leave now, we might make it to the mouth of the pass by nightfall."

"We'll camp there?" Khari asked.

"No. We need to get to the old pathways before we can set camp. Such as it is."

"Such as it is?"

Alex nodded at Khari. "It'll be a cold night, tonight. We won't have a fire. Our best chance of making it through the Wastelands is to move unseen."

"I hope it don't rain again," Eden said. "It was miserable on the way here. Cold, raining, a wind that threatened to strip my flesh from my bones." He shivered in recollection and looked at Khari. "It's horrible, in the Wastelands. It took me days to warm up after leaving those woods."

"There's no other way?" Khari asked, looking at Alex. "I thought Tarenthal was a bit scary for travellers, but the Wastelands sound a lot worse. We can't go another way?"

"If there was another way, I'd take it," Alex said. He turned away, whistling for his horse. "It's not a path anyone would take by choice."

Khari slid from his horse silently, staring around with wide eyes as Takana signalled for them to wait. Eden led Jinx to stand next to Ollie, reaching for Khari's hand between the folds of their cloaks. He glanced up as they walked softly over the mouldering damp ground, the decaying leaves beneath their boots making no sound at all. All noise seemed muffled, and Eden remembered his first trip through the Wastelands with a clarity that had been shrouded by the safety of distance. He let go of Khari's hand and drew the folds of his cloak tighter around his shoulders, lifting his hood over his head as though the thick wool could somehow make him invisible.

Glancing at him, Khari drew his sword, holding it in his left hand as though the three feet of heavy steel weighed nothing at all. He looked into the trees as a high-pitched screech sounded through the skeletal branches, piercing the silence.

"Banshees," Gray murmured, fitting an arrow to his bowstring. "I hate fucking banshees."

Khari looked at his brother for a second, then lifted his chin, walking ahead as he drew his second sword. He looked at Takana. "How far to the pathways of the nymphs?"

"A few hours due west," she replied, scanning the trees.

"I imagine that it will take less time if we walk at a decent pace. I don't like this place." He walked ahead of the crowd, not looking back. "The sooner we can get out of it, the better, aye, Gray?"

238

"Aye," Gray said, glancing around, ready to fire if anything moved.

Eden hurried after Khari, torn between being afraid of the dark decayed forest and terror of Khari falling afoul of something hideous lurking in the tangled tendrils of rotting undergrowth. He shrugged his bow over his head, nocking an arrow to the string as he half jogged along in Khari's wake, Jinx walking next to him as though scared to be left alone in the dark.

Another screech ripped through the air, closer than the one before. He span around in a circle, eyes darting over the black trunks of the trees that surrounded him on all sides, oppressively closing in on him and imprisoning him; waiting to reach for him with their deadened branches, stretching out their rotten fingers to tear his soul from his chest and...

Khari stopped dead and held his hand up in the air, calling out in a language Eden had never heard. He looked at Eden, then slammed his hand to the forest floor.

Lightning shot out from Khari's hand. It sped along the ground; a bright shining trail of white energy, which lit the black forest for over quarter of a mile. It whirled around on itself and ran up the dead shells of the tree trunks, crackling and rustling as it illuminated the branches, banishing the night with its pure light.

Khari met Eden's eyes. "I hate the dark," he said, standing up. He picked up his dropped sword and twirled it next to his hip like a baton, walking onwards once more through the brightly lit forest, now shining with white twinkling electricity.

Eden looked behind them as they moved with

more confidence through the trees, watching the powerful lights fade as they passed. Ahead, the trees were sparking into life, lighting their path in readiness for Khari to pass though. He looked at Takana and raised a brow.

She shook her head, stunned. "I have never seen anything like it."

"Fuck me sideways with a barge pole," Cole said, staring around the forest. He was turning slowly in circles as he walked, looking at the lighted trees and glowing branches in disbelief. "I have never even heard of anything like this. Let alone seen it."

"Prodigious," Alex said, looking at Khari's back. "What did you do, Khari?"

"Hopefully scared off any banshees and ghasts," Khari said. "They don't like the light, do they?"

"No...but how did you do this?"

"Called the lightning," Khari said. He laughed, the sound heating Eden's blood. "Pulled the energy from the air, and the power from the ground. Made lights."

Takana nudged Eden. He looked at her and remembered to close his mouth, blushing at the look on her face. Her eyes were amused and he knew that she had guessed his thoughts as he gazed at Khari's back, drinking in each nuance of movement as the powerful young prince walked—strolled, damn him— through the beastly forest. His entire stance dared any of the evil creatures dwelling in the woods to try and take him on. Shouted that he would be the one walking away, not them.

"We generally try not to announce ourselves, in this part of the world, Khari," Cole said.

Khari looked around, confused. "They knew we were here before we even stepped foot on the path," he said. "Why hide from them, right? It was pointless to try. This way, we can see where we're heading, and they can see that we're not scared little boys that are going to piss ourselves with fear walking through a fucking forest, aye? They can't come into the light—we're safe, aren't we, Gray?"

"I should think so," Gray replied.

"From ghouls, banshees and ghasts," Cole said. "But we're lit up like a frigging beacon for gangs, renegades and murderers."

Khari twirled both his swords again with a shake of his head. "I'm not worried about the living. They won't stay that way for long if they try and take me on. Ghouls and ghasts scare me more, and I'd rather make sure I'm safe from them." He stopped walking and lifted his face to the trees above as the rain started. He cursed under his breath, walking on with renewed energy, tugging his hood over his head.

"Can't stop the rain?" Takana asked, teasing gently.

"He can," Gray said. "I think he's trying not to show off, to show willing, so to speak," he said, jerking his head at Cole.

"He can stop the rain?" Cole asked, his mouth dropping open.

"I can hear you!" Khari sang. "Did I forget to mention I'm an Elemental?" He held both hands up above his head, the blades of his swords glinting in the light from the trees. Turning, he grinned at Cole, looking at his new family, then at Eden, before looking up along the steel of his swords, through the branches and to the sky. He said something under his breath, then lowered his arms. A wind blew through the forest, howling and whistling as it raced through the trees and whipped through their clothes. It circled, a brief twister of noise and motion around where they stood, then lifted into the air. It spread out as Eden watched, dispersing the clouds to show brilliant stars and a bright shining moon, which lit the bright forest in a radiant pinkish sheen of magical light.

Takana reached out her hand, pushing Eden's mouth closed without a word, and stalked away through the trees, dragging Cole by the hand after her. She passed Khari and rolled her eyes. "That was controlling the wind, kid. Not stopping the rain."

Gray grinned at his brother as he followed Takana. "Good job," he said, patting Khari's arm. "Enough now, though. You don't want to drain yourself."

"He just...the *wind*..." Cole cried. "He controlled it!"

"Yes, he did. Now let's try and get to the pathway before he faints from exertion, or something," Takana replied. "Get him to his father, so I can see Airell's face when he realises what he managed to create."

Eden watched as the elves moved off through the trees. He slowly moved his eyes to rest on Khari. He could feel his blood heating his veins, flowing around his body and rushing to gather in a hot pool of desire and lust deep in his gut. The mighty display of elemental magic added to Khari's allure. He wanted him badly enough to feel it as a physical ache. His pulse thudded in his ears, racing as he tried to control the physical effects Khari caused.

Khari watched his face, studying him. The corner of his mouth twitched. Switching both swords to his left hand, he held out his right hand to Eden, beckoning him closer.

Walking in a dream to slip his hand in Khari's, Eden shivered as heated flesh stroked across his palm, a thumb tracing his lifeline for a brief moment. Burning him. Marking him. He closed his eyes for half a second and drew in a breath, fighting against the need Khari had awoken within him.

Khari lifted his hand to his face, kissing his knuckles. He smiled over their linked fingers, then turned, walking after the others, his hold on Eden's hand firm and sure.

"I want you so much, right now," Eden breathed, trying to get a grip on himself, and mostly succeeding. Although he could still feel the pulses of magicks and the thumping of his own blood, racing around his body in a whirlwind of lustful joyfulness that he should be so close to this brilliant man. That he should be wanted by such a man as Khari.

"It's entirely mutual," Khari said, tugging him along until they had caught up with the others. Eden watched as he silently checked to make sure everything was as it should be, all horses present and correct, and Fain still settled on Ollie. "I'm relying on the company to keep me in check," Khari added, whispering low enough that Eden barely heard him. "There's something about you that makes me want to set the world on fire, just so it will burn with me. You make me want to show off, just so I can see your face when I use my powers."

Khari's thumb slid over Eden's palm again, setting off an incendiary response Eden was powerless to control. All his attention snapped to focus on Khari. His world shifted. Khari was at the centre.

"I have a g-spot on my palm," Eden said, breathless.

"So far, I'm yet to find a spot that doesn't turn you on."

"You turn me on," Eden said, speaking the words into Khari's ear. His lip brushed Khari's lobe. He was pleased to see that he wasn't the only one teetering on the edge after several days of secret touching and stolen kisses. Khari inhaled sharply. His hand tightened involuntarily around Eden's. Eden turned away to look ahead, a grin fighting to break free across his face.

"You tease," Khari hissed.

He let his grin have full rein. "Guess two can play at your game, huh?"

"So help me, Eden...when I get you alone..."

"Promises, promises," Eden sang under his breath. "Any chance you can get me alone in a magically lit forest, under stars shining in a magically cleared sky?"

"Don't think so."

"Well, guess I can't have everything."

"This way," Takana said, pointing left. "Not much further. Travelling with you, Khari, certainly speeds things up."

XIII

Guiding his knife through the flesh of a potato, Khari watched the flames of the fire flicker and dance in front of his eyes. He tossed the potato into his pot, then jumped. Startled by Eden touching his arm.

"Sorry. I was thinking."

Eden stroked down Khari's arm before folding his hands in his lap. He watched the fire. "I can imagine you have a lot to think about."

"What if he hates me, Eden?" Khari asked. He didn't look away from the flames, but lifted one shoulder a fraction. "It's all well and good saying that he loved my mother, but I am not her. I'm me, right? Just me...and I'm likely nothing like he'll be expecting. What if he hates me?"

Eden couldn't imagine anyone hating the brilliant elf at his side. Could not picture how anyone could do anything less than adore him; Khari was born to be adored, as far as he was concerned.

"He won't hate you."

"Aye, he might."

"Why would he?"

Khari hesitated. He straightened out the long blonde spikes of his hair, and held his hand to his mouth, nibbling on his thumbnail. "Jaizel," he said. "What he did to me. I doubt a mighty king like Airell would want an ex-whore as his son."

"I never want to hear you call yourself that again," Eden said, as calmly as he could. He clenched his mouth tight, breathed in deeply through his nose, and exhaled slowly. "You were never a whore. You were a fucking *child*, Khari. And that bastard needs to die for what he did to you. It was not your fault, and you were not a whore. Whores choose—you never did. Okay?"

Khari looked sideways at his face. "Aye. Okay. Breathe, before you pop."

"It makes me so fucking *angry*," he growled, closing his eyes as his rage built.

"Because I was a child?"

"Because a lot of things," Eden said, throwing leaves into the fire, just to watch them burn. He blinked, shocked to feel a lump rising in his throat and a stinging behind his eyes. "For all he did, and all you lost."

"Eden..."

He shook his head, swiping his wrist across his eyes. He wondered if he could blame the smoke from the fire, but decided against it, knowing that Khari would see straight through his ruse. He sniffed. "They're angry tears," he said. "I get so mad, sometimes, that it leaks out as tears."

Khari rubbed his back. "Me too. But I generally get thunderstorms, lightning and the odd earthquake thrown in for good measure, when I get really upset."

"Really?" Eden asked.

Khari cubed another potato, talking quietly about the downsides of having immense power. His musical voice, so slightly accented, did the trick, bringing Eden back from the brink of livid red-misted anger. Khari spoke about past earthquakes and tidal waves of earth, tearing through the forests, scaring innocent imps and making fluttering fairies take flight from the trees. He described the night he collapsed his bedroom and had to work fast to prevent himself being smothered by the soft earth. The joys of making water spring, bubbling, from the ground, knowing he would be nourished.

"Don't feel pity for me," Khari said, leaning to peer into the cooking pot. "It hasn't all been terrible, since we ran. It's peaceful. Quiet. We had each other, aye? It wasn't all bad. Not before Mum was killed, either. There were bright beams that flooded through the clouds. It's not all about Jaizel, babe."

"Babe?" Eden asked, finding a small smile was touching his lips. Not much of one, but it was there.

Khari flushed, his ivory skin turning the lightest pink. "It's an endearment. My mum used to call me and Gray it. Babe. Baby." He looked at Eden. "You don't have the word in the Human Realm?"

"We do," Eden said. He took Khari's hand and squeezed it briefly. "It means exactly the same where I come from. Just, I ain't never had anyone say it to me before, like that. It's nice."

"Good then," Khari said, briefly touching Eden's hand. He looked at the food and poked something in the pot. "It's not all about Jaizel, anyway. He's not the sum total of my life."

"Still. I'll die before I see him get his filthy fucking hands on you again, Khari. Whatever it takes, I will never let him touch you again."

Khari patted Eden's back. "It's enough to know you care so much."

"I think Airell will love you," Eden said, hugging his knees. He wrapped his cloak around himself and shuffled closer to the fire. It was a cold night, if a clear one—the clouds, it seemed, had not dared to come back after Khari had cleared them. Even though they were now in Alfheim and safe, the sky seemed scared to get cloudy and upset Khari. Eden wondered if they would come back at all, or if they had been permanently banished from the world. "He'd be stupid not to love you. And he's not a stupid man, from what I saw of him."

"We'll see," Khari said quietly. Throwing the last potato into the pot, he fitted the lid and pushed it to the edge of the fire. "I'll be happy just to have something other than stew. Never mind about people liking me, or anything like that—just give me something that isn't bloody stew to eat. It gets tiresome a lot faster than I thought it would."

"You should have been with us on the way into Chiearatul," Eden remarked, flicking a glance around to make sure Cole wasn't within earshot. "I don't have an issue eating your stews. Not after a few weeks of being fed by Cole."

"He's no cook, is he?"

"Hell no."

"But he did keep you alive, and strong enough to make the journey...so it can't be all bad."

"It was all bad. I never got ill, in case he thought he'd feed me a healing potion. Can you imagine what his *medicine* would taste like?"

Khari chuckled. "Can't taste worse than his regular menu." He shifted in place, wrapping himself up in the thick wool of his cloak to pull his hood over his head. He sat still for a moment, then shrugged out of the cloak, sat as close as he could to Eden to swirl the wool around both of them before working his way under the folds of Eden's cloak so they both had double layers.

Eden held his arm up, waiting while Khari nestled next to him, holding him close once he stilled.

"It's been nice, the journey," Khari said, leaning so his head rested on Eden's shoulder. "Getting to know you a bit. And the others. Being away from home. It's been nice to see a bit of the world I've only read about. I thought there would be more towns. Villages, maybe? It's felt as though we're the only people alive, sometimes."

"There weren't many folks around on the way here. I think Takana was trying to avoid too many people, because of me. In case something happened to me, or we were attacked. Alex's house was at the edge of a pretty big town, but we left in the middle of the night and I never got to see a lot. But there are people, and houses. It's not an empty world."

"What's it like where you came from?"

Eden shrugged. "Noisy. Crowded. Busy. Hundreds of thousands of people, all in a rush to be anywhere but where they are. Cars and trains, planes and bikes. Noise, all the time, to the point where silence seems loud. The Urban Jungle," he said. "Tall towers, filled with people and families. Small flats in huge buildings, stretching up into the sky because there's no room to grow outwards, without losing the last few bits of green that's left. But mainly, it's lonely."

"Lonely?"

"Yeah. Everyone is so busy living in their own world, that they no longer care about having a wider one. Everyone is alone, all together. Still want to see it?"

"Can't wait. Do you miss it?"

He admitted he did miss some parts. His dad— more than he had thought he would. He shrugged, explaining the streets and shops, towns and transport.

The convenience of the world he had known, held next to the peace of the one he had found, even if it was dangerous and the future uncertain. His life seemed to have opened up the moment he met Khari and he said so, moaning at the firm kiss the admission earned him. There was so much he knew he would never be able to explain and so much he would miss from the Human Realm, but he was happier than he had ever been. Simply being next to Khari meant he was home, whatever world he happened to be in.

"Airell speaks English, doesn't he?" Khari asked a while later, looking horrified as thoughts played through his mind. He gazed at Eden. "Please tell me the man speaks English, aye? Because I've all but forgotten what Chiearian I knew—if Alfheimian is anything like Chiearian—and I never got the knack of spoken Elvish. Mum spoke to me and Gray in English, because Jaizel wasn't fluent enough to fully understand it. She deliberately cultured accents too, to make it harder for Jaizel to comprehend. Then when we left...well. We've never spoke anything *but* English."

"He spoke English to me," Eden said. "Same as Takana, Alex and Cole. There's other languages?"

Khari nodded. "Chiearian, Alfheimian, basic Elvish. More, as you get to the Outer Reaches. I don't know what their languages are, but there's several dozen all told, I think. I can read dozens, but I only speak English. Never heard the others, so I wouldn't like to attempt them and embarrass myself totally."

"I understand that," Eden said. Lost in the flames of the fire and warm at last, holding Khari next to him.

"You'll stay with me, when we get to wherever it is we're going? The palace, or whatever?"

"I'll stay with you, yeah. Don't panic. He'll love

you." Eden felt Khari's uncertainty and pulled him a bit closer. "He will love you."

It was two days later when Eden had the pleasure of seeing Khari's face light up when Chainia, the capital of Alfheim, and the seat of power, came into view. He was torn between watching Khari and Gray, or giving his full attention to the first Elven City he had ever seen in his life. His own amazement made the decision for him; he was unable to look away from the crystalline spires and beautifully carved alabaster palace that had been built into the side of the mountain, the roads leading to it marked out by hundreds of smaller cottages and sturdy townhouses.

The horses walked sedately along the cobbled street. Even Ollie seemed to understand that for once he was not going to be able to race like a Hell-Horse along the central thoroughfare. Or he had picked up on his master's nervousness. Both Khari and Gray were silent, shrouded under their thick hoods and invisible to any curious passerby. Only those on horseback would have been able to see under the thick swathes of woven wool.

Eden wore his scarf lifted over his head, like a snood, but had decided against the hood—it would have blocked his view and hidden the sights from his eyes even as it would have hidden his face from gawkers. And he *longed* to see the sights. A lifetime of dreaming about other realms had left him with an insatiable desire to drink in as much as he could from

251

the world he had broken through to.

His fingers itching for his beloved digital camera, Eden turned and grinned broadly at Takana.

"Impressed, wonder-boy?"

"Oh, hell yes," he said. He looked at the palace ahead. "It's...beautiful." He said and shook his head hopelessly. "There's no words."

"I think I might vomit up my lunch," Khari said. "I've never seen anything like this."

Gray pulled his hood down. He lifted his hands to rearrange his complicated braid as he looked at the magnificent palace. A few heads turned as passerby stared at him, but Gray resolutely kept his eyes on the palace, ignoring the hushed whispers and pointing fingers.

"Is it so obvious to people that Gray is a Dark Elf?" Eden asked Takana.

"He looks like his parents."

"Oh. Like Jaizel, you mean?"

"Yes. Very much so, from the paintings and portraits I have seen of Jaizel. There is no denying his parentage—people will stare. And wonder."

Gray coughed into his hand, eyes speculative. "And lock their doors and make sure that their children are never allowed out of their sight."

"It's likely," Alex said, "until they realise you are not an enemy."

"Right now, they probably think you are being escorted to the king for execution, after being captured," Cole said. "I think I will leave them to their assumptions. It will be the only time anyone will ever think I have managed to capture you, my prince."

Khari turned his hood in Eden's direction. "This place is fantastic," he said, muffled by the hood. He looked around again. Even without seeing his face, Eden could sense his awe. "I feel out of my depth," Khari said. "I do not know what it was I was expecting, but this...this wasn't it."

Alex walked his horse ahead as they reached a pair of looming, intricately spun, silvery gates. There were guards—or Eden assumed they were guards— either side of a narrowing pathway. They bowed in deference to Alex as he passed, then looked at Gray with widening eyes. One looked as though he might speak out; call Alex or possibly sound an alarm, but then stilled and stood stiffly to attention although his eyes remained fixed on Gray's face.

Gray stayed rigid on his horse, his eyes unreadable as he passed the guards. Eden watched him, looking for any sign of nerves, but the regal prince could have been watching a play, or listening to an order for his own execution. He gave nothing away at all.

Several minutes passed in silence before they approached another pair of guards. This time the two men blocked Alex's path and studied him.

"Your Highness," one said. "All is well?"

"Perfectly well, I thank you," Alex replied. He slid from his saddle and stretched. "Will you call someone to see to our horses? It has been a long journey."

The guard looked pointedly at Gray. "All is well?" he asked Alex once more.

"Dismount, my prince," Alex said to Gray, waving his hand in invitation. He rolled his eyes when the guard's hand clenched around his dagger and shook his head. "Be still. Prince Gray is here as a guest of His Majesty," he said, voice dropping. "As is his brother, Prince Za'akhar. King Airell's *sons*. You would explain to your king that you kept his sons waiting at the gates?"

The guard gasped and stepped backwards. His eyes darted to Khari's shrouded figure when he jumped down from Ollie's back. Eden watched carefully, swinging his leg over Jinx's back to stand next to Khari. He glanced at Takana, who nodded encouragement before she dismounted. He relaxed, but not by much. By the reactions of the guards, and those nearby, edging closer to them, their appearance in the city was a tremendous occasion and one everyone wanted to be a part of. Townsfolk jostled and pushed their way closer, just to catch a glimpse of the three men who were as alien to their eyes as a Martian would have been to Eden's. Two princes from the Dark Lands, and one guy from the human realm. He was all too aware that he was getting his own fair share of the astounded stares and hushed whispers. Heaving in a silent breath, he pushed his scarf from his head and glanced between the gathering crowd and Takana, needed to be reassured.

The second guard gazed at him in silence for several long seconds. He bowed from the waist, and rose to look at Alex. "I will call for the grooms, your highness," he said, his voice cracking as he spoke. He looked at Khari, at Gray, then once more at Eden. "Welcome to Chainia. It is...an honour."

Khari tugged down his hood and scarf, not looking at the guard as he walked Ollie past. The whispers increased in volume and intensity as he showed his face. He walked with a show of nonchalance and strolled into a spacious marble paved square. He stopped dead and looked around, his golden eyes shining with unconcealed amazement as he took in the beautiful carved columns arching high above his head, supporting walkways and delicate bridges, which led into secret recesses of the magnificent palace. Birds of paradise, brightly plumed, darted from the boughs of purplish willows, skimming plump stomachs over a pond of brilliantly clear water. Creamy carved walls arced upwards either side of where Khari stood. The mountain they were carved from was ancient and impenetrable, yet so beautifully transformed into this elegant court that it appeared as fragile as the thinnest spun glass.

Eden turned slowly, trying to take in everything from the small tinkling fountain near a far wall, to the spiralling pathway high above his head, joining an open doorway to an open-sided platform that seemed to float in the sky, inviting lovers and dancers to glide across its floor under a moonlit sky. Tall trees, wider than any he had seen, grew from the marble, reaching into the endless sky and providing shade for the higher levels of the amazing palace.

"Welcome home," Alex said, standing between Gray and Khari. "And welcome to you, Eden."

Eden held his hand out as a brilliant blue long-beaked bird hovered close to where he stood. He grinned as it lighted on the side of his finger and tilted its head, staring at him for a moment before it took flight again, singing as it spiralled upwards and into one of the thousands of windows glinting brightly in the side of the carved mountain.

Khari stroked his finger down Fain's plumage, lifting her to hold and show her the beautiful courtyard. The bird looked around, dignified in her silence, but Khari placed her onto the edge of a nearby fountain. He folded his arms and watched his falcon, smiling when she hopped from the fountain to the branch of one of the old trees.

"This is...I have no words," Gray said. "I think I was expecting a castle. Fortifications? Stone," he muttered, stroking his fingertips over one pale wall. "Grey stones and dark dungeons. This place is...it's..."

"A fairytale palace," Eden said. He pinched the soft skin of his forearm between thumb and forefinger to make sure he wasn't dreaming. Walking in a daze to one of the tall arching doorways, he held his hand to the crystalline mountain and felt the magical pulses resonating deep within the stone; the heartbeat of the earth thumping all around him. He let out a deep breath he had not been aware he was holding, dropped his hand.

"Are you all right, Eden?" Alex asked.

"I feel as though I walked through to Narnia. Certainly don't feel like I could possibly still be back home. Not now. This is just impossibly beautiful. All of it. How old is it? How was it made? Who made it? It's actually lived in?"

Takana took his arm to lead him through the garden and up a spiral staircase. She walked him across one of the lower bridges, pointing out flowers and glistening leafy plants, her voice a low song as she spoke words Eden's ears could not take in. It was all too much. His brain could not listen while his eyes were so entranced with the vibrancy of the world all around him. For the first time since laying eyes on Khari, his mind was occupied elsewhere. There was nothing that could detract from the joy and wonder he felt. The sense that he had returned home.

Eden walked through a narrow doorway, ahead of Takana. The company all but forgotten, he followed a winding path, sparkling lightly with the glint of fragmented crystals. Letting his feet lead him, he was only vaguely aware of Khari close at his back. He held his hand out behind him, closing his fingers when Khari's hand slid into his own.

"Eden?" Alex asked, somewhere behind him.

Eden shook his head silently. The feeling of homecoming was growing. He knew these paths, and he knew the heart of the mountain.

Takana jogged after him, calling him back, "You can explore later, Eden. You should rest, before Airell calls to see you."

"Down here," Eden said, tugging Khari after him down a narrow staircase.

"The old temple is down there," Alex said, calling after him. "You can see it later."

"Can you feel this?" Eden asked Khari, skimming his free hand over the crystalline wall as he descended. "It's *calling* me."

"I find, as a rule, that if you're hearing rock calling you, you should lie down in a dark room for a while, aye?" Khari replied. "Normally means you got hit too hard."

"I guess so," he said, looking down the stairs into the pitch darkness below. He stopped, hesitating between going further down into the bowels of the palace or returning to the beautiful glistening hallways that would lead to the king of this magnificent land. He looked briefly at Khari before turning to climb back the way he had come. There would be time enough to explore later.

"I'll take you on a tour, Eden," Alex promised as he turned the corner back into the lit hall where the others waited. "For now, we should all get cleaned up, changed, and ready to see Airell." Alex looked at Khari and Gray. "He will be ecstatic to meet you both. Let me show you to your rooms."

"Rooms?" Khari asked, tightening his hold on Eden's hand. It was the only sign that Khari was scared. Eden admired Khari's aplomb, hoping he was putting on as good a show.

"I would feel better if I stayed with Khari," Eden said, looking at the faces around him. "This is all pretty weird anyhow, you know? I don't think I want to be left on my own." He squeezed back when Khari gripped his hand in silent thanks.

"All right," Alex said, a knowing look on his face. "I can't see it being an issue, if you want to stay together. But Airell will want to meet Khari alone, Eden." He waved a hand at a brightly lit corridor. "This way. You can both get the travel stains washed off and change into clothes that are less likely to walk themselves to a washtub."

Alex turned another corner, leading them deep into the mountain. He signalled to a passing girl, bending to murmur something in her ear. She bobbed and hurried away. Alex pushed open a tall oaken door recessed into the wall of the hallway, revealing a room that had been carved out of the mountain.

"Welcome home, Khari," Alex said, sweeping a courtly bow. He stood and turned to face Gray. "This way. Khari is the safest he has ever been in his life. You can wash and rest in peace."

Gray hovered for a moment. "Call me if you need me," he said to Khari. Making the decision that his baby brother was going to be all right, he walked away without looking back.

Pushing Khari gently through the doorway, Eden

gazed around at the rich tapestries and shimmering silks decorating the creamy crystalline walls, and pushed the door closed with his foot, wanting nothing more than to finally strip his travel stained clothes from his aching muscles and wash. The main room was not huge, but it was large enough to comfortably hold a white-wood dining table with four settings, an ornately carved matching sideboard, some shelves and a drinks cabinet. An arched doorway showed a second room with a king-sized draped four-poster bed, a tall chest of drawers, and a pedestal holding a basin and a steaming ewer. That their arrival had been noted, Eden was in no doubt at all, realising that hot water had been brought to the room, and their new accommodations prepared in the time it had taken to reach the room. However, Eden's eyes barely registered anything else, once he had spied the basin and the large ceramic ewer.

"A basin," Khari noticed, pulling his thick cloak off and yanking his grimy tunic over his head as he crossed the floor. He reached the basin and poured from the ewer.

"Fight you for the sponge?" Eden challenged. He unclasped the brooch holding his cloak fastened at his neck, draping the heavy woollen garment over the back of one of the chairs. It was chilly, but tolerable, especially after spending so long exposed to the frozen weather outside. Still, he walked to the open unglazed windows and pulled the shutters closed, flicking the latch to make sure they stayed that way. Satisfied they weren't about to open, he drew the heavy velvet curtains across the casements, locking them both away from the outside world. "I feel like I've been transported back in time," he admitted. "I keep hallucinating steaming showers and shampoos."

"I'd like to see one of these showers you keep talking about," Khari said, bending his head to look down so he could rub at his neck with the sponge. "This is luxury enough to me. The basin," he added, tapping it with his fingertips. "Bit of a step up from a wooden bucket, anyway. Or a freezing stream." He swished the sponge and lathered it with more scented soap before scrubbing at his chest with his eyes closed in silent bliss at being able to clean himself.

Eden left Khari to wash, walking back into the anteroom to open the drinks cabinet. Holding a decanter to the light of a lamp set into the wall, he looked at the amber liquor and sniffed at the neck. Whiskey—and better than the rotgut he had almost got used to over the weeks on horseback. He unbuckled his sword-belt and unarmed himself, piling his knives, daggers, arrows and bow on the seat of one of the dining chairs. He poured two healthy measures of the whiskey into crystal glasses and walked back into the bedroom. His eyes snapped to Khari's torso and his heart stammered for a few beats as he glanced at the glistening wetness of his chest. He gulped hastily at his drink, coughing as it seared his throat, choking him.

Khari gave him a long look from across the room, one eyebrow raised, his eyes shining. "You're meant to drink it, not inhale it." He walked across the rug to stand in front of Eden to take the other glass and sniff at the liquor. Grunting a quiet approval, he sipped. "I'm guessing this isn't what they'd be drinking in the town," he said, tossing the rest down his throat with total irreverence. "As liquid courage goes, it's the best I've tasted," he said, winking at Eden. He patted him on his back. "Not good to inhale, though. Are you all right?"

Eden, just about managed to get a grip on himself. Unable to stop the direction his eyes wished to take, he looked at Khari's chest again. He was pleased when he sipped at his whiskey and did not choke on it a second time. Studying the planes and lines of Khari, Eden glanced at his face, knowing his approval of the sight in front of him must show. Scars and damage notwithstanding, Khari was glorious. Eden wondered if the guy had a clue just *how* special he was to look at. Dressed in rags, living in an underground cave, he was gorgeous. Here, in a mountain palace, surrounded by silks and tapestries, holding finest crystal and wearing nothing but his trousers, Khari was astoundingly beautiful. Eden had never thought he would call a man beautiful, but when it came to Khari, there were no other words; he simply was the most beautiful creature Eden had set eyes on.

"I seem to have managed to get you alone," Khari said, taking a small step closer. His eyes flicked over Eden's face, resting on his mouth.

Eden raised his glass to sip at his whiskey. "Seems so," he agreed. The bed at his side seemed a lot closer all of a sudden. He stood perfectly still as Khari reached for his face, prepared now for the burn of his touch. A jolt of electrical energy, which seemed to run from his lower lip down to his groin. Khari's eyes widened, measuring his response as he stroked his thumb across Eden's lip.

"Took long enough." Khari ran his fingers across the row of stitches at Eden's jaw. "These need to come out."

"They can wait," Eden said. "Other things on my

mind, right now."

"Yes?"

"Hmmm," Eden stepped forward to stand chest to chest with Khari. "Seems as though I have been waiting to be alone with you for years." About to lean and find Khari's mouth, he groaned loudly when they were interrupted by a knock on the door. "You have to be goddamn kidding me!"

Khari dropped his hand. "Yes?" he called, turning around and grabbing for his dirty shirt. "Who is it?"

The door opened and a tray appeared, followed by Airell, his sleeves rolled up and his hair knotted at the back of his head in a scruffy ponytail. He glanced at Eden, then looked briefly at Khari before turning to the table. Seeing Khari's bag, cloak and weapons on the table near the armchairs, he shrugged lightly and walked across the rug to stand in front of Khari.

Eden stepped back and held out his hands for the tray. "Would you like me to..."

Airell shook his head. "Thank you, no. Prince Alexander said you'd both be wanting something hot, and baths. Water will be brought up presently so you can bathe."

"Thank you," Khari said. He pulled his shirt over his head and tugged it into place, covering his chest and back, then took the tray. "It was kind of Alex. Prince Alexander. Um...thank you," he said again, turning away.

Airell looked at Eden. "I think I was just dismissed," he said.

"Khari?" Eden called as Khari wandered across the room.

Khari held a sandwich in his hand, sniffing the filling suspiciously. He shifted his attention from the

262

food to Eden. "What?" he asked, looking back at the sandwich.

"I'm going to go and find Takana," Eden said. "I think you might want to have some privacy."

"Wait." Airell laid a hand on Eden's arm, walking after Khari. He looked around, then pulled out a chair and sat down, resting his elbows on the table to hold his chin in his hands.

"You look much like your mother," he said. "Although I flatter myself that you have my eyes. Hello, Za'akhar. It is an honour to finally meet you...a lifetime too late, but an honour."

Khari considered Airell. He took a step backwards, mastered himself, and bowed awkwardly. "Your Majesty. I expected you to call to receive me. I had no idea you were you. I expected a crown."

"I find it cumbersome when I am weeding my garden," Airell said. He flashed a tiny grin at Khari. It transformed his features instantly. It made him seem impish and he looked like a young man; the aged agony in his eyes fading magically as he studied his son. "You are quite a man, Za'akhar."

"Uh. Call me Khari, please," Khari said, sitting down. He looked at Eden and waited for him to sit.

Eden reached for the decanter and selected another glass from the cabinet, sliding it in front of Airell before fetching his and Khari's from the main bedroom. Pouring for them all, he sat down quietly, feeling awkward.

"You should be alone," he said, readying himself to leave.

"No," Khari said at the same time as Airell. Khari shared a look with his father. "Stay. I want you here, babe. Please?"

Eden hesitated near the door, the small endearment warming him in a way the fire and cosy room could not. He looked at Airell. The decision had to rest with the king, much as he would have liked to follow Khari's desires.

"Yes...please stay," Airell said. He took plates from the tray and placed them on the table, filling each with small sandwiches and cakes. Lifting the lid of the teapot, he picked up the decanter and added several healthy shots of the whiskey, then poured.

"It was a cold time of the year to travel," Airell said, pushing a cup in front of Khari, then Eden. "This will warm you. I was not expecting you for another few days at least. I knew you were on your way, of course," he added, "but I thought it would take you longer to navigate the Wastelands."

Khari bit into a sandwich. "I rushed them through. I don't like the dark." He grimaced and looked at his food. "What is this?" he asked, forcing himself to swallow. "Ugh."

"Tomato," Eden said, watching him.

Khari frowned, opened the bread and removed the tomato. He took another bite of the buttered bread and put it back on his plate, then tasted the tomato. "This is nice," he said. "But I do not like that," he said, pushing at the discarded bread with a fingernail.

"Butter. Your mother grew to like it, but it took a while." Airell turned to face Eden. "Dairy is uncommon in Chiearatul," he explained. "Try a cake," he said to Khari. "You might like them, for all they are made almost exclusively of butter."

Khari picked up a small sponge cake from his plate, biting into it with his eyes on Airell. He chewed, swallowed, and nodded once. "That's nice."

Leaning back in his chair, Airell pulled a rope next to the drinks cabinet. "I'll have something brought to you that you will find easier on your palate." He rested his hands back on the table. Eden saw that his nails were bitten right down to the quick and felt a sudden surge of sympathy for this Elven King who seemed to have so much, yet knew such sadness.

"You don't have a Chiearian accent," Airell said, drinking from his whiskey glass. "You sound like you come from the Human Realm, maybe Cornwall."

"Mum spoke to us in English. I don't actually speak Chiearian...so no accent. I don't know where Cornwall might be, but I'm from Asanthal."

"You don't speak Chiearian?"

"None I can remember," Khari said, glancing at Eden to reassure himself he was still there. "I used to know it and understand it, if it was spoken to me, aye? But that was a long time ago. I doubt I'd understand more than a couple of words now."

Airell sat back in his chair as a knock sounded on the outer door. "Come!" he called. A petite serving girl stopped near the table and bobbed in place. "Prince Za'akhar—Prince Khari—would like plain bread rolls and cold cuts. Kindly ask Cook to supply a variety of spices and some oil to accompany the meats. Inform her that I will talk to her later to discuss menus. A stew will be best for tonight's meal." Turning when Khari groaned loudly, unable to suppress it, Airell frowned. "You do not like stew?"

"I adore stew," Khari said, "but if I have to eat one more bowl of it for at least a month, I will hunt a bloody pig myself and eat it! Anything *but* stew, please?"

"Tell Cook to roast a lamb," Airell said to the

265

serving girl. "We shall have it with Chiearian spices and vegetables. It is to be served in my suite. A private meal. I also think I can hear a rather large bird trying to gain access to the chamber," he added, looking at the curtain and shuttered window. "Do you have a bird, Khari?"

"Aye, Fain. Gyrfalcon."

"Have a perch brought up, please," Airell said to the girl. "Thank you."

Khari stood up, crossing to the window. "Sorry," he said to Airell. "I had left her downstairs...oh shit."

"What's wrong?" Eden asked, standing up.

Khari turned around, a small blue bird in his palm and Fain on his wrist. "She hunted your birds, Sire...I am so sorry. I never thought...she brings me food. Um...was it a rare breed?"

"Rarer now, one would imagine," Airell said. "I would have your falcon hunt my gardens barren, Khari, if it meant that I had you in my world." Still smiling, Airell tilted his head to one side, listening to something Eden could not hear. He called the young serving girl back. "Tell the head groom that our new horse guest may be more comfortable were he allowed loose in the woods. It might prevent more of my stable being demolished. Go quickly."

The girl bobbed and ran. Khari groaned and held a hand to his head, poured himself a cup of laced tea and drank it down in one.

"Any other pets I should know about?" Airell asked, helping himself to more whiskey. "Well, at least my life will no longer be boring. Welcome home...son."

XIV

It was lucky Eden had not expected the meal in Airell's suite to be a totally informal affair. As it transpired, eating in the King's suite was only marginally less splendid than a full Royal Banquet, hosted in a formal dining room. He was pleased for the change of clothes Airell had sent to his room—Khari was just as relieved to not look out of place, although he was shuffling uncomfortably in the tighter than usual tunic he wore.

Accustomed as he was to his jersey shirts and woollen pullovers, Khari was finding the transition to formal attire a hard one. He tugged at the neck for the fifth or sixth time, then yanked the collar open, inhaling with relief when the fabric was off his throat. He glanced Eden's way, studying him to use as his lead in what was going to happen next.

Eden watched Khari's face carefully as cutlery was placed next to fine china plates, and one glass was filled with water, while another goblet was filled with scarlet wine. Knives, forks, and spoons lined up like sentinels. Smaller plates orbited the place settings and silver-domed serving platters appeared, carried in the gloved hands of servant after servant.

Khari bit his lip, showing more and more concern as the procession of foods continued to appear and were set down along the centre of the pale table linens. Eden, more than a little in awe himself, tried to smile reassuringly, but he realised that he had not once seen Khari eat with more than a spoon and his fingers. He had thought little of it. Takana also ate rice with her fingers, balling it and scooping it into her mouth. It had not occurred to him that it may in fact be a cultural divide.

"Alex?" Eden asked, quietly as he leant to murmur in his friend's ear.

Alex looked at him and waited for him to speak.

"Um...in Chiearatul, is it more like China, with chopsticks? Or maybe like Morocco, where they just kinda eat communally with their fingers?"

Alex frowned, shaking his head. "I don't think so. Why?"

Gray leant forward. "Because Khari looks as though he's lost in a sea of silverware," he said, grinning fondly at his brother. "We have had no chance to sit at an Alfheimian table and be served in such grandeur. We sit on cushions, on the floor. Also, my people *don't* have knives at the table. Spoons and fingers, mostly. Forks, too, but not knives."

"It's been so long," Airell said in apology. "I remember, now. Phian," he called, waving over one of the liveried waiting staff, "kindly bring finger bowls and extra napkins. Thank you."

"Your Majesty," Phian murmured, leaving to do as he was bid.

"Sorry," Khari said, turning red. He rolled his shoulders, trying to get comfortable on the chair. "This is all new to me. All of it." He shuffled on his seat, obviously awkward at being unable to kneel or fold his legs sideways, as he usually ate. "I've never eaten like this."

"I know," Airell said. "I am sorry—I never meant to make you feel out of your depth. I remember, now. It was long ago, and I made myself forget a lot of it.

The memories were painful, because of how happy that time was. Please," he said, looking directly at Khari, "sit as you are comfortable. This is your home, now. You too, Gray. I do not require you to learn our ways, simply because I have asked you to come to this land. You are not obligated to change who you both are, to try and fit in."

"Thank you," Gray said, reaching to squeeze Khari's hand quickly. "I have had no occasion to dine formally, Alfheimian-style. It will be enjoyable to learn all the new ways of doing things. I only know what I have read in books, and what our mother taught us, but of course," he said, spooning rice onto his plate as the bowl was passed along the table, "I was young, then, so half of what I learned has since been forgotten."

Khari glanced at Eden, waiting for roasted cubes of lamb to be added to his plate. He reached for a flatbread, rinsed his fingers in his side bowl, and scooped up a small amount of rice to ball expertly in his hand and dip into a tomato sauce. Aware of Airell's eyes on him, he looked sideways, scooping more rice into his hand, slower this time, and rolled it into a ball.

Airell tried to follow his movements, cursing when he dropped rice all over the table. He shook his head. "It seems that the passing of twenty years has not helped my skills. Relaizia often despaired. Let me try again..."

Eden watched Airell as he tried time and time again to copy Khari and Gray. He was pleased to see Khari's face was no longer troubled, and that his self-consciousness was fading.

Khari flicked his fringe back and looked at Gray. He lifted his foot to rest on the chair, wrapping his arm around his knee to eat with his left hand, at ease at last. He drank more wine, and looked again at Eden, his eyes flashing bright in the light of the candles.

Eden drew a small breath. Clenching his hand around his napkin, he wondered if he would ever be able to look at Khari and *not* look foolish. He ate another mouthful of spiced rice, followed by a small chunk of lamb, looking down at his plate. He could not understand what happened when he looked into the inky blackness of Khari's pupils, drawn deeply into them from the pool of blazing heat surrounding them. It was an impossible sensation of falling, rapidly, from a high building. His stomach jumped and his breath left him as though he had been hit, and hit hard. The closest he had ever come to the same feeling of helplessness was when he had parachuted. Spinning into freefall, sure that he would die, yet so exhilarated that the urge to jump again and again had been too strong to resist. As though the risk of death made him alive.

It hit him, suddenly, that after dinner, after they had talked and spent the night in the company of Airell and the others, for once they would not be sleeping under the watchful eyes of someone. That tonight, their bed was not going to be a mattress of piled leaves, nor the hard trunk of a tree at their backs. They would not be covered by their cloaks, trying to stop shivering enough to sleep. Their roof would not be a sky, blanketed with bright stars and illuminated by a pale pink moon.

They would be alone.

Eden felt the heat rise up his chest to his face. He reached for his water glass and gulped. Alone, with

Khari. Uninjured, unwatched and awake. Eden lifted his eyes from his plate and looked across the table at Khari to be met by a blaze of autumn sunshine staring directly into his eyes. Khari watched him for a long second, then lifted his wine glass and smiled; a secret smile that held enough promises to make Eden's blood run hot.

Realising Airell was talking to him, Eden shook himself and forced his eyes away from Khari's bewitching gaze. Airell flicked a glance at Khari.

"I said thank you, Eden," Airell said. "For leading the others to find my sons."

"Oh...I never, sir. I mean, I never led them anywhere."

Airell rested his chin in his palm, pushing his plate aside so he could lean his elbow on the table. "They followed you, even if you did not mean to lead them. You have my thanks." His eyes thoughtful, Airell studied Eden for several moments. "Sometimes, in life, I have learned it is best to not question what is handed to you to deal with. Other times, questions must be asked. And sometimes, more often than not, it is impossible to know what to do, or whether to ask questions, until the time has passed and you have the benefit of hindsight. Meeting you, I find that I have not the slightest idea whether to accept what I see without question, or whether to grill you for answers you likely do not have. I think I shall just wait and watch."

"For now," Takana said, looking up from her food.

"For now," Airell agreed. "And I eagerly await the pleasure of watching you train." He sat back so his plate could be cleared. "I hear you are someone to watch, Eden."

"Oh, I dunno about that," Eden said. "Compared to everyone else, I must look like a lumbering fool. You should see Khari and Gray. Now they can *move*."

"So I hear," Airell said. "And I cannot wait to see them both in action, but you, Eden, have had no training at all, until you crossed into our lands?"

Aware of Gray and Khari's eyes on him, Eden shook his head. "No, sir. None. Just target shooting, but Takana was right in sayin' as it was pretty useless. So am I," he added, pointing to his neck and the stitches that still needed to be removed. "I couldn't do a thing."

"You never bled to death," Cole interjected. "It can be seen as doing something."

"You took out quite a few of the enemy," Takana added. "Let's not forget that were it not for Khari and Gray, we would all be laid out with Denny."

"Orien rest her soul," Airell said. "I am sorry for her loss, Alexander."

"Thank you."

"It was quick," Takana said. "It should not have happened, but it was quick."

Alex drank down his wine, holding his goblet up so it could be refilled. "She was avenged," he said, drinking and placing his goblet on the table with precise movements.

Airell leant over the table to lay his hand over Alex's. "She will be remembered."

"I know." Alex coughed behind his hand and pushed his plate away. A gloved hand reached for it and removed it immediately. He focused on the wine, then pushed it aside. "Brandy, please," he said to one of the servants. He waited for a snifter to be placed in front of him and drank quietly.

"Oh, Alex," Eden said. "I'm sorry..."

Alex forced himself to smile. It was brittle, but it stayed on his face. Maybe if it stayed there long enough, it would become true. "I am sorry too. But it will not bring her back." He raised his glass to Airell. "To lost loves."

Airell raised his glass. "And absent friends," he said, drinking. "And new found ones," he added, looking at Khari, then Gray. "And new loves," he said, the start of a grin playing around the corners of his lips as he looked at Takana and Cole. "Or old ones finally realised, as the case may be."

"Cole is still after a title," Alex said. "He's decided marriage to my sister is the best way to secure himself one."

"Indeed," Airell said. "Well, we shall see, shall we? I might find it in my heart to bestow something. Maybe. When is the wedding?"

Takana poked at her food, not looking up. "I don't know. I never thought I would be able to wed, so I never gave it much thought. I only have the vaguest idea of what is involved."

"Contrary to your belief," Cole said with a bright grin, "you do not have to sign yourself over to me, nor do I receive a certificate of ownership."

She poked her tongue out. The relief was plain on her face at having her fears quelled. She pushed her plate away, nodding thanks to the servant who cleared it. The room was filled with a musical chiming from her hair. Freshly washed, each braid had been newly woven and clamped with ornate silver clips, it looked as vibrant and as alive as Takana herself.

Eden pictured the groomed *princess* dining with him against the wild guard he had first met in the

Borderlands. It was difficult to remember Takana as she had looked when he had first met her. She looked different, now. Likely because she was happy.

He studied the various slices of fruits on a plate slid in front of him before choosing something that looked like a red apple. Deciding it was an apple after tasting it, he ate in silence, listening with half an ear to the conversations floating around the table; wedding plans, ideas of places to take Gray and Khari, plans for tailors and seamstresses to make much needed clothing for them all. The small inconsequential things that made up a life.

"I plan to take Eden to see the old temples," Alex said.

Eden looked up, remembering the enchanting call of the darkness, deep within the mountain. He shivered in recollection of the resonating voice that had chimed inside his soul, beckoning him closer.

"I'm not sure that would be wise," Airell said. "It has been centuries since anyone went down so far. They are not safe. What if the stones crumble and collapse?"

"Is that likely?" Alex asked.

Airell shrugged. "Who knows. They were declared unsafe when I was a child, so I could not say how much longer they are likely to stay intact. It may take a hammer blow to bring the caves down, or it may take a light tap. Who knows."

Khari looked at Eden. Seeing the longing in Eden's eyes, he looked at Airell. "I can go too. I can stop the caves collapsing."

"It is kind of you to offer, but I think the lower levels are beyond the magicks of a young man such as yourself."

"I wouldn't be so sure," Takana said, sharing a look with Cole. "Khari is not what I would call a normal young man."

Gray spooned fruit salad into his mouth, his watchful eyes set on his brother. "If Khari says that he will not let the caves collapse, Majesty," he said politely, "then the caves will not collapse."

"I would take their word for it, Airell," Alex said. "I have seen things over the past few weeks that I would never have deemed possible, had I not seen them with my own eyes. Do not underestimate the power your son holds inside him. I do not think it could be overestimated, in all honesty."

"If Khari felt like creating a mountain, he would probably be able to do it," Cole remarked. He sat back in his chair and folded his arms. "Holding one up won't be an issue, I'd warrant. You sired something that cannot be fully comprehended by mere men, my dear uncle. And women," he added, glancing at Takana. "Stopping a cavern from collapsing under the weight of an ancient mountain could probably be done before breakfast...while he brushes his teeth and chooses what to wear at the same time. Child's play, to the mighty Za'akhar."

Airell looked around the table, then shrugged. "All right. I will not argue with such ringing endorsements. You are sure?"

"Aye, I am," Khari said. "I'm quite at home underground, too. Earth is one of the easiest elements to manipulate, I think."

"Did you carve out your home with magic?" Eden asked. "All those rooms?"

Khari nodded. "I did. We needed shelter, and to build above the ground would have been to risk being found easily. It is easier to hide under the earth. While Jaizel would have never come for us himself, it was easier to hide from his soldiers under the ground than it would have been any other way. I could sense them arriving in the forest and we were able to attack them before they closed in on our home. Had there been evidence of a homestead? No, why take that risk, in case one of the animals slipped past me and managed to attack by stealth?"

"It started off with just the one room...if one could call it a room," Gray said. "I dug most of the earth out by hand, and reinforced it with wood and branches. Khari was not in any fit state to help me, when I first escaped with him. My priorities were to have somewhere warm and safe, where he could heal. Then as time went on, and Khari grew stronger, he started to manipulate the earth."

"It took me a few months to create all the spaces there now," Khari said. "I had to guide the earth and push it aside, without hurting the forest. That was what took the longest. Asking the roots to move aside when I needed extra space for doorways and passages."

"I wish you could have seen it, Airell," Alex said. "Rest assured I did not find your sons living in a damp dank hole in the ground. An underground warren the size of a mansion house would be more accurate."

Airell looked at Khari. "You can manipulate the earth?" he asked quietly.

"Yes, sire," Khari replied. "And the air, the water, and fire."

"Show me."

Eden watched Khari's face as a breeze blew through the dining room, the sudden gust extinguishing the candle flames to leave them in momentary darkness before several glowing balls of heatless flame shimmered into being around the table, lighting them all in golden tones. Khari watched as they grew in size and lifted higher in the air, weaving around each other before settling into place in a circle, shining like a chandelier over the centre of the table. He looked at his water glass, watching the liquid within bubble and boil, steam rising as it reached boiling point, then clicked his fingers to still it, cooling it back down wordlessly.

Khari looked at Airell, assessing him briefly. As though finding whatever he was searching for, he held his hand out to his side, then raised it above his head. Silently, Khari made electricity flare into life around his arm, crackling and sparkling; racing upwards to his fingers and shooting to the ceiling, where it arced outwards in glittering pathways of pure white energy like cracks in a window. Khari grinned at his father, clenched his fist, and sat back as the candle flames sprang up from the wicks of the candles once more, and the glow-lights faded and disappeared along with the lightning.

Airell gaped at his son for several long seconds. Glancing at Alex, then Cole, he shook his head and leant his elbows on the table. "When did you learn you could do this?" he asked. "Did your mother know?"

"She taught me to control it," Khari said. "I can't remember not being able to do it all."

"He has been doing it since he could hold his head by himself," Gray said. "The first time it happened, we thought he might have been too warm, because he made cold winds blow throughout the suite. We never knew, at that time, that it was Khari doing it, of course. It took a few more instances of it happening before we put two and two together and realised Khari could control the wind...and the fire...and the water in the bathtub," Gray said. "He could not have been older than three months, maybe. If as old as that. It was a game to him."

"Mum kept it as a game," Khari said, taking up the story. He looked around the table and, deciding that no one was going to eat the rest of the fruit salad, or touch the cakes in the centre of the table, reached for a slice and put it on his plate. "I like cake," he said, smiling at Eden. "She would play with me and make me use the powers I have, when no one else but Gray was around. Make me stretch myself and push what I could do. But I wasn't allowed to do it when there were others around. It was our game...to be played when we were alone."

"She tried to hide him from Jaizel," Gray said. "We hoped if Jaizel never knew what he was capable of, that he might escape his notice."

Khari shrugged. "Aye, well. It was worth a try," he said. "It could never have worked, but it was worth a try."

"I should have gone after her," Airell said. "I am sorry, both of you. I should have fled with her. She said for me to wait, but perhaps I could have..."

"You could have done nothing," Gray said. "She had no choice, as a mother, but to return for me...and once she returned, she was imprisoned. You could not have known her fate any more than she herself could have known. She was free, before she left. She would ride out and visit the nearby towns and cities. She was not caged, so why would she have thought it would be different, when she came for me? It was only when she came back, that final time, that my father lost his mind and imprisoned her. No one could have known. Nor could you have hoped to rescue any of us. To try would have meant your death, and my mother would never have countenanced you risking yourself. I did not know it was *you* she spoke of, but I know she loved you beyond words. You could not have done anything to help her. Help us."

"There must have been a way to get you out of there."

"There was," Khari said. "Gray did it. It was the only way, and it could not have been done from the outside."

"Really," Gray said, looking directly at Airell. "There was nothing you could have possibly done. My father would have killed you—in the worst way imaginable. You can stop torturing yourself, now. Please?" he asked, softly. "There's no need for you to feel the guilt you've been carrying around. You could never have known what would happen after she left you. No way anyone could know."

Airell held his head in his hands. "I should have known," he said to himself.

"You could not have imagined what had happened, love," Alex said, stroking Airell's back with a gentle hand. "You did all you could with the facts you had. It is unfortunate that those facts did indeed make it seem as though you had been abandoned. You acted as soon as you found out otherwise, and no one could ask that you did more than that. Now stop. This should be a celebration of reunion, not a wake for ghosts long dead. And," he added, reaching for his brandy, "we have someone who is as close to human as we are likely to see at this table. As well as a fully blooded Chiearian, *and* possibly the only elf ever born under Orien's Star. This is a cause to celebrate, if ever there was one."

"We shall talk later," Takana said, glancing at Eden, then at Khari. "Celebrate now."

Airell sat up. He picked up his wine goblet, the mask of inscrutability once more firmly in place, but for his eyes. "Tell me, Takana," he said, "are you thinking of finally resigning your post and settling in one place? Grow some...roots?"

"Oh, you just had to say it, didn't you?" Takana said, rolling her eyes in mock despair. "Never heard that joke before. Roots...good one," she said sarcastically. "How about you pour some wine for this thirsty tree, eh? Then I won't be dried up and brittle later, when you insist on hearing about every step, pathway, and fart we encountered on our journey."

"He was friendlier than I was expecting," Khari said. He opened the door to their suite and waved Eden ahead of him. "They all were. I don't know exactly what I was thinking would happen here, but acceptance without a blink wasn't a part of it."

Eden crossed the room, stroking his hand over the rough walls as he went. He stood in the window casement carved into the far wall and drew back the curtain to look out at the city at the base of the mountain. He gazed at the flickering lights, shining in the glassless windows of the houses built below, golden evidence of life spreading out like a blanket along the mountain pathway. He pulled the thick velvet curtains together, blocking out the world to trap in the heat from the roaring open fire that had been built and lit while they ate. He walked to get a glass of wine, needing the Dutch courage.

"I don't see how anyone could do anything else but love you," Eden said, quietly. He did not turn around, looking down at the surface of the sideboard instead. Suddenly nervous and unsure, now he finally had Khari to himself. Unchaperoned. Alone.

Khari moved at the edge of Eden's vision, leaning on the narrow end of the pale white wooden sideboard, watching Eden's face carefully. It should have been disconcerting, but Eden had got used to the direct unblinking gaze that seemed to study his mind and thoughts; his soul, maybe. He did not know what it was Khari saw when he studied people in his own unique way, but that he saw *something*, Eden had no doubt at all. He slowly met Khari's eyes and waited.

Khari frowned before his face relaxed into something that wasn't quite a smile, but was close. "Are you scared I'm going to jump you and bend you to my will?" he asked. "Or scared that I'm not?"

Eden smiled. He couldn't help himself. He shrugged. "I don't know. I've never been in this kinda scenario before. I don't know what to expect, what I want, what I don't want...hell, I don't got a clue what..." He held his hands out to his sides and let them fall again. "I don't know what I'm doing," he said. "I don't want to screw things up. I waited too long and want you too much to...damnit, my words broke," he croaked, rubbing a hand over his face. Seeing Khari still staring at him, slight amusement lighting his eyes, made him blush. He felt stupid.

Khari pushed himself away from the sideboard and stood up straight, his chest a hairsbreadth from Eden's. Without looking away from his face, Khari raised his hand, tugging silently on the silk laces holding the neck of Eden's shirt. He waited a beat before using his fingertips to slide the silken lawn from Eden's shoulders, the fabric falling in a waterfall of cream to hang around his hips, held in place by the waistband of his trousers.

Leaning to skim his lips along Eden's collarbone, Khari smiled into his eyes. "I might not be sure what I'm doing, but I know the meaning of the word no," he said, quietly as he kissed his way up Eden's neck to a small groove behind his ear. His breath was hot against tender skin, making Eden shiver involuntarily. "I also know the word stop," Khari breathed against his earlobe. "You just have to know how to say either.

I will listen to you, Eden. I have no experience of wanting what it is I want, right now. I'm nervous, I'm scared, and I don't have much of an idea where I'm going with this...but I know I want you so badly, I'm burning. You make me burn, Eden."

Eden groaned, leaning against Khari and sliding his hands around his hips, pulling him closer as he fumbled to pull Khari's shirt from his waistband and lift it over his head. Needing skin. Stroking the silken softness of Khari's chest and, so gently his fingers barely skimmed flesh, his back. Exploring in silence as lips caressed his jaw and found his mouth to tenderly invade in an exchange of breath and tentative tongues.

Barely aware of anything outside of the immediate sensations of Khari pressing against him, the long fingers pushing up the nape of his neck and into his hair, Eden moaned again, trying to wordlessly form the words that had left his head. He felt as though he was at war with himself; wanting to plunge on ahead, regardless, yet wanting to slow things down and draw them out for as long as he could.

"There's no rush," Khari mumbled against Eden's mouth. "I'm not going anywhere."

Eden stepped on the heels of his boots and kicked them into the corner of the room. Impatient for contact, he tugged Khari close again, feeling the stiffness of arousal against his hip. Breathless at the realisation, he grunted soft approval and held Khari in place with his hands on his backside, deepening the kiss and listening with his entire body to each of Khari's physical responses to his touch.

Suddenly, the few weeks he had known Khari for *real* seemed like a lifetime. The dreams merged seamlessly into the reality he held in his arms. Into the hands stroking through his hair and firm as they slid down his spine. Fingertips kneading each vertebrae. Digging into his flesh with increasing urgency as Khari grew breathless and moved hesitantly against Eden's hip, nudging him in silent question.

Eden walked backwards with Khari held firmly in his arms, letting himself be pushed towards the bedroom and the inviting mattress. Khari moaned against his lips, the sound a deep resonance vibrating in his chest. Khari pushed off his own boots with his feet and yanked the yards of lawn fabric from Eden's waistband, letting the shirt fall in a puddle around Eden's ankles, then guiding him out of the material, crumpled and immediately forgotten in the doorway of the bedroom.

"I want you so badly, I don't know which way is up," Khari moaned, leaning in for a long kiss that drew Eden out of himself and set his nerves alight with a passionate fire he had never dreamed existed. He gasped as Khari leant back and shot a look his way, his golden eyes glowing darkly, blazing with emotion. Khari looked at Eden for a moment, then drew in a shaky breath, visibly mastering himself and his breathing, slowing the tempo as he touched his lips to Eden's mouth to skim over the swollen flesh with a gentleness that belied his strength. "Your eyes are silver again," Khari breathed. "You're shining."

"You're burning," Eden replied. He hitched a breath at the touch of Khari's fingertips trailing down from his navel to the laced fly of his trousers. Seeing the nervous apprehension in the golden irises, flashing brightly in front of his face, Eden fell back onto the quilts of the bed and folded one arm under his head, beckoning Khari to him with his free hand.

"I give you my word, Khari, that I will never hurt you. Touching me ain't gonna make me turn into some kind of animal. I promise." He grinned. "I'll only bite if you ask...nicely."

Khari crawled onto the bed to straddle Eden's thighs and effectively pin him in place beneath him. He looked into his eyes for several long silent moments, then let out the breath he was holding and bent his head to find Eden's mouth once more.

"I don't want to mess this up," Khari admitted. "For all my...experience...this is as new to me as it is to you."

Eden closed his eyes against the thought of what Khari's 'experience' might entail. "That's in the past," he said, once he was sure his fury wouldn't be heard in his voice. He looked at Khari, stroking his fingers down the side of his face. "We take this at your pace. I'm good with however slow that pace is. Or however fast," he added honestly. If he was going to be truthful to himself—and he could see no reason to lie to himself at all—he would have been happy to be naked, getting well and truly laid, right this second. However, some things *were* more important than sex. Khari's feelings and past were some of those things.

He would stay a virgin if it meant Khari would lose the fear at the back of his eyes.

"Whatever went before," Eden stated, "you're mine, now. And we have all the time you need. Don't be scared of me, Khari...please?"

Khari stroked his hand down Eden's chest, following its path with his eyes, watching Eden as he hissed in a breath. His mouth quirked and he bent his head, trailing the path of his fingers with his tongue to

Eden's nipple, licking the small bud erect, then the other, sucking gently as his hand continued its downward path across Eden's abdomen to his waistband. Silently exploring Eden's body with mouth hands and tongue, Khari grabbed his hand and held it to the bed, lifting himself to check Eden's face. Seeing whatever it was he was searching for, Khari swept his tongue around the circle of Eden's navel, holding him still when he gasped and squirmed.

Forcing himself not to grab Khari, Eden arched backwards, stretching into the sensations taking over his body as every inch of bare skin was kissed, licked, sucked and stroked, leaving him painfully hard and caged behind the soft leather of his trousers, aching for the fly to be released and ease some of the pressure. The friction was driving him out of his mind with each small movement of Khari above him. Khari's hand skidded over his straining hardness and his own loud moan sounded alien to his ears.

"I like *that* sound," Khari moaned, looking up into Eden's eyes from his place close to the waistband of his trousers. He watched Eden's face and moved his hand again, sliding with deliberate slowness down the length of his cock, his eyes blazing when Eden let go of another loud groan he was powerless to stop.

"Holy fuck," Eden said, letting his head fall back onto the pillows. He closed his eyes, focused entirely on the sensations. "What are you doing to me...oh, good god," he opened his eyes again as Khari slid up the length of his chest, unlacing his fly with deft fingers, springing him free before leaning down to take possession of his mouth once more, while his hand moved with tantalising slowness to grab and stroke him until Eden felt as though he might explode.

He grabbed the laces holding Khari's trousers closed and pulled them apart with frantic haste, desperate to touch and feel him in return. Finding his target, he grinned up at Khari as he shuddered and heaved in a deep breath when Eden found his hand and linked their fingers together between their bodies, finding a rhythm that worked for them both, matching Khari thrust for thrust as they kissed breathlessly, moaning at the sensations surrounding them.

"Eden...I'm..."

Eden clenched his hand, moving faster to match the coalescing heat building in his thighs and pelvis, screaming at him to beg for release from the exquisite torture of holding back.

"Eden," Khari groaned, "I can't...much longer...I'm going to..."

Eden caught Khari's mouth with his own as Khari lost his rhythm, tensing and stiffening above him, growling into Eden's neck as he came with a force that matched his own, leaving him sated and spent under Khari's weight. Feeling as though his spine had been ripped out, he sank into the mattress without speaking, trying to gulp breaths and get his bearings.

Shakily taking his weight on his elbows, Khari looked down at him. "Are you all right?"

Eden closed his eyes, panting. "Kidding, right?"

"No. I never hurt you?" Khari asked again, worried. "Did I...was it..."

"It was fucking fantastic," Eden answered. He pulled Khari back down to lay on his chest, heedless of the slick evidence of combined semen and sweat. "Shut up and let me catch my breath, huh?" he asked. "And stay where you are...I want hugs."

"The mess," Khari said, leaning over to the

287

washstand to grab a towel and silently clean Eden, not meeting his eyes. "Sorry," he said, tying the lacings of his fly. "I, uh...it was...I should have..."

"Ah," Eden said, rolling onto his side. He took the towel from Khari and wiped him clean, then kissed his chest above his heart. "Don't say sorry, Khari. I loved it. Every moment. You weren't rough, and I'm all over the place in a *good* way. I feel as though I shattered and you put me back together again." He stroked Khari's chest with the back of his knuckles. "You don't like it?"

Khari's eyes flashed in his direction. "No. I mean, aye. Aye, I liked it...a lot."

Eden sighed, relieved. "Good. I was worried I was crap, or something. I just did what I liked, I guess. I weren't sure how to go about it. Just knew I wanted to do it. You're not pissed off at me, are you?"

"No, Eden. I just, I don't know, I felt so out of control. Nothing existed except that second, and the one after, and the one after...and I couldn't *do* anything but what my body was screaming at me to do, and that's just wrong. It's not how I want to be. Like him," Khari said, looking at his hands. He shrugged his scarred shoulders. "As though that's all there is, and it's all that matters. To use you like that."

Eden shuffled to lay his head in Khari's lap and looked up at him. "That, in itself, says that you're nothing like that bastard, Khari," he said. He lifted his hand and held it to Khari's jaw, feeling the still-soft growth of downy stubble. "You never used me, I chose to be there, in that moment, with you. It's not the same. Really," he added when Khari met and held his eyes at last. "Nothing like the same. I am coming to you, and going into this, with no experience, good or bad, okay?"

"Aye. okay," Khari said.

"So, you can't project onto me that something is meant to be *bad*, when it's actually so damned good that I flew out of my own head for a while. Use my lead as to what I like and don't like. Not what *you* think I should like and dislike. I will find that out with you, Khari. In time. Don't think you've used me, when I've had a blast right along with you. Don't act as though I need scrubbing in the tub after reaching my first *ever* orgasm that weren't achieved by myself in my bedroom with my own right hand," he said, smiling at Khari's small amused snort. "Been waiting and longing for you so long that all this is beyond words."

"Broken words," Khari said, looking down at Eden and stroking his hair off his face. "Are your words fixed now?"

Eden chuckled. "Reckon they're gonna have to be, because the only way this is gonna work, without you having a meltdown most days—and I do plan on doing this most days—is by being totally honest. It's not easy for me to talk about sex. Any kind of sex. At all. It's not something I could talk to my dad about, my mama died, and in school, the focus was entirely on straight sex, so it was lacking in what I'm meant to do when I like guys and don't have a vagina in my inventory of body parts. But I will try to be as honest as I can. I will tell you if I'm uncomfortable, if it's too soon, too fast, or hurts. I promise."

"I want to explore every inch of you," Khari breathed. His fingers trailed from Eden's cheek to his jaw, then traced an invisible path across his chest. "I want to shut out the world and lose myself in you, but

I also want to wait. Is that all right?"

"It's okay," Eden agreed. "This is enough. Not sure what I want or where I want this to go myself, yet. There's a lot more than just...doing it. I don't want to get hurt any more than you want to hurt me," he admitted, shrugging awkwardly on Khari's thighs. "It's not something I want to rush."

"Do you want some wine?" Khari asked.

"Please, yeah."

"You can warm up the bed, aye? It's been years since I slept in a bed half as good as this one. I want to be under the quilt, not on top of it. With you," Khari added, standing and walking to the door. He stopped, turned, and raked Eden with his eyes. "If you're with me, the ground is heavenly," he said, "but to have a bed like this? I plan on getting comfy and not getting out of it for some time."

Eden stood up to strip off his trousers. He slipped under the quilts and practically purred at the touch of thick silk against his skin. The sheets were certainly a step-up from leaves and a cloak to keep out the freezing wind. Plumping up the luxurious feather pillows, he settled back and relaxed, watching as Khari walked back into the bedroom holding two wine goblets in one hand and a decanter in the other.

Khari placed the decanter on the bedside table, divested himself of the goblets then stood and considered Eden for a heartbeat before pushing his trousers down his legs to stand naked next to the bed.

More than aware just how momentous a gift the trust Khari was giving him was, Eden rolled to Khari's side of the bed and drew back the covers for him to slide into the silken cocoon. "You're beautiful." He fitted himself into Khari's side and took a goblet when it was held out to him. He sipped at the wine. It was amazing. He tilted his goblet and drank the rest, passing it back to Khari to put on the table, then nestled into the soft flesh above Khari's armpit. Just the novelty of being able to touch skin was enough to make his heart race. Having Khari naked, holding him close—so close—was his own personal kind of heaven.

"Not disgusted by me?" Khari asked.

"Not a bit," Eden said, shaking his head. He nudged Khari's side and grinned. "And I'm wipe clean."

"Good to know."

"I thought so."

Khari grinned back at Eden, nestling down under the quilt and drawing the thick silken fabric up to his chin. "Oh, praise the gods," he said, turning onto his side so he could hold Eden closer. "This beats an animal skin and some rough wool. Wow."

"I liked the animal skin."

"What?"

Eden smiled. "You were in it with me, and you mended me in the bed with the skin. I liked it."

Khari touched his stitches and sat up, reaching for his knife, which was on the floor with his trousers. He tipped his chin at Eden. It was a silent order to lie down and trust what was about to happen.

Without hesitation, Eden laid flat, lifting his chin so Khari could get to the stitches. "Will it hurt?" he asked.

"Only if you move and I slice your throat open again," Khari said, deadpan. "Shouldn't hurt otherwise. It's like taking out an earring."

"In my neck."

"In your neck, aye," Khari confirmed. He bit his

lower lip between his teeth and moved his knife hand. Dropping the knife, he worked fast and sure, the small threads of silk tugging as they slid out of healed skin.

"Earrings stuck in place hurt more," Eden said as the final couple of stitches were pulled free. "And it's nowhere near as bad as getting a tattoo."

"A what?" Khari asked, sweeping the threads into his palm to drop into the chamber pot beneath the bed.

Eden rolled onto his stomach, pushing the quilts down his legs to show his left hip and outer thigh. More accurately, to show the dark brown tattoo he had there; a long chain of runic symbols he had dreamt and drawn to try and get the image of them out of his head. He had no idea what they were, or what they signified, if anything, but they certainly made for an interesting and attractive tattoo. Branded lengthways, the runes read downwards from his hip to halfway to his knee.

Khari studied it for several silent moments before looking into Eden's eyes. "I'm guessing you never found this in a book in one of your human libraries?" he asked, sliding down the sheet to look at each rune and trace them with a gentle fingertip. "Do you know what it says?"

"Not a clue. I saw them in my dreams. I saw these, and you. They seemed important. At least, I couldn't make myself forget about them, and they were seared onto the inside of my eyelids for close to a year, each time I closed my eyes. I had them tattooed in desperation. It worked. Once they were on me, I stopped seeing the ghost of them all the time."

"Huh." Khari looked up at him with unmistakable amusement. "And you thought you were human?"

"I thought I had an active imagination," he said.

"Why? Can you tell me what it says?"

Khari hesitated. With uncharacteristic evasiveness, he shook his head and slid back up the sheet to lie at Eden's side. "I think, if you're meant to know what it says, you will find out when it's time for you to know. I think, maybe, this isn't my place to tell you what you saw, or what you have written on you."

"Tell me I haven't cursed myself or summoned demons from the Underworld?" He asked, only half joking.

"No demons," Khari promised. He kissed Eden gently. "I think demons would not dare to approach you. Unless you summoned them, and then I doubt they would have the power to resist you, however much they might be terrified of who they faced."

"You know a damned sight more than you're saying. You're talking in Takana-Riddles!"

"It's not up to me to tell you what you know, deep within you. When you're ready for that truth, you'll know it. Trust me?"

Wishing he could look into the blazing fire of Khari's eyes and demand answers, Eden sighed. He *did* trust Khari, and that trust meant that if he was being told to wait and be patient—a virtue he had never really found the time for—then he would do just that.

"Do you know what I am?" he asked, allowing himself to be swept away in the beauty of Khari's eyes. "Everyone...they all stop and stare, you know? The way folks look at me tells me that they're not staring because I'm from the Human Realm. It's not because they think they have a human among them, but at first I thought that was all it was. It's not, is it? I'm something *other*. Do you know what?"

Khari kissed him instead of answering immediately. His lips, when they pressed against Eden's, held a promise and gave security. "Not what, Eden," he said, drawing back for the briefest of instants. He kissed him again with careful exactitude. "What you are has no name in any modern tongue. But I know *who* you are, aye. Aye, I know you. So do you, but you're not ready to see it in the cold light of day. Not yet. You've always known it, and you've always searched for the answers to questions you had no name for. It's why you called me to you in your dreams—I never called you to me, Eden. You called me, to you, when it was time for you to search for me. You have the answers. You need to learn what your questions are. How far you're willing to fall, and much you're willing to lose of the world you took as your own. You know, in the deepest corners of your mind, and in the deepest depths of your soul, exactly who you are, and what you are searching for...but you have to be ready for the reality of it. It isn't my place to force that on you."

"But you have a place," Eden said, rolling to pull Khari on top of him. He looked up at his face. "I'm not insane in thinking that you're a huge part of this, am I? Your place in this is with me?"

"My place is at your side," Khari agreed. "Wherever you go, now that you found me, I go with you." Khari was quiet for a few heartbeats. He stroked his finger over the arch of Eden's eyebrow and looked deeply into Eden's eyes. The golden sunshine seared past any defences Eden may have been able to put in place, taking his breath away. Khari skimmed his mouth across Eden's lips. "Regardless of anything else, you are mine. That's all I really need to know.

You are mine, and I won't let you go. Not now I have you where you belong."

"Where I belong, huh?" he asked, feeling the first stirrings of arousal.

Khari grinned. "Where you belong," he repeated, rotating his hips slowly, not looking away from Eden's eyes.

"Where do I belong, then?" Eden teased, nudging in response to feel Khari's growing hardness against his own.

"In my arms."

"And your bed?"

"That too. I seriously want to explore every last inch of you." He narrowed the gap between their mouths, but deliberately avoided contact. Instead, he hovered so their noses were less than an inch apart. "I want to taste you. Listen to you as I kiss all of you. Hear you wanting me...to have your taste on my tongue...filling my senses."

Eden felt as though he was tinder, sparks flying close enough to set him afire with one puff of air. A touch would ignite him, carry him away in an inferno of longing. He looked at Khari, mesmerised. One of them, it seemed, had no trouble with articulating themselves. It was a good thing, because Eden had lost all words and language, except for the most basic of them all. He rolled his hips, sliding against the silken skin of Khari's erection to elicit a small gasp from the stunning elf on top of him. Words were unnecessary; body language was working just fine. He nodded silently at the question in Khari's eyes, affirming consent as the blonde head bent to kiss his neck, then his chest.

"Your scent is intoxicating," Khari breathed, his

tongue tracing patterns under Eden's nipple, following the curves of his chest to his ribs and upwards towards his armpit, tickling and strumming his nerves. "Everything about you is. You were made to explore."

Eden drew in a breath, letting it out gradually. He lifted his hand, trailing his fingers over the curve of Khari's bicep and down his arm, as careful as he would touch a skittish horse so Khari wouldn't bolt or shy away from his touch. More than anything, he wanted to feel his way around the tightly muscled body pressing him into the mattress. To kiss and taste and explore in return. But he could feel the fear in Khari. He was not going to make the mistake of giving Khari any reason at all to link his actions to anything that might have been done to him in the past. Better to have him feel safe, however frustrating it might be to hold back.

He gasped, tilting his head back involuntarily as Khari's head dipped below his navel; his tongue cool against the heat of his skin, stretched tight across his hip bone. It felt as though Khari was bringing each individual nerve ending to rest just under the top layer of his skin; each touch of his fingers and lick of his tongue brought with it its own exquisite torture. He heard Khari's laugh, deep and resonating, yet it sounded as though Eden was underwater. His mind span further away with each stroking touch of his body.

"I like that sound too," Khari said, lifting himself to look up Eden's chest into his eyes.

"I...like what you're doing...to make me sound like this," he moaned, watching Khari's mouth glide over his abdomen, unable to look away. Captivated, he watched as blonde strands of fine gossamer hair fell forward, blocking most of his view. Khari's head dipped lower and a jolt of pure sensation shot through Eden's body with the cool touch of Khari's tongue sliding across the tip of his cock. He clenched his hands in the sheet, holding himself still with iron will, panting against the unbelievable wet warmth of Khari's mouth and tongue around him.

"Holy...shit," he said under his breath when Khari lifted his head, glanced at him, then moved to taste and explore the crease of his groin and his balls, working down his thighs even as his hand came up to clasp his erection, moving almost lazily while he kissed each centimetre of flesh, going at his own pace. *Enjoying* himself, Eden realised, closing his eyes and handing himself over to the fantastic man who had haunted his dreams and called from the darkness for so many years. All sense of urgency faded and he gave himself to the moment; letting Khari do what he pleased and simply riding the waves of pleasure that swept through him as every part of him was brought to singing, glorious, life. From instep to earlobe, from chest to the back of his knees, every part of him, most never touched or known, sprang awake, buzzing and straining for more of Khari's attention.

"Still good?" Khari asked, speaking next to his ear.

"...hell yes,"

Khari kissed his mouth at long last. A gentle invasion that was at odds with the sheer strength and size of the man behind it. Asking quietly, not demanding. Sharing, not taking. Breaking down any barriers between them with quiet certainty and a sense of absolute rightness.

This was exactly where he belonged. Eden concentrated on the slowly building desire, reaching its crescendo deep in his gut. It spread hot and fast down his thighs and around to his back. It flowed down his spine and along his arms to his hands. He reached to hold Khari's neck, kissing him as he slipped his other hand down his chest to carry out his own explorations, determined to walk on the edge of release for as long as he possibly could.

As though hearing his thoughts, Khari slid to the side, turning Eden to face him. Kissing him deeply, without urgency. Content to move slowly and tenderly to hold them both on the brink for what felt like a lifetime. Reality faded. There was nothing and no one in the world except the two of them, and no rush to bring an end to the ebb and flow of a constant climax that held them both suspended in time, apart from the world that waited for them when they fell from the precipice of pleasure they balanced on the edge of, out of themselves and flying apart, then back together, with each beat of their hearts, before they finally fell off the cliff edge into oblivion.

Coming back to himself slowly, Eden rubbed his face against the soft skin of Khari's neck and pulled the quilt over their bodies, just about managing to move his arm. Every part of him was relaxed and sated. Heavy limbed and drowsy, he was content to lie tangled with Khari under the plush quilt. Warm and safe at last. He sighed his contentment, snuggling happily when Khari drew him closer and pressed his lips to Eden's head.

"You're okay?" Khari asked.

"I'm more than fine," he murmured in reply. "You?"

Khari held him close, eyes on his face. "I had no idea it could be like this."

"Me neither."

"I think it's rare."

Eden stroked the flat of his hand over Khari's hip and down his thigh, wanting to get closer although there was no room for even air between their bodies.

"You've really never...with anyone else?" Khari asked.

"Never. No one."

"It's absurd, but I'm pleased."

Eden planted a kiss on Khari's nose. He stretched across the bed and snagged the linen towel from the floor, carefully cleaning Khari then himself as best he could. Propping himself against the pillows he combed his fingers through his hair, unsurprised to find it clumped and tangled, still sweat-dampened. He frowned, looking at the ewer and basin, figuring out whether it could be washed over the bowl with nothing but a bar of soap.

It couldn't. He sighed to himself.

Khari reached for the cord next to the bed, dangling discretely from the ceiling, half hidden by the thick draperies of the bed hangings. Pulling it, he waited a minute, then called, "Come in," in response to a quiet knock on the outer door. He looked at the smartly dressed page, holding the quilt up to his chest as he sat up.

"Organise a bath for us, please," Khari said. "And a light meal, as well as some tea. Thank you, um..." He left the query hanging.

"Ascher, your Highness," the page said, bowing politely. "Will that be all?"

"For now. Thank you, Ascher."

Ascher bowed again and backed out of the bedroom, picking Eden's shirt from the floor of the doorway and folding it to rest over the back of a chair. The outer door of the suite closed quietly and silence fell once more.

"You're used to servants," Eden said. It was not a question.

"Sort of. I never had them, of course. Not in the Cells, and, well. You saw my home. It was hardly a place where I could expect to run a staff. But yes, I know how to handle having a staff. My mother was, after all, the Crown Princess—for all she was caged by that bastard brother of hers. She taught me and Gray from birth how to lead. Be in control. Command. It's my birth right, however much my circumstances may have been direly changed from what they may once have been." He looked at Eden, moving to sit and lean against the pillows on his left. "You're not used to servants? Despite all the jewels and riches you have?"

He shook his head. "My dad has a housekeeper who was my old nanny. She does the cleaning and laundry. That sort of thing. But she's hardly staff. I guess it just took me by surprise that you know how all this hierarchy works, and how you should behave in different situations, with different people. I guess I forget you're a prince."

"You find someone living in an underground warren, wearing rags, I suppose it would be hard to equate them with royalty." He flung the quilt aside, standing up to shrug into one of the robes that had been kindly supplied by Airell. Thick purple silk embroidered with creamy patterns at the hem and sleeves, the garment was richer than anything Eden had seen Khari wear. Khari looked down at himself and shrugged. "It's not exactly what I would have chosen for myself, but likely better than wandering around bare arsed in front of the housemaids."

"I like you wandering around naked, myself."

"Aye, I was right in my initial assessment. You are mad," Khari said. "You really mean that, don't you? The scars and everything really don't bother you."

"Only how they got there," Eden said honestly. "Thinking of you hurting makes me feel ill. But that's the thought of you being hurt. Not the sight of the scars you carry with you. They don't bother me at all. And as for having you wandering around naked? Oh, yeah...I have no issue with that at all." He got out of bed and slipped the other robe on, knotting the silken belt at his waist. He took the wine goblet Khari filled and passed to him, sipping the sweetly scented wine with full appreciation.

It was certainly a huge improvement to camping in the woods and at the edges of fields, grimy with the accumulated dirt and dust of several weeks travel. And to have Khari to himself, in his bed, to touch and hold...

He drew in a sharp breath, taken aback by the sudden jolt of electrifying awareness and arousal that flooded him. Good God...just the *thought* of Khari was enough to make him harden on the instant. It was as though he had found a new drug; more addictive than Heroin and just as lethal.

Looking knowingly at him, Khari's mouth quirked upwards. "You too?" he asked.

"Yeah." Eden scanned Khari's body. The silk robe, however thick and richly woven, was not enough to cover the fact that Khari had been hit by the same jolting hit of arousal.

"Don't lick your lips like that," Khari grinned, drinking his wine down and refilling his goblet. "I'd like the illusion of having *some* self-control where you're concerned."

Stupidly pleased at the effect he had on Khari, Eden ran his tongue over his top lip, chuckling under his breath. He drank his wine, forcing himself to hold back from launching himself into Khari's arms and begging for the beautiful elven prince to just *take* him.

Too soon, a small voice whispered at the back of his conscious mind. *Slowly.*

Shuddering, he held the goblet out for Khari to fill. "What are you doing to me?" he asked. "You've bewitched me."

"I don't have the answers for what's happening to us," Khari said. "I just know I don't want it to stop. That already I would die for you. Die without you. I have waited just as long as you have, Eden, for us to find each other. My friend, my lover...my everything. When I slept, and dreamt, it was you I called for and you came. Always, without fail, without question, you came and you bound me to this life when every fibre of my being would have gladly ended it. I *longed* for you, Eden. I prayed for you to find me. I have spent countless hours...days...on my knees, begging for you to come into my life and take me into yours. I don't have the answers for what it is happening now, but I'm too happy to care much. You're bewitching *me*. And you can go on doing it for the next several thousand years, and I will be happy at the enchantment. So long as I have you."

Eden closed the space between them and stood chest to chest with Khari to meet golden eyes. "You have me," he promised.

"There's no one else?"

"Why do you keep asking?" Eden asked. "There's only you. I give you my word."

"I can't...share...you," Khari said, hesitant. "That doesn't sound how it's meant. If you are coming to me with a past, then I can deal with it...I'd make myself deal with it. Just...you're so *special*, Eden, and to think you're *mine*? I can't fall into this and then find that you have a whole other life in your world, and this is just a fling. I can't be used like that and I don't have the strength to lose you. You're...you're *mine*. If you...I think what I'm trying to say, is that if you really want me—and I can't imagine why you would!— then..."

Eden held his finger over Khari's lips, quieting him. "You want exclusive."

Khari kissed his fingertip, his eyes were worried.

"Good. I don't do casual. I couldn't bear for you to go off screwing other guys behind my back, or in front of it," he added. "There has never been anyone else, Khari. Just you. Always you. I won't hurt you."

"Despite everything, Eden...it's only been you for me. I'm *choosing* this, and that's a huge thing. All the baggage I'm bringing with me...I'm scared you'll find it too much."

Eden gathered Khari into his arms and held him close, looking up into his eyes. "I have strong arms." He kissed Khari softly. "Baggage is always easier to handle when there's more than one person to carry it. You don't have to carry it alone anymore. Share some of the load."

There was a silence that stretched for so long, Eden thought Khari was not going to say anything, then he drew a small breath.

"Thank you, Eden. I don't think I'm ready for you to know everything, yet. But thank you. I'm having trouble believing this is real and actually happening. That it's not some convoluted situation that my brain has created to torture me more. This is real, aye? All of it?"

"Oh, it's real. All of it. Every. Last. Bit," Eden said, spacing his words with deliberately gentle kisses on Khari's full mouth. He tilted his head, watching as several maids filled a deep wooden tub, Ascher's quietly spoken instructions being followed without fuss. The scent of woody musk floated through the air, carried on the steam clouds rising up and away from the bath as it was filled.

The fire was stoked and cedar logs added to the flames to build it up until the quiet flames had become a living being, licking the walls of the huge stone hearth to heat the room and perfume the air. Ascher directed two more maids to strip the bed. Another two appeared as soon as the soiled sheets and quilt were removed to replace all the bedclothes. Minutes later, Ascher scanned the emptying bedroom, watching the last maid leave with her huge wooden pitcher. He bowed to Khari.

"Will you be requiring your meal as you bathe, Your Highness, or shall I have it sent to you in an hour?"

"Now, thank you, Ascher," Khari said without hesitation. "And some ale would be appreciated. The wine is as strong as whiskey!"

"Yes, your Highness. And your Highness? My Lord?" Ascher added, sweeping Eden a low bow. "I would just like you to know that it is an honour to serve you both. I will see to your meal." He backed out of the bedroom, closing the door to leave them in a steamy cosily lit space that spoke of silent seduction and sensory pleasure.

Eden closed his eyes and inhaled deeply, loosening his belt and letting the heavy silk fall to the floor in a puddle of purple. He slid into the steaming hot water and ducked his head under the surface before coming up for air.

Khari was sitting on the side of the bath, grinning at his actions. "Untold luxury," he said, adding scented liquid to the water and agitating the suds. He stood and shrugged out of his robe, stepping into the bath to sit opposite Eden. He was silent as Ascher returned to set up a table next to the bath and lay out cold meats, bread, cheeses and fruits, as well as a pitcher of ale and two tankards. Towels were placed over a rail in front of the fire, and then he was gone, leaving them to relax in private.

Khari lifted his tankard of ale in a toast, smiling when Eden held his up. "To the beginning," he said, his eyes flashing gold.

"The beginning," Eden repeated. "A new life."

Into the Woods: Searching for Eden, Part One.

PART TWO

Into the Woods: Searching for Eden, Part One.

Ж

I will find you, Gray. You cannot run from me, be in no doubt of that. I can destroy you, boy. I can ruin you.

Gray reaffirmed his hold on the bar and hauled his body upwards, arms burning with the strain. His father's voice echoed in his head. Jaizel's words were heavily accented, yet gently spoken. A cadence that belied the evil of the man speaking them.

"You will never destroy me," he hissed, lowering himself until his arms were almost straight. "You don't have as much power as you think."

And yet you run. Too scared to face me.

"It works both ways," Gray said, straining to lift himself again. "I don't see you actively trying to face me, Father. You have sent your armies and your animals, as though they would have a chance against me. Yet you don't have the courage to face me yourself, so you? Too scared to even enter the Tarenthian Forests, in case the ghouls sense your diseased heart and tear it from your chest." Gray dropped from the bar, landing softly.

Gray, I will find you. Bring Khari back and save yourself the agony of defeat. I shall spare your life, if you return home. You cannot hide forever.

Gray massaged his abused muscles, using his arms as windmills to try and ease the beginnings of an ache.

"Try me," he said to the voice haunting his mind,

wishing he could switch off the connection that allowed his father to torture him by talking to him telepathically. "I will never let you hurt us again. You will never get your filthy hands on Khari. You will not so much as lay eyes on him, until it is time for him to send you back to whichever hell spawned you." He shuddered, scooping a towel from the floor to mop at the sweat pouring down his face and body. "I will never let him get hurt again. Do not underestimate my loyalty, Father."

You are making a mistake, boy.

The voice rebounded in Gray's head for a second, then the connection was finally severed. Gray turned at a soft knock on the door to his suite. It was stupid, but he was still startled by having other people around him.

"Enter," he said, returning his attentions to wiping the rivers of sweat that seemed as though they would never stop.

The door opened to admit a Light Elf of average height. Dark blonde, her colouring was similar to Gray's own. Well built, yet not obscenely muscled; her head held with a dignity that screamed of good breeding and better than average self-awareness.

The woman was stunning enough to leave Gray flustered. He had thought Takana the most glorious female ever to walk the realms, but this woman sent his thoughts down paths that were new and unfamiliar. He held the towel to his glistening chest, feeling filthy as he swiped his forearm over his face.

"I don't think I have had the pleasure," he said, finding his voice.

"I think I would have remembered," she said, a small chuckle escaping her red lips. "You are really

Gray of Chiearatul? Jaizel's son?"

Gray turned away from the beautiful vision hovering just inside his doorway. Jaizel's son. He could live to be eight-thousand years old, and rule the worlds, but he would always be *Jaizel's son*.

"I am," he said. He yanked a human-style T-shirt over his head. Like Khari, he had found an undying love for the clothes worn by humans. Gifts from the king, he had a closet filled with jeans, shorts, sweatpants, sweaters, shirts and casual *tees*, as Eden called them. They might look out of place in the midst of all the Elven beauty that was present in Mount Chainia, but he much preferred their practicality.

Twisting his long tail of hair, hanging dripping down his spine, he knotted it at the nape of his neck and fixed it in place with a wooden stick. He draped the towel around his neck and turned to face the woman in his doorway again. She was looking at him with a thoughtful expression on her face.

"I meant no offense in the titles," she said, inclining her head. "But I never thought I would ever meet a Dark Elf. Let alone one as high-ranking as yourself...Your Highness. Forgive my phrasing, please. I just arrived home from the Human Realm last night and, as you may imagine, the stories I have been briefed on are, to say the least, rather fantastic for my mind to grasp without a small amount of disbelief. You are Gray, of Chiearatul. Consummate warrior, and possibly the saviour of at least two races. You saved a Chosen Child, when you were no more than a child yourself...and you have seen enough to last a thousand grown men a lifetime. I had to come and see you for myself, just to assure myself that this was not an elaborate hoax. Although, after meeting Prince

Khari and..." She hesitated, biting her lower lip, "it seems so wrong to simply call him Eden," she said.

"He insists," Gray said. "This is your home?" he asked, wondering just who this vision was.

"Oh, how rude of me! Forgive me, Your Highness. I am Elnara. Princess Elnara. You know my father."

Rapidly piecing together the few bits of the puzzle he had in his possession, Gray tilted his head to the side and realised Elnara *did* have a look of Takana about her. Takana looked like Alexander...

"You are Alex's daughter?" he asked.

She grinned and bowed.

"I am sorry for your loss," Gray said, reliving the nightmare moment Denny's head was twisted so violently to the side, breaking her neck. Leaving her to fall lifeless and boneless to the ground in front of Alex's feet. He swallowed the bile that rose in his throat at the memory. Too late. He was always a few steps behind, and people died because of his ineptness.

Elnara took a step towards him and laid a delicate, yet strong, hand on his forearm, squeezing lightly. "Thank you for your sorrow," she said, "and thank you for saving my father, Cole, and Takana. Despite my loss, it is thanks to you that I still have any family." She paused uncertainly before speaking again. "I never thought I would owe anything to a Dark Elf, least of all..."

"Jaizel's son," Gray said, understanding.

"Jaizel's son," she confirmed. Her hand still rested on his arm. She did not move it away. "It is an honour to be able to thank you in person, Your Highness."

"Please," he said, feeling the deep burn where her fingers lay on his still-damp flesh. "Call me Gray, Your

Highness."

"Only if you call me Elnara," she said, dimpling up at him.

"Elnara," he agreed.

The sound of approaching footsteps echoed from the outer hallway. He looked at the door to his rooms as Khari and Eden appeared, looking exhausted and as soaked with fresh sweat as Gray had been. For Khari to be tired gave Gray some idea of how hard the two men had been worked that morning. Airell trained himself and his armies with a fervour that even Jaizel fell short of. Disciplined, strict, with not an inch given for any kind of weakness, the Light King's friendly and playful exterior hid a warring general with a spine of the hardest diamonds.

Khari grabbed for the jug of ale on Gray's drinks cabinet and lifted it to his mouth without looking for a mug, drinking steadily, his Adam's Apple bobbing up and down his throat for several long seconds. Gray saw the amused glint in Elnara's eyes—cornflower blue, shot with lines of sapphire expanding from the inky depths of her pupils—as she watched his brother.

Eden had noticed Gray. He flapped his long Elven shirt away from his chest. Casting a fond eye at Khari, he crossed the reception room to bow to Elnara. "A pleasure to meet you again," he said, glancing at where her hand *still* rested on Gray's arm. He looked at Gray, his face bland, but there was a flicker of something calmly joyful at the back of his stunning silvery-green eyes.

One had to know what to look for, but after a few weeks around Eden, one could learn to use him as an emotional barometer, as well as using the smallest signs in his eyes to predict whether something was a good plan, or one that could lead to certain death. Gray doubted Eden even knew what he did. He did not, Khari said, realise who or what he was. Not fully. He had skills and powers within him that were dormant. Untapped and unrecognised. But sometimes they leaked out through his eyes and could be used to gauge a situation, if one knew what they were seeing in the shimmering silvery depths.

"The pleasure is mine...Eden," Elnara said. "I thank you for not shaking my hand without warning, this time," she added. "Falling in a heap at your feet was rather undignified."

"Yeah, sorry about that," Eden said. "It fades in time. The initial...recognition...is the worst, I reckon. We're not interrupting, are we?" he asked, looking between Elnara and Gray. "You said to come here after training. We can come back later if you want us to?"

"No, not at all," Gray said. He looked at Elnara. "Would you like to join our party?" he asked, his mouth drier than warranted by the exercises he had completed.

"I would not like to presume," Elnara said, although her hand on his arm said otherwise.

"No presumption," Khari said, strolling to stand near Eden. His happiness made Gray's heart swell. "We would love to have company." Khari flapped his shirt away from his chest, fanning himself. "Training this morning was harder going than I expected, though, so I will go back to my rooms and wash before we set off, if that's all right, Gray?" he said, looking for permission to leave—a habit that set Gray's nerves on edge. He hated Khari servile and unsure. "I came here first...in case I was late...but if you want to set off, then a bath can wait."

Eden rolled his eyes and wandered to drink from the ale jug.

"Go and wash," Gray said. "I will do the same." He said as Khari left, then met Elnara's eyes. "He gets worried he'll do something wrong or out of place. Upset someone, perhaps. It's a habit that I haven't broken even after four years." He swept a glance over Elnara's clothes. A long gown in a light fabric that rippled in the slight breeze and dainty slippers. "You may wish to change into something you will not mind getting dirty," he said, finally finding the courage to lay his hand over hers. "I would not want to be responsible for the ruin of such finery."

"Where shall I meet you all?"

"The west gardens. At the fountain. An hour?"

Elnara slid her fingers out from under his hand and stroking his arm. "I will count the minutes, my prince," she said, leaving on silent feet.

"Likewise," he said to the empty doorway. "I cannot wait."

"You got it bad," Eden said. He sat on the edge of the marble fountain, one leg tucked into his chest and the other swinging idly down, his booted foot not quite skimming the ground. "She is very pretty though," he added.

Gray looked sideways at Eden, who smiled, eyes crinkling.

"I'm gay, not blind," Eden said. He looked to the

east entrance of the garden a few seconds before Khari emerged with Takana and Cole. The flare of silver light expanding around his pupils made Gray hide a grin behind his hand.

"And *I* have it bad, do I?" he asked.

"Oh, you don't know the half of it," Eden said, his eyes on Khari. "Not a quarter."

Gray wished he did know a quarter of whatever emotion blazed through Eden and Khari. The force of whatever they felt for each other was tangible and left all those in their orbit breathless. What it must be like to be at the centre of the maelstrom was unimaginable.

"I don't think I could have lost him to anyone more worthy of him," Gray said, quietly. "Thank you. For coming for him."

Eden met Gray's gaze, eyes flashing silver for a moment before they settled back to emerald. He held a hand on Gray's arm, squeezing as he spoke. "I should be the one thanking you. For keeping him alive so I could be with him. Thank you isn't a big enough word, though."

"To not save him would have meant the death of my soul," Gray said. "The worlds need my brother in them." *And you*, he thought, but did not say. "My mother gave her life for him. I could not dishonour her memory by not being prepared to do any less. He had to live. Has to live. He is Khari...he is needed in the worlds."

"He is. More than you can know." Eden jumped down from his perch on the fountain edge. Airell and Elnara appeared in the archway of the southern entrance to the gardens. "Close your mouth," Eden said to Gray. "She likes you just as much. Just be yourself and see what happens, huh?"

"You've seen something in my future."

"Maybe." Eden walked to Khari, taking both his hands in his own as Khari planted a soft kiss on his mouth. Gray turned his full attention to Airell, bowing from the waist as the king approached.

Airell rolled his eyes. "Stand up. Sons rarely bow to their fathers," he said. "It makes me decidedly uncomfortable to see you bowing to me."

Gray straightened. It was taking time to adjust his way of thinking. Airell was his legal father. He knew that, on an intellectual level. Jaizel might have sired him, but as his mother had not been married to her twin, legally Gray was Airell's son. Something Airell seemed to not only accept, but embrace.

It was all very strange.

Elnara grinned and danced over to his side. "I shall call you cousin!" she exclaimed, taking his arm. "Do my clothes meet with your approval, cousin?" she asked, her voice low enough to be for his ears only. Well, and Khari's, but she would have to be a mile out of range for his brother to not hear her words. The boy was unbelievable in his talents.

Gray looked down at Elnara and found a large smile spreading across his face. Her hair had been swept into a high bun, twisted into a casual knot of dark-blonde, accentuating her cheekbones and the almond shape of her blue eyes. Her neck looked as delicate as her mother's had been...

No, he was not going to think of that. Not today.

Her torso was covered in a pale grey sweater, made in the human style, and her legs were encased in low-hanging loose jeans. She wore a pair of what Eden called baseball boots.

Gray grinned wider and told her she looked

amazing, starting to laugh as she twirled to show off her outfit, explaining it was what she normally wore when she was at university. She had made an effort to dress up to meet him, thinking it fitting, despite being told Gray and Khari had a penchant for dressing in the human style, he learned, deciding he could listen to her talking forever.

"It will take some getting used to, wearing these clothes at home," she confided, taking his arm again. "Normally I only wear these clothes when I am at university. I am educated in Human Realm, you understand. My father's eyebrows may take at least a month to descend from his hairline, seeing me *here* in my jeans."

"He has allowed you to venture past your rooms in trousers, however," he said.

"Oh, pish," she said. "It was never going to be an issue. He just likes me to look as though I am made of glass. I am his little princess, both literally and figuratively. He would have Aunt Takana dressed in chiffon gowns and tiaras if he thought she would let him. Cole would likely laugh until he sprained something, but my father sees no reason why women cannot be both beautiful and deadly. What are your views on the matter? What would the consensus be in your lands?"

Gray shrugged, plucking a bloom from one of the bushes they passed. He pulled the purple petals from the stem, conscious of Elnara's hand tucked into the crook of his arm. "The consensus in my lands, as they are at present, would see you executed," he said. "You have your head uncovered, and are wearing the clothes of a male," he added, pointing at her jeans. "Worse, you are dressed as a human. The sentence is death."

Elnara paled. "And your views?"

"I think..."

"Do you agree with the sentence?"

"Not at all," Gray said, closing his eyes against the memories from his childhood. "There are not words to sufficiently express my abhorrence." He paused before looking down at Elnara's face, gathering his words. "I think my views are radical, even in this realm," he said quietly.

"And what are your views? Were we talking about your wife, for example?"

"I would not like a servile wife. Nor yet an inferior one. I want an equal partner. I believe women are, and should be treated as, equals. If you choose to wear a gown, then fine, but that should be your choice; you would look just as beautiful in battle trousers and a tunic. It should be up to you," he finished, remembering the nightmare of watching his mother dragged by her uncovered hair to the whipping post, her clothes torn from her as she screamed, simply because she had worn a pair of trousers and a shirt to clean the floors of their rooms. Unwilling to invite a beating for dirtying the impractical gowns Jaizel insisted she wear, she had changed into men's clothing to clean, knowing the grimy floor would likewise earn her a beating from her brother.

She had tried everything to avoid his fists and whip. Nothing worked.

"You have gone pensive," Elnara said, her hand tightening gently in the crook of his arm. "You have some bad memories, I would imagine. I am sorry for bringing them to the forefront of your mind. It was not my intention. May I ask what makes your eyes so sad?"

"I was thinking of my mother," he said, shaking his head. "It is not a subject for such a fine day as today." He forced a smile. After a moment, it felt genuine. Following Eden as he wove through the garden towards the paths that would lead them to the ancient temple-mountain, he held Elnara's hand in place, liking the fit of it in the crook of his elbow.

"She was a beauty, was she not?" Elnara asked. "I never, of course, had the chance to meet her, although I would have liked to very much, but I found a portrait of her in the king's suite once, when I was young. I was exploring and generally doing things I had no business doing, in places I had no business to be, and I found a small portrait. Her beauty astounded me and held me captive for what seemed like hours. Airell found me, of course, and saw that I held what I know *now* to be something most precious...and he told me that she was his wife, but she had gone far away from him. I think it may have been easier to talk of it to a baby—I was no more than two, I think—because he sat and he told me how deeply he loved the beautiful woman in the portrait. That she was the Queen. His Queen. And that he hoped, one day, she would choose to come back to sit at his side. Wherever she wanted that to be. Whichever world. He would go where she desired.

"I held the picture, and I understood. I could not comprehend how anyone could look at a face like hers and not be willing to walk over coals for her. To fight dragons for her...she was so, so beautiful," Elnara said. "Airell said her name, but I could not say it properly. Just *Laze*. That was about all I could get my tongue around," she said, grinning at Gray. "Airell said Laze was her nickname. I told myself, that day, that I would try to grow as beautiful as Queen Laze. Alas, I am still trying. I doubt I have half her poise or grandeur."

Looking at Elnara, Gray tried to picture her with an added thousand years of life and experience. "I think you have just as much poise and elegance as my mother," he said quietly. Honestly. "And all of her beauty."

"No. And I do not say it to fish for compliments," Elnara added, shaking her head. "Even in a small portrait, she looked so regal, yet so serene. As though she was laughing at the world, and could see all its folly. She was...she was..."

"She was a lot older than you are," Gray chuckled. "I think a lot of her poise was learned over millennia."

"Millennia?" Elnara gasped. "I thought she was Airell's age!"

"No. My mother was far over a thousand years when she was murdered," Gray said. "At least three times Airell's age. Eleven-hundred? Maybe as much as twelve-hundred."

"Yet she looked so young. Did she find the elixir for eternal youth? Even for an elf, to not age at all, at over a thousand years old? How fantastic!"

The thought of Jaizel still fresh in his mind after the morning's communications, he shrugged. "Neither my mother or father aged past thirty," he said. "I asked Mother, once. She joked that it was the magic of being a twin. The last I saw Jaizel, he looked not a lot older than I do."

"How many years do you have, cousin? I thought not to ask, but now I must."

"I am twenty-two. Do not look so scared."

"She was over a thousand when she *started* her family?"

"No. There were others. She had daughters," Gray said, looking at his feet as he walked. "I think perhaps Jaizel could not accept the stain on his masculinity, perhaps. None survived their first weeks."

Elnara held her hand to her mouth. "Oh, your poor, poor mother. To endure such loss. Such heartbreak. Daughters brought him such shame that he...he killed them?"

"I cannot be certain, but I believe so," Gray said. "I do not know how many...my mother could not tell me with any accuracy. Their loss left her more traumatised than she could say, I think. I would wake, sometimes, in the night, and hear her sobbing. When she was carrying Khari, she lived in terror. It was a palpable fear I thought I could have touched and found wrapped around her soul. She lived with an abject terror that her baby would be female, and die, as the others had died. She clung to her pregnancy, praying to hold the child safe forever...she said that she loved its father. That if this child were to die, she could not see a way forward...she...even then, she would have died to save her baby."

Elnara wiped at her eyes with the pad of her thumb. "I feel such sympathy for her," she said. "What a terrible predicament she found herself in."

"This is a maudlin topic of conversation," Gray said. "I apologise. It was unforgivable of me to make you so...so..."

"Soggy?" Elnara asked. "It is not maudlin. It is your past, and in turn, I am honoured that you would see fit to share something so dear to you with me. However, a change of subject for now would probably be expedient. I hope I am not presumptuous in wishing for other occasions to talk of your life before I met you. I would like, very much, to know you."

"I would like that."

"Then it is settled. You may collect me after dinner and we shall talk through until sunrise."

Gray was diverted. "Would you not need to sleep?"

"I am growing older. I sleep only half as much as I did a year ago." Elnara peeked up at him through her eyelashes. "I am twenty-three," she said, answering the question on the tip of his tongue. "I shall rest tomorrow night, should I feel it needful. Tonight, cousin, we shall talk through to the dawn."

Gray took another flower from a dangling tree branch. "Your father will not mind?" he asked.

"Mind me openly chasing the eldest son of our king? Oh, I doubt it."

Gray looked over at Alex, not at all surprised to find the older man's eyes fixed on him. He swallowed nervously. Then Alex grinned, gave a quick wink, and mouthed, "*Good luck.*" His face held all the pride and exasperation of a proud father—and held something else. Something that told Gray he really did not mind his daughter hanging onto Gray's arm.

Something close, Gray thought, to approval.

"So where are we going?" Elnara asked. "Stop checking my father—he is a big softy, really."

"I take it you have not seen him in battle," Gray remarked. Alex was awesome, and not at all soft. "We're going down to the ancient Temple, at Eden's direct request. He has been wanting to explore down in the bowels of the mountain since the day we arrived three weeks ago. However, the arrival of the king's son—"

"Sons," Elnara interjected. "Sons, plural."

"Sons," Gray corrected. "The arrival of his sons, as well as that of Eden has meant that there has been much for him to do, before he could find the time to allow us to explore..."

"I cannot imagine which happenstance affected him most," Elnara said. "Should Eden have turned up on my doorstep, I think it likely I would have screamed, hit him with something iron, then ran as fast as I could."

"You would have *what*?" Gray asked, raising his eyebrows. "You cannot be serious!"

"I most certainly am. I would never have believed him to be who he is. I would have taken him for a demon in the skin of a...oh, Orien's Blood, I do not have the name for what he is. Suffice to say that I should not have believed him to be who he is. I would have stunned him as best I could, and ran before the demon beneath the visage could get into my soul."

Gray shook his head. He walked on, chuckling with Elnara as they wandered past the older trunks of gnarled and twisted elms, their roots deep beneath the pale pink marble underneath their feet.

"Anyway," he said, once he had a grip on himself and his laughter under control, although it still threatened to overflow. "Eden feels drawn to the ancient temples. He says he can hear them calling him."

"Hardly a surprise, one would have thought," Elnara said, staring at Eden's broad shoulders ahead of them.

"No, hardly a surprise," he agreed. "He feels drawn to them, and as the days have passed, he has been feeling more and more agitated that he has not seen them. Having *finally* convinced the king...*Father*...that Khari is more than able to stop a cave-in and we are all perfectly safe, we are exploring the depths of the mountain today."

"How exciting," Elnara said. "Goodness me, I have wanted to go down instead of up for what feels like a lifetime! As soon as I found out I was banned from venturing down those stairs, I have longed to do just that."

"After knowing you for less than half a day," Gray said drily, "I am surprised you did not simply do as you pleased."

"I would have, except for the small issue of possibly having a mountain fall on my head because I trod on the wrong stair, or touched a pull-cord that I should have left well alone. Your brother, Khari, can stop the danger?"

"He can."

"All right." She glanced at the carved archway up ahead of them, a dark space leading to something more ancient than they could reference easily. So old that only vague memories of an aged grandparent's tale existed to describe what could lay beneath their feet. Even Airell could not say with any surety what they might find as they descended. He had only gone down to fifty metres below the ground—the once heard snippets of long forgotten stories said that the temples were hundreds of feet below. Thousands. A day's walking, some said. Others still said that men had got lost and disorientated, and starved, never seeing the light of day again.

Nonsense, perhaps, but then again, it was a risk no one had wanted to take. Until now. Until Eden had entered all of their lives with the burning vitality of something so alive it was close to holy.

It *was* holy.

"Well," Elnara said, "onwards into the void. Don't let go," she said, taking Gray's hand in her own. "I admit to a small frisson of fear...do not let go of me."

Gray tightened his hold around the warm fingers, linking them with his own. He looked into her eyes and lost his breath for a second as his heart stuttered in his chest. He blinked as his world shifted subtly.

"I will never let you go," he promised. "I don't think I can."

XVI

One eye on Khari, the other on the spiralling stairwell descending down, down, down, into the heart of the mountain. Gray kept a tight hold of Elnara's hand and followed Khari's glow lights. Uncomfortably warm, he swiped his forearm over his face. The further down they went, the hotter the air around them became, cloying in his throat and lungs, making breathing difficult. The walls seemed to close in on him as he stepped downwards in a never-ending spiral. The darkness, without Khari's lights, was absolute. The ancient mountain hummed, a deep resonance that echoed in Gray's head and heart.

He wondered how was Eden coping, if it was having this effect on him. Eden could see and hear more than all of them, even Khari. To him, the walls must be roaring as loudly as a crowd baying for the blood of a criminal on an executioner's block. Gray immediately wished he hadn't thought of that. He was close to deciding he was likely walking to certain death. There could be nothing good hidden so far under the palace. Good things were not concealed deep in the earth, hidden from view. The only reason to bury anything this deep would be to stop the rot coming to the surface of the soil and infecting...

"Gray?" Eden was crouched in front of him, holding a hand on his knee. Elnara stood next to him, her knees level with Gray's eyes. "Are you okay?"

Eden asked. "How badly are you hurt?"

He shook his head. "What happened?"

"You fell," Khari said, squatting down on the stair beneath where Gray sat. "Fainted, I think."

"You said that the veil is too weak, then you fell," Elnara said, stroking his hand. "Do you know what veil?"

"Not a clue. How mortifying," he groaned, meeting Khari's eyes to see worry shining in the golden depths that had fascinated him since the moment Khari had been given to him to hold at an hour old. "I'm all right," Gray said, accepting the flask of cool ale Takana passed down the stairwell to him. He sipped, then drank more before capping it and passing it back.

"Passing out and speaking in tongues is Princess' job, Gray!" Cole called from a few steps above. "We stopped, and I thought, oh, great, Princess has gone into one..."

"Shut up, fool," Eden said, grinning over Gray's head.

"Princess?" Elnara asked, raising a brow.

"I was passed out and hypnotised by your dad when Cole first saw me," Eden explained. "He insists I'm a princess, like Sleeping Beauty or Snow White."

"And he looks too beautiful to be a bloke!" Cole said loudly. "No man should have inch long eyelashes and be able to pull off a doe-eyed look."

"He's jealous," Eden said. He studied Gray. "You're sure you're okay? You look peaky."

"Aye, I'm sure I'll be all right," Gray said. "I think it was the heat. And it's so far down. I never thought I suffered with claustrophobia, but I felt a bit panicky," he confessed.

Gray looked down the stairs, as though he could see around the curves of the circular walls to what lay beneath. He shuddered.

Eden shared a look with Khari. He looked over Gray's head. "We should take a five minute break," he said, his tone brooking no argument. "We can eat a small lunch and rehydrate? Takana?"

"Yes?"

"You see the veils and weak spots, and know what it is you're looking for. Are we near a split or divide between worlds or realms?"

Gray breathed out, stunned that Eden had read him so easily. But then, Eden could see him even when he was invisible, so he should not be surprised that his mind could be read.

"This entire mountain is at the crux of the join between all possible worlds," Takana said. Gray heard her braids chime as she moved. "I think that if one wanted to be able to hold the secrets of the codex for every world, then here is the place to be. It's strong, though," she added. "Even for me, it's stronger here...the sense of being surrounded by, I don't know," she said thoughtfully. "It's hard to explain, but it is like being in a room filled with draping gauzes. Each gauze can be moved aside to reveal a secret behind it. Each secret holds the key to something unknown, and there are...dozens."

No, it was more than dozens, Gray thought. He could feel hundreds. Thousands. Worlds that had not yet been walked on; lands unclaimed; realms left locked and barred from the other side, protecting them from the evil beyond. He could hear the ghosts and feel the brush of the chiffon curtains in his mind as they blew aside to show him a glimpse of lands no one else could see.

"Give the man some space, love," Alex said, touching Elnara's elbow.

"No," she replied, "I most certainly will not." She sat on the step, next to Gray, and took his hand in hers, holding it firmly.

"That told you, Alexander," Airell joked.

"You are a seer?" Elnara asked Gray.

"So Takana tells me," he said. He accepted one of the flatbreads filled with rice and curried meat, taking a bite. He grunted his approval. "This is good."

"Thanks," Khari murmured. "I, uh...Dad introduced me to the kitchen staff."

"We have been teaching them some basic recipes," Airell said. "Your mother's old recipes, in the main, but some excellent broths and marinades too."

Gray ate until everything he had been given was consumed, savouring the flavours of Chiearian spices and familiar foods.

"You see other realms?" Elnara asked him. "That must be amazing...and terrifying."

"I am getting used to it, but slower than I would like," he said. "It's easier, now I know what it is I'm feeling. Before Takana helped me, I thought I was afflicted by some kind of seizures. Too many head injuries, maybe," he said, sharing a small grin with Khari. It was an old joke between them. Whenever something the slightest bit out of the ordinary happened to either of them, or something was mysterious or unexplained, then it was happening because they had been hit too hard around the heads when they were small.

Morbid humour, maybe, but it had helped them cope with what their lives had become.

"At least we have that excuse," Khari said, his face bland although his eyes shone with mirth. "Eden hears rock speaking, and he was never knocked out."

"He's odd," Gray agreed.

"You're feeling better?"

"Aye, much. Sorry I scared you."

"Don't say sorry, Gray," Khari said, leaning forward to rest his forehead on Gray's shoulder. He hugged him in a move that brought tears to Gray's eyes and a lump to his throat.

Gray knew at that moment that he would love Eden until his dying breath, just for making his brother feel as though he could reach out for another person. The last time Khari had willingly touched him, he had been ten years old and their mother had been alive. Hesitantly, he raised his arms and slipped them around Khari's back, one hand stroking up to cup the crown of his head, as he had done so many times when he had been a baby.

"I'm all right, baby brother," he said next to Khari's ear, stroking his fine blonde hair with the tenderness of a parent soothing a child.

"You're sure?"

"I'm sure, aye. It was just...an episode, Khari love."

"You should tell your betrothed about this. Prepare the poor woman."

"Betrothed? We just met this morning."

"Eden said. Don't let her go. I want to see you happy."

"Shall we go?" Airell asked as Gray kissed Khari's cheek and patted his head before he dropped his arms. They felt strangely empty without his brother's warmth there. And strength. When had his baby brother got so *strong*?

He watched as Eden took Khari's hand and led him down a few stairs, turning out of Gray's sight. Leading him down further. Taking him away?

Not away. Never away. Leading him to where he should be.

It seemed as though they had been descending for hours. Hot, sweat-soaked and with pressure in his ears from being so far beneath the surface, Gray took a moment to truly believe the hellish downward climb was finally at an end. He staggered a few steps into a wide hallway, carved through impossibly light stone and arched high above their heads. Clasping his discarded T-shirt in his hand, along with Elnara's sweater, he leant against the wall and waited for the rest of their party to stumble away from the final step and onto level ground.

Elnara tugged her clingy undershirt away from her chest, flapping it in futility to try and get some air.

Gray felt pity for her; it was unbearable for the men, topless and, in Cole's case, stripped down to undershorts—for the women in the group it must have been horrific to have the added layers of breast-bindings and essential shirts to preserve their modesty.

Eden slid down the wall and sat with his head on his knees, gasping to try and catch a breath. Khari looked too exhausted to do more than lean his head back against the stone and close his eyes. The glow-lights flickered briefly, giving Gray some indication of just how drained his brother had become. He had seen them flicker once, maybe twice, in the four years they had lived underground. Once, definitely. He remembered the day Khari had been arrow-shot in their woods as though it was yesterday. The sheer terror that had swept through his veins as he watched his beloved brother fall to the ground, blood pumping too quickly for it to be mistaken for a flesh wound. Khari had healed the arterial puncture. Had sealed the gaping wound through his heart with his powers, and had promptly passed out into a coma that lasted sixteen long days and nights.

He had not urinated. Had not defecated. Had not sipped or moved his tongue to lap at the sodden cloths Gray held to his mouth. He had barely breathed, and each small intake of air into his lungs had rattled...yet the lights in their burrow had stayed lit. They had flickered, and dimmed down to the merest hint of light, but they had stayed glowing.

How much had the journey into the heart of the mountain drained Khari?

"Are you going to be all right?" Gray asked him. He didn't bother asking if he was all right at this moment; any fool could have seen he was far from anything close to being all right.

Khari gave smallest inclination of his head. Sweat ran in rivulets of tears down his face and neck, cutting paths down his chest and to the waistband of his jeans.

Airell staggered to Khari's side and looked him over. "Do you need to lie down?"

Khari slumped the instant Airell's arm slid around him to stop him simply hitting the floor. Gray heaved himself over to his brother and checked him over, watching Khari's eyes roll back in his head. The ground beneath them rumbled ominously and Khari startled awake again. The lights brightened even as the strain made his neck muscles stand out like cords.

Gray looked around, understanding. Khari was holding the mountain. Reforming it and strengthening it. Making sure they would not all meet their end here, miles underground, never to be found or seen again.

"I said this would be too much for you," Airell scolded, holding an ale flask to Khari's mouth.

"I'll be...all right," Khari said. "Just need to be still for a while, aye? Just need to sleep..."

Gray swept Khari's hair back from his eyes, studying him. Elnara crouched at his side and opened a small bag tied to her belt.

"What's that?" Gray asked.

"Dried Paheka root mixed with loberry."

"Elnara! What are you doing with loberries?"

"They're medicine," she said to Alex, scooping a spoonful into the ale before forcing Khari to drink. "I don't use them as a drug, but I thought it better to be prepared than otherwise. They're a stimulant," she said to Gray. "Better a bit high than passed out, considering our current predicament. And the comedown is not too laborious, I am assured by those who would know. He may feel shaky in a few hours, but he should be able to sleep as it leaves his system."

Khari opened his eyes, taking a few seconds to focus on anything. He blinked, then shuddered and sat up. "What have you given me?" he asked. "I feel pissed."

"Awake, though?" Airell asked.

"Aye, but awake and totally fucked over!" Khari said, lurching to his feet. He swayed, holding his head.

"It feels as though I've been...no. No, not as though I'm drunk. I feel fucked, but it's not a drunken binge kind of fucked. I feel..."

Elnara smothered a grin as Khari span in a circle and bounced in place.

"Orien's tits," Gray said, staring at her, "he's off his face, Elnara!"

"Oh yes," Elnara said, beaming with satisfaction. "I'll keep him topped up until the area is secure, then I'll lower the doses to minimise the comedown."

"You, madam, are dangerous," Takana said as she passed her niece. She patted Ellie's cheek. "Witch blood, I swear it. I would check your pedigree, if I were you."

Alex frowned at Khari, then at his daughter. "Promise me you do not use this yourself."

"Do I look like a zombie, father? I do not use the stuff, but good medicine is knowing when it is time to use a certain drug. This is controlled, and he is highly unlikely to get addicted after one episode."

"It's addictive?" Eden asked, looking at Khari as he danced along the hallway and back again.

"Oh, extremely so," Elnara said. "Those who use it enough find they cannot face the world without it. It consumes them. However, in the right hands, and at the right time, the effects are very...handy."

Eden chuckled. "Okay," he said. He walked to Khari and pulled him into his arms. "How about me and you waltz and see where this leads, huh?" he asked, as he was swept away along the hallway. Khari muttered something, making Eden blush hotly. "I don't believe you suggested that," he said, just loud enough for Gray to hear. "We have company!"

Gray strained his ears just enough to hear Khari's

next suggestion, and coughed loudly as the heat rose in his cheeks, hoping no one else had heard him. Judging by Elnara's pink cheeks, she had excellent hearing. He groaned to himself.

"You drugged him, Ellie. Whatever he says is on your shoulders," Cole said, grinning as he sauntered off in his undershorts. "Even the stuff that sounds physically impossible." He sniggered as Khari misjudged how loud a whisper was meant to be. "That one, however, is extremely possible. And good fun. Right, my love?" he asked Takana, who gave him the finger. He raised his eyebrows and grinned. "Well, that's the graphic visual description," he said to Elnara. "Did they forget to mention that loberry is one of the single most potent aphrodisiacs in any world, Ellie? When they told you about its...buoyant effects? The poor man is going to be a walking hard on for the next three hours, with the dose you gave him."

"And then, I will watch you as I take you in my mouth and..."

"And that is more than any father ever wants to hear," Airell interrupted. "Loberry. God help our ears for the duration. Alex, you really should have let her go to the college of apothecaries. At least then she would know to dilute it with a good dose of elderflower and primrose oils. It at least stops a man from thinking his cock will pop."

"Khari!" Eden snapped. "God, man! Get a grip on yourself!"

"You'd love it!"

"Oh, I likely would, but I am *not* losing my virginity in front of your family, on a floor, miles underground! No."

"I wouldn't mind."

Gray giggled, unable to help himself. "He's going to be mortified when it wears off," he said. Then added, "Most likely," out of respect to the truth. "Maybe not. He doesn't have much of a brain-mouth censoring switch. And he doesn't get embarrassed. Um...it might just be the rest of us that are mortified. And Eden," he said, trying desperately not to laugh as Eden grabbed Khari's hand before it could plunge down his jeans. "Oh, goodness...this is priceless."

"I had no idea," Elnara said, wringing her hands together, her face blazing with embarrassed heat. "Please forgive me?"

"Don't do it!" Cole called. "Make her sweat and pay a forfeit first."

"Cole! That is my *daughter* you are referring to!"

"Oh, get the stick out your bum, Alex," Cole sang, taking Takana's hand. "You are related to everyone in the palace and half those in Chainia. If I were to avoid slighting your relations, then I would never speak again. And before you suggest it, no, it is not an option. Your daughter is old enough to purchase loberries, make the drug, and administer it—I say she is more than old enough to see the consequences of her actions, and just how much it can affect a bloke. She can be forgiven when it has worn off."

"I agree," Airell said. "You, young lady, will have the punishment of making sure Eden's virtue remains intact while Khari is on this induced rampage of hormones. Gray, help her."

"Yes...Father," Gray said. "He's not in danger?"

Airell shook his head. "The biggest danger is likely to be friction burns on his penis, trying to *cure* a permanent erection."

"Have you ever...?"

Airell grinned. "Once. It was an experience. Get to it, then, my girl," he said to Elnara. "Go and chaperone the elephant in *Musth* you have created. And with each crude suggestion, and every lunge at poor Eden's fly, just remind yourself that it's all thanks to you that he's *awake* enough to keep the mountain from falling."

XVII

It was a maze. A labyrinth of epic proportions that wound back on itself and led to more dead ends than it did pathways. The odd pile of bones in their way testified to how easy it would be to lose their way. It seemed the old tales were true, and people had indeed died down here, in the bowels of the earth, unable to find their way back to daylight. Each curled up or stretched out skeleton he passed, Gray found himself sending a prayer to whoever might be listening.

It did not take him long to equate his silent prayers for help to the slight stiffening of Eden's shoulders. Every time he prayed, the man in front of him tensed and lost the rhythm of his steps for a moment.

"Are you all right?" he asked eventually, too curious to stay silent.

Eden looked at him. "I hear voices," he said simply. "Sometimes they're louder than others. It kinda hurts my head some," he shrugged, absently moving Khari's hand as it crept down to his crotch.

"What does it sound like?"

"I dunno, exactly. Whispers, mostly. Snatched words at the edge of hearing. Very faint. Almost like static...oh, you don't know what static sounds like. It's kinda a constant susurrus of sound. A million voices at the edges of my mind, calling me. Reaching something I don't got much of a clue how to give them." He shrugged again. "I dunno. It's always been there. Just it's louder right now. Likely where I'm a bit stressed," he said, rolling his eyes and slapping Khari's hand away from his groin. "Oh, this way," Eden said, perking up and taking a left. "I knew I would find my bearings as soon as he stopped trying to go down on me in front of your dad."

Elnara shook her head. "I am so, so, sorry," she gasped. "I really had no idea."

"Well, now you do," Eden said. "I'll see the fun in it when I ain't dying of shame."

"Aww, Princess," Cole said. "There's no shame in it. None at all."

Gray saw the seriousness in Eden's eyes and frowned. He moved Khari into Elnara's capable hands—she would be safe enough; Khari had zero sexual interest in women—and took Eden by the arm, walking quickly to get some distance from the others.

"Shame?" he asked quietly. "Shame about what? Khari?"

"What? No!" Eden said, looking appalled. "God, no. No, I'm not the least bit ashamed of him. Ever. And not now, although it's not nice to have him like this. No, I'm not ashamed of him."

"Then why are you dying of shame?"

Eden glanced at him, casting him sideways looks as they walked on through the maze. "Where I come from, it's not...normal...for a guy to be with a guy. Well, it is normal, but there's people who don't...it's not universally accepted, I mean. For two guys to be...uh..."

Gray took his flask from his back pocket and offered it to Eden. "Two men to be fucking?" he asked, noticing Eden's flinch at the words. "Two guys to make love to each other?" he tried. Eden still flinched.

He frowned. "You're saying that in your world, the world you were raised in and knew as your own, that as a man who is sexually attracted to other men, you were on the edges of mainstream society?"

Eden wouldn't meet his eyes. "Gay. We call it gay."

"I was born in Asanthal, not a barn," Gray said drily. "I heard you say you were gay. Happy never seemed to fit the context, so I deduced your meaning. Gay. So what? You are not allowed to be gay in your world?"

"Yeah, you are. I mean, where I lived, yeah. Where I was born, oh, hell no. Other countries, you can be hanged. Shot. Thrown in jail...no, it's not allowed everywhere. And even where I lived there were bigoted bastards who would kick me sooner than shake my hand."

"You're ashamed of being gay?" Gray asked softly.

Eden shook his head quickly.

"Then what, Eden?" he asked, holding a hand on Eden's back. "You look as though you've eaten mouldy bugs. What's the matter?"

"Khari keeps...the things he's saying..." Eden explained. "We've made out and such, and we, uh...we..."

Gray stopped himself from rolling his eyes, but it was an effort. "Tell me. Be blunt. Say it as it is, and don't hold back, Eden. Your hesitancy means I have to fill in the blanks and, as with all blank spaces, any number of words or pictures may fill them. What is the problem?"

"We haven't had sex," Eden muttered. "We've just jerked off and made out." Eden's face could have been on fire under his burnished skin. He glanced at

341

Gray and heaved in a breath. "I'd never so much as kissed a guy before I came here and met Khari. Certainly in my world, you don't *talk* about things like he's been doing...I only have the barest idea of the mechanics, and I sure as hell don't know half the things he's been sayin' today. In front of *everyone*!" Eden nearly cried. "And to make it all worse, I'm wanting more than what's happening between us, yet I don't got a fucking clue what it is I *want*! Khari talking like this today has me humiliated and horny as hell by turns."

Gray walked in silence for a little while, thinking.

"And now I freaked you out," Eden said.

"I'm not freaked out," Gray said, shaking his head. "Not at all. My race, hmmm. Elves see the art of seduction to be as important as the act of sex. More so. There are ways to build anticipation and heighten the senses."

"But Khari...after what happened to him..."

"After what happened to him, it makes the seduction even more of an art, and more important than you could imagine. It takes away the animal and replaces it with the mind. It is something higher than the immediate base instinct to bend someone over and fuck them. You see sex and intimacy as something to hide. Something shameful. Elves do not, Light or Dark—especially Dark. We see it as something to be celebrated and held up to the light of the sun to be nurtured and grow within us. We are direct, and we do not hide behind falsehoods and pretty words. We are truthful in matters of sex. What we want, what we like...the necessity of it, the need for it. It is a celebrated connection between two people. When it goes wrong...when someone uses another simply to make themselves cum? To use another body and not touch the mind behind the flesh? To us, that is a crime beyond words. The crime Jaizel is guilty of is actually unspeakable. He took a child and raped him. He took my mother and forced her to submit...and that actually shows a lot more weakness than it does strength. I don't know how to explain it to someone from a culture so completely different to my own."

"You're saying that everyone isn't looking at me and thinking it's vile?" Eden asked.

"What? Vile? Never, Eden! We are a race of changing faces and deceit. We can drag souls into our world and make them wither as they dance for our enjoyment. We are a race who can shift shape. Take human babes to lend our weakened warriors strength, and then dump that child back in the world it came from, without a clue who it is or how it got there. We are not a *nice* race. We are not a *friendly* race, and we have made lying our legacy. We cannot be trusted, unless you are one of our closest companions, yet we choose to give our trust, able to see through those who would do us wrong...

"We are all of that, Eden, and more besides, but we are completely honest and open in our beds, with the one we have chosen to share it with. We are naked in more ways than stripping away the layers of our clothes. When we speak in our beds, or when we speak intimately, about making love, about sex, about fucking...when we are talking of that, with the one we share ourselves with, then we are honest. Always honest. And honesty can never be seen as vile or wrong. Does that make it clearer for you, Eden? We *love* the act of love. We worship the honesty behind our nakedness, and we celebrate the pleasure we can give to our partners. It is *life* to our race. Can you understand that?"

The emotions flitting over Eden's face made Gray sigh to himself. How humans so managed to damage their young was astounding. To take the most beautiful act and make it as disgusting as Jaizel had been? To render a beautiful young man like Eden to a shamed shell, simply because he had natural wants and needs, the same as every other mammal?

To an elf, making love was the breath of life to a soul that could so easily become caged and corrupt from the power flowing within it. Did humans feel so shamed because they lacked power? Was that where Eden had got the idea he was disgusting for wanting, craving, the intimacy of another body joined with his own?

It was heartbreaking to see the emotional damage humans could cause, with nothing more than words.

"Takana said elves were great in bed," Eden said. "She said you're mostly evil bastards and can't be trusted as far as you could be thrown, but that you're damned good between the sheets."

"That's about as accurate a description as I could have given myself. Aye, I would say it's correct."

Eden glanced at Gray. "What if he leaves me?"

"He won't. He has chosen you."

"But what if?"

"Eden, he will not leave you. He would not dream of using you and then leaving. He will not touch you unless you enjoy every last fucking *second* of his hands on you. That is not our way. Jaizel is an anomaly. He is base. Low, disgusting. He is vile, and there are actually no words in our language for the crimes he has committed—because no elf would ever commit those crimes, and no elf ever had before he did. When an elf takes you to their bed, they have *chosen* for you to be there. That choice has to be a mutual thing; both partners have to choose—mutual consent. Even the whores are there by choice, in the main, where I come from. Once that choice is made, and the promise, however silent and wordless, is given, then we are bound as surely as though we are wed. Unless it is an understood casual liaison."

"But not married, so you can just leave, if you make that choice."

Gray shrugged. "It happens, but it is rare."

"Takana thought Cole had left her. It nearly destroyed her."

"I should imagine so," Gray said. "Yet he had not left her, and now they are to be married."

"I guess so. Do your kind ever wait until marriage before you get to the sex?"

"No, never. Marriage is sacred...you must be sure that your partner is who you choose to spend millennia with. That you are compatible. That you can love each other despite moods and disagreements. That you will always return by choice, if you walk out in a rage. That you would *choose* to go back, and do not return because the law says you must. The law says you are bound...a sacred law. It is one that cannot be broken, Eden. To break a vow given in marriage is unthinkable. A marriage is never entered into without serious thinking...unless there is to be a child, and then it would be unthinkable not to marry. To be a bastard carries more shame than anything else in these realms, except maybe being the parent of one."

"So Alex's father?"

Gray shrugged lightly. "It was a great shame on

him and his house, and especially for Takana. The stain will not leave the family, since Alex acknowledged Takana as his sister, publicly admitting his father's sin. His grandchildren's grandchildren shall still bear the shame of the crime Alex's father committed. It will be less, as he was royal, but not negated. And it shall be remembered."

Eden was watching him thoughtfully. Gray followed the silvery eyes as Eden glanced at Elnara, and shook his head.

"I am born of incest, Eden. My mother was my aunt and my father is my uncle. I do not care about Elnara's grandfather's sin. If she can accept me, considering my father and the evil that runs through my veins from the seed that created me, then I can accept any supposed sin her grandfather was guilty of. I care not for rules. I care for what is right. I care for survival and freedom. For the right to live freely without shame for who you are, or where you are from. I would heal the chasm between the worlds. Between the races. Between the sexes. I would see us all levelled and stood as equals...but that is me, and I am a nobody, now."

"You will never be a nobody," Eden said. Something flashed in his eyes that made Gray believe him. "You were created to rule. And you will. You just...it ain't something you'll do alone," Eden said, closing his eyes. "You will hold the crown, but it will come to rest on your head because of a lot of other people's actions. You will be led there. You won't purposely seek power. Your reluctance will see the start of the greatest empire any realm has ever seen. Those who wish for power should never have it. Those who are forced to it do not normally wish for it...but you will not be forced, and you will not want it. You will simply...you will be you. And that is all you have to be. Your family will be your strength and hold you when you think you will fall...your weaknesses will be your strength and give you empathy, leading you away from cruelty. You, Gray, will never be a nobody. You will rise to the pinnacle of absolute power...and your people will hold you there for an eternity."

Eden opened his eyes. The sparkling molten silver stunned Gray to the core. He watched the amazing creature who had called his brother to him and led him through a world of dreams to give him hope when hope was dead and buried. A man who was little more than a child, for all his muscle and height. The vulnerability in him was crushing, and yet he held knowledge that no person had ever had before.

"You saw me."

"I did, yeah. Sometimes it's clear enough to be confident over."

"Khari?" he asked, needing to know.

Eden's face flickered. He drew a deep breath, evading eye contact. "He will never be caught again. Jaizel will never lay a hand on his flesh in violence. He will be...all you want, Gray, that is what he will become. Two realms, two brothers. You will never lose him. I will not let him be hurt again. I can tell you that, with certainty. He will never be at Jaizel's mercy again."

"Yet you are uncertain of him staying at your side?" Gray asked. "You don't see you both as a whole? You think he will leave you?"

"I think that I don't know enough to share it with you. But..."

"But what?"

Eden took a right turn, then an immediate left. "I want him so bad, Gray," he said. "I want him to..." Eden flushed lightly, pausing to gather his words. "I want him to make love to me," he breathed. "I want him to take me and make me his...I want to know what that would be like, to know that kind of love. I'm terrified to find out."

"Why?"

Eden raised a brow as though it was a stupid question, but Gray simply frowned and waited for an answer. Eden huffed and looked away.

"Last I was aware, for two guys to have penetrative sex, it involved assholes."

"I was of the same understanding," Gray replied, still frowning. "And?"

"Dude, that's gonna fucking *hurt!*"

Gray laughed. Once the first volley of helpless giggles fled from his throat, the rest followed as though a dam had been breached. He held his hands to his face, swiping at his eyes as he shook his head and snorted.

Eden looked at him as though he had grown another head. Gray tried to gather himself up into something sane. He couldn't help grinning, though.

"I don't see what's funny," Eden said, walking away. "My guts fall out my asshole, I ain't gonna be fucking laughing, am I?"

"Well, I think that's unlikely," Gray said. "Readiness, preparedness, oil—a lot of oil—and a lot of time. It should never hurt. *Ever*. If it hurts, then it's not right, and if it's not right, then you should get away as fast as you can. It can be...uncomfortable," he murmured, glancing at Eden. "You have to fight your instincts...it is counter intuitive, not to tense and

348

clench, but it will mean you won't be hurt. Go slowly. Be ready. And make sure you want to be doing that with the man sharing your bed. You can't undo it, once you have gone down that road."

Eden looked at him from under his long eyelashes. "You seem to know a lot about it."

Gray looked away, deciding how much to tell the amazing being who had whirled into all their lives. Nothing but total honesty would do.

"I was thrown into the whore cells when Khari was taken. After our mother was killed...can we get out of this labyrinth please? I will tell you the story over food and wine, if that is all right? I think it is something Elnara should probably hear too...and Airell...Father. I will never get used to calling him that," he said. "I will tell you all my story, but I want wine while I tell it, and I think Khari should be laid down somewhere to sleep off the drugs Elnara fed him."

"*Get out of my way, you little bastard!*"

Gray stood his ground, holding his knife as though it was a sword that might possibly have the power to protect his mother and baby brother. He could hear Khari's screams from where he stood, and Khari was at least thirty metres away from the entrance to the apartment.

"*You will not hurt them,*" *he hissed, facing the hated monster who haunted his dreams and made him so scared he pissed himself. He shook his head. "I won't let you hurt them. Khari is just a baby...please...*" *he begged, feeling his tears burn his eyes. He blinked, ashamed to show his weakness.*

Jaizel sneered. He bent down so their faces were level. Lifted his chin.

"*Do you even know how to slice a throat, boy?*"

Gray gulped, his knife suddenly heavy in his hand.

Jaizel snatched it from him, grabbed the guard at his side, pulled him to the floor and pushed his chin downwards to his chest. He swiped the side of the guard's neck from behind his ear to his collar with the knife and a fountain of blood spurted up to the ceiling like a geyser.

"*Never lift their head. The windpipe blocks the artery. Bend the neck to their chests and then cut. One cut, clean and swift. Death is...*" *Jaizel looked at the dead guard, then at Gray. "Death is quick. Seconds. Would you like to try again?*"

Gray snatched at his knife and glared at his father.

He launched himself upwards and grappled with his long hair, using it to pull his head down. And down. And down. He swiped with the knife and made contact with flesh.

Then he was flying through the air and Jaizel was roaring his rage. Blue fire ripped from his fingertips, scorching Gray's leg as he scrambled to try and get out of the way. He had to run. Save himself.

Khari was screaming. His mother was screaming.

Gray turned and faced the evil, standing his ground as Jaizel came for him.

Use your mind, not your brute strength. You don't have have much brute strength, baby.

He listened to his mother's voice, ducked low and thought, "See me not."

Jaizel screamed his disgust and twisted around, trying to see Gray who had vanished. No one could see him like this. Even Khari could not see him. If Khari could not see him, then he was truly invisible. He picked his knife up from the floor, knowing it would vanish along with anything else he touched.

Bend the neck down. Thanks, Dad.

He crept towards Jaizel and lifted the knife.

And then he was floating. Held in the air by a force he could not touch. It squeezed him. He coughed and felt the world around him become true once more. He choked back a sob. He could be seen. He had failed.

"Gray! Gray! Help me!"

Gray sobbed. "Khari!"

"Mummy! Mummy...no, no...Gray!"

Gray struggled, fighting against the tugging sensation as he was pulled through the air to the doorway of his mother's bedroom. He saw her in the corner, Khari clasped to her chest as though he was a

351

scared chimpanzee. She waved a knife. Another blast of magic swept through the room. Khari, bless his soul, was fighting to save them too. Covered in shit, pissing himself, his baby brother was not going to give in without a fight.

"You will not take him, you bastard!" his mother screamed, spitting at the monster. "I will not let you take my baby!"

"I need the power he will give me. It's the only way. Give me the boy—give me my son!"

Jaizel stalked forward. He reached out a hand and punched Khari, stunning him enough to stop the flow of violent magicks being fired at him by the small child clinging to his mother.

"He's not yours, Jai!" his mother cried, snatching for her son. "He's Airell Jarlen's son, you fucking animal. You could never sire something as special as Khari. You're not fit to lick his shoes!"

"You whoring bitch," Jaizel screamed, grabbing his twin and dragging her across the room. "You filthy whore!"

"No...please..." Gray begged, seeing his knife in Jaizel's hand. He shook his head as Jaizel lifted it and grabbed Relaizia's hair with his other hand. He forced her head down.

"Mummy!" Gray screamed, unable to look away as the knife swept across his mother's throat.

Jaizel snatched Khari from Relaizia's slackened grip and watched her fall to the floor, holding Khari to his chest as Gray screamed, realisation hitting with fists harder than anything Jaizel could hope to wield.

"Mummy!" Khari screamed, battering at Jaizel with his tiny fists. Kicking with his feet, struggling and twisting as his new shirt and smart trousers were

ripped from his small body. "Gray! Gray! Make him stop...it hurts! Please, no...Gray!"

Gray closed his eyes and turned his head. At least his baby brother would know Gray had never seen what had happened. Known, yes. Heard, yes. But he had never seen it. In the future, they could pretend it had never happened. He closed his ears to his brother's screams, staying silent when Khari's sobs had become small gasps in the corner of the room.

Gray stayed silent as Jaizel released him. Stayed quiet as his father pushed him down onto the bed and raped him, hand twisted in his hair to keep him still as he fought as helplessly as Khari had, moments before. Gray clenched his jaw at the agony lancing through his body, pushing his face into the quilts as he was forced to submit. His weakness, his helplessness complete; Jaizel's power over him proven absolutely. Gray tried to think of nothingness. To forget the day had happened. That his mother was still alive and Khari still innocent. He stayed silent throughout the torture his father was putting him through.

Khari would never hear him scream.

"You're a whore, now," Jaizel said, an eternity later. "What do you say to that, you little bastard?"

Gray lifted his head and glared at Jaizel. His rage overwhelmed the fear and the pain.

"I say that I will use it to my advantage. I will get power. I will learn...and then I will make allies. And I will leave this place...you murdering..."

He was so tired. He crawled to Khari's side, wondering where he was going to start and how he could fix his brother's body, crumpled next to the corpse who had been their mother; the most beautiful woman in the worlds. He scooped Khari into his arms and glared over his head at Jaizel.

"We're not beaten," he whispered in Khari's ear, switching to English so Khari would understand him. "We are stronger than he will ever be."

Khari heaved in a shaky sobbed breath. "It hurt..."

Gray took a small breath of his own and held Khari tighter. "This is the start. It will get worse. We are stronger. He is weak," he said, holding Jaizel's eyes. "He cannot break me, and I will always love you, Khari. Always. Just stay strong for me."

"Mummy..."

"Is free," he murmured. "She can be happy now."

"I want to be with her."

Gray shook his head, eyes on Jaizel, who stood wordlessly next to the bed, horrified realisation dawning in his dark brown eyes. He looked at his twin, holding a hand to his mouth, momentarily letting his grief show.

"It's not our place to be free, yet. We have a job to do, Khari." Gray rocked Khari against his chest, trying to shove his thin little arms into the torn shirt he had been wearing, wanting to cover him and give him some dignity back.

Khari gasped back a scream of pain, and burrowed into Gray's neck. "It hurts so bad...what job do we have?"

"We're going to grow and kill the fucker who just stole our lives."

Jaizel looked at him for innumerable moments, then stood from the bed. He turned to the soldier in the doorway. Gray memorised the face of the man who had watched him and his brother get raped by this monster and vowed he would die.

Painfully.

354

"Take them both down to the cells," Jaizel said. "Keep them together. I doubt the half-breed bastard could feed itself without help. I need it alive. It has something I want."

Khari wept into Gray's neck. "I don't have anything...he hurt me."

"You have more than he could dream of owning," Gray assured him. He forced his legs to stand and hold him upright. The pain, deep inside his arse, made him dizzy. He tightened his hold on Khari, mindless of his own blood, less than it had been, trickling down his thighs and over the back of his knees, tracking a path to the floor.

Gray walked carefully, growling at the soldier who tried to take Khari from him. "I know where I am going," he hissed. "Keep away from us, you fucking animal." He walked from his mother's apartments, moving as fast as he could bear. One slow step after the other. He took the agonising journey down into the maze of cells, holding traitors and foot-soldiers. A prison camp for those who had fallen into disfavour. A place where those who Jaizel did not want in his sight were thrown.

The detritus of a broken society, tossed under the ground to rot.

Gray kept his chin up and eyes straight as he walked naked along the dirt path. He met the eyes of each and every man, woman, and child who stared at him. He clasped his brother to him and made no attempt to cover or disguise their injuries.

Jaizel had committed an unspeakable sin. He was not going to hide it.

He turned into a small hole of a room, a million miles away from the Spartan luxury of their apartments. He looked at the nest of straw and the thin sheet and held his tears in check. He would never let Khari see him cry. Khari would never hear him scream.

He laid Khari down on the sheet and carefully wrapped him up. He wasn't sure if it was good or bad that Khari had passed out. He thought it might be good. At least he might heal, Gray thought, watching a red patch grow on the sheet where it curved around Khari's backside.

He staggered back to his feet and out of the door. He stopped an worn out woman by tentatively touching her hand. She looked down at him. He swallowed his fear.

"I am...I am Prince...I am Gray," he said, determined he would not cry. "Jaizel has murdered my mother...and I think my brother might be haemorrhaging. He was raped. I think he needs help..."

The woman bent down and turned him around so she could see his back. She bent him carefully forward, her breath a hiss as she assessed Gray's own wounds.

"Which is your cell?" she asked.

Gray pointed.

"Go and lie down, my love. I will be with you soon. We'll get you and your brother fixed up, yes?"

Gray swayed on his feet. The woman scooped him up, grabbing a rough linen towel from a hook nailed to the wall. She padded it around his arse and rocked him in her arms for a long while, then walked towards his cell. She looked over her shoulder and spoke to someone Gray could not see.

"Get water boiling, and a medical kit. Bring broth. And a soft blanket."

"Who will pay for that luxury?"

356

"Don't you worry about that, girl. Just do it." The woman bent her face down to look at Gray. She flinched back. Chewing her lip, she walked him to the nest of straw Khari was curled up on and laid him next to his baby brother. She stroked his arm.

"You ain't got no cause to trust me," she said, sitting down to lift Khari onto her fat thighs. "None at all. No, sir, not a reason in the world. But I ain't going to do wrong by you or the little prince here," she said, assessing Khari. She blanched, shaking her head. "His age?"

"Ten. He was ten last week."

"He's small."

"He...he isn't allowed out in the sun."

"Jaizel's orders?"

Gray curled into himself, praying the pain would stop. He wanted to pass out, like Khari had managed to do. He wanted to die.

He wanted to see Jaizel die more.

He heaved in a breath and held onto his rage, letting it settle and grow within himself; a warm, live being that would fuel him. Something that would stop him from picking up a knife, tucking his chin down, and swiping his own carotid artery wide open.

He would live for Khari.

Khari needed him.

They needed money. They had to live.

He needed to make friends and allies.

He had to make money so he could bribe guards.

He looked at the old woman. "I need your help," he croaked.

"Oh, my Prince?"

"There's a way, in this place, to earn coin, isn't there?"

The woman gaped at him. "You cannot be serious!"

"Perfectly. You live here. You know what the...customers like. Teach me. I need to be the best. I need to fuck the best. Guards, patrolmen, soldiers...I need their coins. I need money. And books. I must have my books."

"You're a child."

"I'm thirteen. I was a child. Now I am Gray. And I will be the best. My father thinks he has destroyed me by forcing me to whore for my food. I will turn that around and be a whore to save myself. I will choose this. Will you help me? It will happen anyway, but you may be able to help me make it hurt less. Make them finish faster than Jaizel did. There are...tricks?"

"There are tricks," she said, abhorrence in every line of her face.

"Show me," Gray commanded.

The woman looked at him. The boiling water and medical kit arrived, and she still stared at him. She pushed something down Khari's throat and waited for him to go totally limp in her arms, then laid him over her thigh. She jerked her head at Gray. "We can keep him dosed. He won't know as much as he would fully awake. When the bastard king comes for him, feed him a wad of this," she said, pointing to a ball of grassy-type strands. "It is sweet," she added, sewing carefully. "Asanthal Grass. He will eat it. You take some too, the first few times, at least. It will take you time to get used to what is happening to you. My Prince...there must be another path for you?"

"I can sit at that bastard's right hand and watch my brother die."

The woman sighed and ran her podgy hand over

358

his head. "No choice. I understand," she said. "You are sure you will be forced into this, if you are not willing?"

"I am sure."

"All right," the woman said.

"I will share..."

She glared at him and cuffed him around the ear, just hard enough to make spots dance in front of his eyes.

"I will take not a penny from you, Gray. Not one coin. I will not have it said that I pimped out a child. I am going to help you, simply because it seems to be in your interests to learn a few things so you don't bleed like a stuck pig every time some horny fucker takes a fancy to your arse. That I am willing to help you, does not mean I will like it, and I ain't going to enjoy this, Gray. But I think you both need someone to look after you...and I don't see many others around who ain't going to exploit you both." She laid Khari down with extreme carefulness, and beckoned to Gray, rinsing her hands and soaking a fresh cloth. "Let's see the damage," she murmured. "Get you fixed up."

"I took my first *customer* the following week," Gray said, twisting his mouth, remembering. He sipped his wine. "It was nothing like as bad as Jaizel had been, and I made five coins. A female adult whore could have asked for a half-coin. I was in business, and I was soon in high demand. I made enough to keep us fed as best I could. To keep the rougher clients at bay. To make sure we always had water and fresh straw to sleep on...I would fuck the soldiers, and laugh, and dance...and I was soon commanding twenty coins. A fortune," he said, tracing a pattern on the floor with his fingertip. "I had the guards under my thumb. I owned the cells and built myself a loyal inner circle.

"But I couldn't stop what was happening to Khari. I had a pile of coins growing under a flagstone in our cell...I had customers who really weren't that cruel or nasty. .Most were gentle and revered me...but I still had to watch as Khari was dragged away and then brought back to me, broken and bleeding. He withdrew quickly. I knew I was losing him...and that I had to do *something*. One of my...customers...was a highly ranked guard. I convinced him to teach me swordplay. Another, I asked to teach me unarmed combat. Incendiary skills...explosives...survival skills. I learnt to shoot an arrow and dodge them. I learnt to kill a man with my bare hands, and then I made more money by fighting in the ring, down in the cells. I grew in strength and skill, and built a small arsenal. I built up my money. I made more friends. I took over more of the Cells...but I couldn't save Khari from the torture Jaizel was putting him through."

Gray paused, glancing up. "We had been in the cells for three years, when they came..." He sipped his wine, noticing his hand was shaking. He tried to steady himself, but with little success. The memories were flooding back and he was at their mercy. "I was held by four of the strongest soldiers and tied to a hook that was fixed to the ceiling of our cell. Khari...he started screaming as they began to whip me. I laughed and vowed to keep laughing. I'd not give them the satisfaction of my screams. They could hurt me. They could tear the flesh from my bones, but they could *not* force me to scream in front of my brother. He had to know I was strong enough to cope with anything. And I thought I was...I really thought I was."

Gray gulped his wine. He held his glass out when Elnara tilted the bottle at him. He glanced at her face, pleased to see open pain, but no disgust. He raised his glass and drank quietly, gathering his words around him. He took a small bite of cake and sipped his wine again.

"They lifted Khari from the straw." He closed his eyes, taken by memory. "They dragged him and strung him up in front of me. Told me to watch. I refused. They whipped him...they told me to watch. I couldn't. I couldn't...I couldn't *see* that...the whip struck again. Oh, Orien's Blood, he screamed so loudly. They said unless I watched, they would keep going, and then fuck him. Fuck his powers from him. Force him to release what he held...if I watched, they would spare the whip. They started whipping me again when Khari looked away. If we looked away from each other, the pain would be tenfold. It was an easy lesson to learn. By the time Jaizel came in, I think we were too scared to look away from each other."

"Oh, God," Airell said. He gulped from his brandy flask, leaning his head back on the stone wall to close his eyes. He shook his head when Alex reached to comfort him. "Leave me be. Go on, Gray."

"By the time it was over, it was three days later. I truly thought Khari was going to die. I paid one of the guards. I ran through the cells and shot anyone that stood in my way. I do not know how many I killed. I ran out of the open door, past the guard I had bribed, and just...ran. Khari had been raped by several regiments. The blood...oh, God, the blood," he cried, looking at his hands, half expecting to still see the stains. "He had...he had n-no skin on his back." He clasped his hands to his head, trying to hold in the betraying emotions. "I could see...I c-could see his...h-his spine...he *grated* as I ran with him...b-b-bones...b-broken," he stuttered. Barely aware of Airell pulling him into the circle of his arms, he gasped out a choked sob of anguish. "I had meant to *leave!*" he cried, clenching his fists. "The day before they c-came...I meant to...to...I meant t-to *leave!* I stayed. I thought...I thought," he choked, heaving each breath he took. "I thought we could rest. Leave the next day. I needed s-sleep..."

Airell rocked him, comforting him wordlessly.

"It's over, now," Cole said, his voice thick. He stroked his knuckles along Gray's jaw. "You're not alone anymore. You can let it go, sweetheart."

Gray pressed his lips together holding himself in, forcing his anguish back. He would not, *could* not, let it out. He was stronger than that. He was Gray. He was a survivor. He was...

Eden reached over and slid him from Airell's lap to his own, cradling him close. He moved closer to Elnara. "You don't have to be strong, all the time," he said. "I promise you will not break if you let it out."

Elnara leant to rest her head on Gray's chest. "Strong men know when it's okay to cry," she said, her hand resting over his heart.

Gray shattered and fell apart. Through the haze of his tears, he saw Khari, sleeping with his head on Takana's thigh. Safe and loved.

Through his sobs, he heard the murmured words of people who truly loved him. Telling him it was all right, now, to let go of some of the load. He could rest. He could sleep.

He was safe.

Safe.

The single word followed him as he was swallowed down by the yawning darkness, opening its jaws to enfold him in blissful nothingness and lift him away from the world. From his pain. From his memories.

He clenched his hand over Eden's pectoral muscle, feebly fighting oblivion. Eden curled around him and held a hand to his head. He muttered something under his breath, and the weight of fear lifted from Gray's mind. His memories, horrific and tortuous, seemed fogged. Blocked. They were all there, but they belonged to someone else; he was watching them through someone else's eyes. They hurt less. They were no longer his. The crushing weight of his struggle to live and survive was lifted, leaving only a sense of strength and competence in its wake.

"You are the strongest man I know," Eden said. "It's time for your life, now, Gray. Live it, huh?"

"With me, if you don't mind," Elnara said, curling herself into Gray's side.

"Even now you know?"

Elnara pressed her lips to Gray's mouth. "Especially now I know," she whispered. "Sleep, my love. Rest. We will move in an hour, so you better get over your sogginess before then."

Gray sniffed a small laugh and let the darkness finally take him.

XX

"You took his pain," Takana said, leaning against Eden's arm as she watched the brothers sleeping. "I saw you. You did *something* and it took some of the pain..."

"I took his guilt and shrouded the worst of the pictures in his mind. Don't ask me how," Eden said, glancing sideways at her. "I don't know how I did it. But...those memories were more than anyone can bear and stay functioning. I'm shocked he made it this far without going insane. I saw I could mute it. So I did," he said. He picked at the stuffed chicken thigh he held. For once Takana was not yelling at him to eat.

He doubted any of their party would have an appetite for a few days.

Eden watched as Elnara rhythmically stroked her fingers through Gray's long hair, braiding it in complex patterns behind his ears and around the nape of his neck. Gray slept on, unaware of the tender fingers moving with a silent declaration of love. In Gray's arms, back pressed into Gray's chest, Khari slept peacefully, finally free from the raging hormonal surges that had been alarming and sexy as hell by turns.

Eden looked at the chicken thigh he held. He peeled a chunk of flesh from bone. The vision of two young boys hit his mind's eye; hogtied and hanging from a low ceiling dripping with damp...their skin flayed from their backs as they were forced to watch each other...

He scrambled away from the others and managed to aim the violent torrent of vomit against a far wall. He held his hand on the cold stone wall, bending nearly double as he retched, losing his lunch, then his partly digested breakfast. His body purged itself of anything he had fed it, leaving him gasping with beads of sweat dripping from his nose, barely able to breathe as the bile filled his nose and throat, his eyes watering freely as though he cried.

Maybe he was crying. He wouldn't hold it against himself.

"Eden?"

He shook his head even as he pressed back into Takana's hand to increase the contact. "Chicken," he muttered stupidly. "The meat...peeled. Flayed from the bone," he breathed, spitting. "Can't eat it."

"Okay," Takana said, massaging circles between his shoulder blades. "Vegetarian from now on."

Eden hung his head. He pushed himself away from the wall and wiped his hand over his face, grateful when Takana passed him a handkerchief to blow his nose and clear some of the foulness. He took the ale Cole passed him and swilled it around his mouth, spitting it out, then drinking. His neck and throat felt raw. He coughed, drank more, and passed Cole the ale.

"Thanks."

Cole was serious for once. "Anytime, Princess," he said, but the name held no humour, now. "Will you be all right, Eden?"

"Yeah."

"Okay. Do you want to walk with me and Takana? Explore a few of these rooms?"

Eden looked down the hallway they had gathered

in, and at the tall arched doorways; portals into secret spaces and hidden histories. He glanced at Khari. A large part of him wanted to hold Khari close as he explored and discovered...his *past*? His future? Eden did not know what it was he would find. Just knew that it was his. Whatever was down here, whatever lay buried and long forgotten, held the key to whatever was locked around his soul.

It would let him know the questions for the answers he had; answers that made no sense.

"I'd like that," he said, looking at Cole. "Thanks."

Cole walked away. It said a lot for Cole's looks and breeding, that he could wear a pair of boxer briefs with the same sang-froid as a tuxedo. Damn, the man was good looking.

Takana nudged him. "That one is mine."

"He's so good looking."

"He certainly is," she agreed.

"How old is he?"

"He'll be three-hundred in a few months," Takana said, grinning. "Airell is close to four-hundred and thirty, or thereabouts. Alex is a few years his senior. About four-hundred and forty..."

"And you?"

"I'm a baby," she said. "Two-hundred and twenty, give or take a couple of years."

"Khari's mama was ancient."

"Yes."

"How long do you live for? Elves?"

Takana shrugged. "That depends. If we're not killed, then we are immortal. But we are a war-like race. We don't generally get to put the immortality to the test often. Nymphs age and die, with time. Elves do not, as a rule. I don't know what my future holds, but I have a few lines here and there to betray my age."

"You look no older than thirty," Eden said after studying Takana for a few moments. "Are you sure they are wrinkles?"

"Well, it could be bark," Takana quipped. "I am part tree."

"Princess?" Cole called softly. "Come and look at this. You will piss your scholarly knickers."

Eden sniffed and immediately wished he hadn't. He spat against the wall and blew his nose again. "Ugh," he said under his breath. "Vile." He walked through one of the archways and peered into the gloom, then drew a breath and took a small step into the...chapel?

It had to have been a chapel. Altars were in chapels, weren't they? He walked closer, reaching out a hand to trail his fingers through the dust coating the cold surface of the altar, engraved with runes, looking around at more runes painted on the walls and at the display of eight-pointed stars that decorated the space behind the altar. All so familiar, whilst being completely new.

He knew it all, yet had never seen it before in his life. He turned in a slow circle, looking upwards. He drew in a slow breath. Hundreds upon hundreds of eight-pointed stars had been carved and created from glimmering diamonds, emeralds and sapphires. They were scattered over the deep blue painted ceiling as though they were real stars, thrown across the blanket of the sky. Eden jogged out into the hallway and snagged one of the bobbing glowing balls of heatless flame from the air close to where Khari slept. He glanced at Airell and Alex and jogged back to the chapel, throwing the globe of soft light ahead of him to light the room.

The jewels set into the ceiling blazed, lighting Eden's face as he turned, speechless, and watched the chapel spring to life under its coating of dust.

"Oh," Takana said. "This is beautiful."

"Worth the journey," Cole agreed. "Do you think this is the temple? Seems...small."

"This is a sanctuary," Eden said. "This was a private place for contemplation. It was never meant for the eyes of the public. That will be down the end of the hallway and down the red stairwell...the double doors at the end of the passageway."

"You're freaky, Eden, you are aware of that, aren't you?" Takana asked. She rubbed his upper arm in silent reassurance. "You know this place?"

He did. He always had. "Can you please pass me the book from the cupboard over there?" he asked Cole, pointing at a small low cupboard tucked in a corner. "It's on the lowest shelf...near the back. Wrapped in—"

"Oilcloth," Cole said. He held up the wrapped package and looked at Eden with wide eyes. "Princess, this is kind of weird, even for you. How did you know it was there?"

"I left it there...I think. Another me. Not *me* as I am, now, but...before. I left it safe...for me to find?"

It all felt right. Like holding a bow and firing an arrow. He had known the skills, and he had held the bow in his hands before he had ever touched it. He had known his way to the chapel without having ever seen it. He had known how to ease the horror in Gray's mind.

"I just know," he said, taking the book from Cole

and flipping back the oilcloth wrapping. "Just, I don't know *what* it is I know, until I see it again. Like a long forgotten dream, just coming alive, I guess. Sorry. I know it don't make sense."

"It makes about as much sense as everything else does lately. What's in the book?"

Eden shook his head, turning the vellum pages. "I can't remember," he said, frustrated at the indecipherable script and runes that danced across the page.

Cole leaned over to look. "That script is ancient, Princess. I don't mean a few millennia. I mean it's as old as the creation of the worlds, almost. The book is about three-thousand years old, I think," he continued, taking it gently from Eden's unresisting hands, "maybe a little less," he corrected, peering closely at it. "The script used here is much older, though. It's a long dead tongue, and one I doubt we could find reference to in the palace libraries. There's no one who would know how to translate this."

"May I see?" Khari asked from the doorway.

Eden turned, startled by how drained Khari was. He looked as though he had known a rough night on the town, had not slept, and had then spent the day drinking.

"You look ill. Are you okay?"

Khari shrugged. "Aye, not so badly off. I have a headache, dry throat...I'm shaky on my feet. I keep getting the shivers. I feel as though someone drugged me and I'm withdrawing, funnily enough." He walked into the chapel and gave a low whistle as he looked around and upwards, the glow of the heatless flame brightening to a bright white, bathing them in artificial daylight. "Orien's..." He was unable to complete the sentence as he walked in a trance to the altar, stroking the table as Eden had done. He traced the runes carved into the stone.

"You can read them, can't you?" Eden asked.

Khari leant to dust the altar, bending to better see the carvings. "There's not much I can't read."

Eden jerked his head at the book Cole held. "Do you think you can make sense of a language as old as the creation of the worlds?" he asked.

Khari chuckled and looked at the book, holding his hand out reverently. He looked at the page and scanned the writings. Right to left, Eden noted, not left to right. Others he scanned from bottom to top, others top to bottom. One page, he turned ninety degrees and read on the diagonal, seeing a sense to the scriptures that had evaded Eden and Cole. After several silent minutes, Khari closed the book and passed it to Eden.

"Aye. I can read it," he said.

"Could you tell me what it says?"

"Yes."

Eden waited, then huffed impatiently. "But you won't, will you?"

"No."

"Not your place to tell me?" Eden guessed.

"Is withholding this information from Eden likely to place him in danger, through his ignorance?" Cole asked.

Khari shook his head. "If anything, it's the opposite. His ignorance and innocence is his protection. He knows that...it's why he doesn't want to open all the secrets of Pandora's Box at once."

"I am here," Eden joked.

"Shall I repeat what I said, but say it to you?"

Khari asked, smiling tiredly at Eden.

"No." He rubbed his hands over his head in frustration. "I know I *know* all this!" he cried, waving at the chapel. "I have *seen* it all before, and I have been in this room, and I have *spoken* these fucking words!" he said, pointing at the book. "What *am* I? What the fucking hell am I, that all this is as familiar to me as my own face in a mirror, yet I have *never* seen any of it through these eyes?" He slumped against the wall and closed his eyes, shaking his head hopelessly from side to side. "I'm just a kid. Couple months back, I was writing essays on Marlowe and hanging out in my college tutor room. Looking forward to going home and watching a movie and eating a Big Mac," he said. "It was lonely, sure...but it was *simple!*" he snapped. He banged his fist on the wall behind him and stamped his foot.

He wanted to hit something. He wanted to tear the pages from the exquisite book and toss them to the flames. He wanted to walk out of the beautiful chapel that set his soul singing with awareness. He wanted to vault onto Jinx and gallop back to the river, jump across the Divide, and forget all of this.

Whatever the hell *this* was.

"Fear will hold me, in my future," Khari said.

Eden opened his eye a crack to see Khari holding the book and reading from a page.

"Fear takes me, and it holds me," Khari continued, glancing at Eden, then down at the page. "It will wrap its fingers around my new soul, and it will drag me away from the light, shrouding me in darkness, hiding me from the light...in the light, I can be seen. The darkness will hold me safe in my ignorance. The fear will prevent me from stepping into the light, because in the light..."

"My soul will be laid bare," Eden said. "In the light, my true self will be seen, and be known. Once I have walked into the light, I cannot pretend that I have not seen the sights laid out for me, nor can I un-see the truth in my heart, or my soul. In the light, I shall know myself." Eden hesitated, then let out a long breath and stated, "The fear that holds me protects me from that ultimate knowledge. My fear protects me from who I am."

Khari closed the book gently. "You know what it says. You know who you are. You know what you are. You know these walls and you know these rooms. You have touched these stars and you have fixed them to the ceiling above your head. Down here, in the darkness, away from the world, Eden, you have known all these things, aye? And you have known you were not ready to hear what you wrote for you to read, this time. You have known you could not step into the light and see your truth. My place isn't to force you into the light and force that truth into you. I will not read to you from a diary you wrote thousands of years ago, and toss your fears and thoughts into your face. I will not wake you up from the dream that is holding you safe, Eden. Not until you are ready to wake up."

"If I wake up, I might be thrown into a nightmare." Eden pushed himself away from the wall. He took the book from Khari. Walking out of the chapel, he turned left and walked to the furthest door, pushing it open with a nudge from his hip when it stuck. It had always stuck. Even when it was first built, it had swollen and stuck. He walked down a narrow flight of stairs and ducked his head under the lintel of a door set into the stone to his right. Placing the book onto a sideboard, he looked at the dust that had accumulated in the room, and flung himself onto a long, low couch, covering his eyes with his forearm. The skins covering the horsehair and straw had perished in places, but it had survived quite well, down here in the darkness.

Tugging the furs from the back of the couch, Eden covered himself and folded his arms behind his head, staring at the ceiling. A soft golden light cast itself over the carved stone above his head, announcing Khari's arrival in the doorway.

"Nice room," Khari said quietly. "May I come in?"

Eden nodded, closing his eyes. "I always liked it here. It's peaceful."

"It is, aye," Khari said, his light making the darkness behind Eden's eyelids glow red. "You built it?"

Eden unfolded his hands from behind his head and flexing his fingers. "Not these hands, though. Other hands. Am I good or bad?" he asked, quietly. "Evil? What is it living inside me? Is it to be revered or feared, Khari?"

"Both."

"I was afraid you would say that. Close the door? I don't want to be around people right now."

"Do you want me to leave?"

"No. I don't know much of anything right now, but I know I want you here, Khari. Just...make my excuses to everyone. They can all go back up to the surface. There's nothing down here for them to see, unless they want to look at the main temple...it's kinda pretty."

"It is, aye," Khari agreed, leaving him with the glowing light.

Eden frowned to himself. *Aye.* As though...

"You've seen the temple?" he said, as soon as Khari came back. "I said it was pretty, you agreed. You've seen it."

"Not exactly, but aye, I know what it looks like. Same as I knew who you were as soon as I opened my eyes and really *saw* you. Same as I can read the ancient writings. I just...know."

"Saw it in another life?"

Khari sat down on the couch by Eden's hip. He placed his bag on the floor and rested his elbows on his knees. "Yes, and then again, no," Khari said. "It wasn't my life. But I hold the memories of it, and the knowledge."

Eden sat up, looking at Khari's profile. Khari held his head in his hands, his blonde hair falling forward over his fingertips in a fine fringe. "It took me a few days to put the pieces together," he said into his palms, not looking up. "After you found me. Once I had pieced them together, I could see the picture, and I wondered how I could have been blinded, even for three or four days. It was obvious. It has always been obvious.

"You have lived this before. Several times. You know you have. Who you are, I mean...you have come and walked this world, and you have always tried to be...too much, maybe. And alone, you never had the strength to be who you knew you were meant to be. Did you?"

Eden shook his head. "Last time...the time I built this," he muttered, "I...I couldn't live with the loneliness. A thousand years alone. Even with everyone around me, all the time. Even with the priests and worshippers. I could not be who I was meant to be. I couldn't...I couldn't even touch another being. The touch was too..."

"It was too powerful," Khari said, understanding.

"I killed them," Eden said. "If they looked at me...it sent them mad. I was so, so, alone. In this place, millions of souls above me...but none who could be close enough for me to speak to. To hold. To touch. I locked myself away, down here."

Khari lifted his head from his hands and met Eden's eyes. "You died down here."

Eden looked at the doorway. "Up the stairs again, along the east passageway. The bones in the smallest chamber are mine. I laid down, and I never got back up. I was tired. I need...people. I need to love. Without love, without people, I die. Alone, I wither and I fade."

"You were hidden behind a maze, and buried beneath their feet. Again. What is further down, Eden? More rooms? More chapels? More bones?"

Eden closed his eyes, remembering. "Yes," he said, quietly.

"And further down still, where the heat from the heart of the world warms your feet?"

"There too," Eden said. "It's been going on awhile." He took a breath and glanced at Khari, daring to utter aloud the words floating through his mind. "The curse of the gods is to walk alone."

Khari's eyes flickered at Eden's words. "Until now," he said. "You're not alone, Eden. Not this time. This time, you have me at your side."

"You were born for me," Eden said, holding a hand to Khari's face. The jolt of awareness shot through his hand and up his arm, swirling deep in his chest. "You...you really *are* mine," he said to himself.

"I can't be who I am without you. You're...I am..."

"You are a tongue-tied, beautiful, fool much of the time," Khari said, holding his hand over Eden's and pressing his cheek to Eden's palm. "You're lucky I don't need to hear your voice to hear you speak, aren't you?"

"You...you were born with the powers of a god," Eden breathed, staring at Khari, awed. "You hold them inside you."

"Do you mind?" he asked. "I think I'm keeping them safe for you."

Sighing, Eden bent his head, startled when Khari lifted his chin and shook his head, his golden eyes holding barely concealed anger.

"Don't bend your head like that," Khari said. He pressed his fingers against the side of Eden's neck, under his ear. "This is your carotid artery. Bending your head down means it is easy to slice through. Keep your chin up. Every time I have seen someone bend their head, or have their head pulled down like that, they've been dead seconds later. My mum included. So don't do it."

Eden lifted his chin.

"Besides," Khari said, "you look better with your head up. Confidence suits you more than you know. You should always walk and sit with pride, Eden. Be proud of who you are, hmmm?"

Eden smiled as best he could. "Okay. I'll try. And no, I don't mind you keeping them safe. The powers. I think I have enough to cope with trying to learn to use those I have inside *me*, without worrying about the ones you have in you. I'm actually a god, aren't I?" he asked. "I'm not just having a mental moment that will have me waking up in a padded room wearing a straitjacket?"

Khari raised a brow. "No padded rooms. You know who you are, now?"

"I'm..." Eden breathed deeply and pulled his shoulders back. He looked around the room that had become a prison for him, once. He felt the resonances of older rooms; of deeper prisons and lonely bones, laying alone and forgotten in small dust-filled rooms. He felt the heat from the heart of the mountain and felt the pulse of the worlds beat in time with his heart. He looked at Khari. "I am Eden, but I was once called by another name. Once, they called me Orien. Once, the worlds bent to my will and my touch could bring life, or take it away. Once...I was the Alpha and I was the Omega. Once..."

Khari kissed him. He laid his hand on Eden's thigh, where his tattoo was. "And this? Do you know what it says?"

"It is time," Eden breathed. "It is time. I am come. Behold the End of Days. One Soul. One life. One World." He looked at Khari and linked their hands together. "One dream."

Khari leant forward, sucking gently on Eden's lower lip. "Welcome back," he whispered, holding Eden's head on his shoulder, keeping him close. "Welcome back, Eden. It will be better, this time. This time you are not alone. I will never leave you. I will be at your side. Welcome back."

XXI

You have something of mine.

However Eden looked at the words on the sheet of parchment, they made no sense. He sat back in his chair. "Does it mean Khari, or Gray?" he asked, picking up a small bread roll and taking a bite. He waved away the servant offering him lamb. "No flesh," he said firmly, swallowing a rising tide of bile. "Don't offer it again."

"Yes, my Lord."

"Eden. My name is Eden."

The servant bowed. "Yes, Eden."

Eden held the parchment up between his thumb and forefinger, as though it might bite him.

"It came pinned to one of my Border Guards, this morning," Airell said. "By pinned..."

"Arrow?" Gray asked.

"Through the heart. It is Jaizel's hand?"

"I think so," Gray said.

"It wasn't written by someone confident in writing English," Alex said, sliding the parchment to rest in front of Elnara. "What are your thoughts?"

Elnara held her chin in her palm and frowned at the words on the page. "The formation of the letters is clumsy. We can assume that it was not written by an infant, so I would hazard that the composer of this note is an adult. Right handed. This is not their first language, and they are not comfortable writing it...I would guess at male, simply because men tend to have messy handwriting, but it could be an ill-trained

378

woman, who has no skill with a pen."

"Well, that reiterates all we have so far said," Airell snapped, scowling across the table. "How about you tell us what the words mean? Give me some insight of what is going on here!"

"Airell..."

"No, Alex. We have sent her to the best schools in the human realm, because she wanted to solve mysteries.   Here is her chance.   Come on, Miss Forensics. Thoughts."

Elnara bowed her head. "Apologies, Your Majesty. The fact it was sent to you pinned to a dead soldier tells us that it is a direct threat. You have few enemies. You do have something Jaizel sees as his...two somethings. Three, if we are to count Eden. And, sir, you are confusing my love for forensic science with a psychic ability. If you wish to be told where this note came from, and what evil it forebodes, then may I respectfully suggest you ask Eden?"

Eden laughed into his tea. He loved Elnara. She always managed to make him giggle and totally ruin Airell's composure. It was fun.

Airell glared around the table and then sat back, holding his thumb and forefinger to his eyes, rubbing as though to relieve pressure. "Just the one guard?"

"Yes," Alex said, sitting back in his chair and crossing his legs at the ankles. "One guard. His post was close to the Tarenthian edge of the Wastelands. There were no signs of torture, nor of extended death. It was swift and clean. Then he was tied to his horse, who would know to come home...it was a professional execution, which rules out a low-bred soldier."

"He's after me," Khari said. He reached for the teapot, and looked at Elnara. "I assume you have resisted the urge to drug the tea?"

Elnara grinned. "Drink it and find out, cousin."

"Don't tease," Gray said. "It's safe, Khari."

Khari poured himself tea, adding a slice of lemon. "I prefer to be in charge of my own penis. I'm weird like that, aye?" He sipped from his china cup. "The note is in Jaizel's handwriting. I don't pretend to have an eidetic memory, but I saw enough of his writings when I was dragged to his rooms. He is after the powers I hold in me. He is under the mistaken belief that he can force them from me...but they are *not* mine to give away. I hold them until Eden is ready to begin to take them back. The powers of a God, for a God. Jaizel is no God."

Eden reached for Khari's hand and squeezed lightly, adjusting his position when Khari leant against him and tried to nuzzle into his neck. He held the beautiful elf as close as he could, and waited for him to get comfortable. Once he was, Eden sipped his own tea.

"So he has made his move," Eden said. "What do we do about it? What *can* we do about it?"

"My instinct says to get you all away from here," Airell said. He pinched the bridge of his nose between thumb and finger again. "I don't want you here. I can see an invasion attempt, and we are ill equipped to survive under siege. We are a peaceful people, for our kind. We weave cloth and grow fucking cabbages. We are tailors and farmers. We tend plants and make things look nice...we are not equipped for Jaizel attacking. Hell, we're barely equipped to fend off a bloody herd of fauns. I don't want you here. We can't protect you."

Khari started to sit upright, but Eden held him

380

back. He frowned at Airell. "If we leave, we will return. You will fortify Chainia, and we will return here. We're not in exile?"

"Never," Airell said. "I failed my wife. I will protect my children. Whatever that entails. And you, Eden. We can't lose you."

Eden sniffed. "Yeah, right, because an impotent baby god is really in demand these days."

Takana grinned. "Impotent? Sweetheart, no wonder you're still a virgin!"

Eden pointed his finger at Takana. "Shut up."

"He's so not impotent," Khari muttered into his teacup, sniggering as Eden blushed hotly. "So we leave?" Khari asked Airell. "Where to? Back to my house?"

"I don't think that would be a good idea," Gray said. "We were compromised the moment we left. The forests have eyes. It would be suicide to return."

"Damn that bastard," Khari said. "All right. Where, then?"

"The Human Realm," Airell said decisively. He chuckled when Khari's head jerked up, despite the gravity of the situation. Eden could practically feel the excited adrenalin pumping through Khari's veins. "You wished to see that world, did you not? You, with your love of all things human, Khari, can hide in their world. You know how to glamour?"

"I know how to glamour," Khari said quickly.

"You don't need to," Eden said. "Not really. You're just exceptionally good looking. There's nothing that really screams out that you're an elf. You could pass as human—you're just a sight better looking than any human I've known." He looked thoughtfully at Gray. "You, however," he said, "look every inch the

Elven King you were bred to be. You would get stared at. It's, um...well, it's your ears," he said, flicking his fingers at the elongated points atop Gray's ears. "And you're kind of pointy," he added. "Your face, I mean. All angles and sharp lines. Human faces are softer. I look human."

"They're all brown?" Gray asked.

Elnara patted his hand, smiling. "No, Gray. Your colour is fine. Eden is Indian, I think."

"Half," Eden agreed.

"It's a lovely colour."

Eden ate a small cake. "Racist fucktards in my town would argue otherwise," he said, the cries of *Paki* and *Muslim faggot* still a faint echo in his head, even after months of being free from the bullying he had run from. The ignorance that made everyone who met him think he was either a terrorist or a Muslim, Buddhist or Sikh, when in fact if he had to give himself a label, he would have termed himself an Atheist. Ironically.

It turned out there was a god, after all. It just happened to be him. Had been him? Would be him?

It all still made his head spin to try and work it out. He snared an unsuspecting bread roll from the central platter and stuffed a few slices of blue cheese into the middle, breaking off a chunk for Khari automatically, so he could try the cheese and see if he liked it.

Khari bit into it, chewed, and reached for a napkin, discretely spitting it out. "Nope. Horrible," he said as a footman stepped to his side with a small plate to carry away the napkin. "Thank you."

"Your Highness."

"So, Human Realm," Takana said, leaning forward

with her elbows on the table and her chin in her hands. "For how long? Where will we stay? How large shall the guard detail be?"

"The stay shall be as long as it needs to be," Airell said. He held the bloodied paper, its written threat stark against the white background. "You will keep my family safe," he said to Takana. "I cannot hope for a future where Eden shall not start to announce his presence in the worlds. Much as Khari declared his existence in a thousand small ways that were accidental, the same shall start to happen with Eden. There cannot be a Tempest building in the worlds without drawing attention. Wherever you choose to stay, the danger shall be equal to anywhere else. Nowhere is safe, but that realm is safer than this one. For now. We *must* keep Eden out of Jaizel's grasp. He cannot be allowed to get my sons back in his grip. Or we will all be lost."

"I agree," Alex said, tapping his fingers on the table. "Elnara knows enough of the Human Realm to assist in this mission." His daughter beamed, looking adoringly at Gray, softening Alex's eyes. "I am not such a tyrant that I would part you from him, Ellie," he said. "You may be a part of this mission. But you answer directly to your aunt. Am I understood? If Takana tells you to leave, for whatever reason, then you will follow her orders. It's time for you to learn to be a soldier, I suppose," he added, resigned.

"You will stay here, Cole, for a few days," Airell said. He held up a hand, forestalling objections. "You will join Takana as soon as you may, but I need you to help us here first. Scout the land and make sure we have sentinels where they will be most needed."

Cole bowed his head in mute agreement while

Takana looked resigned. She reached for Cole's hand, holding it on the table top.

"I will organise bank accounts and finances for you all," Airell said, pushing his chair back to stand. "And I will send you teachers, as soon as I find some who are able to push your skills as far as they will need to be pushed. You need to learn to fight and protect yourselves. We will take you from merely astounding, as you are now, to unbelievably fantastic.

"You have twelve hours to pack what you wish to take with you and say your goodbyes to people. Any questions?"

Everyone shook their heads. Khari looked at Eden as Airell left the room.

"I'm really going to see humans?"

"Looks like it," Eden said quietly.

"You don't seem happy about it."

Standing up, Eden clacked his tongue bar against his teeth. "I'd like to see my dad," he said eventually, walking out of the room and along the winding hallways to their apartment. He would. He had missed his dad and his calm capability more than he had thought he would. It would be good to see him again. At the same time...

"I guess, when I made the decision to stay here, I let that world go," Eden said. "I never felt as though I belonged in it. My skin colour, my sexuality, my accent, my intelligence. They were all used as ammunition against me. They made me stand out from the crowd and were used to make my life a living hell, with taunts and curses. When I made my choice to stay here, I was free of that. I knew that, given time, I would be pronounced probably dead, and people would forget I had ever lived there, and that was just fine. I let that life go...and now I am being forced to live it again, and leave the first place that has felt like home. I belong *here*," he said, sitting on the squashy sofa in their living room. He took the brandy Khari handed him and shrugged.

"I don't want to leave this mountain," Eden said, softly.

Khari drank quietly for a few minutes, then shrugged. "If I can be blunt? Half your troubles in past incarnations have been because you felt as though you could not leave this mountain, right? Maybe it's time you did. Walk out in the worlds, knowing who you are. Be around more people than one small circle of high ranking elves. This mountain has been your prison in all your lives. Maybe you cling to it because the worlds away from it seem scary. Your fear, holding you in the darkness?"

Eden knew it made sense, but the knowledge wasn't making leaving any easier.

"I'll be with you," Khari said, sitting next to him and taking his hand. "You can show me what a car is?"

"I prefer horses," Eden joked, and met Khari's eyes. He saw the excitement there and rubbed his hand over his face in defeat. He could not ask Khari to stay in the Elven Realms. Not when he had spent half a lifetime dreaming of the human world. "Okay," he said. "I'll show you the world I was born in."

"I can meet your father?"

"You can. Fuck knows what he'll say, though. I actually never told him I was gay!"

XXII

Eden cast a last lingering look at the mountain citadel he had grown to love, then turned Jinx's head away with a pang of loss, following Takana and Gray. He checked his weapons out of habit, making sure he had his sword, bow, arrows and knives. He tugged his cloak around his shoulders, fastening the brooch at his throat to try and prevent the whistling Arctic wind penetrating his bones. He lifted his scarf and hood and cursed, for the first time, the lack of nice heated cars or a railway. This was no season to be travelling on horseback. It was frozen enough to make him think that snow could only warm things up.

Khari tapped his heels to Ollie's sides and trotted ahead, murmured something to his brother, and reached into one of Gray's saddle bags. He turned back, walking towards Eden's place in the cavalcade, and held something out.

Eden looked, reached out a shaking hand and closed numb fingers around the small package. He raised an eyebrow at Khari.

"I made them when I was younger," Khari shrugged. "Before I could regulate my body heat."

Eden looked at the gloves, nestled in the folds of a silken scarf, and slid them onto his hands, startled at the instant warmth caressing his fingers and palms. He widened his eyes and looked closely at the thin fabric. It looked normal enough. Nothing magical.

"How?" he asked Khari.

"I drew the heat from the earth into the cotton

bolls. The warmth was in the actual threads. It never faded after I wove the cloth and made the gloves."

"Thanks," Eden said, tucking his hands under his armpits in the hope that the warmth from the gloves would spread through his body.

Khari watched him for a moment, then shook his head and vaulted from Ollie to land behind Eden on Jinx's back. "Move forward. It's easier for the horse if you're on her shoulders instead of her back."

"S-Saddle," Eden stammered through chattering teeth. "We won't both fit."

"Get off a minute, then, aye? Let me sort her out. Horses hate saddles anyway—you should learn to ride without. Get your blanket out of the bag."

Eden slid off Jinx, and followed Khari's orders. It was ridiculously cold. A cutting icy wind whirled around them, stabbing needles into his face. He let Khari heave him back onto Jinx, without a saddle, and offered no resistance when he was manhandled to sit as far forward as possible. Khari draped Eden's blanket around his shoulders and pulled him back into his chest, surrounding him with his heat, kicked his feet into Jinx's sides, and moved off in a gallop to the head of the train. Ollie followed him, like a well-trained dog, and Fain soared above their heads, screaming joyfully at random intervals.

"Close your eyes," Khari said, next to Eden's ear. "Try and sleep. I won't let you fall, and it will make the journey seem faster. Warmer, now?"

"Some," Eden said. He let his eyes close. It was likely the cold, and the deep ache in his heart at leaving the mountain, but he found the idea of sleeping attractive. He slumped easily against Khari's well defined chest, fitting into the curves and planes of his body with a small sigh of contentment.

"I've got you, Eden. Relax. Sleep. Figure out the million things I can feel racing through your head, eh? You do that best when you sleep, I think. I'll wake you when we stop to eat."

"I will never be warm again," Eden said, hunched over the fire. He ran his eyes over the grouped soldiers and his friends, wondering what secret they had found to keep warm. He was chilled through to the bone. Surely this was colder than Alaska? The North Pole was probably warmer.

The deep freeze was warmer.

Khari passed him a mug of steaming soup. "Get this into you. It will help."

"What would *help* would be a fucking snow-suit and a centrally heated house," Eden snapped uncharitably. "This is stupid weather." He looked around quickly at a touch on his shoulder to find Elnara standing behind him with a thickly woven wool blanket. She draped it around him, walking back to Gray without a word.

Khari frowned, scanning the trees. "I can't make you warm up and I don't know why," he said. "I've been trying, but whatever this is, is not just a cold snap. The *weather* isn't cold, right? The weather is normal. I'm not sure what's going on, Eden, or why you're so cold. Drink up," he said, pulling the edges of the new blanket together under Eden's chin. "We'll move on. The sooner we reach the Divide, the better, I think. You're turning blue."

"It's not the weather?" Eden asked.

"If it was, I'd fix it."

Gray stood up and peered into the trees, a crease marring his smooth forehead. "We should leave this place," he said. "I don't think we're alone."

"What is it?" Khari asked. He patted Eden's back and joined his brother, squinting to see into the forest.

"Wind spirit?" Gray said, glancing at Khari.

Khari chewed his lip. "Shit."

"Aye. We should leave."

Eden struggled to his feet, holding the blankets and cloaks tightly together under his chin. "Wind spirit? What do they do?"

"They can formulate directed attacks," Gray explained, picking up bags and tossing them onto his horse. He glanced at Takana, who was tidying away their small campsite.

She looked back at him. "I can't fight wind spirits. We need to shift."

"Why would they be attacking me?" Eden asked, shivering violently. His spine felt as though it was made of ice and the pain of frozen bones in his neck was becoming unbearable. "I haven't done anything to make one attack me, have I?"

"No, babe," Khari answered, drawing him close to hold him tight, trying to share his warmth. "I think it might be trying to keep you here and stop you leaving."

"Let's go," Gray said, helping Elnara mount their horse. "We'll try to outride it."

"I think he's passed out," Khari said from somewhere above Eden. The rocking motion of the horse continued relentlessly underneath him. The weight of another blanket pressed around his body and Khari's arms tightened around his chest, holding him in place.

The wind howled, tearing through the thick fabrics heaped around him. It screamed past his ears, slicing through his flesh, trying to tear it from his bones. Trying to make him turn back and re-enter the mountain. To give up and return to his ancient citadel. His cage.

Imprisoned, but safe.

"Move as fast as you can, all of you," Takana ordered. Her shouted command to her horse was followed by the beat of her soldiers, all riding as though the hounds of Hell were on their tails.

"Hup...c'mon, girl," Khari said to Jinx.

The rolling gait of his beloved horse increased and Eden felt his head slip from its place against Khari's chest. He was unable to stop it.

"Oh, no you don't, baby," Khari said, holding him tightly, his large hand cupping Eden's head to hold him in place. "Stay with me. We're nearly in the Border Lands."

"It's...so cold..."

Khari's mouth pressed against Eden's temple. "Just stay with me—we'll outrun it."

"Why is it trying to get me? It don't...make no sense."

"It knows you're trying to leave."

"What is it?"

"I'm not sure. Other than it's some kind of wind spirit. I'll keep you safe."

Eden gave himself over to the heaviness in his limbs. He recognised the sensation of suggestion, and knew Khari, or Gray, were forcing him to sleep. He was too weak to stop it, but for once, he did not care. He slept.

"Is this it?" Khari asked, looking at the gushing waters of the wide river. He held Eden in his arms, bouncing him upwards a bit when it seemed he was slipping. He shook his head when a soldier stepped forward to help with his load. He had no intention of letting Eden go.

"This is where he came through, yes," Takana said. She scanned the area, one hand on her gun, ready to shoot, should it be needful.

Ever watchful, she held Khari enthralled. She had done since the first time he had set eyes on the half-nymph, spitting her hate into the face of Jaizel's henchmen. There was something visceral about her that reminded Khari of his mother. A strength, born in the bone, that could not be learned or taught. A primal elegance that wove seamlessly with her lethalness.

"Is he still breathing?" Takana asked, flicking a glance at Eden, hidden under every blanket, shawl, cloak and scarf they possessed.

"He's alive," Khari said. "But fading. I don't think

he'll survive another attack from whatever the fuck wants him dead."

"It's an Echeneis, most likely," Gray said, turning in place to look into the trees, as if he would be able to see the wind-spirit and stop another attack.

"It's circling," Elnara said, "we need to move."

Takana walked to Khari's side. "To cross, you jump the river. It looks wide. In reality, it's little more than a creek. I will open the world on the other side as you launch into the air. You will land in a small glade, surrounded by Birch trees. Walk straight for a minute. Do not turn back. Do not pause. Just walk. Can you do that?"

Khari swallowed his fearful excitement. Anticipation fluttered in his chest. He looked down at Eden, gathered him as close and as tightly as he could, holding him as though he was a child, then looked at Takana.

"I am ready," he said. The words came out as a broken croak. He coughed. "I am ready," he said again, stronger.

"Do not stop walking for at least sixty seconds. Until you pass the Rowan. Do not look back, whatever you hear, Khari, you must keep walking, your step firm and sure. The Divide can take you, and there is no way for me to bring you back to either realm. Do you understand?"

"I understand."

Takana held her hand to his face. "Go," she shouted, as the wind screamed and ripped through the trees. "Go!"

Khari jumped, pushing himself from the riverbank with all the strength he possessed. He flew, hanging in the air for a long second, everywhere but nowhere.

The sky flashed above him. Thunder cracked the silence. Lightning seared the world. The trees vanished, came back into focus and flickered from sight. Leaving nothingness where moments earlier there had been verdant beauty. The water disappeared from under him. The river nothing but a barren slash of dark rock across the ruined landscape. He felt the worlds crackle and tear open. Felt Takana flick through them all as though finding a picture in a book. Getting the right one in place before Khari's foot touched the ground.

It was terrifying.

Khari squeezed his eyes shut, the scream of rage from the frozen wind monster following him as he flew through the air, its iced hands trying to claw him back and snatch Eden from him.

He would die before he let Eden go.

The sky turned a strange shade of palest blue. White clouds skidded high above small leaves of young birch trees. Khari landed on soft mulch, the soil dark beneath his boots. He heaved Eden back into his chest, securing his precious load, and walked quickly without giving into the temptation to look back. He could feel the gaping void of all the open worlds at his back, and had no intention of being dragged into it.

Thirty...thirty-one...thirty-two...

He walked carefully onwards. The air smelled odd. There were scents entirely new to him. The trees were strange. The ground unusual. From somewhere behind him, a loud roaring noise built to a crescendo of sound, then faded again. A monster? Eden had not mentioned there were roaring monsters in this realm, but it sounded like nothing Khari had ever heard before. Far away from where he walked, he could hear a steady thrumming sound, like a thousand machines all cranked up and running as one. Motors. He could hear motors. But nothing like the motors he had seen in Alfheim, in the kitchens. The mechanical machines that would keep a joint of meat turning, or the fires stoked.

Fifty-four...fifty-five...

He saw the rowan bush ahead of him, and sped up, passing it with a long outrush of breath. He stopped walking, turned, and slid to the ground with Eden draped over his thighs. Watching the pathway he had taken, he waited for the others to appear.

He had done it.

He was in the land he had always dreamed of.

He was home.

XXIII

Approaching his front door was surreal. Eden touched the glossy black wood and pulled his keys from his bag to fit one into the lock. Months away, and he felt as though he had left that morning. Everything had the touch of the unreal to it. He pushed the door open and walked into the wide hallway, putting his keys into the glass bowl under the window next to the door. He shrugged out of his coat and hung it on its peg, dropping his bag at the foot of the stairs, then waved Khari in. The others followed Khari through the door; Gray, Takana, Elnara and five bodyguards, who he doubted he would be allowed to stray far away from for the duration. He waved everyone but Khari into the large formal sitting room on his right, taking Khari by his hand and leading him up the stairs to his bedroom.

He picked up the phone on his bedside table and held it in his hand for a long moment before dialling a number long committed to memory and holding it to his ear.

"Peter speaking," his dad said. He sounded tired.

Eden had a lump forming in his throat. He closed his eyes. "Hi, Dad," he whispered.

"Eden? Oh, god, *Eden*! Where are you, son? Are you safe? Not hurt? Oh, god," Peter said, crying. "I was so worried. The police have been looking for you...we searched everywhere. They even dredged the creek. Where are you?"

"In my bedroom," Eden said, sniffing. He wiped

his nose on his wrist, then took the handkerchief Khari passed him, grateful when he was tugged into the circle of his arms and held close.

"Where did you go, Eden?" Peter asked him, his tone gentling.

"I...uh. I opened the forest," he said, realising how mental he must sound. "I wasn't mad, Dad. It is a magic wood...um. I walked through and I..."

"Okay," Peter said. "I'm just getting in the car. You're safe?"

"I'm safe," he said into the phone. "I'm not here alone, though, Dad. There's a lot of folks with me, so don't be startled that there's a load of people in the sitting room and a couple of horses in the garden. Oh...and a gyrfalcon has taken up residence on the garages. She's called Fain."

There was a long pause. "A falcon and horses?" Peter asked. "Anything else I should know?"

Eden drew a deep breath and rested his head on Khari's collar bone. "Uh, yeah...I met someone," he murmured. "I'd really like you to meet him," he added, holding his breath.

The silence stretched for almost a minute before Peter spoke. "All right," he said, quietly. "Is he nice?"

"Yeah."

"Not too old?"

"My age," Eden said.

"Okay. I had a vision of you bringing home a guy old enough to be your dad. So the rainbow button on your bag? It wasn't just to show solidarity?"

Eden choked back a nervous laugh. "No...I got it for me."

"I thought you might have had a gay friend. Not that it matters," Peter added. "I don't mean to sound as though it's a big deal. Uh. Good. It's good you met someone. How many other people are there?"

"Uh...eight, plus me and Khari."

"Khari? And he was in the woods...this is going to take me some time to process," Peter said. "Khari. Woods were a gateway to another realm...yeah. My life sure is mad. Okay. I'm on my way home. Do you want me to bring anything? Soda? Chips and dips? What do you want for dinner? The folks with you. Uh...are they, you know, human?"

"They're the Fae," Eden said, slipping a hand around Khari's back, starting to relax.

"Fae. Got it. Um. Do they have a special diet? I'll run to Sainsbury's—I think there might be enough to snack on in the fridge, but I'm not sure I can feed ten. Dietary requirements?"

Eden smiled through his tears. "Anything that doesn't have meat. I turned veggie. The others eat anything. Takana can't have vinegar. She's a wood nymph. Part tree."

Peter laughed tearfully. "All right, I'll make sure I don't douse dinner in weed killer. I'll see you soon. I...it's good to have you back, Eden. I missed you like crazy. You're really okay, and not hurt?"

"I'm okay. It's good to hear your voice, is all." He ended the call, swiping at his eyes. He looked at Khari. "That was more emotional than I thought it would be," he said, putting the phone back in its holder on his bedside table.

He sat on the edge of his bed. "Well, this is my room," he said, watching Khari look at everything with wonder. He would have to show him how it all worked, from the toilet flush to the laptop. For Khari, it was going to be a steep learning curve. And Gray, although Elnara would help Gray—Eden could concentrate his efforts on helping Khari settle in. He laid down, head on his pillows, and beckoned to Khari, needing to hold him and be quiet for a while.

"Are you okay?" he asked, once Khari had curled into his side. "This must all be a bit weird for you."

"Pleased you're not dead," Khari said bluntly, lifting his head to kiss Eden. "I was scared for you with that creature trying to get you. So I'm pleased you're alive, for a start. The flight over the river scared the living shit out of me," he said, lying back down. He chuckled. "I nearly pissed myself. Cars are a lot louder and faster than I had imagined, and I'm still trying to get my head around the idea of aeroplanes and helicopters you told me about. Everything is a thousand times brighter and more vivid than I had ever dreamed of, and it's all so *noisy*...but I'm all right. I like your house. It's big, though."

"Yeah, I guess so," Eden said. "Not so big compared to a palace carved into a mountain, though. So I could argue that your house is bigger, but I'll show you around later on. You'll love the kitchen. I'm pleased I'm not dead, too. Wind spirits are pretty scary."

"Aye. We'll try not to piss them off again."

"Sounds sensible. That's a light," he said, smiling at Khari's insatiable curiosity. He leant over Khari's chest and flicked the switch.

"You have magic!"

"Hardly. I have the National Grid," he said, as Khari flicked the light on and off repeatedly. The toilet flush was going to be hilarious. He grabbed Khari's hand, holding it to his chest, stilling his enthusiasm with a light kiss. "It will blow out," he explained. "The bulb."

"Oh," Khari said. He laid back down, but kept looking at the bedside lamp. He looked at the overhead light. "How does that one work?" he asked. Eden pointed out the switch next to his door. He was silent for a moment, then began pointing at everything in the bedroom. All of it was new; all of it amazing.

"Television," Eden said. He sat up to list all the items and gadgets that came with twenty-first century living in the Human Realm, explaining what each thing was for, briefly. "All electric. That's my cell phone," he added, when Khari picked it up from his bedside table. "I thought I'd lost it when I crossed the Divide, because it weren't in my bag. Looks like I left it at home that day."

"A phone, like that one?" Khari asked, pointing to the cordless land line receiver. "You use it to talk to people, aye?"

"Uh, yeah," Eden decided the world of Apps, games and gadgets could wait a while. Khari looked as though his brain was about to pop as it was. "It needs charging," he said. "Um...do you want to see downstairs?"

"All right. What's through there, though?"

"My bathroom," Eden said, "save that for later. I want to be relaxed and alone when you discover that for the first time," he said. He tugged Khari into his arms and slid his hands into the back pockets of his jeans, holding him close. "There are three words I can say to you that will make you mine forever," he joked.

"Oh?" Khari nipped his lip gently. "Three words?"

"The most seductive, beautiful, words anyone can

say."

"Uh huh..."

"Hot," Eden said, kissing Khari, "running...water."

Khari blinked at him, a small frown creasing his forehead and wrinkling his nose. "Is that even possible?"

"It is, yeah. You'll love it."

"Show me?"

"Later, okay?" Eden said, kissing him again and letting him go. "We can share a bath. Or a shower..."

"A shower? I finally get to see what one of these showers you keep on about are like, aye? I can't wait."

Oh, yes, a shower would be fun, Eden decided, tugging Khari down the stairs and through the main hallway to the back of the house and the kitchen. He stopped close to the large scrubbed oak dining table and watched as Khari looked at the black granite surface of the island and the gleaming worktops; the white cupboards, holding their contents secret; the range cooker, deep ceramic sinks and shining appliances. Knowing his father always kept the fridge stocked, Eden opened it and laughed loudly at the sheer amazement on Khari's face as Khari crept closer, his mouth opening and closing as he tried to form words.

But then, after a lifetime of struggle and never knowing fully where his next meal would be coming from? Yes, he could see why the fridge would be fantastic beyond belief. Eden made a mental note to take Khari to the supermarket at the earliest opportunity.

"This is...I don't have the words," Khari said, reverently holding an apple from the salad drawer. He looked at a pot of yoghurt, shaking his head in wonder.

"This is all food?" he asked, prodding a banana and raising one eyebrow.

"Yeah," Eden said. He reached for a chocolate mousse and held it out to Khari, leaning back against the island to watch. "Spoons are in the drawer to your right," he said, pointing at the cutlery drawer. "You peel off the lid and eat what's inside."

"All right...oh, that's a lot of spoons. Are these silver?...oh. oh, good gods," Khari mumbled around a mouthful of mousse. "...is goo'..." he said, closing his eyes in bliss.

Eden giggled. "Chocolate."

"Better than cake," Khari said, scraping the small pot. "Cake has nothing on chocolate, does it? Oh, aye, I like this."

"Oh, I dunno. Try chocolate cake."

"Feed me chocolate cake!" Khari demanded. "I *must* have chocolate cake!"

"Do elves get fat?"

"I won't be getting fat, babe. Feed me cake!"

Eden took Khari in his arms. He opened a cupboard and passed him a Mars Bar. "I can see you becoming a secret binge eater."

"No secret," Khari said, mouth full. He covered his mouth with his hand. "Sorry," he mumbled. "Excited. Forgot you don't want to see my food. Oh, Eden...this is so nice. What's that?"

"Crisps. Shouldn't you slow down? Too much will make you get cramps and then...well. Tonight, you're gonna be kinda uncomfy, and I was thinking we could, maybe, um..."

Khari arched a brow. "One day, you'll be able to talk about sex without squirming," he said. "Well, making out, as you call it. Sure it's not sex?"

"Not fully," Eden popped open a can of diet coke, drinking deeply before handing Khari the can. He smiled at his amazed reaction, knowing he was never going to tire of showing Khari the world he had longed for—and everything in it.

It took his mind off some of his own fears about being back in the realm he was born in. He could not shake off the thought that he was in entirely the wrong place. That safety, however carefully cultivated, was never going to be more than an illusion the whole time he was in the human realm.

He shook himself and grinned brightly, helping Khari open tins of tuna and beans, mushy peas, kidney beans. Showed him popcorn made in the microwave, made a milkshake.

And then, there was the sound of the front door opening. A flurry of movement from the front of the house told him that his guard detail was guarding. His dad's laugh, deep and disbelieving, floated to the kitchen, and Peter's voice said something too low to hear properly.

Eden placed a tub of ice cream down on the counter, slowly. Khari rubbed his back in mute support as he turned to face the kitchen door, and saw his father for the first time in months.

"Hey, Dad," he said, taking a small step forward.

Peter stared at him as though he was an apparition, about to vanish. He held his arms out, catching Eden as he fell into the circle of secure strength that had carried him through all of his fears and tears over this lifetime.

"You broke through the woods, huh?" Peter asked, mumbling past his own tears. "Found the voice that was driving you mad? The dreams?"

Eden held his hand out behind him to where Khari was standing, beckoning him closer. "Dream," he mumbled into Peter's shirt. "...sreal..."

"I never thought it wasn't, son," Peter said. "It's lovely to make your acquaintance. You must be Khari?"

"I am, sir, aye. It's a pleasure to meet you."

"His real name's Prince Za'akhar," Eden said through his tears. "He's an elf. And Elemental."

"It's lovely to meet you, Khari. Oh, Eden, I've missed you so much. I was worried, but kept telling myself that there weren't no way in Hell you coulda gotten killed by anything as *ordinary* as Ridley Stewart. The police were searching and even had divers in the creek near where y'all vanished, then they dredged it. I swear this entire island has been pulled apart looking for you...I was scared, but not *scared*. I knew you weren't dead. But...you just *went*, Eden. It had me worried." Peter pushed him back, holding his shoulders so he could better see him. "You look well. Magic suits you. your...um...he's magic? Fae?"

"My boyfriend? You can call him my boyfriend. It's okay, Dad."

"Yeah." Peter looked between them both. "I admit it's a shock that you're, um..."

"Gay?"

"With someone," Peter said. "I thought you were asexual."

Khari almost choked on his mirth.

Peter grinned. "Not asexual, I take it?"

"No!" Khari said. "Orien's Blood, asexual is about the last thing he is."

"Just gayer than Lapland at Christmas?"

"Guess so." Eden sobered as Gray peered around the kitchen door. "Dad, this is Khari's big brother," he said, waving Gray into the kitchen. "He's the Crown Prince for one of the Elven lands. Khari is the Crown Prince for the other. Khari has a different biological father to Gray, so it works out they should get one each..." Eden started introducing each of the people he had grown to love as his family, explaining who—and what—they were to his dad. Laughing and joking with the motley bunch of soldiers and royals, Peter looked stunned but coped well, chatting with everyone while Eden snuggled in the safe circle of Khari's arms, just watching his two lives merge together.

"We should be thanking you," Takana said, holding out her hand for Peter to take. "And your late wife's memory. You are the ones, after all, whose belief and hope led to Eden's birth. You protected him well, although you didn't know what you did. You raised him without hate, yet never hid evil from him. You loved him and let him grow, knowing he was not of your kind. I thank you, Eden's Father. And I thank your wife. You did well."

Peter shrugged. "We were never sure. We wondered, but we were never sure."

"Certainty would have made you scared. This way was better. You simply raised an exceptional child, and gave him as much of the world as it was yours to give. I can only hope to be half the mother your wife was."

"I thank you," Peter said formally. "But it was an honour to have the gift of Eden entrusted to us. May I show you all to your rooms? I am afraid that the soldiers you bring with you will have to share two of the guest rooms, but I can squeeze you all in without too much trouble. Eden?"

"Yes, Dad?"

"There's horse feed and hay in the car. Get it and make a start in getting the old stables suitable for tenants. Then vacuum the goddamn hay from the back seat of my car. Khari. You look like a capable sort of man. You can fetch nails and oil from the garage and fix the hinges of the old stalls. I saw the big black horse, and he'll break out in seconds. Miss Takana, ma'am? Would you mind helping me arrange bedding and towels? Prince Gray, please make a note of everyone's eating preferences and whether anyone is deathly allergic to seafood, or anything like that." Peter grinned and looked at Elnara. "You, ma'am, would you mind taking a walk to the end of the road? There's an off license there, and I *really* need a stiff drink."

"Hot. Running. Water," Eden said, his voice low as he pulled Khari gently into his bath to stand under the shower, eyes on his face.

"The sexiest words in any world."

"You like?"

Khari tipped his head back under the spray and let the nearly scalding water pelt his head and scarred back. His eyes fell closed. "You have no idea."

Eden kissed his throat, licking the water as it ran down between his clavicles to his chest. Reaching for the shower gel, he squirted some into his hands and rubbed Khari's chest and shoulders until it foamed.

Khari's low moan of bliss made him smile to himself.

"Nice?"

Khari opened his eyes to treat him to a full golden gaze of blazing sunlight. "Don't stop," he said throatily. He held a hand around Eden's waist. "Clean me...please?"

Eden caught the underlying current in the request and shook his head. "You're clean enough...but I'll wash you," he said, voice quiet. "Turn around and hold your hands on the tiles."

Khari turned. "Be gentle," he said. "It's bad today."

Eden lathered gel in his hands and slid his palm over fragile skin, skimming across the damaged surface. "I haven't hurt you, yet," he whispered, kissing Khari behind his ear. "I'll get your cream when we're done. Is this okay?"

"It's on the edge of painful," Khari said softly. "It's nice though. Don't stop."

If there was one thing he wasn't planning on doing, it was stopping. Eden used the pads of his thumbs to carefully massage Khari's spine, watching the visible muscles under the tissue thin skin move and relax at his touch. He focused on the opaque flesh under his thumbs and forced his mind to *see* how to fix it.

It had to be possible. Khari may hold the essence of who he was, but he was some kind of god, right? He *had* to be able to lift some of this agony. Fix some of the damage.

He was responsible for it. If Khari did not hold his powers, after all, then he would never have been tortured beyond endurance.

The skin under his touch rippled. Sure he was not

imagining it, Eden watched as some of the tracing paper opaqueness faded; the brown torn muscles beneath were harder to see. Less ruined beneath the surface.

"Oh, God," Khari said. "Literally," he added, casting a glance at Eden. "Magic hands."

Not daring to believe that he could be healing—and it was so, *so* slight anyway. "I would never hurt you," he said, kissing the curve of Khari's spine at the base of his neck. Held back by the small voice in his mind telling him *enough*, he slid one hand down Khari's back and around to his stomach, pulling him back into his chest and holding him there as he washed his hair with his free hand, watching each breath and nuance of pleasure as the hot water cascaded down over Khari's face. He felt his erection slide against Khari's backside and started to pull away.

"Don't," Khari said, so softly that Eden had to strain to hear him. "I know you won't do anything I don't want. Hold me. I like feeling you close."

"You are so...beautiful," Eden breathed, trying to focus on washing Khari when every nerve and sinew screamed at him to make love to the man until neither of them could breathe easily. "I want you. So much."

"Want me how?"

Eden opened his mouth, willing the words to come. He just had to say them. *Take me. Love me.*

Khari turned in his arms and met his mouth, kissing him deeply. Quietly. Softly. "You're not ready," he said, pulling back just enough to speak. His lips grazed Eden's as he gazed into his eyes. His soul. "Tell me how you want me..."

Eden shook his head. "I don't know."

"Then," Khari said, reaching down between them

and closing his wet hand around Eden's cock, "waiting is very...sensible...don't you think?"

Eden watched as Khari slid down his chest, kneeling in front of him. He heaved in a breath as pink lips skimmed across his pelvis and brushed lower.

"Shit," he groaned. "Khari...you don't have to."

"I want to," Khari said, looking up at him, one hand wrapped around him, moving languidly. "Do you want me to?"

Eden looked downwards.

"Do you want me to?" Khari repeated, his free hand sliding up Eden's chest. "I will never do anything you don't want me to do."

"Will you promise to not do anything *you* don't want to do?" Eden asked, holding onto his sanity. "I don't want you on any other terms."

Khari's tongue licked him from root to tip. "I promise," he said. "Do you want this?"

Eden tipped his head back, linking his fingers into Khari's and holding the hand snaking up his torso. One hand stroking him was more than enough to focus on.

"Eden?"

"Yes," Eden breathed as he was surrounded by warm wetness. He closed his eyes, the wall cool against his free hand, despite the heat. "Oh, god, yes," he whispered. "I want this. I want...everything." He thought he should maybe get out of the bath, out from under the shower...get onto the bed...

Then Khari moved his hand, taking him deeply in his mouth, and he thought no more.

XXIV

You have something of mine.

Khari shot up in the bed, his hand reaching automatically for his sword. He frowned into the dark shadows, lit by the strange lights that were *everywhere* in this realm. A small crack under the bedroom door allowed the light from the hallway to seep in. Outside, in the distance, there were bright orange lamps to light the street. The stars were dimmed in the sky, so bright was the light on the ground.

He looked down at Eden's sleeping face, catching his breath, as he always did when he looked at the man who had claimed him as his own. Who had poured powers untold into his body and given him life, although Eden was yet to realise the fullness of what he had managed to do.

Khari slid from the bed and grabbed his second sword, gripping both.

You have something of mine.

He turned quickly, as though if he moved fast enough he would catch Jaizel at his back and kill him before the pain started.

"I have nothing you could ever hope to claim," he hissed crouching; prepared to fight to the death before Eden was harmed.

A shadow under the bedroom door flickered. Khari watched Gray's outline as it slid through the closed door, then faded.

"He spoke," Khari said to the empty space he knew his brother occupied.

"I heard. He is not here."

"You checked."

"I did, aye." Gray said.

"He can't get Eden."

Gray was quiet. The air shifted to Khari's left. He turned, sure Gray had walked that way.

"Eden will give himself to protect you, and you would give yourself before seeing Eden taken," Gray said. A hand stroked Khari's hair. "He will hurt one of you. Both as much as each other, my love. Different ways, but the pain shall be as deep. The cut as fatal. The wound beyond bearing. The one, or the other..."

"We can't live without each other. You know that as well as I do, Gray."

"Aye, I know, and he will hurt both," Gray said, the air in the room moving again as Gray flitted away from Khari.

"There are times," Khari said, "that I *really* miss Mum. She would have known what to do."

I will take what is mine...

"You will fuck off," Khari breathed. "He's mine."

"Eden alone is no good to him. He must know that?"

Khari propped his swords back in their place next to the bed and pulled a pair of sweats on. He walked to the window. "I don't think he does. I think he's found out that I'm not the only one born that day. Night. He thinks Eden holds powers he can use. He thinks Eden is holding powers, like I hold powers. He knows that he can't get mine...so he's going to try and take Eden's."

"Eden's are in you."

"Mostly," Khari looked around as Gray became visible. "He has a few powers of his own, in him, but they're coming slow and steady."

Gray looked at Eden, sleeping deeply under the human style *duvet*. "The best powers are in you, Khari."

"They are, aye."

"He can't fight his way out of a sack next to Jaizel."

"No. But he's getting there." Khari looked at his brother. "He's not totally without any kind of innate skills. He's good."

"For a human."

"Oh, humans are nothing like him. It's no wonder he felt outside of everything."

Gray looked at Eden's face and sat on the edge of the bed. "You can't give him his power?"

"Not until he asks for it. He has to take it from me. I can't offer."

"Then make him ask for it!"

Khari turned and leant against the windowsill. He looked at Eden, asleep and peaceful. "No," he said.

"Khari..."

"No. What will happen, will happen. It will happen for a reason. *He* will know that reason...I can't go against that."

"You could die."

"Aye, I could."

"You don't care?"

"I have him. I *know* him. Gray...I have been able to love a god. I have watched as *my* touch brings a *God* to life. I have watched him cry my name...so no. No, I don't care. If I die now, I will die well."

I will take what is mine. I will take him...and I will watch him scream...

Gray met Khari's eyes and shook his head. He

pulled Khari into his arms.

"We will stop him."

"We have to."

"Khari. You have to train him."

"I know...I will. Can we keep him safe, Gray?"

"I want to say yes, but honestly, I don't know. One of you, alone, I could keep safe. The two of you, together, are going to start kicking out a *lot* of power sooner rather than later. I don't know if I can hide you both. I don't think I have the power to stand against Jaizel. Not yet. Even with the Alfheimian army at my back. I can't say yes," he said. "But I promise I will die trying, if that's what it takes."

Eden stirred, rolling to slide his hand over the sheet where Khari had been. His eyes fluttered open and he propped himself up on his elbow. Seeing Khari with Gray, he sat up, the duvet pooling around his groin. "Hey. You okay?"

Khari fought down the instant arousal that he could barely control when Eden was dressed—Eden naked, in bed, and dishevelled with sleep was too much for any red-blooded male. Gray walked to the door.

"I was just making sure Khari was all right," he said, leaving the bedroom. "Night."

"Uh...night," Eden said, watching the door close. He looked at Khari. "He lies worse than you do. What happened?"

Khari slipped the sweats down his legs, kicking them away from the bed, and climbed into the warm space next to Eden. He ran the pad of his thumb across one high cheekbone, knowing he could not lose this man and stay sane.

"I heard Jaizel's voice. It scared me, because I

thought he'd found me," he said, watching Eden's eyes flash with icy silver fire. The colour change of his irises worked well as an emotional gauge. The silver, when it overtook the green, spoke of high emotions that could not be contained. Whether that silver shone with a molten heat, or with the coldness of a frozen diamond told Khari more than words ever could.

Right now, Eden was very, *very*, angry.

"He's here?" Eden asked, leaning over the bed to his bedside table. He yanked open the drawer and grabbed his handgun, an object he had taken from the safe earlier in the day and kept close to him since. He pushed the clip holding bullets into the handle and pulled something that made a *final* sort of sound.

"He's not here," Khari said, eyes on the weapon. "He was in my head. And Gray's."

Eden grunted and put the gun on top of his bedside table. "You're safe?"

"As safe as I can be," Khari said, not able to lie. "Eden...you can't try and kill Jaizel with a gun. I know it's a powerful weapon, but he's not going to be taken down with a bullet."

"Damnit, Khari, I know that," Eden snapped. He clamped his mouth shut. "Sorry," he said after a second of silence. "I never meant to sound that harsh. Just...he scares me. He makes me so fucking angry that I feel as though I could tear him limb from limb. Fucking *smite* him, or something. But at the same time, he has me scared enough that I worry I'm gonna lose all bowel control and just shit myself with fear." Eden looked at Khari flopping back down to the pillows to drag a hand down his face. "Sorry. What did he say?"

"*You have something of mine*, again. Same as the

note said. He said he will take what is his."

"Fuck," Eden said. "He was in your head?"

"It's like telepathy."

"He's not here?"

"No," Khari said, stroking Eden's face. "He's not here."

Eden took his hand, bringing his fingers to his mouth, and kissed the tips of each finger, lightly. It was enough to send ribbons of electric heat up Khari's arm and to his soul. He drew in a short breath, watching as Eden turned his hand over and kissed his palm, licking the tender skin there to set off an incendiary response he was powerless to control. Khari watched the steely ice of Eden's eyes melt into a flowing mercury radiance and knew he was lost.

He bent his head, holding Eden beneath him and finding his mouth with his tongue to taste and savour. Eden rippled under his touch. A reaction that brought all his blood rushing to his groin. He moved Eden's hand slowly downwards, until warm fingers danced over a hardness that was soon going to be able to crack ice.

"Can you feel what you do to me?" he asked under his breath, circling one dark nipple with his thumb. "Do you have any idea, Eden, what you do to me?"

Eden closed his hand to hold him in a tight grip of iced fire. "Is it anything like what you do to me?" he asked, full lips brushing against Khari's collar bone.

The solid erection digging into his hip told Khari that, yes, it was likely along the same lines. He waited for Eden to close his eyes. Block out the world. Fall silent. Let Khari explore and do what *he* wanted, without daring to reciprocate. Too scared. Too nervous.

Eden looked at him, his free hand rising to stroke down Khari's chest, silver eyes flashing in the darkness. Khari sensed *this* time, something was changing. Something in Eden was changing.

He lowered his head, kissing Eden with a slow passion. Forcing himself not to speak, he stayed silent, simply holding Eden's eyes, hoping he read the unspoken words correctly. To get this wrong would kill his soul. He could *not* be Jaizel. He could *not* do that to Eden. Cause him pain, hurt him, destroy him.

Eden reached to the drawer of his table, taking something from it to press into Khari's hand.

"What..."

"Better than oil," Eden caught Khari's earlobe in his teeth and sucked gently. "Trust me."

Khari flipped the plastic lid, pouring something slick and cool into his palm. He rubbed his thumb against his finger, feeling the smoothness of the liquid. It was strange but, yes, it was better than oil. He stroked his palm down the length of Eden's straining erection. Lifting his head, Khari was surprised to find Eden's silvery eyes still staring at him. He had almost given up hoping Eden would *see* him while he made love to him with his hands, mouth and words.

"Are you all right, babe?" he asked, worried by Eden's attention.

"Finding my words," Eden replied.

"Oh?" he asked, stroking his hand down Eden's thigh and back to his hip, lifting his leg by degrees. Trailing his fingertips down Eden's inner thigh, he held his breath when Eden moaned quietly and lifted his hips, rocking in a primal rhythm to grind softly against him.

"That is...nice," Khari said, not looking away from

Eden's face. He stroked back down, then up, feeling the hairs on Eden's leg lift under his skin. He started to move his hand down again, stopped in his tracks when Eden moved under him, changing his course. He looked down at Eden, hand still, his fingers barely a hairsbreadth away from secret dark and warm places that had filled his dreams to slowly send him out of his mind with desire.

"Don't stop," Eden whispered, voice shaking. "I want you. I want you to...I want to feel you inside me," he said, barely breathing. "I want to know what it would be like...to have you a part of me. I want to know what...what you feel like. In me." He held a hand over Khari's heart. "I know we're...it's..." He huffed a breath and tried again, groping for what he was trying to say. "I want you to make love to me,." He rushed out the words in case they escaped before they were said. "I want to know what it's like to have you make love to me. Be in me. Move with me. Want me. I don't know how long we'll be safe. I know we're going to be hunted down, Khari...and as much as it all scares me...it makes me want you more. I don't want to wait and then find I waited too long...and I'll never have this moment again...and I..."

Khari shut him up by lowering his head to kiss him deeply, tasting his mouth and sharing his air. He lifted his head. "You're sure?"

"Don't...don't hurt me. Or try not to, too much." Eden hesitated, clearly trying to find a way to say something else. Khari waited, moving his hand in slow circles over Eden's backside. He guessed there was at least four hours until dawn. He was in no rush.

"Do we, uh...should we, um, use a condom?" Eden asked.

"What's that?" Khari asked, lying next to Eden again. Pulling him onto his side to face him. He waited while another new thing was explained to him, then shrugged. "I can't get you pregnant, and I can't catch any kind of disease like that," he said eventually. He saw relief flash in Eden's eyes. "You were worried, because of what happened to me?" he asked. "I'm not at all mad at you, so don't look as though you've done something wrong," he added, pulling Eden's thigh up and over his hip. He nipped at Eden's lower lip. "I don't have anything like a disease. I'm an elf. We can't contract illnesses, and certainly not human ones. What do you want to do? Whatever makes you happy, Eden."

"I...I think I would like to...just feel you."

Khari met Eden's mouth gently. "You're going to have to try and relax, at some point."

Eden gave a small chuckle, flushing warmly. Nervous, even now. "Sorry," he said. "This is something that books couldn't much help with, and watching porn was a mistake—it looked fucking agonising."

Khari decided he would leave the question of what porn might be unanswered, instead kissing his way from Eden's mouth to his jaw, and down to his collar bone. "It's not meant to hurt," he said, licking the bud of Eden's nipple and drawing the sensitive skin into his mouth to suck gently. He let go, moving to pay the other one attention.

It wasn't meant to hurt. Ever. He knew that, despite what had been done to him. He *knew*, the same as he knew to instinctively draw breath and eat and drink, that it was never meant to be like anything he had known at Jaizel's hands.

He vowed Eden would never have any reason to be afraid. Not after he was through, anyway. He moved down the bed, licking and sucking, catching skin tenderly between his teeth as he worked at making Eden's body sing and stand to attention. Sliding his hand across Eden's backside, he raised his head to find Eden's lips with his own again, moving his fingers with infinite slowness, leaving Eden to push down onto him in his own sweet time, circling the tight muscle without intent.

"Oh, god," Eden moaned, pressing down, his eyes wide. One arm around Khari's neck, he bit his lip between his teeth and hissed a breath, pushing further.

"Slowly...aye, like that," Khari said, kissing Eden calm. "This isn't to be rushed...gods, you look so beautiful, right now," he said, enthralled at the flashing desire and want in Eden's eyes. Obeying an unspoken command, he slid his finger deeper, watching Eden arch back, although his leg held Khari pinned close, keeping him there. Eden looked at him again, blazing silver fire.

Khari felt something deep within him snap and fly up to the heavens. Something broke free and his head span, even as he was pulled into the fathomless depths of Eden's eyes, bound by the blazing beauty that held the secrets to the worlds. He gasped, hardly aware of his movements as Eden held him, moving him above his body and curling his legs upwards to hold his arse and pull him closer. Wanting. Needing.

He held himself up on his elbows, obeying each touch from Eden, moving where he was wanted, until he found he was at the point of no return. He tried to force himself to stop shaking, gliding into Eden by small degrees, eyes locked onto the mirror of his soul as Eden tipped his head back, raised his hips, and pulled him in, joining them with a long moan of pained pleasure.

"Oh...my...god," Khari panted.   He was only vaguely aware of soft silvery blue lights floating from the pores of his skin, like miniscule dust particles on the air. They leaked from him as he moved his hips in a languorous circle to draw an immediate low moan from Eden. It was a sound that went from his ears straight to his soul.

His. Eden was his.

And he was Eden's. Always.

This *was what it was all about.* This *was worth dying for.*

More lighted particles floated serenely from his skin, flying lazily into the air surrounding them before sinking softly into Eden's body. Lighting on his dark skin.   Leaving him glowing for a second.   Then dissipating and vanishing from sight.   Each time it happened, Eden gasped. Panting. Then moved to pull Khari deeper into himself. Clawing at him to try and make them one being. No end to one before the other began; nothing between them.

"More," Eden breathed, his eyes on fire as he glanced at Khari. "Again."

Khari pulled back, then pushed hard, watching Eden's response. The flared pupils and gasped breath Eden gave nearly pulled him over the edge, but he held on. He could feel Eden's cock; hot, hard and heavy between their stomachs, and moved to create deliberate friction.

"Oh, fucking hell," Eden panted, writhing beneath him. "Again!"

"God, Eden...God," he cried, struggling to hold the remnants of his sanity as he moved faster, harder, slower, deeper in response to each small movement under him, each breath, every clench of a hand and bite of a lip, reading Eden's body as his powers leaked from him into the man they were meant for, filling him and binding them as they moved and moaned together, climbing the pinnacle of hedonistic pleasure to find new heights. He buried a scream in Eden's neck when Eden pulled him, hard, into himself, knowing he could not hold on; knowing he could not keep going. Not when it felt like this. Not with Eden shouting his name and moving so ruthlessly underneath him; taking him; owning him.

"Eden...I..."

Eden grabbed his neck to bring his face down, kissing him desperately. His climax curled in his gut, swirling in his spine, filling his body with unnameable heat and power. He lifted himself on his hands, pushing into Eden as deeply as he could, throwing his head back as Eden screamed his own release beneath him, joining him in a moment of absolute perfect blankness. Nothing and no one existed except for them and that single moment. The world faded. Only Eden existed, and the glowing silver eyes that pulled him out of himself as he came with enough force to stop his heart beating for a long, long moment, filling Eden. Claiming him.

He gulped a breath, falling down onto Eden's chest, unable to do more than heave air into his lungs as his heart resumed beating, thudding in his chest and in every nerve. Eden touched his leg, and he quivered, a small sound escaping his lips. A bead of sweat ran down his face, dripping onto Eden's chest.

He drew in another breath, hearing his small sob. He blinked, his eyes stinging with sweat and encroaching tears. Eden held a hand on his back, holding him still. A shiver ran through Eden's body, and Khari knew Eden was crying before he forced himself to lift his head.

He moved shakily, slipping out of Eden as he propped himself up on his elbow. Eden looked at him, catching a single tear from Khari's cheek on his thumb, and licking the wetness off. Khari gazed down, kissing a trail of salt as it brimmed over to trickle down Eden's cheek.

"I...that was..."

Eden wiped his face, not breaking their connection.

Khari remembered the sight of the infinitesimal glowing particles sinking into Eden's body. "Did they all find you?" he asked. "Your...were they your powers?"

"Some," Eden said. "I can feel them. Feel you," he added, quietly. "It feels beautiful."

"Not hurt?"

Eden, half sobbing, shook his head. He pulled Khari down, hiding his tears in his neck, holding him tightly. "I never thought it would feel anything like it did," he said, when he had got a small degree of control of himself. "Khari...it was perfect. You were perfect."

"You were," Khari said, closing his eyes. "You're beautiful." He moved his head against Eden's chest. Eden pulled the duvet over them, enfolding them both in a warm cocoon. "You're mine," he said, holding a hand over Eden's heart. He felt the strong beats under his palm, pounding in perfect time with his own.

"Yours," Eden said sleepily. "Will you run away if I tell you I love you?"

Khari smiled. "No. You can tell me."

"I love you."

Linking his fingers through Eden's, Khari brought their hands to his mouth and kissed Eden's knuckles. "I love you too."

"I would ask if you slept well," Takana said to Khari as he walked into the large kitchen, still tugging his sweatshirt into place, "but I heard that you didn't sleep well at all."

Khari rolled his eyes as Takana and her guards laughed over their bowls of golden coloured shards of...something. A box, picture on the front, proclaimed the legend *Corn Flakes*, so he assumed that was what filled the bowls. It looked odd. He opened the fridge and considered the array of strange and exotic foods within.

"I hope you never wore Eden out too much," Takana continued. "He has to be able to train and fight."

Khari looked at Takana. "Jealous that someone other than you is being bedded?" he asked, grinning. "Don't worry. Cole will be here in a few days, and you can torment us all with your public foreplay again."

"Jealous? My room is smack bang in the middle of the hallway. I had you and Eden on one side, and Gray and Ellie on the other. Nearly gave myself a sprain trying to relieve the building tension," she quipped, and winked. "Lucky I have strong fingers, right?"

"You never just actually said that?" Khari asked. He turned back to the fridge, shaking his head. He selected a pack of mixed chopped fruits, something called a yoghurt, an apple, and a chocolate mousse—he loved chocolate—taking it all over to the table and sitting down. He reached for a slice of lightly golden toast and took a plate one of the guards handed him. Frowning at a small jar, he hesitantly allowed Takana to take his toast and smear it with something that looked like gooey black tree-sap.

"Marmite," Takana said, handing him back his toast. "Try it. Would you like something hot as well?"

"Please, yes," he answered, chewing a mouthful of Marmite. He liked Marmite. "Whatever's going," he added, looking at Takana. "I'm famished."

"No doubt. So where is wonder-boy?"

"Sleeping."

"You did wear him out, then?"

"Eventually, aye," he said, eating fruit. He saw, in his mind, Eden arching backwards beneath him, his eyes locked onto his face as he moved with a languid sensuality that had held Khari captive. He forced himself to sip at the coffee Takana slid next to his plate, shivering internally with barely banked fiery lust.

It was lucky Eden had slept, or he would have been unable to leave the bed, making love until he withered away or starved to death.

"What's this?" he asked, when Takana placed another plate in front of him, taking away his toast plate.

"Beans on toast, eggs, bacon, and mushrooms."

"It's all...colourful."

"And tasty. Eat up, because you need your strength. Morning, lovebirds!" she said as Gray walked through the door with Elnara.

Khari buried a laugh. Gray looked dazed and as though he had been pulled through a wringer. His hair was mussed and held in a scruffy knotted tail at the nape of his neck, which was covered with small red bite marks. A claw mark was just visible above the neck of his T-shirt, and his eyes shone with a stunned wonder Khari had never thought to see there. Not in Gray's face. Gray, who was regal and proud, standoffish and controlled at all times, never letting himself relax or letting his guard down. Gray had always seemed to be the male equivalent of an Ice Queen—even when he was whoring to keep them both alive, nothing had broken through his facade of calm superiority.

And here he stood, looking as though Elnara had fucked him through the mattress.

Takana walked past her niece and slapped palms. She grinned over at Gray, busying herself with cooking up more food.

"Oh, bacon," Elnara said, gravitating towards the stove. She grabbed two plates and started piling them with food as Gray sat at the table and stared at Khari, still dazed and vacant.

Khari pushed the teapot towards his brother. "Good night?"

"Uh," Gray managed. He poured tea and sipped from the ceramic mug. Meeting Khari's eyes over the rim, he grinned briefly. "Very good."

"I thought it best to do something to block you out, Khari," Elnara said, sitting down with every appearance of demureness. "No Eden? Did the poor boy wear himself out?"

"Can we not talk about me over the breakfast table?" Eden drawled, leaning against the doorframe. "Some things are meant to be personal, you know?"

"Well, maybe you shouldn't have made so much noise," Takana said.

Eden raised a brow. "I reckon I was quiet,

considering. Yeah, eggs would be great," he said when Takana held up the pan, offering to cook. "And some beans and tomatoes. Morning," he said softly, taking the empty seat to Khari's left. "You should have woke me."

Khari touched Eden's cheek briefly, simply because he was physically unable to go longer than a few moments without touching Eden in some way or another. "You looked peaceful, so I thought I'd leave you for a while longer. Are you all right?" he asked, pitching his voice as quiet as he could and still get sound.

Eden looked at him for a few seconds, then let a slow smile spread over his face. "So long as we're training in armed combat, and I don't have to ride a horse."

Khari inhaled his coffee. Trying to not choke to death at the table, he gazed at Eden, hardly believing the grin lighting his dark face and making his eyes shine brighter than ever.

"Reckon horse riding is gonna have to wait a few days, don't you?" Eden asked, holding out a napkin. "Don't die. I refuse to allow you to die, even more so after last night. I'm fine," he said, softly. "Just great, as it happens. Feel...good." He looked around the table, realising everyone was staring at him. "What? I grew another head? Have snot hanging off the end of my nose? What's wrong?"

"You look...happy," Takana said, looking down into her coffee cup. "As though, oh, I don't even know how to explain it. You just look different."

"And not different because you got laid," Elnara added. "Before you get all worried about that."

Eden looked at Khari for reassurance.

426

"It's not that sort of change," Khari confirmed. "It's more likely because of what happened," he said, thinking again of flowing, floating, blue particles leaving him in a peaceful dance to reach Eden.

"Oh," Eden said, smiling secretly. "Okay."

"Your eyes are totally silver."

"I am aware."

"It looks good."

Eden smiled. It could have illuminated a room easily. "Good to know," he said, cutting into the eggs Takana placed in front of him. "I can't change them back to green. They seem to be stuck this colour. It was...a shock," he added, shrugging. "They look a bit weird, to me, but as there ain't nothing I can do about it, reckon I'll just have to get used to it."

Khari watched the silver mercury shift and swirl around the inky-blackness of Eden's pupils. The silver seemed to dance and move to a silent beat, and he knew he wasn't being poetic when he thought Eden's eyes held a lot more secrets than they had before. They held a knowledge of something deeper and older than Khari could fathom.

He was watching a God come slowly back to life. Full, glorious, beautiful life.

And he had been the one to wake him.

"Okay, kidlings," Takana said, stacking the dishwasher with empty plates. "Eat up and get ready for action. I want you all in the garden in twenty minutes. Ready and willing to be worked until you can't fucking stand. Am I understood?"

Khari shared a look with Gray and raised one eyebrow. He looked Takana over. She crossed her arms and looked back at him.

"You think I can't break you, my prince?" she

asked, her voice deceptively soft. "I have watched you and studied you for months. You think you have no weaknesses? You think you are the best you can possibly be?"

Khari stood and faced her, seeing a general of an army and not the fun-loving princess who could reduce him to giggles with her quick wit and ready tongue.

"I think I am intrigued," Khari said, "as to what you think you can possibly teach me."

Takana waved a hand. Spiralling from nowhere at all, ribbons of mist lashed out faster than his eye could follow, to loop around his neck. They were not burning him, but the heat flowing off them in waves was all he needed to feel to know that Takana was going easy on him. He stayed still and waited.

"Not going to fight them, my prince?" she asked, swaying over to stand in front of him. She held up her hand, cutting off objections from Eden and Gray. She flicked her knife close to Khari's throat, her face growing pointed and elongated as her eyes narrowed and a killer took the place of his friendly cousin.

"Not going to try and save yourself, Prince Khari? If you can't save yourself...how do you hope to protect what is yours?"

Khari relaxed into himself, finding the small space inside himself that had always held him centred through the fear of running, and the terror of the darkness, which held Jaizel's taunting voice, whispering in his ear. The calm place within his soul. the place Eden had led him to, during nights where he could have given in and easily sought oblivion through death.

"Still nothing?" Takana asked, her voice a hiss as

her knife trailed across his throat. "I could kill you where you stand, and then where will your precious boyfriend be, huh?"

Khari crouched. He heard Takana's startled gasp as his speed made him vanish from sight. He whirled around in a circle, dragging the power of the wind from the air around him and grabbed Eden at the same time. Holding out his hand, he span and pushed Eden up against the far wall of the kitchen, blocking him with his body. He let the tornado he was nurturing break free of his body. It pushed Takana across the room. She slammed into the opposite wall.

Khari stamped his foot, feeling the heat in the ground, and lifted it into his body, firing white hot tendrils of living flame into the space between them. He watched as they laced together, forming a netted cage, narrowing his eyes when it curved around Takana to hold her in place against the wall.

One hand still pressing Eden to the wall behind him, his body still a protective barrier, he looked at Takana.

"I would advise against moving, Princess of Alfheim," he said, watching as she studied the white hot cage enclosing her. "Your mistake was not having your witchcraft ropes hot enough. And talking out of your arse instead of killing me. And threatening the man I love. And thinking I cannot protect what is mine. So, Princess of Alfheim," he hissed, "I ask again. What do you think you can possibly teach me?"

Takana glared at him from across the room. She pointed to where Eden was hidden.

"I plan to teach you," she said as Khari looked around to see one of the guards had a gun held to Eden's head, "not to be so easily distracted. Bang.

Eden's dead. You have twenty minutes to get ready, *my prince*. I am going to thoroughly enjoy fucking you into the ground, you upstart little shit bag. Get this cage off me." She rolled her shoulders when Khari let go of his hold on the fiery netting. "You were too intent on attacking me. Do you seriously think Jaizel will waste his time talking to you? You'll let Eden get killed while you're listening to some nobody threatening you with words. You'll be watching mouths and faces of those you think will harm you, and while your attention is diverted, Jaizel will fucking swoop in and take the *only* thing that matters enough to you to keep you alive. Twenty minutes," she said, stalking away.

"Shit," he snapped, watching her go. "Fucking *bitch*!"

"Get used to it," the guard with the gun said. He rubbed Eden's upper arm. "Sorry," he said. "I would never have hurt you, Eden."

"Yeah, I know," Eden said, looking pale nonetheless.

"Are you all right?" Khari asked, taking Eden into his arms to check over. He glared at the guard. "Get used to it?"

The guard shrugged. "She is about the best we have, because she's a ruthless bitch," he said. "She can make you the best you are capable of being."

Khari ran his hands over his face, feeling stupid that there had been a gun against Eden's temple. That he had *allowed* there to be a gun held to Eden's temple. He could not afford mistakes or distractions. All the company and the illusions of safety were going to make him soft.

He could not allow himself to get soft. Softness

meant death, and pain. He saw Gray staring at him and noted the not-quite-concealed disappointment in his eyes. Not much, but enough to tell him he had been lacking—something he knew well enough without finding censure in Gray's face. He hung his head, climbing the stairs to get his swords and bow.

"Hey," Eden said gently, touching his bicep. "It's okay. I'm okay, Khari. What's wrong?"

"If that was real, you'd be dead," he said, not looking at Eden as he slung his bow across his back and belted his quiver to hang at his hip.

"Yeah, I know."

Khari glanced at him. "Sorry."

"Um. Okay, but why?"

"Why?"

Eden pushed the door to his room closed and leaning on it to look at Khari carefully, his head tilted to the side. "Why are you saying sorry?"

"I let someone get a gun to your head, Eden. You'd be dead if it was real."

"Yeah, and I get that part," Eden said, "but the way I see it, is that you were doing mighty fine in keeping the main threat of Takana the hell away from us, and I was too enthralled in watching you do that, that yet *again*," he said, rolling his eyes, "I ended up nearly dying. Sure, this time hurt less, and I don't need stitches or blood transfusions, but the fact remains that I should be able to stop folks getting close to my neck or head with weapons that can make me dead, huh? *I* got caught, Khari. It's cute that you want to protect me and all, but I really should be able to take some responsibility for myself, don't you think?"

"You shouldn't have to. I should be able to keep you safe."

"And who is gonna keep you safe, huh?" Eden asked, crossing the room to stand in front of him. The slight difference in their heights was barely noticeable when Eden stood tall, as he was now. "Don't I get a say in wanting to protect you? And don't you dare laugh," he added, watching Khari's face.

Khari stopped the small laugh that had indeed been about to break free and looked at Eden. He brushed back the long straight strands that never seemed to want to stay tailed with the rest of his hair, tucking them behind Eden's ears.

"How could you protect me?" he asked. "Eden, you have taken about one percent of the power I hold for you. You're fast, aye. You're a crack shot, aye. But how do you think you'll be able to protect me from what's coming? I am a *warrior*, Eden! I should be able to protect what's mine. It's a simple job description. Fight, guard, protect and win. If I can't do that, then we have no hope at all of getting through what's coming. You can't protect me," he said, tracing Eden's lip with the tip of his finger.

"You don't want me to," Eden said, looking at him intently.

"I don't want to see you lose the...softness," Khari admitted. "I would do anything to allow you to keep that part of you."

Eden frowned. "You make me sound like a girl."

"How so?"

"Soft and incapable of goddamn anything."

"Do you know any girls?" he asked Eden, frowning at him. Disbelief was rising in his chest as he held Eden's chin and made him meet his eyes. "Why does me wanting you to stay as you are, soft, gentle and loving, make you sound *like a girl*?" he asked again. "I assume you know females. You know Takana and Elnara at least. I think you were born and not hatched, so you would have had a mother. One who loved you very much, I should imagine, aye?"

"Well, yeah," Eden said, "but..."

"One who would have had the strength to die for you? Who would face agony, just to get you *into* the world? One strong enough to fight for you, protect you? Have you *seen* mother bears, Eden?"

Eden grunted and jerked his face free of Khari's hand. "Of course I have. I mean you talking to me like that makes me feel like you might as well cut my bollocks off and keep them in your back pocket."

"So men aren't allowed to be soft and gentle? That's just women?"

Eden looked away from him. "It sounds bad when you say it like that."

"Sounds bad when you say it at all," Khari said. "I made you sound like a girl—soft and incapable? If that's how you see females, Eden, then me and you need a long talk about the realities of the world and nature in general, because women are fucking terrifying compared to most men. Soft and incapable?" Khari opened the door, walking back down the wide staircase.

"I meant," Eden said from inside his room, quiet enough that he could have been talking to himself, Khari thought, "that you don't get to treat me like a woman just because you're screwing me."

"You mean screwing you, when I'm a man...makes you a woman?" Khari asked, jogging back and looking around the doorframe at Eden, who sat on the bed with his head in his hands. Khari pulled the door closed as he stepped into the bedroom again. "You wanted me to make love to you. You asked me to. More than once," he added, in case Eden had forgotten.

"I know."

"So what's the issue?"

"That you shagged me like I was a girl and now you're treating me like one."

"Eden? Look at me?" He waited until Eden lifted his face from his hands. "I never shagged you like you were a girl. I promise you that. I shagged you like the man you are. But being a man doesn't mean you have to be..."

"Like you?" Eden asked. "Hard and capable? Able to fight and wreak mayhem? Khari...look at you, and all you can do! Look at me, next to that. Is it any wonder I feel inferior? I did anyhow, but after what you did with the wind, and pinning Takana like that? And last night...you were in charge...I just feel a bit like my balls have been torn off."

"You want to fuck me? Is that what this is about? What goes where?" Khari asked, seriously hoping Eden said no, because running away at this point was not an option, but neither was ever being possessed like that again. By anyone. Even for Eden, he doubted he could bring himself to...

"No," Eden said. "No, I'm not a natural top. Never imagined it the other way round. Not really. Do you want to sigh a bit louder? I think the neighbours over the road might not have heard the relief." Eden looked at him. "No need to panic, Khari. You look like a deer in the headlights."

"Then what's the matter?" Khari asked. He did not understand. Eden had wanted him to make love to him, so he had done just that. Several times. And it had been good—great—he had made sure of that. In fact, if Eden had felt any better, going by the noises he had made, there was a chance of combusting from pleasure. Feeling as though he had somehow floated out into the centre of a deep, fast-running, river, he fought to find something stable under his feet that he could stand on. "You have to talk to me. I don't know what's the matter," he said eventually.

"I want to be able to fight like you can. I want to be your *equal*," Eden snapped, "not some fucking *wife* whose place is to wait for you to roll in with the rest of the *men* and then serve you dinner!"

"Uh, all right. I missed something. You can barely boil water. How do you plan to cook me dinner? And does me cooking for you mean I'm a girl too? Or the...the fact I like soft music and to have flowers in vases to brighten my room?" he asked, understanding finally dawning. "The fact that I'm happiest when I'm sat in front of a fire, making something or sewing something? Curled up reading a book, or maybe just lying on the grass and watching the world around me? Does that mean I'm a girl, to your mind?" He took Eden's hand. "The fact that I love being on my knees and taking you in my mouth, feeling you and tasting you? That makes me a girl, aye? Is that how it works, Eden?"

Eden looked at him. "No," he said, at last. "No, that's not how it works."

"Good," Khari said, lifting Eden's hand and kissing his knuckles. "I'm pleased we have confirmed that we both are, in fact, men."

Eden shook his head and looked at his knees.

"It was an odd thing to get upset over, but it's good we've cleared it up, in case there's any future misunderstandings, don't you think?" he asked, smiling at Eden's soft giggle. It was a lovely sound. He let go of Eden's hand and bent to kiss him on his head before walking to open the door again. He stepped into the hallway. "Oh, and Eden?"

Eden looked up. "Yeah?"

"You have about a minute to get your manly arse down into the garden, or Takana might just castrate you, and then the whole argument will be moot."

"Moot?" Eden asked, starting to giggle. "What sort of word is moot?"

"A good one. Come on. Let's see how many times we get killed before we're allowed to go and do something fun. I hate training."

"You do?" Eden asked, grabbing his weapons and jogging down the stairs at Khari's side. "Really? But you're so...can I say capable?"

Khari rolled his eyes. "If you must."

"Khari, you beheaded the soldier who was going to kill me in your woods. You move like a fucking whirlwind and you have the ability to just cut down anything and anyone in your way. You're amazing."

"I know." Khari pushed open the back door and stood in the doorway. He drew his swords and looked across the grass at Takana, then looked at Eden. "I know I'm good. I know I'm one of the best. I know I have to train, and I know I have to be strong all the time, because to be weak would mean death, and the death of everyone I love, Eden. I am fantastic because I have to be, and because I have made myself be as good as I can be."

"But? I sense a but."

"But, Eden...don't you think I long for the other life I could have known, where I wouldn't have to behead soldiers and fight *every single day* for something as simple as survival? To have known a life where I could still open a door and see my mum sat there, ready to hold me and tell me it'll be all right? To have that softness back in me? Be allowed that? Aye, I'm good, and yes, it's all fantastic. I have extraordinary powers and can call the lightning into my soul and release it in a wave of fire. I can do all that, and I can survive and kill and hurt and maim. I can take on armies and be the one left standing...but that doesn't mean I have to like it. I hate training—it reminds me of all the *normal* I will never have." He held his hand to Eden's face. "I'd like to know what it is to have the chance to be normal and not fight. If someone could take the need for it from me, I would be pleased for the gift it would be. Come on. Before things get soggy, as Ellie says. Let's go get ourselves killed."

Eden looked across the lawn of his garden, then at Khari. "Soggy has its place," he said. He leaned close and kissed Khari, then turned back, walking into the kitchen. He laid his weapons on the table and grabbed a can of Diet Coke.

"Eden? She'll have your balls if you don't get over there," Khari said. "I'm not joking. It's time to train, babe."

Eden glanced back at him as he walked out of the door, scooping car keys into his hand. "You train. I have something important I need to see to."

"Eden?" Khari stared at the doorway leading from the kitchen into the main hallway of the house and blinked. "Eden?" he called.

"I'll be back for lunch!" Eden shouted back. "I have to do something."

437

"Now?" Khari yelled. "Eden this is...Eden!" he shouted, hearing the engine of a nearby car roar to life. He listened to it fade away, knowing Eden was moving away with the sound. He bit his lip, holding back a sound of pained abandonment, not quite able to believe that Eden had...left. He blinked rapidly, his vision suddenly blurred at the edges, and sniffed, wiping his eyes with the heel of his hand.

Eden had gone.

"All right, my sweet princeling," Takana yelled. "Get over here and show me that you're not an out-and-out arrogant little prick and there's maybe hope for you yet!"

Khari looked into the empty house for another heartbeat, then turned away, starting to twirl his swords in preparation as he walked lightly across the grass. Steeling his spine, he faced Takana.

"I'm ready."

"I'd expect nothing less, my prince."

Pushing the shampoo suds out of his hair with his palms, Khari leant back under the strong shower of blissfully hot water and sighed to himself as the warmth penetrated his achy muscles and rinsed the soap from his head and body. Showers, as well as chocolate, were up at the top of his growing list of things he loved about the human realm. Sure, he had only seen a few humans, so far, as he had travelled from the woodlands to Eden's house. He had only really spoken to Eden's father, so had not had much of a conversation with the inhabitants of this world, but he liked it here. From the blue sky and white sun, to the odd hard concrete ground and tall buildings reaching upwards as though trying to get closer to the sun.

It had all been going perfectly, and then Eden had left. He had been tentatively starting to explore a few things, here and there. Items that were as mysterious to him as the single glowing moon in the sky. What a button would do if pressed. What a *stereo* was. Small things, but there was so much to learn he thought it was likely sensible to start slowly.

Eden had left. He had said he would be back for lunch, which had been eaten hours earlier. He had not returned for dinner, either. Now it was dark and the stars were out, twinkling in the sky.

Khari wondered if he planned to return. The ache in his chest had nothing to do with the blows he had taken during his training and everything to do with the heartache of being parted from the other half of himself. He stepped out of the shower and rubbed at himself with one of the soft fluffy towels, which were hung over a heated rail screwed to the tiled wall. More amazing things that let Khari know he was as far away from his previous life as it was possible to get.

He got dressed in some loose tracksuit trousers and a baggy sweater, tugged a comb through his hair and sat on the king sized bed. He picked up Eden's *mobile phone* and examined it, wondering how it could be used to call Eden. He turned it over in his hands, stroking the glossy black glass, then placed it back on the bedside table and crossed his legs at the ankles, leaning back against the pillows, thinking.

"You okay, son?" Peter asked, popping his head

around the doorframe.

"Aye, thank you."

"Call me if you need anything," Peter said, giving him one last long look before he walked away, closing the door to leave Khari alone with his thoughts.

Need anything, he thought, shaking his head in wonder. How could anyone need anything in such a world as this one? A world where most things happened at the touch of a button, or by picking up a *telephone*. A world where, just that day, there had been a knock on the door and Peter had admitted a man who had carried in crate after crate of food and drink, filling the kitchen almost completely. So much food that most had been taken into the room where a machine washed clothes and another dried them, placed in a deep wide box called a *freezer*.

Khari would have sold his soul to have a freezer in his underground home. Something that meant there would be food for months—food that was not just rice and some dried plants.

He reached for the mobile phone again and was about to pull the back off to see if that would make Eden hear him when he heard a car in the driveway. He sat up, putting the sleek black object down again, he listened to Eden's voice in the hallway. He sat up, hearing Eden coming up the stairs and swung his legs off the bed just as Eden opened the door to stand flushed and grinning in the doorway.

"I am *so* sorry I took so long," Eden said, crossing to stand in front of him. "I got lost."

"Lost?" Khari asked, pulling Eden against his chest to hold him. He pressed his face against Eden's neck, inhaling his scent as though to reassure himself Eden was there on a more primal level. "Lost where?"

"The motorway. I got carried away in my head and ended up somewhere in the Midlands—it happens to me more than I'd like." Eden laughed, the sound not much more than a soft rumble deep in his chest. "I got a surprise for you," he said into to Khari's ear. "I was thinking about what you said...about softness and normalcy. And my mind got to working, thinking it over."

"All right..." Khari said, lifting his head.

"Come with me," Eden said, leading him from the room. He stopped, looked down, then grinned. "Maybe get some shoes on?" he said, pushing Khari back into the bedroom.

"Uh, all right. Where are we going?" Khari asked, shoving his feet into his new *trainers*. They were up there on the list with chocolate, showers and diet coke. It was like walking on fluffy cushions of air. Amazing invention. He looked up and saw Eden appraising him. "I should change?" he asked. "I was just going to stay here, so if this is all wrong, I can change."

Eden opened the door to his wardrobe—another room leading from his bedroom. He threw items into a bag, and more in Khari's direction, stripping quickly out of his own jeans and T-shirt to replace them with black trousers. They were cut like no trousers Khari had seen before. Eden selected a fitted pale pink shirt, slipped his feet into smart looking black shoes and pulled the band from his hair to brush it quickly. He sprayed it with something that made it even sleeker than normal, then looked at Khari.

Khari blinked at the vision in front of him, his eyes roaming over the tightness of the trousers around Eden's hips and arse—somehow more indecent because they weren't skin-tight and clingy from waist

441

to foot like battle trousers. These were thinner cotton and made Khari's hands ache to smooth them over Eden's skin.

The shirt...well, he just wanted to rip that off and see it lying on the floor while Eden laid in his bed. Naked.

"Orien save me," he muttered when Eden smiled, his face saying he knew *exactly* what effect he had on Khari. He blinked and changed into the trousers and shirt Eden had passed him, pausing when Eden walked to stand in front of him and fasten the buttons.

"Arm," Eden ordered, taking Khari's wrist when he held his hand out.

Khari watched as something silver was pushed through holes in the long sleeves and twisted to hold the cuff closed.

"Other arm," Eden said, repeating the process. He kissed him gently. "You look amazing."

"Um, thanks," Khari said, taking Eden's hand and slipping on black shoes before leaving the room. "Where are we going?"

"Well. First of all, you're going in the car."

Khari beamed. "Really? You're going to make it go?" he asked as Eden opened the front door. He walked to the driveway and Eden's car. He examined it, touching the faded red roof to stroke the cool metal.

"Drive it?" Eden asked. "Yes. Well, that's a loose definition of what I can manage to do, but I have a licence, so they have to let me on the roads. Jump in."

Khari looked at the door Eden held open for him and at the seat inside before sitting down and glancing around the interior. He jumped when Eden closed the door, then laughed at himself. Eden opened the other door and slid into the seat behind the wheel, leaning over the centre of the car to reach over Khari's lap, grab something, and fasten it across Khari's chest with a small click.

"Seat belt," Eden said. "Stops you going through the windshield. While I don't doubt you could heal yourself, blood will be a bastard to get out of the carpets."

"All right."

Eden turned a key to start the engine and pressed his foot down, then they were moving away from the house. Fast.

"Wow," he said, looking out of the window. "Faster than Ollie."

"Maybe, but not by much," Eden joked. "I'm sorry about earlier," he said, the smile on his face fading. "I had time to think about it while I was driving the length of England. I just went off on one, and it was uncalled for. I'm sorry."

"That's all right," Khari said. He turned in his seat to watch Eden drive for a while. Studying his face. "I'm sorry you were so upset."

"But you're still not sure why I was," Eden said, glancing away from the road. He looked ahead again. "I love that you can't work out what I was mad about. It makes me look neurotic, but also means I had no reason to be worried. Guess I had a bit of an existential crises. I'm not a misogynistic pig, by the way. I never meant to make it sound like being a girl is a bad thing. I saw it in your face, that you thought that was what I was saying. I wasn't. Just...I've kinda been raised by the television and books. Men are men, and women are women, and men should be strong and women aren't all that strong...anyway," he said, leaning over the wheel and taking a left hand turn onto another road. "Not a misogynist. Never wanted you to think I'm weak, is all. You getting all protective is nice, but I guess I think I should be able to look after myself." Eden grinned out of the windshield, taking another turning and speeding up. "The fact that I'm pretty hopeless at looking after myself is something I possibly need to work on, but I think I should be able to, all the same."

"But I want to," Khari said, watching Eden's eyes to see if they would narrow dangerously as they had earlier in the day. They stayed relaxed and calm.

"I know," Eden said, glancing at him again. "I don't got much of a hope of saving myself. At least until I get all my power from you, and I don't think I'm in a rush to get it all. The few I got last night have taken all day to settle into something that don't feel like a million butterflies flying through my veins. So yeah...I don't got much of a hope. I can shoot an arrow, and I can run and swing a sword blindly with the rest of you, but the good fighting? Even trying that will get me killed, so I ain't gonna try, I don't reckon." He frowned out of the window, reading the signs above the road.

Khari watched the shrubbery zoom past, then there was a blaze of light, brighter than anything he had imagined. He gasped and sat straight, looking at the signs and bright lights. He blinked around, trying to look everywhere at once, then sat back in his seat to look at Eden, who slowed the car and drove it backwards into a space between two others before killing the engine.

"You're not going to train?" he asked, making sense of what Eden had said.

"Not with the rest of you, no. I'd just get hurt. I

444

can't use witchcraft, or get the power from the core of the earth, Khari. I can't move faster than light and control two swords spinning faster than a helicopter blade. I can't throw a fireball and make my enemy burn. I'm pretty shit, really. I'll focus on learning what I am, and what I have inside me, and dealing with it all and learning what I can do as it happens. Way I see it, is that if you can't protect me, then no one can," he said, his beautiful face serious for once.

"I'll protect you," Khari said, taking Eden's hand when it slipped into his own. He squeezed. "I won't let you get hurt."

"No. I'm not asking you to put that kind of weight on your shoulders, Khari. I'm saying that if you can't protect me, then *no one* can. If something happens, it doesn't mean you failed, or whatever, it means that there is not a single person, breathing, in any realm, who could have prevented it. Do you understand that? It's important."

Wondering what Eden knew, what he had seen, what he foresaw, Khari looked out of the windscreen. "It won't be my fault," he said. "I understand, aye. What you think might come. It's not going to be my fault."

Eden looked relieved. "Yeah."

"You will *not* die. Not this time."

Eden's hand squeezed Khari's. "Let's try to keep that promise, huh? I don't fancy dying. If nothing else, it will be a pain in the ass to reincarnate all over again. I like this time the best out of all the memories I have floating to the surface. I'd like to keep it going if I can."

"I'd like that, too." Khari looked out of the window, back at all the bright lights threatening to put him into sensory overload. "Where are we?"

"Well. I was thinking," Eden said, getting out of the car. He walked around and opened Khari's door, leaning in to free him from the seat belt. Once that was done, he reached into the back seat and stood tall with the bag of clothes he had thrown together in his bedroom.

"Thinking?" Khari asked, watching how a car was locked. He took the keys from Eden and pressed the button on the car key, smiling when the car bleeped and lights flashed. He pressed it again. "Locked?"

"Locked," Eden confirmed.

"Clever," he said, examining the key.

"Don't pull it apart to see how it works, okay?" Eden said, bag held firmly in his hand. "And don't lose them. It drives my dad nutty when I keep losing keys."

"I won't lose them. So, anyway. You were thinking?" he asked, hoping to get Eden back on track.

"Yeah. What you said about softness. About wanting things to be *nicer* than they've been for you. I figure that I might not be great at bodyguard duties, or fighting...or much at all really," Eden said, mouth twisting. "I'm not the most macho guy, am I?" Humour lit his face. "I try, but honestly, I'm better off with schools and exams than I am with swords and fighting. It's not *me*. They're things I learned, simply because I'm meant to know how to do them, I suppose. I like the bow and arrows, though. Otherwise, I don't reckon I'm a soldier. Anyway, I'm none of that, but I *do* know how to be myself, and I know what I like, and I know how to be soft, as you call it. So I thought, you know what? He wants soft and gentle and loving, then I can do that."

Eden pulled open a glass door, waving Khari

446

ahead of him. He walked up to a desk to talk to a pretty woman with red lips and painted eyes. Eden produced his wallet, chatting as he leant on the desk, checking details on a screen the woman showed him. He took a card she passed to him, tucking it into his pocket.

"Enjoy your stay," the woman said. She looked at Khari. Her eyes widened as she looked at him. Enough to make him wonder if he should have used a bit more glamour. Then he noted her dilated pupils and parted lips. He smiled at her as he followed Eden, managing not to laugh when she drew in a fast breath.

Humans, around elves, were fun.

"The poor woman is gonna be on edge all night," Eden said, pulling Khari through an open door. "You need to to maybe *not* look at folks like that. It's like me running around the elven realms and just kissing everyone. It's mean."

Khari grinned and looked around the box he was in. "Why have we walked into a mirrored box?"

"It's a lift," Eden said, hitting a button with a smile. Everything had a button in this realm. Khari jumped, holding Eden's arm when the floor moved. "What the fuck is happening?" he asked. He grabbed for Eden, worried. He could feel himself moving even though he stayed still. "Eden?"

The doors opened again to show a different hall to the one they had walked through before.

"It took us somewhere else?" he asked, amazed.

"Instead of stairs," Eden said, opening the only door in the small hall. He swung it wide and looked at Khari, watching him. "Walking up to the twentieth floor would be exhausting." He smiled as Khari walked forward and gasped at the view from the huge plate glass windows. "Welcome to the Human Realm."

"I have a table booked for nine. Aris," Eden said to a man at a high lectern of a desk.

Khari shuffled in place behind him, looking out at the street and around at the brightly lit windows of shops that were closed for the night, but shone as as if they were open for business. A beautifully sculpted car passed him by, its lines sleek and sharp. He looked back into the restaurant, at the people sat around tables, and inhaled the gorgeous scents that floated to fill the intimate spaces of the lovely large room. He smoothed his shirt, knowing he was fidgeting but not able to stop.

"This way," Eden said, a hand gentle on the base of his spine to guide him forward.

"What is this place?" he asked, sitting down on a padded chair. He took something passed to him automatically, then looked at the leather cover. *Menu.* All right, so there was food, that was good—he was starving again. He opened the menu and frowned, not knowing what anything was. Except rice, but there seemed to be an awfully large selection of rice to choose from. And what was a *prawn*? He closed the book, picking up his glass when it was filled with a pale gold liquid of some sort. Very pale. He hoped it wasn't horrible and tasted it nervously.

Not horrible. That was good. Moving boxes, disembodied music, cars, buttons...if the food was different, he would not have been shocked. Although...

"What is a prawn?"

"Shellfish," Eden said, smiling at him across the table. "You'll like them. They're similar to elven clawed fish. A bit sweeter, maybe."

"What's an aubergine?"

"A vegetable. They're nice." Eden leant over, going through the menu with him. A lot of the food was new, but there was a lot that was the same as he had known in Chiearatul, it just had a different name. He slipped his hand into Eden's, linking their fingers, browsing the choices on offer. It was odd to have so much choice. Dinner had once been what he had been lucky enough to catch, now he was feasting for all he was worth.

"Why are we being stared at?" he asked, feeling hard gazes on his face. He didn't lift his head to look at a couple sat close by. He knew they were disapproving.

"Because we're two men having a romantic dinner."

"And?"

"And they're likely affronted by it."

"Why?"

"Because I have a better looking boyfriend?"

Khari giggled, then clamped his mouth shut. Shutting his mouth did not change the fact he had giggled. He felt his cheeks warm, looked at Eden, then laughed fully. He turned around to the couple and raised his wine glass.

"Lovely evening, isn't it?" he asked, grinning when they quickly looked away. He looked back at Eden. "Really? Because we're both men?"

"Yeah." Eden looked back at his menu. He didn't look up when a plate of flat bread was brought to their

449

table with a selection of pickles.

Khari took one of the breads from the plate and tore off a chunk, using it to scoop some dip. He chewed, taste buds almost exploding, and waved over the servant—or whatever they were called. He asked for the man to tell him what all the dips were, letting Eden have the time to compose himself. When it became clear he wasn't going to, Khari frowned.

"All right. Thank you," he said, dismissing the man. He broke off a bit of a poppadum, waiting for Eden to lift his head. "You think their opinion matters?" he asked when Eden remained staring at his menu. "You think it's wrong that you're...what did you call it?"

"Gay," Eden said.

"We don't even have a name for it in my realm."

Eden looked up.

"No word. No name. It just is. We have no name for a male and female couple, either. Or when a man or woman isn't a man or a woman...um." He waved a hand. "If a man wears a gown. Lives as a woman?"

"Transgender?"

As soon as Khari heard the word, he knew what it meant. It was a handy skill to have. "That," he said. "There's not a word in my world. It's illegal," he added, "but there's not a word for it. My mother was flogged for wearing men's clothing." He swirled the wine in his glass and sipped. "She never felt she was a man, but she wore trousers. Jaizel flogged her for it."

Eden glanced at him across the table. "Just for wearing trousers?"

"It didn't take much."

"God, Khari."

"Happened a lot. Mum liked trousers. She was

strong," he added, holding Eden's eyes. "When I call someone a woman, it's a compliment."

"Not a misogynist, but okay, I get the point," Eden said, drinking from his wine glass. "I would have liked to meet her. She wouldn't have minded you're gay?"

Khari wondered how his mother could be thought to mind something as natural as falling in love.

"It's sad that, in this world, you even have to ask that question," Khari said honestly. "You love who you love." He shrugged. "I won't pretend it's not harder to realise that you love men if you are a man, and more so in *my* situation, but there's nothing strange, odd, or wrong about it. I found it hard because of Jaizel and his soldiers...what is *in* this drink?" he asked, as he set the glass down. "Have I been drugged again? If I have, please get me out of here."

Eden chuckled. "Are you ready to eat?"

"Yes. But I don't know what most of this tastes like. I'd like to try something I wouldn't have had before."

"Do you like spice?" Eden asked.

"I'm Chiearian."

"That means yes?"

"Aye, it means yes." Khari said. "I'm guessing you brought me here for a reason. It smells like...*home*, and nothing like the stuff I was fed last night. What was that?"

"Mashed potatoes and butter."

"It wasn't nice."

"It was, but you're not used to it."

Khari conceded the point. "So you bring me here?"

Eden waved over the serving man. "Can we order?" he asked, looking at the menu. "A prawn

451

jalfrezi, with mushroom pilau, some saag aloo, onion bhaji...make that two onion bhajis...a vegetable biryani, and more garlic naan. And more champagne when this bottle runs out."

Khari watched the man walk away. "This smells great," he said, inhaling.

"The closest I could think to Chiearatul. Rice, spice, heat, fingers..."

"Fingers?" he asked, looking up.

"The way you eat. With your fingers."

Khari picked up his fork with slow deliberation. "This on the table means that I'm expected to eat with it." He frowned, putting it down, and turned to look at the couple close by who were still staring at him and Eden. "Can I help you?" he asked. He watched as the man looked away first, then turned back to Eden. "This is odd for me. To be stared at because I'm *gay*," he said, trying out the word. "Strange thing to be worked up over, I would have thought. Don't they have anything better to do?" he asked, drinking from his glass and holding it up so Eden could refill it. "Rice, spice, heat and fingers?"

"I thought it might make you feel a bit more at home," Eden answered, glancing at the couple before dropping his gaze to the table.

"Do you want me to create a tornado and make them blow through the window?" Khari asked, only half joking. He didn't like the look in Eden's beautiful eyes at all, and wanted it gone. He reached for his hand, gripping Eden's fingers when he tried to pull away. He linked his fingers through Eden's and squeezed, holding him there. "I'm not going to sit here and have you act as though there's anything wrong with what we have together, babe. Ignore them, or I'll throw them through the window."

Eden looked at him. Seeing he meant it, he widened his eyes. "Don't. No tossing folks out of windows."

"Okay, but you ignore them too," he said.

The food was brought to their table. Small dishes that were laid out in the same way his mother had served their meals when he had been a small child. If he was sat on the floor, on a cushion, he could have closed his eyes and pretended he had been transported back in time to ten years ago. He blinked rapidly when Eden touched his forearm and asked if he was all right. He looked at the dishes, listening to Eden ask for finger bowls, passing the cutlery to their server.

Khari glanced at Eden and reached to pick up a small handful of rice, balling it and popping it in his mouth to chew and savour, swallowing the small lump that had formed in his throat at the memories the food evoked.

Home.

"This...this is not like the food you eat in your house," he said, once he was sure his voice would stay steady. "You eat the same sort of food as they did in Alfheim. This is not like that. This is...this is what I was fed when I was small. This is Chiearian cuisine."

"This is Indian cuisine. My mama's sort of food."

Khari watched as Eden expertly used a torn chunk of naan to scoop some vegetables from one of the bowls and bite into it with an ease born of long familiarity.

Eden met his eyes. "Ask what you want to know."

"Your father. He is American."

"He is."

Khari held out his hand, looking at his skin.

"White. Like me."

"And blonde, yep."

"He said we were eating American food last night. When we had the buttered potatoes and the beans."

Eden scooped up a ball of rice, eating as he waited for Khari to say more.

"You're not American. Or white."

"I am American. I was born in Alabama—moved here, to England, when I was teeny, but I was born in America."

"Ellie said you're Indian."

"I'm half Indian," Eden said. "My mother was Indian. Darker than me, skin colour-wise. I was never going to pop out white and blonde like my dad."

"What's Indian mean?"

"Oh!" Eden said, "Sorry. Of course you wouldn't even know what the hell American and Indian mean, would you? I'm sorry—I should have thought. Okay...so in this realm," he said, lowering his voice, "there's these things called continents, and each continent is filled with different countries..."

Khari listened, eating and drinking while he soaked up all the information Eden could give him. He drained his champagne when their *waiter* came over with another bottle. The couple who seemed to have issues with *gay* people left, and the street outside became quieter, yet Eden continued talking, and the waiter left them in peace, bringing plates occasionally and taking away the emptied ones. He watched as Eden used his fingers to eat, so similar to his own way of eating. He listened to stories of other cultures and religions, and creeds, and tribes. The world opened a crack as he saw it through Eden's eyes, and felt his memories of places seen and countries discovered.

"Let's get back to the hotel," Eden said, his voice soft.

Watching Eden somehow pay for their food with a small card, he managed not to pass out at the total written on the bill. Khari allowed himself to be guided back out into the night, along the pavement, and into the hotel.

"So...are you a half-breed? Like me?" he asked, kicking off his shoes. He walked to look out of the window at the world below. What a world it was. A blazing, vibrant, beautiful world filled with life and light: noise and laughter. There was bad here, yes, but it was all so *there* that unfamiliar emotions clogged his throat. Of course, the fact that he had spent the evening eating food from his childhood—food he had never thought he would taste again—left him emotional too.

"I wouldn't recommend calling people half-breeds," Eden said, sliding his hands around Khari's waist and drawing him back against his chest. "Same breed. Different race," he added, resting his chin on Khari's shoulder to look out of the window. "My mother and father are both human, regardless of whatever the fuck I turned out to be."

"All right. Same breed."

"Are you okay?"

"Aye. I was thinking how I never imagined half of all this," he said, pointing out of the windows. "None of this had crossed my mind at all...and then, the food," he said. He looked sideways at Eden's profile. "It's strange, but just eating the food I used to? It has made me feel...as though this is my world, I suppose. If they eat the food I do, then it can't be so wrong that I am here. How did you know? To take me to that

455

place? It's just made me feel at home."

"Your job is to protect us both. Mine is to make sure you have a home. With me." Eden met his eyes, turning his head so he could kiss Khari's cheek. "It was what you said. About wanting life as it could have been. I thought...I might not be able to do much, but I can give you a good life. A fun one. One that's a bit softer than the one you've been living, maybe. And the food, honestly, was because you've been trying so hard to eat everything folks have been pushing at you, but it's been plain you don't like it much. I figured, from the heat of the stews and such you made, that Indian food should be more your thing. And, of course, it's kinda mine too. I just wanted you comfy."

"It worked."

"Good," Eden said, his voice dropping to a sultry purr next to Khari's ear. His fingers lifted the hem of Khari's shirt to stroke across his abdomen. "I've been pretty uncomfortable all night."

Khari grinned. "Oh?"

"Hmmm. You dressed up, looking like this, made sitting and eating a meal harder than you'd think."

"Harder, huh?"

"...harder..." Eden said, smirking. He caught Khari's earlobe between his teeth and sucked gently. His hand slid upwards, finding Khari's nipple, while the other slowly began unbuttoning his shirt.

Khari let the light cotton slip from his back. He waited while Eden removed the silver cufflinks and tossed them onto the dressing table, shuddering when Eden's hand slid back around his waist to move him once more, so his back was pressed the length of a shockingly warm chest; hard and defined in all the right places under his shirt. Eden's lips skimmed across his shoulder, to the nape of his neck, and then back, while his hand never stopped its languid movements up and down his chest, touching his nipples and brushing his waistband, but never staying in one place. Driving him slowly out of his mind, wanting the strong fingers to stay in one place for long enough for him to find a rhythm. He longed to turn around. To push Eden down into the centre of the huge bed and lose himself in him.

He pressed his hands against the window, and closed his eyes. It was the first time, since waking in his arms deep underground, in a bed covered with animal skins, that Eden had actually had the courage to touch him.

It was the first time Eden had ever touched him like this. It was the first time anyone had touched him like this.

"Nice?" Eden asked.

Khari felt the softness of Eden's mouth trailing over one of the deepest scars on his back. It felt amazing, yet...

"How can you kiss them?" he asked, not opening his eyes. Hoping Eden wouldn't stop. He didn't.

"Easily. They're part of you."

Khari looked at the lights of the world below them, braced against the glass. He was lost in the sensation of Eden's tongue licking its way up and down his spine. At the deft fingers popping the button at his waistband, and the burning touch of Eden's hand over his heart, keeping him still.

"I want you so bad, right now," Eden said, breath heating Khari's neck. "Being away from you today was unbearable...not able to touch you, or hold you. I want you, Khari."

Senses on fire, Khari turned and found Eden's mouth, tasting spice and expensive champagne. He pulled Eden closer, winding one hand in his hair and grabbing both his wrists with the other to hold above his head, stretching him out to press against the wall.

The sound—almost a growl—Eden made against his mouth almost made Khari lose all control. He started to pull away. Just enough to calm down. Just enough to be sure he could stay in control. Just enough to...

"Make me scream," Eden whispered, the words hot, burning the flesh of Khari's ear. "Make me yours."

"Oh, Orien's Blood," he moaned.

"You want to take me...mould me to you."

Dazed, he managed to find Eden's mouth again, claiming him and tasting him. He moaned loudly when Eden's tongue invaded his mouth, demanding more. Operating on a primal level that he had never known, he *needed* to do this.

He span Eden around, grabbing the front of Eden's shirt. He tore it open. Pushed him back toward the bed. Laid over him to grind him down into the mattress, holding him in place with his hands pinned above his head.

"You're mine," he hissed, forcing down the gorgeously tight trousers Eden wore, which had driven him slowly insane over the course of the night. Using his feet to push them off Eden's legs, he wrangled free of his own trousers, sucking one nipple into his mouth with just enough force to make Eden arch off the bed beneath him with a loud moan of pleasure.

Eden lifted his head, looking at him with eyes that blazed with desire.

"How do you want me?" Khari asked, gasping when Eden moved his hand to his head, knotting it in his hair to hold him in place.

"Not gentle," Eden said, pulling him into a hard kiss. "I need you."

Grabbing at the small bottle of lube at the top of Eden's bag, he popped the lid. He studied Eden's face carefully. Seeing the raw need there nearly broke him.

"I want you," Eden bit out, "every which way I can have you. Give me all of you, and make me yours. I need to know I'm yours, Khari," he moaned. "Own me..."

Wondering if the burn he felt for Eden would ever fade, he grabbed Eden's legs, pushed them into his chest and slid home all in one movement, plunging deep into a tight warmth that had him panting and clinging to sanity as Eden threw his head back, screaming his name. He bent his head, biting the soft skin of Eden's neck, pulling his hair, holding him tightly as he claimed him. Hard.

"Again," Eden screamed, forcing him to slam into him with enough force to shake the bed. "Don't...stop! Oh, fucking hell, Khari! I'm...I'm gonna..."

Screaming into Eden's neck, he felt the slick wetness of semen splatter against his stomach and was unable to hold himself back. His orgasm rocked his world. It turned his vision black and stopped his heart as he collapsed. He pushed as deep as he could into Eden, filling him. Claiming him. Marking him.

Owning him.

Something broke free. Stronger than before, he felt a pull in his chest as power shot out of his body to whirl around the room with the force of a hurricane, pounding into Eden, making him scream, grow hard, writhe against Khari as he was filled with forgotten magicks. Lights blazed brightly and bulbs blew out. A glass exploded on the nightstand and the world actually did move.

Khari, holding onto Eden, still inside him, cried out, not sure if it was a cry for help or a shout of triumph. As gentle and calm as his powers leaving him had been before, it was a violent reckoning now. The blue particles were a tempest of noise and heated supremacy; stronger than anything Khari had known. A tornado of forceful commanding power that set the earth alight.

Eden slumped into the mattress, lying in Khari's arms as though dead. The last of the lighted power slammed into him. Eden barely acknowledged it. He turned instead to hold his face in Khari's neck, his breathing shallow and uneven.

"Holy gods in the heavens," Khari panted, once he was sure the storm had calmed. "Are...are you okay?"

Eden made a small sound.

"Eden?" he asked, concerned by the silence.

"I...I think I came hard enough to make my balls pop and my dick explode."

Khari laughed helplessly at the awe in Eden's voice, lifting his head to look down into his face. "Gods...you're a mess," he said, taking in soaked raven hair, glistening face and neck, chest slick with semen, shaking hands and panted breaths.

"You should...see yourself," Eden managed. "What just happened? Was that, like, all the powers of the fucking universe hitting me?"

Taking stock, Khari lifted himself up, sliding out of Eden with a pang of loss, and rolled to the side, half sprawled across Eden's body. He closed his eyes and concentrated on his store of immense power, the vortex of white heat he held deep within his soul.

"All the power of the universe, right?" Eden asked.

"Or about three percent of it, depending on how you look at it," he said, sucking Eden's lower lip into his mouth. "Not hurt? I never hurt you?"

"Oh, hell no," Eden said. He stroked his fingers across his neck, where Khari had bitten down. "Turns out I like it rough. And slow. And gentle. And hard," he added. He started laughing. "And fast."

Khari grinned. "Sounds to me that you just like it, full stop."

"I love it. Love you." Eden held his hand to Khari's cheek, his eyes flashing in the dark room. "Again?"

Moving quietly, Khari bent his head, kissing down Eden's neck. His touch was light and fleeting over Eden's chest. He knew, as he stroked hot skin, that the flaming passion he felt would never leave him. It would never die, or be banked, but would become an inferno and consume him.

He moved with Eden, entering him slowly to join them together. Unhurried and tender. He knew he would throw himself onto the pyre and burn with pleasure. That he had never had a hope of outrunning the flames. That he had been born to burn.

Into the Woods: Searching for Eden, Part One.

PART THREE

Into the Woods: Searching for Eden, Part One.

XXV

The days, weeks, and then months passed in a blur. To Eden, it seemed as though he had only opened the curtain between his world and the Elven Realm a week ago. Had only stumbled into Khari's life yesterday. Had only seen the sun that morning. For the first time in his life, he was able to say with true honesty that he was content. Happy, almost.

His days were spent watching Khari train. Watching him as he advanced from fantastic to awe-inspiring under Takana's firm unyielding instruction. Watching him learn more about himself than he had been able to uncover living alone in the woods with his brother.

He spent days connecting with Gray, getting to know Ellie, talking with Cole and being taught alternative histories by Alexander. Watching as Khari came out of his shell and bloomed into life along with the blossom on the trees as autumn ended, winter passed and spring arrived, announced by gentle breezes and warm skies.

Nights were spent in Khari's arms, being held and loved. Taken out of his head, turned over entirely to sensation and instinct, living in a darkened world filled with whispered promises of forever. A world of floating lights, powerful magicks and locked secrets that flooded his soul. Nights when he would lie in the strong circle of Khari's arms and dare to hope for a different future this time round. Nights where he could dream of forever. For everything to remain exactly as it was, so he could stay in his safe and secure little world and would never have to leave the people he loved.

Where he could pretend that he wasn't plagued by Jaizel's voice, threatening him; voices heard at the edge of hearing, hissing descriptions of what would happen, if he was caught. He would pretend nothing was wrong, never letting Khari know he had found a way to cut Jaizel's link to his son and nephew. That he was intercepting the threats and listening to the man talk to him and threaten all he held dear.

At night, in Khari's arms, safe and loved, Eden could try and pretend that he wasn't waiting for his world to be ripped apart. And, during the days as he watched the warriors train, using powers stronger than anything ever known, he could try and tell himself that he could stop what was heading towards them.

That he was strong enough.

XXVI

"Are you all right, babe?"

Eden turned to Khari, pulled from his thoughts. He took his hand and held it for a few moments. "I'm okay. You?"

"Good. I'm all good."

"It's good that you're good," Eden said. He listened to the shouting coming from the back of the garden. "Unlike some people. What's going on? Can you hear actual words?"

"There's too many people yelling. And I've been trying not to eavesdrop."

Khari could try not to eavesdrop all he liked, but it was unlikely to have an effect. It was like him trying not to hear, or see. Impossible.

"Did you get what you wanted in town?" Eden asked, turning his mind away from the raging row that was quickly reaching epic proportions.

Khari tossed his car keys on the kitchen table and sat on Eden's lap. He plopped a bag in front of him and pulled out a box with something akin to reverence.

Eden hid a grin as Khari unwrapped his new Kindle and quickly went through the set-up. Khari swung the laptop round to face him, tapping rapidly on the keyboard, then grinned and bounced in place.

"So many books." He scrolled through the Kindle Store. "We can afford them? This one is *pounds*."

"We can still afford them," Eden said, smiling across the kitchen at his dad. "Buy the ones you want."

At least a Kindle took up less space than the several thousand books that had appeared over the months. Sometimes, Eden swore they bred during the night, and there were a few hundred baby books born whenever he got out of bed in the morning. Much like clothes and toiletries appeared with astonishing regularity, whenever Khari drove into town. And shoes. And gadgets.

"This is amazing," Khari said, biting into a chocolate muffin, his eyes fixed on his new Kindle. "I should have got one of these ages ago. Why didn't you tell me about this?"

Eden had. Several times. Khari had been outraged at the thought of books not being *books* and had wanted nothing to do with it. Until he had found Elnara's, and then he had fallen in love.

"Coke?" Eden asked, getting comfy while Khari fidgeted and arranged himself on his lap, leaning back against his chest to read.

"Uh? Oh, aye,. Yes thanks...amazing. How does it work?"

"Don't pull it apart," Eden said at the same time as his dad.

"I'll see if we can pick you up an old one you can pull apart," Peter said, putting two cans of Diet Coke on the table. He glanced at the small pile of computer parts and a dismantled television near the back door, waiting to be taken to the tip.

Khari liked to know how things *worked*. Eden would have preferred it if he had as much interest in putting things back together after he had torn them apart to see inside.

"You will *not* tell him what to do!" Elnara shouted, whirling into the kitchen from the garden.

She was pointing at Alex and shaking her head. "This is our life, and we will do what we damn well please! You will not tell me what to do!"

Gray rushed in after her, barely looking at Alex. "Ellie...he's right."

Ellie swiped at her eyes to try and clear tears that were falling too fast to dry. "It's archaic!"

"It's how it is!" Gray said, taking her by her arms. "It's just how it is, my love."

"I won't have you *forced* into this...this...stupidity, Gray! We don't even live in the Elven Realm!" She buried her face in Gray's T-shirt. "What does it matter? I don't care."

"I do," Gray said.

Eden looked at Gray, who was looking at Alex. He glanced at Alex, who stood perfectly still, holding onto his emotions, but barely. He cast an eye over Elnara, then raised an eyebrow at Khari, who was staring at Gray, appalled.

"Oh, good god," Khari said, turning paper-white. "Gray...no."

Gray glanced at his brother, lifting his chin, defiant.

"Oh, shit," Khari said. "How far?"

Eden frowned. "What did I miss?"

"Four months," Elnara cried. "Nearly five."

Everything clicking into place, Eden looked at Khari. "A baby? They're having a baby?" he asked, feeling a grin fighting to break free across his face. "That's brilliant!"

"No, it's not," Khari said, eyes not leaving Gray's face.

"Sure it is! Oh, I adore babies. Five months? That means that it'll be along in four, right? Like humans? Oh, congratulations, Ellie! Well done, Gray! This is so..." Eden looked again at Gray's face, at Alex's frozen expression, and at Khari's horror, and frowned. "Why isn't nobody pleased?"

"Because it's a half-breed bastard," Khari said. "And Jaizel's grandchild."

"And your new niece or nephew," Eden said, moving Khari from his lap so he could stand up. "Your grandchild too, Alex," he added. "Congratulations," he said again, taking Elnara from Gray to turn her around and hold against his chest. She shuddered, crying quietly as he stroked her head.

Cole poked his head around the kitchen door. "Is everything all right, Princess?"

"We're going to have a baby keeping us all on our toes soon. Cool, right?" Eden said, daring Cole to disagree.

Anything but slow, Cole grinned. "Oh, that's fantastic," he said, coming into the room. "I'm going to take a leap in the dark and guess at it being Gray and Ellie, because you're not showing any signs, Princess."

"Yeah, unfortunately it's not my baby, but I'm going to share it, I reckon."

"This is against Orien's Law," Alex said, quietly.

"Oh?" Eden asked. "And when did I make that gem? During which life did I lay that one on the table? Because I don't recollect making it law that folks have to be married to have a baby, and frankly, if you're all that concerned about having kids out of wedlock, maybe you should screw around less, or get married before you get down and dirty. Just a thought." He held a hand over the slight rounding of Ellie's abdomen. "Can't wait to say hi. It's dead exciting, huh?"

Elnara gave him a watery smile, then her face crumpled and she started crying again.

"I want to marry you," Gray said, taking her back into his arms.

"No. You think you have to. You're not doing it because you want to."

"Ellie, my love, I can't think of anything I would like more than to marry you."

She shook her head. "It's too late. Everyone will know that it's a bastard anyway. I'll be six months gone by the time we can marry. It'll be born three months after the wedding—saying it came early is a stretch."

Eden laughed, quickly covering his mouth when everyone glared at him. "Sorry. It was funny."

"Carrying Jaizel's half-breed bastard grandchild is not funny," Khari said, chewing his bottom lip. "Oh, Gray..."

"Okay. Enough," Eden snapped. "It's a baby. It has nothing to do with fucking Jaizel. It will be Ellie's and Gray's, and that's a pretty much perfect mix to have. It'll have Alex and Airell as granddads, Takana as a great-aunt, and you, Khari, as an uncle. And me too," he added, smiling at the thought. "As well as Cole...poor little bugger."

"Hey!"

Eden poked his tongue out at his friend. "Look. You're all up in arms because you're not married under *Orien's* Law, but I'm stood right here—a bit younger and still a bit hazy on the details of how to create worlds and smite people, but I'm me all the same. New name, new face, same soul. *I* am saying this is amazing and cool. *I* am saying that I'm over the moon that you're having a baby, and that I can't think of better people to be parents. You want to be married?" he asked Gray. "Ellie? You want to be married?"

"Yes. But not if Gray thinks he has to."

"He would have married you half an hour after meeting you," Eden said. "He adores you and that won't change. So okay...you both want to be married. Cool. Luckily, you're in the right world to have an entire cornucopia of gods to choose from, whose name you can get married under. Pick a religion and run with it, kind of thing?"

Elnara wiped at her eyes with a tissue Peter passed her. "I only have one god. Younger, maybe, with a different face and a new name, but still the only god I believe in."

"Me too," Gray said.

"You have no idea how weird that sounds," Peter said. He filled the kettle and took mugs from the cupboard. "I want a T-shirt that says I changed your god's shitty diapers. He sure as hell wasn't all that holy when he was shitting all over the rugs because he found a potty too complicated."

"Okay, anyway," Eden interrupted. "So you get married under *Orien's Law*, yeah? Is there a service? Do you have to sign contracts? Have a ceremony? Be in a temple?"

Cole shook his head. "You need a priest, Princess. And witnesses. Declare love and fealty, and that's it. Hands are bound with a ribbon, a blessing is said, and then you're married."

Eden held out his hands, taking Elnara's hand in his left, and Gray's in his right. "I think we can forego the priest, don't you?" he joked, glancing at Khari. He looked back at his friends.

"Gray, since the day you met Elnara, you have been so deeply in love that it's been amazing to see. She brings you to life and clears the clouds so you can see there's sunshine...something you were missing before she came into your life. You saw, straight away, what a gift you were being given, and it's one you will cherish forever.

"Elnara, you knew within moments that you had found the one who was destined to walk at your side and stand with you as an equal. You knew that Gray was the one you could love and be yourself with. The man you had wished for. You see him as he really is, and not the façade he hides behind." He looked at them both, watching as they glanced at each other, faces softening when they met each other's eyes. "It's a rare thing you have with each other," he said, "and it will be something that will continue to fill your lives with joy, each day you wake up and can hold each other. Love each other. Do you give Gray your fealty, and promise to be the best version of you that you can possibly be? To give him honesty, and hold him up when he would fall?"

"I...of course I do," Ellie said, wiping at her eyes again.

"Gray? Do you give Elnara your fealty, promise to be the best version of you that you can possibly be? To give her honesty, and trust that she knows when you need to be held up to stop you falling?"

"Absolutely."

Eden glanced at Khari. "Create something ribbon-like and tie them together."

Khari blinked suspiciously reddened eyes and held his hands around Gray's and Elnara's, holding them together as a soft white mist swirled around their hands, a perfect ribbon of delicate pearls that danced and stroked over their skin. He took a small breath and looked at his brother.

"By the word of our God," he said, "and with the powers of our God, I bind you together in marriage. May you live in contentment, and watch the worlds grow old around you. Hear laughter all the days of your life. Feel the sun on your faces, and walk each day with love in your hearts. Congratulations," he said. "I think you're married."

Eden looked at Alex. "Can I say congratulations *now*?" he asked when his friend gathered him into a tight hug and clapped him on the back.

"Thank you, Eden," Alex said. "I don't think anything could actually be more officially sanctioned."

Eden waved off the thanks, feeling uncomfortable. He took the coffee his dad passed him and leant against the kitchen counter. He looked at Khari. "Remind me to find this book of laws I supposedly wrote. It's all outdated bollocks and needs a do-over."

Alex sat at the table, resting his chin in his palm. "I'm going to be a grandfather."

"And you look about thirty," Peter said, handing out coffees. "It's all right for some, I guess." He looked at Eden. "Are you okay?"

"Not all that pleased that there seem to be a lot of things that were apparently dictated by some incarnation of me. Pretty shitty things too. Ones that, however hard I try to find some familiarity in the words, I'm coming up blank. I don't recollect ever having said them, or even having thought them. Kinda odd, if something is being done in my name."

"That must be a mind trip," Peter agreed. "Just

knowing who you are...were. Whatever. Is there, like, worlds of people waiting for the second coming?"

"Or the eighth coming, or something. It feels a bit like a merry-go-round, sometimes. One I can't get off."

"Well, for now, just concentrate on being young, okay? I'll be in the study if you need me. Some of us have to actually work for a living," he added, glancing at the grouped elves hugging each other near the kitchen table. "Mouths to feed, and cars to fill. You know. The boring stuff."

"Thanks, Dad," Eden said, watching his father leave the room. He drank his coffee, catching a glimpse of a rather large wolf-like dog as it ran past the back door. When he had first seen a wolf in his garden, he had freaked the hell out and nearly shot it. Luckily he had paused, because shooting elves generally just made them pissed off. Another two huge dogs ran across the lawn, followed by a lethal looking large cat. The cat who had made the local paper, with residents swearing it was eating the cows on the nearby salt marshes. The cat who was being called everything from beast to endangered species.

Eden called the cat *Your Majesty*. He had learned it was best not to stroke him. It was odd, in any culture, to give your boyfriend's father belly tickles. He wished the elves would shape-shift more, because it fascinated him, but he had soon learned that they only did it occasionally and only for fun. Recreational shape-shifting, Airell had called it. They didn't do it much, because Cole would feel left out. Lacking magic couldn't be easy for the man. It was a shame.

He looked at Ellie as she spoke to Cole, awed afresh by the friends he had found and the family he now had. After such a lonely adolescence, he knew he would never take them for granted. Even just being able to watch them and know he was a part of their world was balm to the wounds he had suffered before he had crossed the Divide.

"I can't believe they're having a baby."

Eden turned to see Khari leaning against the counter at his side. "The amount of time they spend shagging, and you're shocked at the consequences? It's hardly a shock."

"You know what I mean."

Eden did. He took Khari's hand and held it. "Are you okay?"

Khari shrugged. His eyes kept darting to Elnara's waistline.

"What is it?" Eden asked, quietly. "What's got you worked up?"

Khari tugged Eden by the hand, out of the kitchen and through the main entrance hall, into the formal sitting room at the front of the house. He closed the door, leant against it, and bit his lip, worrying the soft pink flesh with strong white teeth.

"It's not like you to not have the words to say," Eden said, holding his forefinger to Khari's mouth, stopping him before he could break the skin of his lower lip. "What is it? They're as married as married can possibly be, Khari. The baby will be born in wedlock, or whatever you want to call it. That's not going to be an issue."

"It's not that," Khari said, shaking his head.

"Then what?"

"What if..."

"What if *what*? Speak to me, Khari."

"Gray is the result of incest, Eden. He's the

476

strongest man walking the worlds, next to Jaizel. His father. The baby's grandfather. Inbreeding morphs abilities—you've seen some of the stuff Gray can do. My mum was the most powerful woman ever born. Half of what I can do is because I got the skills from her, not because of the powers you...another version of you...locked inside me. What if...what if it turns out all powerful and evil, Eden? Like Jaizel? What if that baby turns out exactly like its grandsire, and..."

Eden sat down, holding his chin in his hand to study Khari.

"It's a legitimate concern, Eden."

"I know it is," Eden said. "I wasn't going to argue otherwise."

"Dark and Light aren't meant to mix, either," Khari said. He slid down the door to sit on the carpet, his knees under his chin. "The combination of magicks *is* lethal. Trust me, I have them in me."

"Yeah, I know."

"What if the kid grows up and razes the realms to ash, Eden? What if Gray is the one to unleash the furies of Hell into the worlds...just because he loves Ellie and made a baby? It's Jaizel's grandchild."

"You're Jaizel's nephew, and Gray is Jaizel's son. Your mother was Jaizel's sister, honey. I think he's the anomaly, not the rest of you."

Khari shook his head. "I would agree, but...I think it's a Dark Elf thing, Eden. The soldiers...what went on in the castle. It all went against everything that elves are meant to cherish and adore. It's the antithesis of what elves should know as *right*. Something happened in Chiearatul, babe, and Jaizel is not abnormal. I knew enough of them all to be able to say that with certainty." Khari linked his fingers together on his knees. "I know Gray knew a lot of people, down in the Cells. He knew every single whore, soldier and fighter down there, and commanded what was almost an army. He was strong, and he kept us alive, and I know that..."

"But?" Eden asked.

"But he stayed *down* in the Cells. I was taken up to Jaizel's rooms. I saw the castle. I saw the *normal* people—and I really use the word in the loosest possible sense, because they sure as hell weren't fucking normal. Something happened, I think, when he killed my mum. Something happened in that world, because what was happening to me wasn't out of the ordinary. I think my mum protected us both, and then when she died and we were sent down to the Cells, Gray never went back up into the castle proper. He mixed with the whores and all the people who had displeased Jaizel."

"Yeah, I know. He told me...months ago. I know what happened."

"Oh, I know you know all that," Khari said, waving it off dismissively. "It wasn't something I was ever going to be able to keep a secret from you, was it? I figured that you knew, but accepted me for who I am now and let the past stay in the past."

"You figured right," Eden said. He slid from his chair and sat in front of Khari, legs crossed, taking his hands. "But Gray found friends. He had folks helping him. Folks who got you out."

Khari looked at him. "Aye. None of whom fitted into the lands above the ground. Think about it, Eden. What kind of land is it, that the decent and good people are enslaved and kept buried underground? That the ones who would laugh, love and sing are the ones hidden, as though they are shameful? Eden...I don't think it's just Jaizel who is evil. Do you understand what I'm saying? I'm saying that Gray doesn't know what the Dark Elves are like...because he was protected by Mum, and then he was with the *decent* people, down in the Cells. He doesn't have a clue what Chiearians are like. Jaizel was *normal*, from what I saw, aye? What if the baby is true to its blood?"

Eden blinked as what Khari was saying sank in. "Do you think that could happen? With Gray as its dad? Khari...I'm not saying it couldn't, but, well...I just don't *see* anything like that. I've kinda seen what lies ahead for Gray, and bringing what sounds like an antichrist into the worlds wasn't a part of it. The kid will be powerful—look at who made it—but I don't see, or feel, anything evil about it. I get the heebie-jeebies when I sense something that's wrong. This isn't wrong, Khari." He followed Khari's jawline with the pad of his thumb. "It's just a baby. Your brother's child, Khari." His words hit home and Khari's eyes widened. "Your brother has a wife, and soon, he will have a child. I think, instead of worrying about what the baby might grow into, you should maybe go and get Gray a beer and clap the guy on the back."

"Oh, gods!"

"What?" Eden asked, startled.

"I'm not going to be the baby anymore!"

"Fool. Go and hug your big brother. And your new sister." Eden stood, opening the door for Khari, and watched him jog back through the house to find Gray. He saw Takana, her eyes fixed on him. She flicked her gaze to Ellie's stomach. The worry and uncertainty in her eyes were reflected in Alex's. Eden held his hand up in acknowledgement and closed the door to the sitting room, shutting himself in, alone. A few minutes after lying on the larger of three sofas, he heard the door open, close, and Takana's quiet footsteps.

"The kid isn't gonna burn the worlds to ash," he said without opening his eyes. "She's gonna be a cute kid, and grow into a normal and decent adult."

"Considering the father, I had no doubts that his child would be just fine," Takana said. She sat next to Eden's head, lifting it up and plonking it back down so he could use her thigh as a pillow. "I know you well enough to see when you're worried about *this*, or scared about *that*. It's not what the baby is that scares you, is it?"

Eden shook his head. "No. The baby will be amazing."

"Girl?"

"Yeah. Should please Gray."

"He'll be overjoyed," Takana agreed. "So what is it, about this pregnancy, that has managed to make you look a bit grey, Eden? You give good happy, when you know you're being watched. Not such a great actor when your guard is down. Talk to me."

"Talking about it will make it real."

"Will it ease you, though? A worry shared is," she paused. "Well...it's actually a worry that two people have to think about instead of one, rather than having it halved, but I think it might help you to let it out. You can't keep the worries of the worlds inside your head, Eden. Not all the time."

He knew that all too well. He opened one eye and looked at Takana, drinking in her strength, then blew out a long breath.

"Jaizel talked to Khari and Gray. In their heads."

Takana glanced down. "I know. There's no way to stop it."

"There is," Eden said, closing his eye once more, shrouding himself in the fake safety of the darkness behind his eyelids. "I know it can be stopped. I hear him instead. I intercepted him."

"You?" Takana asked. Her voice was quiet, still steady, but her thigh muscle twitched and her hand stuttered in his hair. "But if he's talking to you, Eden, then..."

"Then he knows about me, yeah. Well, he's known about me for a while, but I think he's realised I'm not some guy holding a few untouchable powers. I hear him, Takana. I can hear what he wants from me, and I hear what he plans. I can't stop what's coming, Takana. I think you know that."

"Oh, Eden," she whispered, bending double to kiss his head. "See the pathways, and lead them to another future. You must be able to do that."

"Sure I can," Eden agreed. "But what future will it be, for me, if all those I love are dead, Takana? Am I meant to stand and make the choice to sacrifice Khari? Gray? A newborn *baby*? I'm meant to sacrifice everyone to save myself? No...I can't do that, Takana. Would you sacrifice Cole?" he asked. He lifted his hand and held it next to his face, resting it on Takana's stomach. "Sacrifice this one, who you aren't telling a soul about—don't worry, I won't say a word. I won't even tell you if it's a boy or a girl. Promise."

"You bloody arse," she said. "How long have you known?"

Eden opened his eye again to look up at her. "Months. People will notice when you pop it out at the side of the garden, though. What's the plan? Ten minute break in training, have a sprog, get back to it?”

Takana tapped his cheek. “Brat.”

“Gonna pass it over to Cole and just keep fighting, yeah?”

“Something like that. We’ll see.”

“You're running out of time to wait and see. I don't know how you're stopping it from showing, but you have to be close to popping it out.”

“Oh, I have at least a few weeks,” she replied. “All right, so you can't sacrifice those you love. What other options do you have?”

“Watch the worlds burn. Watch everything burn and be destroyed.”

“That doesn't sound like fun, either.”

“Not really. Takana, Jaizel knows about me. You know what that means as well as I do.”

Takana looked at him. “You said, before, that it would mean we fight. What's changed?”

Eden held his hands in front of his face, palms open. He slowly closed his left hand, making a fist. “In this hand, this side of the scale, is Khari, Gray, you...the adults. Able to fight. Able to stand, and fight what's coming.”

“All right.”

“In this hand,” he said, closing his right fist, “is Gray's daughter. Khari and Gray's soul, if they watch him get his hands on her. Both those men would give themselves over to Jaizel without a blink to stop him getting that baby, Takana. And that's what Jaizel will be counting on. He wants Khari back, where he can try and force *my* power from *his* body. He needs the power. It can't be taken from Khari by anyone but me, but Jaizel will try and Khari will be killed in the worst possible way. If Khari doesn't go to him, then Gray's child will be murdered. Gray's soul rests in her hands, for all she's not born, Takana. Before, we had a small chance—not much of one, but a small one all the same—to be able to evade him. Fight what's coming on our own terms. Grow in strength...plan. What's inside me is programmed to work over aeons, because what God gets raised by humans and comes to full power at twenty years old? It's ridiculously young when I have millions of years of creation and growth to remember and discover."

"You're a baby."

"Exactly. Before, every time, I stayed hidden and grew to full power without much notice. I never blazed into the worlds with a chorus of angels and trumpets heralding my coming. But this time, it all went to shit before any of us had a chance, because Jaizel knew what he was waiting for, and he knew Khari for what he was, when he was born. He craves our power, badly. He was prepared to force it from a kid, for goodness' sake. I had to wake—if that's the right word—earlier than ever before, because I'm only *half* of myself, unless I have Khari, and we're needed to battle the future I can see behind my eyes."

"I know he holds your power."

Eden shook his head and held her eyes. "Takana...he's more than a vessel holding powers for me."

"I know. It's all very romantic."

He groaned. "No. Listen to me, Takana. He is *more* than a vessel filled with my powers, holding them in some magical storage container. He is the *other half* of myself. My memories. My passions. They are in Khari. We hold one soul, Takana. We are *one*, although he hasn't worked it out, yet. We were born within seconds of each other, when you allow for the time differences between us. We *both* came into being at the same time. We are *one*. Do you understand? We hold the secrets of each other, in each other. I can't let Jaizel get Khari, Takana. If he gets Khari, before Khari hits his true power, he will kill him. Then it's all lost. And this time, it won't be a case of waiting another couple thousand years for me to get enough strength to reincarnate and start over. This is the End of Days. We're balanced on a knife edge, and we either go one way or the other, and if we fail, there will be no worlds to reincarnate back into. I need to find the path that will lead to Khari standing at the end of it all. There's a way to make him survive...I'm just trying to find it out."

"You?" Takana asked, tracing the line of his brow with her forefinger.

Eden shook his head. "Not me. It was never going to be me."

"Eden, what are you saying?"

"There was never a way I saw me standing at the end of all this," he said, kissing her hand and holding it in his own. "I never thought there would be. I never went into this with my eyes closed—asked Alex about that—I never went into it with the hope of seeing it end. That's not what my purpose is." He sat up, holding out his arm so she could lean into him. "Remember when Gray first found us, and I was about ready to turn and run back the way I'd come?"

"I do, yes."

"That was my only chance of escaping what's going to happen and die in ignorance. I had the choice. I could run and I would have been *safe*. For a while. I'd have come back here, lived a life, died without knowing what was coming or what could have been. I'd not have had this last year. I'd've never gotten with anyone, Takana. I wouldn't have had a family. I would have died, in this world, lonely and alone—the same as I always died before in the heart of a mountain. Unremarked and forgotten. I had to *know* Khari. I had to find the other half of myself, so I would know what it's like to be in love. To have that one person you know you'd die for. To be loved."

"Oh, Eden." Takana snuggled against him, clasping his hand. "You're loved so much."

"I know. I'm so grateful for it. It's worth anything that's going to happen. At least I've gotten to love, along the way. I never had that before, in any of my lives. I was too powerful to even touch another creature. It was unbearable and death was welcome, when it came for me. Khari changed all that. I know what it is, now, to love someone with a fierceness that everything else fades into the background. Nothing else matters. I *will* protect Khari. He sees his task as protecting me from anything that might harm me and to stop me being killed. To stop me being stretched out on a rock, having my liver pecked out or something weird. But it's not. His task is to hold me, and keep me strong enough to do what has to be done. So he will stand and rule worlds at Gray's side."

Takana held her head pressed to his shoulder. She swiped at her eyes, sniffing loudly, then deflated as the fight left her with the acceptance of his words.

"You'll help me?" he asked. "With what I have to do?"

"I gave you my oath."

"Then you got married."

"Cole has my fealty. You hold my oath. You

outrank him."

"Oh, good. I like getting one up on Cole. So you'll help?"

"You don't have to ask."

Eden turned, kissing the top of Takana's head. "Thank you." He pulled her closer into his side, winding his arms around her so he could press his face into her neck and sit still for a few minutes.

"I don't know if I can let you go," Takana said, holding his head and stroking his back. "I don't know if I'm that strong."

"You have to be. For this little one." He rubbed her perfectly flat stomach, lifting his head to look at her. "Cole knows?"

"Of course he does."

"How come you're not showing?"

She wiped her eyes again and took a deep breath. "I'm half wood-nymph. I can basically petrify myself. I've not let the muscles expand, that's all."

"Can it move?"

Takana held a hand to her stomach. "Oh, it moves around, all right. It's not much different to breathing in all the time and tensing my stomach muscles to hold it back. Not at all dangerous. I wouldn't do anything to harm my baby, Eden."

"I never meant it to sound as though you would. When are you thinking it'll come? Must be soon. And why not tell anyone?"

"It's due in about two weeks, depending on whether I'm breeding as a nymph or an elf. If I'm going the elf way of things, then maybe another ten days. If I'm being a nymph, then maybe as much as three more weeks. Eden...I couldn't be taken away from you because I'm pregnant. I swore an oath, but

Alexander and Airell would insist I sit in the palace, sewing bonnets."

Eden grinned. "I see you loving that. You're such a housewife, right? I even saw you load the washing machine last week. You'd love keeping house and going to baby groups."

She slapped his arm. "I would so not love it."

"I won't let them make you leave. Not my personal soldier."

Grabbing him, she held him in her arms, stretching them both out on the sofa. "Thank you for finding me," she mumbled into his hair. "I'll do the best I can for you, Eden. Keep you safe until I can't...and then I will guard Khari. I won't let you down."

"I know," he said, quietly. "Thank you."

Takana held the back of his head so he could bury his face in her neck again. "Going to enlighten me as to the plan, then?" she asked after several minutes of silence. "Tell me what idiocy you're thinking of committing, and I'll see if I can change it into something that might just work."

"Look at it like a quest," Eden joked, sniffing back encroaching tears.

"Oh, I can see me getting used to quests," she said. "The greatest ones. Where Gods walk among men and histories are decided. Yes...I rather like quests. Are you just going to keep rubbing my stomach as though I have your indigestion?"

"That's the plan," he said tearfully. "I love kids. I'm pleased I'm gonna get to meet yours."

Takana laid her hand over his and relaxed, the solid wood of her abdomen softening just enough for Eden to be able to feel the nudge of a hand or foot.

He widened his eyes, looking at the rolling motion of the baby under his palm, and glanced at Takana. "It moves."

"Told you," she said. "You play with Fidget, and tell me what you see happening at the same time. Start with...oh, bloody hell. I don't know where to tell you to start. Just tell me what you have planned out in that pretty head of yours. You never know. I might be able to stop you getting dead."

XVII

"Do you think you can protect them all?"

Eden listened to Jaizel's sharply accented voice in his head. He wrapped his arms around himself and stared out across the sea, watching the waves and the moonlight glinting off the surface of the water.

"You don't have the power to save them from me. You're a child, and I am powerful."

He sat on the bonnet of his car, keeping his eyes on the water. It was pointless to argue—Jaizel was every bit as powerful as he thought he was. Time had run out and it was time to try and deal with the devil.

"They have nothing you need," he said. "There's nothing Khari, or Gray, can give you. Why don't you just let them go? Leave them to be free and live their lives?"

"Where would be the fun in that, child from the Human Realm? They belong to me. I will do with them as I choose. Khari holds the power I need, as I have told you before. As for Gray...he is my son. He belongs to me. As does Khari. Mind and body, that bastard belongs to me."

Eden bit down the scream of rage that threatened to burst free from his throat. Khari was not Jaizel's. He had never been Jaizel's. Khari was his, and his alone. Mind, body and *soul*, Khari belonged to *him*. Never this monster.

"You do realise that you have been duped by a whore, child of the Human Realm? Taken in by a fine face and a tight arse."

Sometimes, proof was given that Jaizel may be able to be in his head, but he sure as hell couldn't *see* what went on. The guy knew nothing.

"I have been taken in by nothing and no one. Khari is mine. You're not going to touch him.

"We shall see, child of the Human Realm."

"You'll see I'm right," Eden said to the sea, watching the waves.

"So, my bastard son has begat a child on the Alfheimian wench?"

Eden watched a boat sail between two buoys, its lights reflected in the inky waves. "You know he has. Stop playing games."

"I will kill it." Jaizel hissed, the sound as soft as a feather on the light spring breeze. *"As I should have killed the whore my sister produced and tried to pass off as mine. Vermin. Half-breed shit, not worthy of drawing air. My blood in their veins. They're not fit to live."*

"You'll not touch them," Eden said quietly. "Any of them. I won't let you."

"You cannot stop me. You do not have the power."

Eden had thought he would be terrified, bargaining with Jaizel. Yet now the time was upon him, he was strangely calm.

"You won't touch Khari. He is mine."

Jaizel laughed again. *"There is nothing special about a whore's arse, child."*

"Khari is mine," Eden repeated. He lifted his legs so his feet were balanced on the edge of the bumper and curled his arms around his calves, hugging his knees under his chin. "You will never see him, touch him, or hurt him again. Never again, Jaizel."

"I gave you no leave to use my name!"

490

"Jaizel," Eden repeated. "I will call you whatever the hell I like. Coward. Fool. Monster. Jaizel." He tilted his head to listen to the silence in his head and took a deep breath. Taking the moment of quiet to gather himself. "You will not go near Khari," he said. "Or Gray. And you will *never* touch Gray's wife or child."

"I am not sure whether you amuse me, or anger me."

"Like I care or give a fuck," Eden snapped. He felt a simmering rage building, and knew he could sense Jaizel's anger. It scared him, but at least Jaizel was no longer intrigued.

"You make demands of me, child of the Human Realm. As though you have the right to demand from me. As though you have the right to do more than kneel at my feet and beg for mercy. You are either brave, or foolish."

"Or," Eden drawled, "I have the right to talk any which way I choose. Maybe you should be kneeling at my feet, begging for my mercy. Did you think of that?"

"I kneel for no one."

"Perhaps it's time you started," Eden retorted. He let go of his legs and stood up, walking a few paces to the sea wall so he could lean over and watch the waves lapping the shore of the beach below. "Tell me what it is you want, Jaizel of Chiearatul. What it is you desire so badly that you are willing to cast your soul to Hell by stealing innocence, stealing lives, and turning your lands into a a nightmare where the sun wishes it did not have to shine. Tell me, Jaizel, what it is you seek that is worth so high a price. Tell me..." Eden paused, eyes on the surf as it broke over the shingle. "Tell me what it is you want. What you think you can achieve,

491

Jaizel. Tell me *why.*"

XXIX

"No Eden?"

Khari looked at Gray, shaking his head. He helped himself to a large serving of salad and sat back in his chair. "He wanted to go for a walk along the beach." He turned his head at a small sound from Takana and frowned at her. "Are you all right? You've been really peaky the past couple of days."

Takana looked at him as though she'd never realised he was there, grimaced, stood, and bolted out of the room.

Khari listened to her muffled cries and glared at Cole. "If you've hurt her, I swear I will choke you on your own balls."

Cole merely looked at him. It was worrying, as Cole would normally fire back an insult or threat of his own, then end by making them all laugh.

"Is she all right?" Khari asked, gentling his tone. "Cole?"

Cole dropped his napkin onto his still-full plate, and left the table.

"What the fuck is going on?" Khari asked the room in general. "Takana's gone weird since you two got married," he said, flapping a hand in the vague direction of his brother and Ellie.

Alex glanced up from his salad. "She's pregnant and thinks she can give birth in a closet without any of us noticing," he said. "She's near her time, too," he added. "Thinking we'd make her go back to Alfheim, she's kept it secret so she won't be made to leave. It's a lot of stress."

Khari pushed his chair back and picked up the bread bowl. Taking the two flights of stairs three at a time, he knocked on Takana's door and opened it to see her curled on her bed. Cole rubbed her back. Her shoulders shook with the force of silent tears. Or almost silent tears.

"I wouldn't have let you be sent back to Alfheim," Khari said, stepping in and closing the door. He looked around; Takana and Cole's room was a fair bit smaller than Eden's. Plain light lemon walls, finished with white edging, it held a tall chest of drawers, a wardrobe that had been painted white, and a matching wooden double bedstead. A single width widow overlooked the garden, and that was it. No doors in this room leading to bathrooms or walk-in closets. But it was cosy and warm. Takana had hung woven branches on the walls, shaped into hearts and love knots; Cole's touch could be seen in the framed artwork and the rug next to the bed.

He walked to the bed, holding out the bread as a peace offering to Cole. "I'm sorry I thought you'd upset her. Why didn't you say you're having a baby?"

Cole took a slice of French bread. "Takana's the general in charge of your security. To leave would have been abandoning a post. It was better to stay quiet, but then as time passed it got harder to say that we're having a baby." He shrugged.

"Are you all right?" Khari asked, touching Takana's arm. "I'm sort of thinking there's something going on that I should know about, aye? More than the baby, which is great," he said quickly. "Shouldn't you have grown fat, though?"

Takana rolled onto her back to look at him with

red-rimmed eyes. "Really? You find out I'm days away from giving birth, and you're going with *shouldn't you be fat*?"

"That's what happens, aye? A baby grows, you get fat, then it's all a bit gruesome and it falls out."

"That's exactly right," she said. "It falls out."

Khari grinned. "Okay, so maybe not falls out, but it pops out when it's ready? You should be fat." He picked up another slice of the French bread and held it out to her. "Eat. Get fat!"

She shook her head at him, but took the bread and bit into it.

"So is it all the emotional bits and bobs that have you on edge? Hormones, maybe? They surge, close to the end of pregnancy," he said, taking his Kindle from his hoodie pocket. He flicked through the book he had been reading—better to have some knowledge, what with Ellie being pregnant after all. Now to find out what an epidural was. He sat down on the bed. "This is all based on a human pregnancy, of course," he said, "so it's just a guideline."

"Oh, may the gods help me," Takana groaned. "How many baby books have you read since you found out you're going to be an uncle, Khari?"

"Six."

"And how many books did you read about manners and etiquette when we arrived here?"

"Uh, I think about a dozen..."

"Fashion?"

"A lot."

Takana looked at Cole. "You need to take this poor guy out more. Wouldn't shock me to find he's read a library's worth of books about sex and a hundred ways to achieve orgasm. Poor sod."

Khari raised a brow and grinned slowly.

"You never!"

He shrugged. "I wanted to make sure I knew what I was doing."

"Judging by the fact Eden is *not* a quiet bunny in bed, I would say you know exactly what you're doing." Takana swung her legs over the side of the bed, sitting up. She took the hanky Cole handed her and wiped her face. "It's hormones, Khari," she said, not looking at him. "I'm fine, and then I'm crying for no reason."

"You're lying," he said, looking into her eyes. "Don't lie to me—you can't."

"Fuck," she hissed. "All right. Not hormones."

"You can't tell me what's happened."

She shook her head, looking at her knees. "I can't."

"But you want to. And badly. This is to do with Eden."

She flicked her eyes at him, then back to her knees. His stomach dropped and he gazed at her bowed head for a second, then at Cole. "Do you know what's going on?" he asked, feeling sick. "Is he hurt? Has something happened with the powers he's been taking? What's happened?"

Cole held his hand out and clamped it around Khari's forearm, squeezing. "Calm yourself. I don't know what's going on, but Takana has given Eden her oath. If he was in danger, she would not be here, even if the baby was falling out," he said. "He had something he had to do."

"Where did he go?" Khari asked, already walking from the room. "Is he actually at the beach?"

"Yes. West side, past the fair."

Khari vaulted over the banister, landing softly in

the ground floor hallway. He picked up his swords out of habit, frowned, and put them back in the umbrella stand. He scooped up his car keys from the glass bowl next to the door and dashed out into the night. Seconds later, he was speeding towards the funfair at the end of the promenade.

"So, child of the Human Realm," Jaizel said. *"Now you know. My question is, what can you possibly have to offer me?"*

"Give me a week," Eden replied. "Leave Khari, Gray and everyone alone. They don't have what you want. They never have."

"You do not know this, child."

Eden lifted his chin. "I do know. I know more than you could imagine, Jaizel of Chiearatul. I am Eden, but once I was known as Orien," he tipped his head back to look at the stars. He memorised them, letting their image sear into his brain. Who knew when he would see them again. He listened to Jaizel's silence and spoke again. "I know you can never get power from Khari. Only I can take it from him. That to try and destroy Gray will achieve nothing at all. To kill the baby Elnara carries will mean the death of your soul, as well as Khari's and Gray's. I speak the truth, Jaizel. I am young, and I don't have all the answers you seek, but I hold them within me as Khari never has, and as Gray never will."

"You are...Orien Incarnate?" Jaizel asked. *"I hear the truth of it, in your words. You are the locked chest. You hold the power."*

"I do, yeah," Eden replied. "But you can't take them from me, no more that you could get them from Khari. I can...I give you what you want, though," he said, nearly choking on the words. A golf ball sized lump lodged in his throat as nightmare became reality.

He was actually doing it. Bargaining. Playing out the fate he had seen coming for him. There was no going back. "I'll do what it is you need me to do, but you leave Khari alone. You don't touch Gray and you never lay a hand on his daughter, when she's born."

"This is not a trick? They are your terms, Child-God?"

Eden straightened his back. He looked out at the waves, and spoke softly. "One week. I ask for one week, and I shall come to you, and I will be yours...to do with as you will. I hold the answers. I have the power you need, inside me. I am the Alpha, and I am the Omega...take me, but you will never touch those I love, Jaizel. Never again. You might wanna hurry with your reply—another thirty seconds and Khari know I've spoken to you and the deal will be off. I can't stop what will happen if he finds out what I'm planning."

"Done. One week, little Child-God. One week, and you are mine."

Eden walked back to his car. He looked along the empty seafront road, at the lights of the speedy sports car Khari had been bought for his birthday by Airell. A light blue Porsche, it suited Khari so well, it was unthinkable to imagine him in any other car. Eden walked to the rear of his own Bug and leant on the boot, waiting for Khari to hit the brakes.

Khari flung open his door and unfolded himself from the driver's seat. It was going to kill him to leave. He walked to Khari, sighing when strong arms wrapped around him, holding him tight.

Safe.

He closed his eyes and ran a hand up the back of Khari's hoodie, feeling heated flesh and the slow beat of Khari's heart through his ribs. He clamped his teeth down on the soft muscle inside his mouth, tasting blood, silently pressing his forehead into the warmth of Khari's neck. He breathed in, inhaling the scent Khari exuded. It owed nothing at all to anything made in a lab, or bought in a store. It was just *his* scent. Pheromones. Beauty and strength: freedom and safety.

Home.

"You're all right?" Khari asked, looking around to see where the danger was. To find what had threatened him and destroy it.

Eden found he was comforted even though there was no comfort to be found. Not now. "I wasn't expecting you," he said, lifting his head. "Shouldn't you be holding court over pasta and sauce?"

Khari tucked his hands into the back pockets of Eden's jeans, tugging him so they were pressed together. "I got worried something was wrong. Just a feeling. I had to find you...I can leave, if you wanted time alone." He looked out at the water. "The sea's nice, tonight. Aye, it's a good night to stand and stare."

"Stay with me," Eden said, quietly. "I don't want you away from me. I need you here."

"All right," Khari said. As usual, there was no question in his tone. Just an easy acceptance. "Takana is having a baby next week," he said, resting his chin on Eden's shoulder. "She's not fat, but she's about to have a baby. Next week."

Eden felt a laugh bubble in his chest. He let it break free. "Yeah."

"I guessed you'd know," Khari said. He lifted his head to press their foreheads together. "Not much

500

gets past you."

"Not much."

"When...when we're older, Eden?"

Eden looked up. "What?"

"Do you want a family?"

"Well, yeah," he said. "You don't?"

"Of course I do. I was just thinking, if you never wanted one, it's better I know now, so I can get past it."

"I'd love to have kids," Eden said, dropping his head. "A few. Couple of each, maybe."

It was good to dream. Even knowing it could never be.

One week.

"Marry me?" he asked, mumbling against Khari's collar bone.

Khari lifted Eden's chin, staring at him. "Marry you?"

"Yeah."

"Really?"

"You don't want to?"

Khari met his mouth, kissing him. "I want to. Aye, I want to, Eden." He inhaled, hand held to Eden's cheek. "Gods, I love you. Yes, I will marry you."

Eden smiled. "Thank you. I love you. I just want you to know that. It's important you know. I love you more than life, Khari...more than anything."

"I know. You understand I feel the same?" Khari asked.

"Yeah."

"So are you going to tell me what's going on?"

Eden dropped his head back down. "I just wanted you to know," he said, making sure he had full control of his face and body language. He gazed into Khari's face and touched his jaw with gentle fingertips. "I was just here, thinking how much I love you, and how I maybe don't tell you enough...all that. I had planned a big thing, asking you to marry me. I was thinking a meal, maybe the theatre..."

"You hate the theatre. You said it's a load of pointless pratting around and should be banned. You hate it!"

Eden grinned. "You don't."

Khari chuckled. "Aye, all right. Point conceded."

"Then I was going to ask you, maybe stood by the Spinnaker Tower," Eden said, lips brushing Khari's. "Down on one knee, on a clear night. At midnight when there's a full moon. It was all there, in my head. But...I like this too," he murmured, kissing Khari gently. "You said yes."

"I said yes," Khari agreed. "A thousand times, Eden, I say yes."

"Take me home? Please? Just take me home and make love to me until the sun comes up, Khari."

Khari looked at him for several silent seconds. "Come on," he said, quiet. He led Eden away from the Bug and to the Porsche. "Let's get home."

XXXI

"Can you tell me, yet?" Khari asked Eden, pulling the duvet over them and winding their legs together. "I'm not so blind that I can't see something has you seriously worried."

Eden pillowed his cheek on Khari's bicep and pulled him so he laid on his side, pressing the length of his body. He just wanted to lie in the gloom of the pre-dawn and hold Khari. Set memories in place to get through what was to come. Memories to live and die with. He stroked his hand up Khari's chest, tracing the ridge of one of the scars across his ribs. He turned, kissing it as though his mouth could erase the violence that had put the scar there. His heart thudded with terror at what he might face. He squashed the fear down deep. It would distract him from his final days with the other half of himself and he had no intention of letting that happen.

"You'll tell me, when you can?" Khari asked, kissing the crown of Eden's head. "You have me here so you don't have to go through life alone, babe. Tell me. Let me in, aye?"

Eden held his fingers over Khari's mouth. "Shhh. Just hold me."

"Not this time," Khari said into Eden's hair. "It's something you've seen? Something's going to happen?"

Eden groaned, rolling onto his back, throwing one arm over his face. "I really don't want to talk about it."

"There's nothing I can do to help, then?" Khari asked, softly. "Talking won't help?"

Eden shook his head. No amount of talking would help. Not now. It was too late for words.

It was too late, full stop.

"All right." Khari gathered Eden back into his arms, clasping him to his chest. "But you're not alone, Eden. Anything. You can talk to me about anything."

Eden watched the slow play of light on his ceiling. The white ceiling brightened as the sun began its journey into the sky, heralding the dawn of a new day. Bringing the night to an end and taking away time he could spend safe and warm, holding Khari. Being whole.

"I'm not going to make you talk," Khari said, stroking back Eden's hair to look at his face. "If you say that talking won't change what you see, and that there's nothing can be done about it, then I'll believe you, Eden. But do you know what you're doing, aye? Whatever it is you're thinking is the way forward...are you sure of it?"

"I'm sure," he said.

"All right. Saturday."

"Huh? What?" Eden asked, confused. He ran the conversation back through his mind and decided Khari was actually making no sense at all. "Saturday?"

"Marry me on Saturday."

"Oh," Eden said.

"You don't want Saturday? Were you thinking of waiting for the summer? A big event, sort of thing?" Khari asked. He kissed the tip of Eden's nose, asking if he wanted a royal wedding. All the trimmings. A dream that could never be his. Not now.

Eden stilled his words with a lingering kiss,

tasting himself as well as the fading mint of toothpaste. "I was thinking tomorrow afternoon," he said. "Or today, after breakfast. Then we can come back here and spend a few days in bed, making sure it's all consummated."

Khari raised an eyebrow at him. "We could just do it now, and save time."

"Could do," he agreed, sliding his fingertips down Khari's chest, trailing them through blonde curled hair and down to Khari's hardening cock. "We can do a lot of things here. Don't see why we can't marry each other."

"As it'll all be done in your name, I mean," Khari added. He rested his hand over Eden's, stilling his explorations. Turning onto his side, he settled so they were lined up, touching in all the right places, but stayed still. He simply looked at Eden. "I love you," he said. "I want to marry you right now. We can. It's your name that makes it sacred.

"There is that," Eden said. He let Khari lean back and take his hand.

"Humans wear rings, aye?" Khari asked, touching the fourth finger of Eden's left hand.

"Usually, yeah."

Khari lifted Eden's hand, thumb brushing over the place a wedding band would sit on his ring-finger. Eden closed his eyes, only to open them quickly as something wound around his finger; brushing his skin with a gentle touch that felt like the breath of a kiss. He looked at his finger—at the misty, barely there, ribbon of pearly light. It grew stronger, becoming more corporeal as Eden gazed at it, awed. A band of antique-looking silver, engraved with the smallest of runic script, which caressed his skin. He looked at

Khari in wonder, then ran his finger over the ring. It was definitely *there*, and not an illusion. No glamour had created the ring. It was as real as any that could have been bought in a jewellers. Except that this band would never be able to leave his finger. It was bonded to his flesh, and there was no way he could have slipped it over his knuckle to get it on—let alone get it back off.

Khari held his own hand up, showing the twin of the ring Eden now wore.

"I think that has to be the single most romantic thing you've done," Eden said, linking their hands together. He looked at the rings, and noticed the small eight-pointed stars carved between the runes. Bound by his own symbol. "What do the runes say?"

"Our names. The date. *Forever*," Khari said. He curled his arm under his head, using himself as a pillow so he could look at Eden. "I love you. I was thinking of some vows, or something I could say, but in the end...I love you says it all. And I will love you forever."

"I love you," he said. "Always." He laid on his side, mirroring Khari, resting his head on his arm, curled under his head. Just staring at him. He wondered how he would ever find the strength to walk away. Eden touched Khari's cheek with his knuckles, stroking along his jaw and down his neck, watching Khari's eyes as they softened to the glow of autumn firelight. Seeing a small flicker of something in the flashing irises, Eden stroked lower, skimming Khari's nipple. "What are you thinking?" he asked, whispering, stroking lower still.

"That I'm happy," Khari replied, just as quietly. "That I'm whole. That I love you and want you so badly, right now, that I don't even have the words to explain it. That I need you as much as I want you. That I can't believe you could ever be interested in me...and that we just got married."

"We'll have to go through it with witnesses, later, but right now...yeah," he said, kissing Khari deeply. "Married as married can be, I think, seeing as we are who we are. As for the wanting me, I think we can deal with that."

"Aye?"

"Oh, *aye*," he joked. He rolled onto his back, holding Khari over him, feeling his weight and strength, and blocked out the future he could see barrelling towards him.

Khari lifted his head, staring down at him.

"What?" Eden asked. "Don't stop. Khari?" Sitting up as Khari rolled off the bed and grabbed for a pair of jeans, Eden blinked and looked across the room. Khari shoved his feet into a pair of plimsolls and yanked a T-shirt over his head. "Khari? What..."

His words were drowned out by shouts from the back of the house, and the bone-deep grumble of the earth shaking from the impact of...

"Bombs?" Eden shouted, rolling out of bed and into a pair of jeans in one movement. "Was that a *bomb*?"

Takana rushed into the bedroom, braids flying. Her eyes fixed on Eden's face. "The Divide has been ripped open," she said without preamble. "We are under attack."

"No," Eden said, casting frantic glances around the bedroom. "Not like this...it doesn't...it's *not next week*!" he yelled, backing away from Takana. "It doesn't happen like this!"

"You *know* what's happening?" Khari asked, arming himself. "What's happening?"

Takana held out her hand. "Eden. Come with me. Khari, come. There's no time to explain, now. There'll be time enough for me to tell you later. Right now we have to get out of here. I can't secure the house and grounds. I can't fucking *stop* them coming!" she yelled, her face contorting. "I have to get you out of here!" she cried, staggering from the room with her hand pressed to her stomach.

Khari grabbed Eden and ran from the room, dragging him in his wake. He looked at Takana. "Where's Gray?"

"Ellie!" Eden shouted over the dreadful noise of the earth shuddering. The agony of the worlds tearing open ripped into his chest. "Ellie!"

Elnara ran to him, Gray on her heels. "I'm here...I'm right here," she said. "Takana! Oh, Takana, we need to get you out of here."

Cole skidded to a stop in front of his wife, scooping her into his arms. "A fine time to go into labour," he said, looking around as though an escape route would become clear in the entrance hall. "Shit...what are they doing to the Divides?"

Gray pressed his hands to the top of his head. "They're tearing it apart," he hissed. "It *hurts.*"

"You stay with me, Gray," Elnara snapped. "You are not to fall today, my love. Come on. Dad! Dad, what are we meant to do?"

Alex's voice shouted from somewhere outside. Eden heard the roar of his guards, and the heavy tread of marching soldiers. He felt himself fall into nightmare. He moved blindly, letting Khari lead him after Cole, who was following Takana's screamed instructions, running with her held in his arms.

"This way!" Airell cried, running to them and pointing east. "Get out of here, all of you! *Run!*"

"To the king!" Alex yelled, as a wave of heavily armed soldiers flowed from nowhere, appearing in the street out of the flickering air. The houses nearby faded, replaced for a moment by the forests of the Elven Realm, then returned. The barriers between the worlds broke down. Crashed. Leaving the layers of realms occupying the same space.

Cole ran fast, weaving through the ranks of soldiers with Takana held firmly to his chest. He dodged oncoming soldiers, holding Takana so she could fire her guns over his shoulders, still fighting, even now.

Khari sprinted after him, Eden's hand held tightly in his own. Eden heard Jaizel shouting, but could not hear the words. He was unable to say if the sound was in his head, or actually had been heard over the clawing, tearing horror of the veils being torn down around them all, leaving everything exposed and weakened.

"Dad!" he shouted, realisation Peter had not been seen hitting him like a fist. "My dad's still back there!"

"Move!" Cole screamed, urging Khari onwards.

"My dad!" Eden yelled. "Y'all can't just leave my *dad*!"

Cole looked at him. "I'm sorry. Eden...going back wouldn't help."

"We've got to get him...we can't leave him..."

Ellie touched his arm and shook her head, running alongside him. "He fell through the Divide. I am so sorry Eden. He shall be remembered."

Eden tried to fight Khari's hold on his wrist to run

back to his house. Find his father. He couldn't lose his father—not now. Not like this.

"Come on," Khari ordered, pulling him after Cole, running with him through the crowds of screaming people. They dodged cars as they screeched to a halt in the middle of the road. He ran through an alley between two old warehouses, climbing rusting iron stairs after Cole, never looking back, never slowing down as the world fell into chaos all around them.

Takana cried out. "I need...Cole, I need to..."

Cole shouldered open a rotting wooden door and ran with Takana to the far corner of the abandoned warehouse. "I know, sweetheart," he said, lying her on the dusty floor. He looked around, searching for something. "Will you be all right for a few minutes? We at least need a sheet to wrap the baby in and tie it to me, so we can run again."

"Go," Takana said. She held out her hand to Eden, squeezing when he took it. "I'm sorry," she moaned, moving onto her hands and knees. "Peter was...a good man."

Eden closed his eyes, trying to take stock. He let Takana grip his hand. It couldn't be happening, not like this. He would have *seen* it. He would not have missed this. He couldn't have done.

"I'm just going to ease you out of your trousers, Takana," Ellie said gently. "Eden, hold her next to your chest and let her lean on you. Khari, can you start a fire and get some of the damp out of the air, my lovely?"

Khari spread his arms out to his sides. The air in the room warmed and moved gently around the huge upper floor of the warehouse. Several blazing fires sprung up around the space, lighting and heating them. He made sure nothing was about to catch alight and sat behind Eden, supporting him as Eden supported Takana.

"Give me your jacket, Gray," Ellie said, kneeling down to look between Takana's legs. "That's it, honey...just relax and breathe. It's all going just fine from what I can see. I don't know as much as Gray," she added. "Gray? Can you take over?" She looked up as Cole ran back in through the door. "And here's your gorgeous husband with supplies...what did you do, Cole? Smash and grab on Mothercare?"

Cole dropped the armfuls of towels and blankets he held and knelt next to Takana. "You're all right?"

Takana looked sideways at him, resting her cheek on Eden's arm. "I'm shitting out a watermelon. Ask me again in a while," she panted, closing her eyes. She held a hand on Eden's chest. "I'm so...sorry," she gasped as another pain took her breath away. "I couldn't keep the Divide stable...I should have been able to...oh, this fucking *hurts*," she cried.

Eden glanced at her. "This was not your fault," he said. "Nothing was meant to happen like this." He patted her braids, rocking with her as pains wracked her body. "Can you help her?" he asked, looking at Khari. "Stop some of the pain?"

Khari held his hand on her lower back and closed his eyes. A gentle mist seeped from his palm, enveloping Takana's back and stomach, cradling her and supporting her. She moaned again, but this time in relief, as the mist circled and caressed her, giving her respite from the violent contractions and agonising pain of childbirth.

"Okay...you're going to be my birth partner," Ellie said to Khari before ducking to look between Takana's legs again.

Gray bent down, doing something mysterious that Eden was pleased he couldn't see. "Push for me, Takana...and again? That's it. Not long. Khari, help Eden hold her up a bit. Cole, you come and help me deliver your child," Gray said, calm and controlled.

"You're doing great," Eden said, stroking Takana's face.

She wrapped her arms around his neck, staring at him, her eyes afraid for the first time since he had met her over a year before.

"It's going just fine," he said again. "Look at me. You're doing brilliantly, honey."

"I'm dying!"

"You're having a baby," Eden said. "Not dying."

Another wall of sound roared through the world, making them all flinch as people screamed and cried out in the streets below; panic and fear had taken over, and the sound of humans running, screaming, and elven armies advancing was clear.

"Push," Cole shouted. "We need to get Fidget out so we can run. Push for me, my love."

"Squat," Gray ordered, lifting Takana so she could get her feet under her. "Bear down for us. The head's nearly there. A big push," Gray said. "Take her weight with me, Eden. Khari, stop some of the pain again. Come on, Takana...let's get the baby out, aye? Breathe in with me...out..."

Eden watched Gray, wondering at his knowledge.

"I was a whore in the Cells," Gray said, glancing sideways. "Births happened a lot. And," he said, stroking a braid away from Takana's face, "you'll be pleased to know that none of the women died. A *big* push for me, now...one more..."

512

"Oh...my...fucking *God!*" Takana screamed, grasping Eden's hands as Gray and Cole cried out, working together. Khari shouted encouragement. Seconds later, a high healthy wail ricocheted from the old brick walls. Takana collapsed on the floor, covered in Gray's jacket.

"A girl," Cole cried, holding his daughter. "A perfectly beautiful...girl. Takana...she's amazing!"

Takana looked up with tired eyes. "Good. It's worth the pain, then."

Eden held his hands out, taking the precious parcel from Cole and holding her close to his chest, bending so Takana could see her daughter, valiantly ignoring Gray and the appearance of a placenta. He looked up from the baby and met Khari's eyes.

"Want to see her?" he asked.

Khari reached for the small girl. She was small enough to be held in one of Khari's hands. Khari gasped at her size, disbelieving, and wrapped her hastily in the blanket Cole handed him. "She's so small," he said. "Gray...look at her!"

Takana grinned. "I'm chopped liver," she said to Eden, folding a thick towel with precise movements of her fingers. She held it between her legs, winced, then asked Elnara to slide her trousers up to her knees. Catching Eden's look, she gave him a shaky smile, her eyes sliding away to rest on her daughter. She looked overwhelmed, but happier than he had ever seen her. "Blood is normal. I'm not bleeding to death."

"She's fine," Elnara confirmed. "Gray, you carry the baby. Cole, carry your lovely wife. Let's get somewhere a bit safer than this place. Eden, Khari, bring all the loot from Mothercare." She winced as another crack of thunder ripped through the air—the

Divide not prepared to fall without one last hurrah. "We need to evade the Dark Elves," she said, looking at Gray. She held her hand over her abdomen and closed her eyes briefly, praying. "Is it your father?"

Gray shared a long look with Eden. "I think so."

"I...I don't know," Eden said. "This isn't what I saw. This is unexpected. Something happened. But yeah—it's Dark Elves."

Takana touched Eden's face as Cole lifted her into his arms and jogged away, taking her to safety. Or somewhere safer than a city being torn to shreds.

Eden looked at Ellie and held his hand over hers, over Gray's baby. "He will not touch your baby," he promised. "He will not touch any of you. Let's get away here, though. There's an old bomb shelter near the creek...follow me."

Eden curled to hold his legs to his chest. He pressed his forehead to his knees. "Why?" he asked, not understanding the drive behind the slaughter of so many innocent humans, or the desire to see the realms ripped at the seams, taking away safety and security for all worlds. Leaving them exposed to each other. Making the crossings more lethal than ever, now the pathways had been jumbled and made impossible to follow.

"What have you done?" he cried quietly. "Oh, Jaizel...what have you done?"

"Hey," Khari said, crouching in front of Eden. "Here—have a bite to eat," he said, pushing a biscuit against his hand.

Eden lifted his head and looked at the digestive without seeing it.

"Eat," Khari said again. "Here...drink something too," he tried, holding out a bottle of water.

Eden took it, staring at the label.

"Are you in shock?" Khari asked, kneeling in front of him. "Babe? Look at me. This wasn't your fault. Just because you can see some things, it doesn't make you omnipresent. Not yet, it doesn't. You can't be expected to see all and know it all, all the time. This was *not* your fault, Eden."

"It wasn't meant to happen like this," Eden said, dropping his head back onto his knees and closing his eyes. "Can you hear all the people screaming?" he asked. "Can you hear them crying for help? Praying? They need my help—and I can't *help them*! I couldn't even save my own dad, Khari!"

"Oh, Eden," Khari said, wrapping his arms around Eden's waist as he cried.

"Do you think he screamed, child of the Human Realm?"

Eden hunched into himself, trying to block out Jaizel's insidious voice.

"Do you think your weak human father wondered why his godly son allowed him to be pulled apart, torn in two, and devoured by the Divide? Do you think he wondered, as he screamed his agony, Child-God?"

"Eden? Baby, are you hearing me?"

Eden let Khari enfold him and turn him sideways to sit between his legs, cradling him. Trying to keep him safe, when he could never be safe again.

"This was not your fault, okay?"

"Oh, but it was your fault, wasn't it, Child-God?

*You cannot use the power you should be able to wield.
You should have been able to see this. To see it coming,
and to stop it happening, but you are weak, and small.
A God unable to use his powers...what does that make
you? Look at all the death around you. All your fault."*

Eden shuddered, shaking his head.

*"Perhaps I shall take my whore back, and take the
power he holds, Child-God. What use are you to me, if
you cannot even protect your own father? I will take
the powers of the earth from Khari and kill my enemies.
I shall use them to rule empires. The worlds shall kneel
at my feet, and I will be invincible. How does that
sound?"* Jaizel asked.

"We had a deal," Eden said under his breath.
"You tricked me."

"Babe?"

"Just thinking aloud," he said to Khari.

"We did have a deal," Jaizel agreed. *"I cannot wait
to meet you. To own you. To make a God kneel at my
feet. No, I cannot wait. Three days. New terms. You
have three days, Eden of the Human Realm. Let me see
if you can save those you love in that time. Show me
you are worth the trade, hmm? How far are you
willing to go to save the whore you use in your bed?
How much will you sacrifice to save the mixed blood
bastard in the Alfheimian's stomach? What do these
people mean to you—a God among men—what price,
their lives?"*

Eden lifted his head from Khari's chest and he
stared out over the shallow waters of the creek, where
they had all camped for the night. Jaizel laughed; a
serpent's hiss, entrancing prey.

*"You leave them, Eden, for a moment, and I will
take them all from you. You stay with them, and you*

will watch the city you called home burn to ashes. You will lose one, or the other. Which will it be? Do you believe in giving up the few to save the many?"

Eden looked around, gazing over the city he had called home for so many years. There were close to a quarter of a million people, separated from him by a few bridges onto the island. The creek held the city away from the mainland, a small, unimportant island where people went about their lives, same as they did the world over.

Two-hundred thousand souls, trapped. Held hostage for the lives of a few dozen elves.

"Eden? What is it?" Khari asked, turning to look over the water at the city with him. He watched with Eden as the nearest bridge exploded in a blast of magical greenish-blue fire. Khari held a hand to his mouth, choking back a cry of horror.

"There's nothing you can do," he said, standing. He walked to Takana to see her eyes wet with tears. He held his hands out for the baby, taking her when Takana held her up for him to take. He cradled her downy head next to his cheek and walked back to stare over the city. He watched the roads on and off the island be destroyed by magical blasts. He watched as fires sprang up in the distance, close to the sea on the eastern side of the island. Watched them spread. Heard the screams of those trapped.

He cradled the baby and turned to kiss the side of her head, leaning on Khari when he stood at his side and held a hand on his back. He stood still as his friends grouped around him—the only people in any world who might, one day, have the strength to kill Jaizel—and watched his city die. He never once looked away as the inferno raged through the night and into the following day.   Khari held him, becoming his strength as he watched the world he knew turn to ash.

XXXII

Airell held a length of red ribbon in place. His eyes were fixed on Khari's hand, bound to Eden's. He looked up. "Under the law of my lands, you are bound together," he said, looking from his son to Eden. "It is an unbreakable bond, which ends not even in death. May you walk with peace in your hearts," he finished, letting go of the ribbon and dropping his hands to his sides. "I wish the setting could have been better."

Eden could not have cared less about the setting. Khari was alive and at his side, and that—for now—was all that mattered. The seconds were ticking past, changing into minutes and then into hours, and his time was running out. Had run out. No, the setting did not matter, not now. It was doubtful it ever had. Eden turned and held his head against Khari's, gazing silently into his eyes. It was done, and they were bound twice over.

The elves who had witnessed the marriage drifted away, leaving him alone with his husband in a small field next to a children's play park. Eden linked his fingers with Khari's and stayed quiet, just looking into the glorious light shining in his eyes. Eyes that had imprinted themselves on Eden's soul the first time they had looked at him. There were no words big enough for all he wanted to say. If he said one, then more might flow, and then he might not be able to stop. He could not speak. Not now.

Khari led him to the trees and the makeshift tents that made up their camp. He looked around, checking,

Eden knew, to make sure that their small section of the Human Realm was still stable and wasn't bleeding into the Elven Realms, or something much worse. Satisfied they were safe as they could be, Khari held a hand to a tree and watched the branches spiral down, growing and spreading around the small space they stood in, weaving and coming down to enclose them in a darkened, safe, room. Alone and private.

Heatless globes of flame flickered and blossomed, floating above their heads, casting the softest of orange light over their skin. Khari wordlessly lifted the hem of Eden's T-shirt, slowly pushing the soft cotton up his chest, then over his head. He looked at him for a heartbeat, then stepped forward and found his mouth, brushing his lips over Eden's in an unhurried kiss as gentle as a butterfly lighting on a flower. Eden closed his eyes, pulling Khari's sweatshirt off, then opened them again, unable to look away.

He wanted to remember. To see it all, and watch Khari. To see his face as they made love on their wedding night. He shook his head to make his hair fall around his face as Khari pulled it free of its band, pushing into Khari's touch when fingers combed across his scalp, massaging and holding him steady as the kiss was deepened and the world shifted. Eden popped the buttons on Khari's jeans, stroking his fingertips across the hard muscle above soft blonde curly hairs, running his hand from one hip bone to the other, watching Khari shiver with unspoken pleasure. He slid his other hand down the back of Khari's jeans, feeling the cool round of his buttock under his palm before pulling him closer, kissing him without rushing; losing himself in the moment as, item by item, their clothes were piled next to the wall of twisted branches to the side, leaving them naked.

He pulled his head back, casting a lingering look over Khari's face, then slid slowly to his knees, running one hand up Khari's chest and the other around his hip to rest on the curve of his backside, bringing him close. He looked up at Khari, searching for the closed expression of discomfort that could appear. Waiting for the rebuttal, and the hand that pulled him back to his feet, stopping him before he could taste and touch. Never allowing himself to be out of control, Khari had stopped him. Every time.

Khari looked down at him, moving his head just enough to make his long fringe of soft blonde spikes fall and partly cover his eyes. His mouth parted as he watched Eden lick and kiss his way to his goal.

Keeping his sanity, barely, Eden watched Khari's face, looking into golden eyes as he moved his tongue and worked his mouth, using his hands to touch and explore, inhaling scents that set his soul flying. He widened his mouth, tasting salt and musk as he licked and worked his tongue over Khari's hardness, taking him as deep as he could. Pulling back, only to take him deeper. The sound of Khari's breathing filled the small cave of branches and Eden gripped his thighs, fighting against the need to grip his own cock and grant himself release from the lust writhing in his gut.

"Stop," Khari said, thighs trembling. "I don't want to finish. Not yet."

Eden slid up the length of Khari's body, kissing him deeply. Khari's hand slid down his back, working lower, finding dark places and secret nerves inside him that brought him back to his knees, supported, this time, in Khari's embrace. His head span as he was lowered to the ground, the earth under him, the trees around him, the sky above him, and everywhere, Khari. He moved his foot, lifting his knee, starting to pull Khari to him, only to be stopped with a silent kiss and a hand on his thigh.

Eden gazed upwards, breathless, and watched Khari lean over him again. He straddled Eden's hips to lower himself inch by inch, holding Eden still as he pushed downwards, taking Eden into him with maddening slowness. Eden clenched his fists, not daring to move as Khari moved above him and joined to him with wide unblinking eyes.

Khari bent and kissed him, lifting his arse up and down slowly, holding Eden's hands pinned to the soft ground either side of his head. Holding him captive with tight heat and a maddeningly slow rhythm that quickly brought Eden to hover on the edge of a high cliff of pure sensation. There was heat, tightness, the soft wetness of a mouth and the firm touch of hands. Stroking fingers, clenching muscles, hot breaths and murmured sighs. He flew and rode the waves with Khari. With his husband.

With his soul.

He was everywhere and nowhere, all at once. Inside Khari he was whole. He was alive.

Khari leant back, tipping his face up to the heavens, bringing them both to a climax that was as strong as it was silent. He rippled under Khari, a bundle of nerves and senses and nothing else as he slowly fell apart, exploding and shattering into a million shards of fragile crystals with a silent scream, lifting his hips to plunge as deep as he could into the other half of himself. To join them. To bind them so closely together that nothing could ever separate them.

Khari slumped forward, covering his chest and

breathing heavily. Eden's hand was lifted, the wedding band Khari had created kissed with a long sigh of happiness, then Khari was still.

"You're mine," Khari said, his voice a broken rasp in the silent wooden cavern of twisted branches. "Only mine, Eden."

Eden closed his eyes before tears could form. "I know. I'll always be yours."

"And I'm yours," Khari said.

"You always have been."

"I know." Khari lifted gently so Eden slid out of him. He laid down at Eden's side, hand over his heart. His eyelids fluttered and Eden watched as his breathing deepened and sleep reached for him.

"You're beautiful," Eden said, touching Khari's eyelashes and tracing the curve of his lips with his fingers, no longer trying to hold back his tears. "I wish you could see you as I see you," he said, quietly. "See all you're going to be, and see the world you'll rule over. I wish you could see the future I see, Khari, so you would know...so you would know why I'm doing what I'm doing. I wish we could have had our forever." He kissed Khari's forehead and stood up, blindly pulling on his clothes. Taking his notebook from his bag, he wrote quickly and folded the paper to rest next to Khari's outstretched fingers, along with all his jewellery; tongue bar, eyebrow bar, earrings, bracelets, all his rings except his magical *perfect* wedding band.

Eden crouched down, holding his hand on Khari's back, watching the ruined muscle and skin heal and become whole. He bent his head for a heartbeat, his tears landing on newly perfect ivory skin, then stood and walked away without looking back.

Into the Woods: Searching for Eden, Part One.

EPILOGUE

I was born for you. It seems a simple thing to say, but do you know how rarely those words are true? I was born for you, Khari, as you were born for me. One half of an empty soul. A shell, just waiting to find the one person who could fill the void and bring light into the darkness. One person who could see me and make my world make sense. You made it all make sense. Every moment I spent with you, in your arms, in your bed, was right. It was perfect.

I have to leave you. It's killing me, but to stay will kill us both. I can't let you be hurt. Not again. I wish I had longer. I wish I could say more. I wish I knew the answers, but in this I am as blind as I ever was.

I leave who I am behind. I leave the man I am with you, in the hope that one day, maybe, I will find myself again. It is not me, leaving. I am part of you.

Khari, I love you. Always, I will love you.

Remember me. Remember us, and hold us safe. I hold your hand and I touch your face, and I know I will never let you go. You'll walk with me for eternity.

Forever yours,

Eden.

Khari read the words again and looked over the ruins of the city Eden had brought him to. The first home he had ever truly known. The first place he had ever been happy. He watched the world flicker The Divide was healing. Separating the realms once again, as it must.

As it ever was, so it ever will be.

He heard Jaizel's laughter. Felt his triumph.

Khari folded the letter and placed it carefully in his wallet with hands that shook. He looked at Elnara, running his eyes over her growing belly. He watched Cole lift Felicity from her nest of leaves and soft grasses, holding her to his chest. His smile was gone and the light in his eyes extinguished.

He looked at Takana, now lying silent although her tears still flowed and the welts where she'd clawed at her face and arms still stood out vividly against her light brown skin. At Alexander, sitting under a tree, his eyes blank and his shoulders slumped in defeat. He looked at Airell—at the man who had given him life and loved his mother with a passion that had not been dampened, for all she had been dead for years.

Airell knew how he loved Eden.

Khari found Gray with his eyes and watched his brother walk over to him from his right. Airell came from his left. He waited until they both stood with him and, then, finally, he felt the crack in his heart split wide, and he broke down.

The dream was over. The nightmare was just beginning.

To be continued...

Into the Woods: Searching for Eden, Part One.

ACKNOWLEDGEMENTS

This list seems to grow and grow. There are people I couldn't have possibly written this book without. My family, of course. Shout out to the Hubs and kids, as well as my mum! They keep me insane enough to hear the voices in my head.

I have some brilliant friends, who hold me together. There are hundreds of you who have contacted me and lent me your support. I can never say thank you enough. Keep the messages coming—they really make my day. Thank you to all of you who have taken the time to find me and say hello, and to let me know what you think (good and bad) of my work.

Thank you Chris Artiss, for the daily little nudges that let me know there is more to the world than me and my PC. Also, it's always fun to have another person to add to the madness that seems to be my life.

Chris Hurst and Rob Boggs, for being mad and having some rather interesting conversations.

I'm going to give special mention to Jay Aheer, my Ninja Lady. She is the most brilliant magician born when it comes to cover art. She brings my stories to life and makes you notice them on the virtual shelves of the internet. She also has a dirty mind and a beautiful heart.

Finally, I have to thank my editor, Sam Flaco. He (and his hilarious margin notes) helped make this edition of Into the Woods what it is. Any mutterings, murmurings and stares are entirely my fault.

A SMALL NOTE.

Into the Woods is an English based novel. For my American Readers, *college* in England is *not* the same as an American *university*. University is 'University' and 'College' is a continuation of senior school—also known as Sixth Form. It's where we send our 16-18 year olds, so they don't feel the need to work for a living too soon. Our colleges can teach any number of subjects, from woodwork and bricklaying, to A-Levels that will hopefully get a child into university. It's nothing like getting a degree.

At the beginning of the adventure, Eden is enrolled at an English college, in a small city called Portsmouth, which is attached to the mainland by three roads. Down here, on our own little island, we speak *'roight funny'*. We can be heard to say, in conversation, "Well, I ain't never seen the like," and, "That's proper nice, I loves that, I doos." Yes, really, people where I live speak like that. I do myself, when I'm drunk (cause I'm a Pompey Girl, innit).

For those who are interested, Eden was in his second year, about to sit his final exams in English Literature, Language, Mathematics and History. He had no plans to go to university.

Also Available:

The Call of The Dark:
Searching for Eden, Part Two.

Coming Soon:

Legacies (a prequel)

Shadowfae:
Searching for Eden, Part Three

Into the Woods: Searching for Eden, Part One.

9597208R00312

Printed in Great Britain
by Amazon.co.uk, Ltd.,
Marston Gate.